Praise for

SEARCHING FOR TINA TURNER

"Jacqueline Luckett writes about relationships in a way we can all relate to . . . Does Lena divorce Randall? Does she find herself? I loved finding out, and you will, too."
—Examiner.com

"With her tender heart, cultural sophistication, and sardonic sense of humor, Lena takes us through her journey . . . and shows us one of the most creative ways you can make it to the other side."
—Farai Chideya, author of *Kiss the Sky*

"In her debut novel Luckett delivers a strong, likable heroine who comes through her crisis by recognizing her true worth and empowering herself. Luckett's triumphant tale will rally readers of all backgrounds."
—*Booklist*

"Ms. Luckett spins a sparkling tale of a woman's rise from emotional pain and obscurity to independence and power. Tina Turner as a mystery character is pure ecstasy!"
—Deborah Santana, author of *Space Between the Stars: My Journey to an Open Heart*

"[A] fresh take on a familiar fiction premise."
—*Essence*

"A rare glimpse into the world of African-American privilege . . . provides a first-class ticket to the good life, revealing the inner strength and struggle that allows a woman to redefine herself."
—Lalita Tademy, *New York Times* bestselling author of *Cane River* and *Red River*

"The pace quickens until it becomes un-put-down-able. You want to know what happens to Lena. An impressive novel. I can't wait for Luckett's next." —*Midwest Book Review*

"An incredibly gifted writer. SEARCHING FOR TINA TURNER is the book we've been waiting for—a deeply moving story that's also a page-turner. Bravo, Ms. Luckett!"

—Renee Swindle, author of *Please, Please, Please*

"Readers will enjoy Lena's quest to find herself . . . a charming contemporary tale that looks closely at self-actuation inside of family dynamics." —HarrietKlausnerwwwi.com

"Both eloquent and elegant, Jacqueline Luckett's SEARCHING FOR TINA TURNER charts the course of a swiftly changing life with straightforward honesty and gut-wrenching precision."

—Nichelle D. Tramble, author of *The Dying Ground* and *The Last King*

"Luckett sculpts loveable, complex, and beautiful characters. She creates clear, evocative scenes, transporting the reader to Lena's world . . . transcends age differences and makes this novel easily accessible to any generation. So grab a copy, walk alongside Lena Spencer in her fear and renewal, and together, you and Lena can go SEARCHING FOR TINA TURNER." —NewWorldReview.com

SEARCHING for TINA TURNER

JACQUELINE E. LUCKETT

GRAND CENTRAL PUBLISHING

NEW YORK BOSTON

This book is a work of fiction. Names, characters, places, and incidents are the product of the author's imagination or are used fictitiously. Any resemblance to actual events, locales, or persons, living or dead, is coincidental.

Grand Central Publishing
Hachette Book Group
237 Park Avenue
New York, NY 10017

www.HachetteBookGroup.com

Printed in the United States of America

Originally published in hardcover by Grand Central Publishing.

First Trade Edition: January 2011
10 9 8 7 6 5 4 3 2 1

Grand Central Publishing is a division of Hachette Book Group, Inc.
The Grand Central Publishing name and logo is a trademark of Hachette Book Group, Inc.

The Library of Congress has cataloged the hardcover edition as follows:
Luckett, Jacqueline.
Searching for Tina Turner / Jacqueline Luckett.—1st ed.
p. cm.
ISBN 978-0-446-54296-8
1. Self-realization in women—Fiction. 2. Midlife crisis—Fiction. 3. Turner, Tina—Fiction. I. Title.
PS3612.U259S43 2010
813'.6—dc22
2008053712

ISBN 978-0-446-54295-1 (pbk.)

Book design by Charles Sutherland

To my mother, Bernice Luckett, and my sister, Bernadette . . .
for being there . . .

Chapter 1

On their first date more than thirty years ago, Randall took Lena to an Ike and Tina Turner concert. From the minute they sat down in the fifth row from the stage, she knew he wanted to impress her even though he hadn't needed to. She would have sat with him in the park, gone to the drive-in, eaten Wheaties in the narrow half-kitchen of his studio apartment, done whatever he wanted; she'd been that eager to be with him.

The Ikettes crowded onto the narrow stage while Ike's deep bass warmed up the audience; like a chant his words tumbled soft and low. A hush fell over the auditorium as the guitar riff brought down the house lights. *Blamp.* The trumpets spit. Up, down, left, right. *Blamp blamp.* Suddenly, Tina pranced across the stage swinging her store-bought hair, the mic, the fringe on her sequined dress. Her taut legs pumped like a runner about to hit the finish line, her short dress coming close to revealing all that was underneath. The music increased to a faster, throbbing tempo. Girls cried. Men beckoned to Tina. The Ikettes moved with Tina, step for step, pounding the stage in three-inch heels.

Lena inched toward the crowded center aisle along with everyone else to get up on the stage and dance with Tina. Randall caught her by the waist, leaned down, and pressed his lips against her ear. "You're as cool as Tina Turner," he whispered, he as cool in a hip, sixties way as he meant she was. Trembling from the heat of his body, the ripple of his chest, the fuzz of his mustache, Lena kissed him. The clamorous crowd and loud music disappeared into the distance, and for years she remembered thinking that, as corny as it seemed, they were the only two people in the auditorium.

Now, those memories rush back as she watches a wrinkled TV personality melt in Tina Turner's smile. Lena lifts her glass; it would be nice to ooze such charm and self-assurance in a way so subtle and subdued that it ought to be bottled. Randall believes that good liquor deserves a toast. So here's to Tina. And Randall.

Tina looks directly into the camera, poised and straightforward; her eyes twinkle with humor and self-confidence. She is a perfect combination of wild and sexy. Of secure and comfortable freedom. The reporter sees it, remarks on it, and asks if it comes from celebrity or the people around her, and Tina lets him know that it comes from within. He goes over her history: regaining her place at the top of the pop charts, her refusal to focus on color or race, a misunderstanding with Elton John. Tina smiles again and changes the subject.

She talks of life, faith, and love for her man. Her brownish blond hair softens her ageless face, accentuates her full lips. The camera captures the warm beige and gold of her skin in a tight close-up and pans her hilltop home and the royal blue Mediterranean beyond. A happy blue, Lena thinks—the opposite of the blue she feels right now.

Without a thought of the fifteen-hour time difference between Oakland and Hong Kong, Lena dials Randall. The international connection to his cell phone click-click-clicks her to the Far East.

"Who the hell is this?" Randall's voice is slurred with sleep.

"Rollin', rollin', rollin' on the river." Lena mimics Tina, believing her husband knows good and well who it is. Because, unless his ears have suddenly lost their perfect hearing, their home number has a special ring tone on his phone.

"Remember that Tina Turner concert we went to?" She reaches for the Drambuie and dribbles more into her glass. "Tina's arms spinning, her energy . . . she's so beautiful."

"Is everything all right? Are the kids okay?" The metallic echo of fumbling comes through loud and clear. Lena closes her eyes and imagines Randall in a fancy king-sized bed, his suite big enough to house a family: left arm stretches out under the covers, right arm adjusts the pillow to fit in the crook of his neck, his thick eyebrows push toward the permanent wrinkle in the middle of his forehead. She can almost smell his nighttime musky scent in the whoosh the pillow emits when he finally settles into it.

"Kendrick is fine. Camille is fine. I know you said we'd talk again in a couple of days, but I got excited when I saw Tina Turner."

"What does Tina Turner have to do with me at four in the morning?" Randall clears his throat, and Lena visualizes his neck lengthening, his Adam's apple sliding up, then down and up again, his arm bending to show the luminous dial of his watch. She had not thought of that concert in years or the feeling she'd had of being complete and whole. Stretching her own arm again to the glass beside her, she glares at the TV and the dip Randall's body has worn into his side of the mattress.

"She's on TV. Right now. I wish you could see her. She made me think of our first date. That was the first time we made love, remember?"

"Of course, I remember, Lena, I was there, too. Are you drinking?"

"It calms my nerves."

"Maybe you can frivol away the day—and that, coincidentally, is compliments of this trip and all that work you've been complaining about—but I have to get up in two hours."

For the first time in twenty-seven days, Lena wonders if this abruptness is because she has disturbed more than his sleep; if some woman has gone to where Lena should have. No invitation had been extended to join him, like other business trips to New York, Rome, Berlin, and more, savoring free moments between conference calls and meetings. No matter what he has told her, his work—the complexity of TIDA's pending acquisition—allowed Randall to escape. He needed to be upbeat, he told her, to be ready to think clearly, to strategize, to make decisions—or change them on a dime—and he did not have time, or the desire, to deal with the irritability that seemed to plague her.

Sharon? Not four months ago, at a TIDA dinner, Randall's colleague insisted he taste her béarnaise-smothered steak. Lena watched the very sexy Sharon risk a death knell for her career, and maybe her boss's, by leaning into Randall and offering her fork to his willing and open lips. Randall is friendly, she thinks, but that gesture went way past friendly.

"Are you alone?" Her lips tighten, shoulders hunch; Lena presses the phone hard against her ear, as disarmed by the question as she hopes Randall is. Tossing back her drink in one, swift motion, she slams the glass on the nightstand. The table creaks with her protest, her alarm.

"No, my mistress is here; right beside me: the TIDA contract. Hundreds of pages all over me, all over the bed, all over the floor. I'm doing her every place I can. Sorry she can't talk now, but if you want, I can fax her to you."

"That's not funny."

"And neither is your question."

"I'm going to call your secretary and make our next appointment with the therapist."

"Fuck no. If that leaked to the board . . . they'd assume I'm incompetent. That's all the ammunition they need to keep from appointing me CEO. Just figure out what's going on with you."

Before Randall left, Lena suggested a marriage counselor to help get to the root of the heightening tension between them. She described to him what he called her indifference and watched his eyebrows knit together in what she assumed was his indifference. Both let go of their unspoken routine. Never going to bed angry. Apologetic embraces that turned to lusty sex. Revering the gem they called love, considering each other's opposing points of view until they reached truce or, even better, agreement.

"Therapy," he said, "is what white people do." Lena reminded him that he had quickly agreed to therapy for their son, and that, the last time Lena looked, Kendrick wasn't white. Randall agreed to a session before he left and one more when he returned.

After introductions, Dr. Brustere opened his hands like a priest ready to bestow the sign of peace, to balance the power in the room, and asked about their marriage. Randall eyed the therapist as if determining a battle-ready opponent. Good brotha, bad brotha. Dr. Brustere pressed his expensive pen into the dimple in his chin—his signal to Randall that he was expected to talk.

Randall told the therapist that most people who knew him would be shocked to know that he considered himself a simple man, given the thick gold bracelet on his right wrist and the Rolex on his left (his only jewelry), his designer suits, and luxury four-door sedan. He believed goals were essential to success—personal or business—that only through hard work and consistency could a man, or woman, meet those goals. He valued loyalty as the most important quality in human nature (his father taught him that, if nothing else) and jazz as an imperative for sanity in an unstable world.

At the age of eight, he had decided he would never be like his father, an unreasonable man who got religion and a sure sense of self-righteousness about two years after he left Randall and his mother; though he did return to take care of his son after Randall's mother died. Randall had basic needs: kids who believed he could do no wrong, the love of his wife, a little attention, a lot of sex.

He pointed his finger at his wife and, for all his smarts and degrees, the wrinkle in his brow proved that he did not understand what had caused the change. "Lena is the one with the problem. She has everything she could want."

"I love my husband. I love my kids, my home. I do not love that they have come to define me or that *what* I *have* has become more important than *who* I am." She twisted her wedding ring as if the large replacement suddenly itched the finger that she had worn a ring on for twenty-three years. "My spirit, what makes me me, is dying."

Randall leaned back deep in the wingback chair. Before that one gesture, before the lips pursed, the brow wrinkled, she thought she saw a glimmer of understanding, of empathy. He made a loose one-handed fist beneath his chin and moved his head up and down as though they had all day, not fifty-five minutes. Lena knew that move and all his moves; she could write the dictionary on Randall's unspoken commentary. That one meant checkmate. Lena wanted to point out that his reaction was typical of what was wrong with their marriage lately: the more important Randall became at TIDA, the more he disregarded explanations based in emotion.

"I love you. I love our family. But, I've given myself away, slowly, freely, and now . . . I want myself back." Lena dug her fingernails into the sides of her chair, and somewhere in the back of her mind it became clear to her why they were so frayed. "Otherwise, I'm going to lose my mind."

"This is the same conversation we had last week, the same conversation we keep having. It's circular. It hasn't gotten us anywhere and, quite frankly, if I have to hear it again . . ." Randall made finger quotes in the air. "I'm going to lose *my* mind."

On TV speeding police cars in the midst of a freeway pursuit replace Tina's interview. Their shrill sirens mask the space the phone static fills. Lena switches the phone to her right ear and measures two fingers of Drambuie into her empty glass with her left hand.

By the end of that session Randall offered Lena an ultimatum, and now she shudders under the pressure, the urgency to make a decision. She opens her planner and darkens another dated square of the calendar. That square, and twenty-six others recklessly colored in with black ink, creates a stark disparity between what was, what is, and the five white squares left in this month. Five days left to get her act together. Five days to decide if she even wants to get her act together.

"I wish . . . ," Lena says, wanting Randall to understand her change of direction, her altered focus. Not away from him, just closer to herself. "I love you. You *know* that, don't you?"

"I *know* there are plenty of women who would be very happy given the same set of circumstances." Randall huffs, and Lena imagines his body twitching like it does when he gets mad. Legs first, then arms, then left eyebrow. "I did what *you* asked. I sat in front of that wimpy-assed therapist while you complained about how unhappy you are, how I won't let you play with your photography. I told you. If you're so unhappy, take the time that I'm gone to figure out what you want."

"I want us, and I want *me*."

"It's almost dawn. I'll talk to you later. And don't forget Kendrick's prescription."

In the second it takes to realize the phone call is over, Lena's armpits dampen with icy sweat as a quarter-sized spider skitters across the pillow where Randall's head should be. She worries where this damn thing has come from and questions if this is a sign her husband will never nestle his head in that spongy spot again. The spider's blackness, its scampering pace, forces a frantic search for newspaper, tissue, or shoe. She snatches the daily planner beside her, holds it so the contents won't spill, and whacks the spider again and again; lets the up and down motion, the dull slap of leather against pillow, do what her husband would if he were there.

Her parents poked fun at her when she was young. Said their California-born girl was city-spoiled. Sky-splitting lightning, the Great Dane around the corner, the creak in the closet at night—those fears they understood, but not of pests so small that, even as children, her parents smashed without thinking. Back in Mississippi, they told Lena, black folks thought spiders in the house were omens of wealth and good luck.

Omen, confirmation, or sickening fluke, Lena collects the

squished black dot with tissues. Holding the wad at arm's length, she shoves Randall's pillow to the floor and stumbles into the bathroom, where she pitches the tissue into the toilet and slams the lever. At the sink, she scowls in the medicine cabinet mirror, not caring for what she sees: one of Randall's undershirts hangs loosely from her round shoulders, puffy eyelids, lopsided bed hair, flaky patches on her nose. If Randall could see her, he would not be pleased. She sticks out her tongue at her reflection, reaches for a can of window cleaner underneath the sink, and sprays a thick coat of foam on the mirror's surface. "You can't run, but you can hide."

Two shakes of the bedcovers and tissues, magazines, bras, and panties flip in all directions. Lena grabs Randall's pillow, wraps her arms around it like she would his body if he were there, and tries to understand when her ability to be on her own diminished, and how she slipped from self-sufficiency to comfortable reliance. With one turn to the left, her body readjusts to the groove she's worn into her side of the mattress. The headboard rattles as she falls back against the smooth upholstery and ponders this loss of self that can't be brushed aside by Randall like a toe stubbed in the dark.

The squat bottle of Drambuie on the nightstand has replaced the alabaster pot full of bottle caps that a then three-year-old Camille gave to Lena. Lena assumes that gifts of words or anything else must not be hip for teenagers anymore. These days, if her daughter—or son, for that matter—were to bestow such kindness, Lena would be grateful. She reaches for the bottle and splashes the liquid into her glass. She swirls the sweet, golden Drambuie liqueur around in her mouth and holds it, not quite accustomed to the burn at the back of her tongue, and lets it slide from throat to stomach.

It's not just her; Randall needs to get his act together, too. Lena punches the phone pad with the international code plus 8 and 6 and his phone number again to tell him she will schedule a second appointment with Dr. Brustere. Randall's phone rings and rings, and when his recorded voice, his proper English, instructs callers to leave a message, she pitches the phone and watches it skid across the hardwood floor.

Drambuie or reality, the pages of her red leather planner seem to gawk at Lena and demand action. She owes a call to the woman she tutors, an apology for missed sessions so her student will understand that neglect is not her intention. Save for the blackened squares, April is empty. Manicures, meetings, the hairdresser, luncheons, and volunteer work have disappeared. In all of the twenty-seven days since Randall has been away—the longest time they have ever been apart—she has ignored invitations, requests for donations, and callers who say in singsong voices, "Just checking in."

Assorted pictures are jammed between the planner's thin pages: Kendrick, at two, beaming in a Halloween costume; Camille, all of five, posed in a novice arabesque; a Jamaican vacation five years ago—she and Randall hand-in-hand in the midst of a dive off the cliff at Rick's Negril Café. He'd held her hand all the way down and into the turquoise water. Her hand tingles now with the memory of the security, the assurance of Randall's solid grip. There is also a withdrawal slip from their joint checking account, confirmation of enrollment for a Tuesday evening photography course that starts tomorrow night, and Kendrick's most recent prescription.

Outside the windows beyond her bed floodlights cast shadows on the house and the undersides of the trees and their leaves. Lena walks to the window and looks down on the magnolia tree spiking in anticipation of a mid-spring bloom. The tree sold Lena on the house when they first saw it from the real estate agent's car nineteen years ago. It reminded her of Lulu's recollections of stately southern homes that black folks could only walk by, not live in: huge white flowers that attracted more beetles than bees, the earthiness of the double-colored leaves, scent like strong citrus perfume.

Her dreams blossom in this home framed with purple hydrangeas, leggy oleander and this magnolia tree. The memories flash in her mind: her children, now grown past the days of tumbling across the sprawling lawn, fearless and eager to show off; brilliant

Fourth of July fireworks beyond the silhouette of downtown Oakland and San Francisco's foggy skyline; the smell of cut grass on Tuesdays and Saturdays.

She does not want to think about the orchids in her sunroom wilting from lack of water. Nor the jars of homemade apple chutney, bottles of olive oil, and tins of spices in the pantry that await her creative hand. Nor does she want to focus on the jade lion that guards the front door, the photography books stacked on the coffee table—Parks, Arbus, DeCarava, Weems—or the gold-flecked Venetian glass ball that all sit covered with the fine dust of disuse.

Presence was the word the Italian-accented agent used when they first drove up the winding driveway. "This house fits you and Mr. Spencer well. You both have presence, too."

Randall may still have presence after all of these years, but what Lena feels right now is the complete opposite. Her ability to create the future diminishes each day: yesterday she could not raise her arms to shower or comb her hair, this morning she could not keep food in her stomach, minutes ago she could not explain to her husband what is in her heart without sounding whiny or spoiled, and now she can barely stand.

In the scheme of things, twenty-seven days is not a long time. A flower can bud, bloom, and die in twenty-seven days. At this very minute, Lena is overwhelmed by indecisiveness, incapable of moving her fifty-four-year-old body. The odds of her leaving or staying are as unpredictable as that skittering spider's path. Call it unhappiness, menopause, midlife crisis, lack of respect, fear of losing who she is, fear that she no longer fits in this dream. Whatever.

Pick one.

Chapter 2

"Lenaaaaaa Spencer!"

Lena cringes at the scratchy, off-key intonation of the familiar voice and tiptoes around the lofty shelves toward the hand-painted FICTION/TRAVEL/PHOTOGRAPHY sign at the back of the store. Ducking in front of the K through P shelf, she closes her eyes and breathes in the dust and must of The Big Black Dog bookstore, her special place to spend time on an overcast day like this one. Candace asks questions—so many and so fast—that, in the past, it has been easy for Lena to be lulled by the woman's insatiable thirst for scandal in the guise of concern. And she'll be damned, Lena thinks, if she'll let Candace spoil her afternoon.

Lena scans the shelves. These days she feels like one of these used books: in good shape, full of excitement, yet no longer appreciated. Instead of a worn spine, the cover of a misplaced paperback, *I, Tina*, catches Lena's eye. Tina Turner crouches, fish-netted legs tucked beneath her, hair as wild as it was in that *Mad Max* movie. Her smile implies a question: Where is your joy? Something audible clicks inside Lena's chest like the tumblers of an opening lock.

The kids' first nanny asked the same question nearly every day that Lena drove from the bus stop and up the steep, winding hill that Letty was too overweight to walk. "Where's your joy today, Miz Spencer? Mine is right here." Letty held her Bible upright in her lap and let it fall open with the car's swerving motion. Then she would drop her forefinger onto a random passage and softly thank Jesus for his inspiration.

Lena lets the paperback fall open and points to a paragraph. *"People look at me now,"* Tina writes, *"and think what a hot life I must've lived—ha!"* Right on.

"There you are!" The voice breaks the bookstore's silence once more at the same time that a heavily jeweled hand grabs Lena's shoulder. "What in hell are you doing on the floor? Didn't you hear me calling you?" Candace's gold bangles jingle when she leans toward Lena. "I haven't seen you since that handsome husband of yours went out of town. When is that luscious man coming home anyway, and why haven't I seen you at any Circle Club meetings?" Her clothes are coordinated: slim, tight pants under a yellow, belted slicker, ankle-high rain boots match the slicker's herringbone lining intentionally exposed on turned-back cuffs. "And since when do you wear Kendrick's clothes?" She pinches Lena's sweatshirt between two fingers as if she is touching something nasty or unclean.

Lena scolds herself for defying the rules: her mother's "Pay attention to what you wear when you leave the house; you never know who you'll run into." Even Randall's: "Put gas in the car when it registers low so you won't get stuck in the middle of nowhere on an empty tank." Sometimes things just happen: the car runs out of gas in the middle of nowhere, or somebody like Candace shows up.

Lena stands and speaks her lie without hesitation. "I'm in the middle of a project." For the last month she has left her trademark starched white shirts, skinny-legged jeans, and high heels in her closet and exchanged them for clothes she should have taken to the homeless shelter. She brushes lint from her pants, circles behind Candace, promises to call soon. Blah blah blah.

"A project in a bookstore?" Candace grasps Lena's arm, looks from Lena to the books and back to Lena. "Give me a break." The petite woman follows her down the aisle to the old-fashioned cash register.

Sam Black and his big black dog sit side by side behind a massive antique English wooden table. The skinny owner and muscular dog wear the same woolly look on their faces. Each time Lena visits the store she asks Sam who is in charge—owner or pet. Today he responds with the same answer, "Depends on the day," while he labors with a calligraphy quill over a receipt for Lena's seventy-five-cent book.

"Girl, get the DVD," Candace says, thumping the paperback. She squeaks an off-key line from "What's Love Got to Do with It" and snaps her fingers. "I'll tell you what: love doesn't have a damn thing to do with anything. Have you heard about poor Dana?" Candace pauses in anticipation of Lena's reaction.

Sam raises his head. His brows protrude above his wire-rim glasses. Candace's leer warns him to mind his own business. Lena tosses a dollar bill on Sam's desk and stuffs the receipt into her purse.

"Dana and Carl are getting divorced." Candace scrunches her cheeks and eyes with the expression of someone who is about to speak of doom. Lena shakes her head no, and Candace does the same for a long minute, reminding Lena of how her grandmother shook her head and grumbled "unh, unh, unh" at sad news. "They say she's had too much of her husband—he's such a tease. There was no way you could tell anything was wrong. I mean, a few months ago, they were flirting and smooching like lovers. Such a pity."

Lena remembers that extravagant holiday party: the dolefulness in Randall's eyes that the loud celebration had precluded them from pursuing, that left as swiftly as it had come. "Here's hoping for a better year," he had said, holding her as they glided across the dance floor, and Lena, knowing even then her downward tilt, had hoped for the same.

"Nothing is predictable anymore." Lena lowers her eyes; afraid to let on that this sad reflection is as well suited to herself as it is to Dana.

"Oh, bullshit. Predictable or not, I've been married to Byron Stokes for thirty years, and I'm not about to put myself in Dana's position. Doesn't matter what her husband did or didn't do." Candace points to her sparkling diamond tennis bracelet and fingers the five-carat wedding ring Randall gave Lena for their twentieth anniversary. "I'm not giving any of this up, sweetie. At our age, it's hard for a sister to find a man with the same *abilities*."

"It's got to be about more than . . . 'abilities.' Whatever happened to trying to work things out? What about love?"

"You heard me: what's love got to do with anything?" Candace conveys Dana's story with a half-pity, half-tattletale smile: early last year, Dana told her husband that she would leave him after their twins graduated from high school, unless he changed. "From what I hear, he told her she had nowhere to go without him and his connections. Translation: money. Well, the twins graduated early, and she's living with her mother. She has to get a job, make new friends, and find a new man."

As if, Lena supposes, those simple things are the solution to a woman's problems.

"And she's almost sixty." Candace tightens her long ponytail, her sign that she denies her almost sixty years. Lena knows that underneath the slicker, Candace's body is tight, thanks to her trainer. Her makeup is perfect, her skin flawless thanks to modern chemistry and a good esthetician.

"Should we call her and take her out to lunch, try to cheer her up?" Lena asks.

"You can if you want to. Sometimes divorced women are double trouble. Some *husbands* don't want their wives to see how women can improve after divorce—and unless you're Ivana Trump, with a big settlement, that doesn't always happen. Let's face it, some *wives* don't trust their men around them. Happens all the time."

"You mean you won't have anything to do with her just because she's divorced?" Lena gawks at Candace. For eleven years they have lunched, visited, bestowed gifts, and socialized. She knows Candace is notorious for cutting off women who don't give her the attention she loves, but not because of divorce. "You're still friends with Gail Coleman, and isn't Ada Munson divorced?"

"People grow apart. We don't do the same things." Candace dismisses Lena with a wave of her hand. "I'll catch up with Dana, of course. I love her to death. But Byron and Carl are friends; more than friends, actually. They've helped each other's careers—you know what I mean—the networking our men do. Byron wouldn't want me to jeopardize that. Besides, she's competition now, honey."

"Why do you think she would compete for your husband?" Lena presumes that Candace is the only one who wants her portly, beady-eyed husband, money or no money.

"I don't need any single women around Byron. His eyes wander enough, and he's always talking about Dana: how nice she is, how she takes such good care of herself, how her husband is a fool for dogging her. A lot of married men believe divorcées are lonely and horny, and they try to do something about it. I wouldn't want a woman like Dana around my man."

Lena makes her way to the pharmacy as she has done all these months without Randall's reminder. As if, in his absence, she could forget her responsibilities; as if in twenty-three years she hasn't been mother and father, doctor and nurse, teacher and tutor every time he goes away.

Without prompt or invitation, Candace follows. At the counter, she stops alongside Lena and squints at the prescription in her hand. "For Kendrick? Is everything okay? Did he decide to go back to Chicago or transfer to a school out here?"

"Kendrick is fine. If you'd wear your glasses, Candace, you'd see that's *my* name on the prescription." Lena turns away from Candace's line of vision and shoves the paper into the clerk's hand. "You're being pretty hard on Dana. What if I got divorced?" Lena coughs in hopes that sound will throw Candace off track.

"Ha! You and Randall are perfect: the black Barbie and Ken. Big everything: house, cars. And trinkets." Candace flicks Lena's heavy gold watch. Randall, Lena recalls, likes Candace because she is never embarrassed by what she has or what she does.

Six months ago, Lena might have considered those words a

compliment. This isn't the first time someone has labeled them perfect: the symmetry of their physicality—she tall, he taller; complementary brown skin tones—neither fair nor dark; stylish, hip clothes from New York and San Francisco designer boutiques—coordinated, but not; their speech proper and grammatically correct—hints of slang at the right time and in the right company.

"I've known Dana for as long as I've known you." If only Candace would stop her blabber and look beyond her frown, Lena thinks, she would understand. The glint in Candace's eye says she doesn't see anything but Lena's clothes and the questionable prescription as fodder for more gossip. "I wouldn't chuck her friendship just because she's made a decision to save herself."

"Dana was naïve. She should have planned better—if she'd done that she wouldn't be at her mother's." Candace looks Lena up and down and follows her out the front door. "You're no fool. And *if* you're thinking that way, or something close to it, take my advice: don't. Be happy."

If she were the kind of woman who got into physical fights, Lena might find this the perfect time to smack Candace for her ability to think about plans and consequences. She chuckles at the thought of the petite woman falling, more worried about her hair and her jewelry spiraling across the dirty linoleum floor than the fact that she had been assaulted. Then again, perhaps Candace would lie on the floor, the way Lena lies in her bed unable to figure out how to tell her husband that honoring herself does not mean dishonoring him. Once on the floor, she knows, Candace would take action: yell for help with her wretched, squeaky voice, or devise a case to sue, courtesy of pictures taken with her rhinestone-encrusted cell phone.

"Stop frowning. You take everything too seriously. We all have our bad days." Candace harrumphs in a way that means she's never had a day as bad as the one Lena seems to be having and shoves a business card into Lena's purse. "My personal shopper."

Outside the pharmacy, a sullen-faced woman steps back from the sidewalk and stares like she would at an escaping shoplifter as Lena rushes to her car. In Montverde—a hillside shopping district that is called by a different name to distinguish it from the flatlands of Oakland but is still Oakland—white people act like they are not used to seeing black people in fancy cars. As she steps into the car, Lena assumes that the contrast between what she is wearing and what she is driving is so great that it raises the question: does the car belong to her?

"Come on now, I don't look that bad." Lena waves to the woman. "Can't a black woman have an expensive car and a bad hair day, too?"

Lena negotiates her sleek car between the broken lines on the freeway's asphalt and ponders Candace's focus on possessions. In that way, Candace is like Randall. And, she supposes, how she used to be. How many times can she tell Randall?

Last November, Randall asked Lena what she wanted for her birthday. "A weekend," she'd said without missing a beat. A weekend together—just the two of them—no laptop, no BlackBerry, like they used to. A simple celebration. A shared, uninterrupted soak in the tub. Maybe in Sonoma or Napa—taste new wines, ride bikes, take pictures, laze in the sun.

She should have suspected something when Kendrick stayed home longer than usual after Thanksgiving. The evening of her birthday, Randall slipped off his silk tie, blindfolded her with it, and escorted her to the back door. Camille and Kendrick, obviously in on whatever surprise Randall had in store, giggled as the three of them led her out of the house to the driveway. Lena giggled, too, stepping carefully into the brisk twilight.

When Randall loosened the tie, Lena screamed at the top of her lungs. There, in the driveway, sat a low, red Mercedes SL convertible with shiny alloy wheels, buttery leather seats, and keys dangling from a red ribbon tied around the rearview mirror.

Lena eased behind the steering wheel, while Randall, Kendrick, and Camille faked a silly squabble over who would be the first to ride with her in the two-seater. Randall claimed his right, having paid for the car, Kendrick claimed his as first-born, and Camille claimed hers as the only daughter. In the end, a giggling Lena made them pick a number between one and ten and drove down the driveway with the same enthusiasm and high speed each time one of them buckled themselves into the passenger seat.

Two days later she thanked Randall again for his extravagance and explained that she loved the car, but she really wanted more of him, not material things, while his voice rose louder and louder. "Just keep the damn thing." Lena knew he didn't understand, knows he doesn't understand.

Speed is the excitement in her ordinary errands. Zip. Grocery store—milk, juice, bread, peanut butter. Zip. Hardware store—light bulbs, batteries, that thingamabob for the stereo that Randall drew a picture of before he left.

The radio is off. After Candace's frenetic proclamation, all Lena wants is the hum of the engine, the alternate whine—like ascendant chords—of the gears, the constant attention required to handle the car. She avoids pillows of exhaust; manipulates, teases, plays in and out of the gaps in the afternoon traffic. Her foot presses down on the accelerator: 300+ horsepower. Her biceps tighten with the thrill of the push past fear and carbon fumes. Gravity takes over with the increased speed; it forces her back into the cushy seat, pumps adrenaline through her body, moistens her palms. A little more, a little more. She moves from the fast to the slow lane, eases up on the accelerator, and exits the freeway.

In the ten minutes between the pharmacy and home, Lena works herself into a state of disgust—with herself, with Candace. She swerves into her driveway and races up the stairs and into bed. The phone beside the bed calls out to her: pick me up, call Candace and offer an explanation, call Randall, beg for more time. Apologize? Instead, she reads. In the bed, across the bed, on the toilet, then back to bed, Lena reads about Tina's ups and downs for the rest of the afternoon.

What comes through Tina's autobiography is the realization that she already had everything she needed for success inside. Tina thought about leaving for years, but she also thought—or so Lena interprets—that when you love someone you stay with them. Through good times and bad. Lena blesses herself with a small sign of the cross for the differences in their circumstances and because Randall has never treated her that way—but the emotions, the doubt and fear of the future, are similar.

Maybe, she thinks, she should make a plan. Maybe she should get a yellow legal pad and a red pen and label two columns + / – like Randall does when he thinks through a decision. Like the night they decided, together, to buy this house. Like he did the night before his vote on the TIDA merger, Lena, his sounding board, next to him on the couch. What would she put in her columns? What does love have to do with anything? she reminds herself—he is far from perfect, but so is she. There is the mole on his left shoulder, his generosity, his love for Kendrick and Camille, how he doubles back to leave money by a sleeping homeless person's side, the way he huffs when he exercises and talks nonsense in his sleep and used to reach for her and take her in his arms in the midst of a dream, how he cherishes Lulu as if she were his own mother. If these qualities all fall on the + side, why isn't she happy? Or, was Candace right—are they the same?

Lena shakes away the thought of any resemblance to Candace and imagines what her +/– list would look like.

++Camille and Kendrick; – Camille and Kendrick's attitudes

+ Tina left at forty-five; – she is fifty-four

+ Tina had marketable talent; – her photography is pretty good

+ Tina fell out of love with Ike

+/– She loves Randall

Chapter 3

The bedroom windows rattle lightly with the *ba-boom, ba-boom* of the surround-sound speakers. The system Randall had installed two floors beneath this one can be turned to a volume loud enough to make the walls of this fifty-year-old home shudder. She has no idea how long Kendrick has allowed the music to pound or why it needs to be so loud. On her left, the red planner beckons from the nightstand. The enrollment slip extends beyond its rounded edges. When she registered for the six o'clock class two months ago, she hoped that Randall's attitude would mellow, and he would be happy that his wife wants to follow a dream that complements their life. Lena checks her watch: one hour to pull herself together and get to campus. A smile breaks across her face: one hour of lecture and two of lab. Oh!—the bitter smells of developer and fix.

Dressed in the same sweatshirt and cotton pants that Candace criticized her for earlier, Lena gets out of bed and strolls to an armoire in the corner of the bedroom. Inside there are freshly pressed linens, her boxed wedding dress and Randall's old tuxedo, Camille's cotillion gown, and Kendrick's first communion suit. Her old Pentax 35mm with manual controls, not the palm-sized digital she has used over the last couple of years to capture her family's history, sits at the back of the top shelf.

"Mother?" Camille pokes her head into the doorway. "What's for dinner?"

Tonight Lena's excuse is valid. "Call Hunan City, Camille, and have them deliver. My photography class starts tonight."

"Starless, Mother." Camille's tone is matter of fact and insistent—use the name I've chosen, it says, not the one you gave me. No matter how hard Lena tries to accommodate Camille's recent capriciousness, her younger child's desire to change her given name is not easy to accept.

"Mom, Starless."

Most days, Camille is cranky. Cranky and reclusive. How can she criticize her child for the very behavior she is guilty of? The discontent that started last fall continues. Lena longs for the two of them to be close again. Either way, come September, she'll shed tears when she walks past the door of Camille's disused room or when the clock's hands sweep close to the normal hour her daughter would come home from school. For seven months Camille has been searching for answers. This new name, Starless, Camille told her parents, signified her preparation for college and separation from them. Her given name, she constantly reminds them, no longer reflects who she is. She is without a fixed point: one foot almost in college, one foot at home.

Camera in hand, Lena kneels on the floor and unscrews the lens cap. She points the camera upward at Camille's heart-shaped face, plays with the f-stop, and adjusts the shutter speed. Snap. Wind. Snap. Camille shrugs, seemingly equating the prospect of Lena's class and the possibilities of Chinese food equally dull. Her resemblance to Lena, save for her demonstrative hands and round eyes, lessens each year. But still, Camille resembles Lulu's side of the family more than Randall's: small bones, an imperceptible smatter of freckles between her eyebrows, clear skin, and oversized teeth that fit well with her lips when she smiles.

"I think I'll puke if I have to eat Chinese food again." Camille's hint of a grin slips quickly to a pout. "You've hardly cooked since Dad left. Kendrick and I have to eat, too."

"I'll rustle something up before I leave. Maybe I'll bring back ice cream."

Camille turns her back and heads down the hall. "And I need cat litter."

The almost nine months since Randall gave her Kimchee on her birthday have made Camille more demanding, not responsible. Her room is a mess, and she rarely makes it to school on time. Tomorrow Lena will chauffeur Camille to the store because she refuses to learn how to drive and complains when she has to carry sacks of cat litter on the bus. Camille will take the two twenty-dollar bills Lena will hand her to buy cat litter and a few extra items for her pet, and perhaps wander beyond that store to buy something for herself. Lena will sit in the car and read about Tina while Camille considers which of the fourteen generic and specialty brands of cat litter is the best for her precious Kimchee.

Ba-boom, ba-boom.

"Kendrick!" If she could remember where her cell phone is, she would call Kendrick because she would have a better chance to reach him that way. Lena grabs two tall containers from her purse and jams them into her pocket. She walks down the staircase, a half-circle of seventeen regular and five pie-wedge stairs that end at the front hallway, and continues to a second, shorter, and straight flight that stops at the open door of the family room. "Turn that down, please."

Eight of Kendrick's friends loll on the floor, the couch, and the recliner. They greet Lena in unison, while their eyes focus on the TV and two wrestlers in skimpy underwear entangled in the ring.

"Chill, Moms. This is the no-nag zone." Kendrick is at the door in two lengthy strides. His body is lanky like his father's once was. He is tall, taller than Randall is now. He has his father's thick curly hair, high and sunken cheekbones passed down from Choctaw ancestors, a narrow forehead. His large ears, his dimples, his smooth brown skin are his father's. At twenty, his face is still like the boy who used to cry when he saw a dead bird or squirrel in the yard. "My friends want to stay for dinner."

Lena searches the corner of Kendrick's eyes for their old impish crinkle. She can't decide if he wants to impress his friends or shame her. His eyes are clear and brighter now than when he came home from college at the end of last semester, but they still lack spark.

"I don't have much time." With a hasty glance at her watch, Lena takes a mental inventory of the freezer and pantry. "I've got a photography class tonight."

"Aw, Moms, nobody can teach you a thing. Your photographs are already great." Kendrick stares at Lena with the look of a neglected puppy. "How's about a little soul food? Fried chicken, cornbread on the side, a sweet treat . . ."

Eight sets of eyes peer at Lena as if to say, "We love your fried chicken, Mrs. Spencer." As if their votes count.

"Yeh, Moms, it's been a while."

Lena checks her watch and calculates the twenty minutes it will take Kendrick to get to the grocery store, shop, and return home—if there isn't any traffic, if the store isn't crowded. She guestimates before she commits: "The first part of the class will probably be introductions and a review of the syllabus. I've got forty minutes, maybe an hour, max, if you leave for the store right now."

"Does that mean the vehicle thing is over?" Randall laid down the law when Kendrick came home. No driving until he had clearance from his parents and his doctor.

"No." Lena sighs. "I'll go. But take the garbage cans to the bottom of the driveway. Now." Lena purses her lips so that Kendrick understands she is in no mood to awaken at five tomorrow morning to drag the heavy containers from the backyard to the front of the house.

"I'm watching the fight right now. Later, for sure."

What did her sister say when Lena complained how Camille, Kendrick, and even Randall forget to clean up, pick up, take out, bring in? When she fusses, and she always fusses, they complain, and they always complain that she fusses too much. It's not the messes and the forgetfulness but the assumption that she will take care of it all. And she will. Bobbie said, "Get over it. That's what Mother's Day flowers are for."

She removes Kendrick's medicine and a bottle of vitamins from her pocket and tosses them in his direction. Kendrick's therapist believes in integrative medicine. Kendrick follows most of his instructions: support group on Mondays, therapy sessions on Wednesdays, and long runs.

"You're embarrassing me." Kendrick drops his voice to a deep, quiet timbre and tucks the bottles into his pocket.

"If you don't do what I ask, you're going to be even more embarrassed."

Kendrick steers Lena to the door like an impatient escort on the dance floor. "Just call us when the food is ready." The door slams shut when she steps beyond the threshold. Behind the door, a voice mocks Lena in a high-pitched, falsetto: "Yeah, Kendrick, you're going to be even more embarrassed when I kick your ass across this room."

In the kitchen, the granite counters are covered with the remains of Kendrick's pantry raid: wrappers from two packages of Double-Stuf Oreos, empty, oversized potato chip and pretzel bags. The clock blinks 5:45 and Lena calculates her time: drive to the store, shop, wait in line, cook, clean up. A lone can of soda sits on the counter. Lena pops the top, sips, and scribbles a grocery list wishing all the time that she knew someone to call and find out what she missed in class.

When the last of the plates have been loaded into the dishwasher, Lena sets cookies on a saucer and covers them with a napkin. The kitchen still smells faintly of frying oil—another reason why she no longer cooks this way—and fresh-baked chocolate chip cookies. She saunters through the back hallway, stopping halfway through to shut the laundry room door on the heap of dirty clothes that will stay there until hours before the housekeeper comes. Thursday she will wash them and leave the clean clothes piled atop the dryer for the housekeeper to iron or fold. She ignores a dead bouquet of flowers on the antique table she found at a garage sale and the vase's murky water and heads for the stairs.

"Camille?"

Camille has not made a sound since she emerged from her room to grab a hefty helping of chicken and cornbread. Kimchee mewls behind the bedroom door, and Lena thinks the cat might mean for her to stay away. "I mean, Starless. I have cookies." Lena realizes, maybe for the first time, that her conversations with Camille through closed doors have become a metaphor for their relationship—another barrier to keep them from seeing eye to eye. "Can I come in?"

A chair scrapes against the hardwood floor. Not once, but twice. Camille is not heavy footed, but Lena can tell from the abrasive sound that she has backed away from, not moved closer to, the door. So much for Camille's promise to differentiate herself from friends who withdraw into their rooms and never talk to their parents. The door opens no more than five inches when Lena leans against it. Kimchee slides through the gap and trots down the hallway like he owns the house. Cookies tumble from the saucer when Camille dashes after her cat.

Lena stifles a sneeze against the immediate tingling reaction that starts whenever she comes in contact with the furry feline. When Randall surprised Camille with the cat to motivate her, Lena had no idea she was allergic. No animals of any kind were part of her childhood household except for the summer night when she was eight and a neighbor's cat dashed through a torn screen door and onto Lena's bed. Her Grammie shrieked when she found the scraggly cat at Lena's mouth. The incident was funny to Lena until

Grammie warned there was nothing funny about dying young because a cat sucked away your breath.

Kimchee jumps into Camille's arms. Claws drag across Lena's sweatshirt as Camille scoots past. She scowls with the face of the girl who changed from sweet to sour, once she turned fifteen; tension flits around them like a bothersome moth.

"Please try to control Kimchee, Starless."

"*You're* the one who opened my door, Mother. Nobody else cares."

Sleep comes faster when you read in the bed. That was Bobbie's reasoning in the days they shared a bedroom, and Lena complained she couldn't sleep with the light on. Lena splashes Drambuie into her only glass of the night and rubs her eyes. Beyond the open curtains, the trees are black silhouettes against the sky. The house is hushed and still. What worked for her big sister never worked for her. At nearly two in the morning, and near the end of Tina's story, Lena is wide awake.

"Let's see what else you've got to say, Tina." Without bothering to turn on the lights, Lena slinks down the hallway to her office. "I'll take all the help I can get." One flick of the push-button switch and lamplight blanches the desk and everything across it: neon-colored sticky reminders to call the handyman and pay those bills not automatically deducted from their checking account, twenty or thirty square and rectangular envelopes. Lena brushes aside the old mail: an invitation to an art gallery exhibit last weekend, another to a cocktail party the day after Randall left, a charity fashion show this weekend.

Eyes closed, she tries to conjure up Tina's Mediterranean blue, but all she sees is black. Once she had confidence like Tina. Before Randall's schedule and his corporate social obligations, before the rush to and from soccer practices, sleepovers, dentist appointments, and drama lessons became what she did best; before her chores became more burden than blessing.

A shallow drawer beneath the cherry wood top runs the length of the desk. Lena tips the lamp base, removes the key hidden underneath, and turns it in the brass lock. Inside an open cardboard box sits embossed letterhead and business cards. *Lena Harrison Spencer, Photographer* is printed in an elegant and simple type. The spiral-bound booklet beside the box opens easily to the first page: *The Lena Harrison Spencer Gallery, A Business Plan, May 15, 1999.* Her plan was written in hopes of bank approval on her father's birthday—fifteen, her good luck number. The table of contents summarizes financial requirements, an implementation schedule and darkroom costs, possible mentors, and clientele from her former job at Oakland's Public Information Office—contacts she wanted to make before they forgot what a capable director she was.

Randall came home early that showery April day four years ago, excitement written all over his face. Lena stood at the bedroom window hoping the rain would stop so that she could get in a short run before dinner. The sound of his voice, from all the way downstairs, preceded his arrival. "We did it, Lena!" Once in the room, Randall swept her off her feet and spun her around until they were both dizzy. Camille and Kendrick ran into the bedroom, energized by the joyful commotion. Randall grabbed Camille; Lena grabbed Kendrick. Laughing and spinning, spinning and laughing.

The four of them were infected with Randall's news: they were in the presence of TIDA's new executive vice president, worldwide operations, six-figure bonus, IPO options, possibilities of golden parachutes. Kendrick and Camille jumped around the room and chanted "IPO, IPO" like they understood what it meant.

Before this promotion, when the dot-com building boom filled Silicon Valley, TIDA's board of directors broke the mold and expanded northward from San Francisco to Novato. Randall spearheaded the Novato operations, putting him another step closer to running TIDA; neither he nor Lena felt he could turn down the offer, though the daily, almost eighty-mile roundtrip commute from Oakland would be wearing.

For all of the talk and plans beforehand, Lena underestimated the impact of Randall's worldwide operations appointment. In the beginning, for every day he was out of town, Randall called home. Five-minute conversations where business took a backseat to the ordinary details of their lives; enough time for "I love you" to all three of them and "I wish you were here" to Lena. No coaching Kendrick's soccer team or boisterous applause in the middle of Camille's solemn ballet recitals or input at teacher conferences; no banter, no repartee crisscrossing their dinner table, no middle-of-the-week dates. He couldn't back Lena up when she disciplined Camille or control Kendrick's defiance.

Randall's responsibilities increased. He worked. Hard. The bonus was that he returned to work in San Francisco, but in any given month, he stayed at least two nights in the corporate apartment in Novato. He traveled to their twelve national and international locations. He assembled a new staff, analyzed, brainstormed, strategized new company directions. He dabbled in golf; started smoking cigars and let himself be cajoled into joining the 95 percent white, male-only club on San Francisco's Nob Hill—all to expand his connections, to expose him to the business powers that be. At TIDA, there were introductions to the board and other key players. Lena entertained executives in their home, gave dinner parties, and assured that Randall sat next to those who could further his career.

"Teamwork is what got us here and what will keep us here," became their motto, their mantra. Randall practiced his speeches; Lena corrected, edited, offered feedback that he made his own. She hobnobbed with executives' wives—picked their brains for insight into what their husbands thought of Randall and encouraged them to share TIDA pillow-talk gossip. She was Randall's behind-the-scenes ears, and her public relations skills sold Randall to them, so that they would do the same to their husbands.

But that was Randall, she thinks now, tucking the stationery and business plan back inside the drawer and locking it. When he committed, he went all the way. Home. Family. Work. If he had thoughts about giving up, he never told Lena, and, at the time, she felt blessed knowing his loyalty extended past TIDA to her and their family.

Once the computer awakens, ten hasty keystrokes yield 11,200 hits and 952,000 Tina Turner mentions: flawless skin and charismatic smiles, albums, song lyrics, an international fan club, the location of Tina's star on St. Louis's walk of fame. The official fan club site is filled with one-line blurbs of adoration and appreciation.

So much information, so much tiny print. Each mouse click directs her to different links and websites, each portal leads to more information: a home in Zurich, another in the south of France. Lena scribbles the album titles on a monogrammed tablet, crosses off duplicates. Scroll. Flip. Click. Buy, buy, buy: thirty-eight albums with and without Ike, five DVDs. At another site the lyrics to Tina's songs are available for free.

PRINT PRINT PRINT. Pages spew from the printer with repeated taps on the button in an erratic rhythm of whoosh and whine, then flutter across the floor. Lena stoops to pick up a page and sinks back into the chair, overwhelmed by the wisdom and specificity of her random selection: the song, "I Don't Wanna Fight"; the line, "*This is time for letting go.*"

Chapter 4

The phone rings for the first time all day. Either Kendrick or Camille will answer it. Lena is unsure until she hears Camille's voice. Kendrick never liked talking on the phone, and now, more than ever, he avoids it.

"Hey, Dad." Camille paces the hallway and responds to what Lena assumes is her father's litany of questions. Her voice is conspiratorial. "School's okay . . . my senior project . . . any day now. Get ready. It's either Columbia or NYU . . . in the bed . . . in his room. Yes, Dad, I'm taking care of Kimchee. I miss you, too." Camille pounds on Kendrick's door—the pesky little sister she pretends to be. "It's Dad."

Kendrick's deep pitch is barely distinguishable from Randall's. Like Camille, he paces the hallway, too, allowing Lena to overhear fragments of his conversation: Dr. Miller, car, the fellas. He walks into the master bedroom, hands the phone to his mother as if she cannot use the one beside her bed, and pauses long enough to take a pair of sunglasses from the top of Randall's dresser.

Lena greets Randall in what she hopes is a version of Camille and Kendrick's light, happy tone.

"Today's been a fiasco." Randall yawns. "Thompson fucked up the terms for a critical section of the contract. He forgot federally regulated language that could have blown this whole deal wide open."

The negotiation for TIDA's acquisition of another high-tech communications company has taken most of the past eleven months. So long that Lena wonders how his veteran assistant could have made such a grave error.

"He's on his way home." The irritation in Randall's voice is unmistakable, although Lena can't decide if it's because of the error or his fatigue. "I had to postpone my return. So, I'll be home Tuesday night instead of Sunday. The limo service will pick me up."

Lena winces. The next photography class is Tuesday night. "Other than that, what's it like over there?" Her intention is not to trivialize his return. *What's it like over there*? Stupid. Maybe the connection will soften her words, soften him.

"Hong Kong is just another big city with signs I can't read. I can't wait to meet up with Charles. I hear Bali is beautiful." When Randall found out Charles would be in Bali at the same time he was in Hong Kong, he took his best friend up on his suggestion to tag on a short vacation at the end of his trip. Randall snickers and yawns again. "You'd love it—except, of course, for the spiders."

"Ha, ha. Very funny." Through the window, thin fog curls like smoke in the cone of light under the street lamp. The wind carries the sound of a train whistle, and Lena is astonished at how the warbled echo travels from the station five miles below and beyond their house. "There was a big black spider on your pillow the other day." She flinches with the recollection and glances around the room.

The silence between them is so loud that Lena taps the handset to see if they are still connected.

"I'm ten thousand miles away, Lena, with more on my mind to worry about than a little spider."

"I'm sorry . . . I know you're busy."

"Call the exterminator. Have him spray outside the house, the windows, and the attic. That should take care of it."

"Do you think it was some kind of omen?" Some kind of omen that means the opposite of wealth and good luck, she wonders.

"It was a spider, Lena. I'm my own omen—*I* make the shit happen." Randall laughs. Not the hearty laugh that brushed her cheek those Sunday mornings they used to sleep in, nestled eye to eye, full of gossip and plans for what they will do—play poker, visit Tahiti, romp in the sand in the south of France—when Randall retires. His laugh is cool and distant; the one reserved for clients, the one that makes him appear noncommittal, more than competent. Controlled. "Have you made any decisions?"

"Decisions?"

"You heard me. I won't put my life on hold until you figure out how good you've got it."

Months after his promotion, in a trendy San Francisco restaurant, Randall spoke to Lena of how being the only black man in the inner circle, where no one made less than a seven-figure salary, made him watch his every step. The double stress plagued black men, he told her, especially where the fraternity of black power brokers was limited and fragile.

"Success is a game—aka the black man's burden—act white, fight white to get to the top. Then fight, any way you can, to prove that you deserve to be there."

Lena watched Randall, with barely a blink or a breath, while he described, not for the first time, the need to fight stereotypes that could turn a black man into something less than whole and accusations that lacked substance: forgetting where one came from and selling out; smart but not smart enough, the expectation of failure. The pressure he felt from all sides was palpable, but he remained determined to do whatever it took to be successful.

At the next table, a man held a match to his cigar and puffed madly until the chubby stick of tobacco caught the flame. Lena inhaled the strong, bitter scent that reminded her of Saturday night chats with John Henry when she was a teen, reminded her of the puffs he let her take when Lulu wasn't watching.

"I won't be around as much as I'd like. I know how much you do. And I appreciate it." Randall took a slender, black box from his jacket, slid it across the table, and opened it. Couples to the left and right stared when Lena gasped at the large, radiant yellow diamond attached to a delicate, narrow platinum chain. The stone glistened in the candlelight in that way that only a clear diamond can. Randall stepped behind Lena and fastened the necklace around her neck while the same couples applauded and asked if it was their anniversary or her birthday.

She turned and pressed her lips to his, the promise in her eyes of more than that to come. "Thank you, sweetie. I love you, and I'm behind you one hundred percent."

Randall raised his glass in a toast. He waited until she finished her wine and poured a little more into their glasses and reminded her that none of the other executives' wives worked. "I know you're ready to launch your business. Put your plans on hold. For a while. Forever if you want. At least until I'm established, more trusted at TIDA."

His scattered and disjointed phrases were so unlike him that Lena wondered if he was nervous. She watched his face, the clear skin, the absence of wrinkles that made so many people mistake him for much younger than his then fifty-three years. His eyes focused on the stone on her chest. His expression affirmed his satisfaction in the incline of his head, the angle of his neatly clipped mustache, and she wondered what other sacrifices she would make for the sake of his career.

The diamond pulsed with the rapid beat of Lena's heart. Randall's lips moved but she could not hear what he said. She fingered the yellow stone and smiled. "Is this a bribe or a thank-you?"

"Both." Randall grinned. "You'll have more time. You can come with me on my trips. We'll see the world on TIDA's dime. When the time is right, I'll help you start again. I promise."

The cigar smoke wafted closer to their table. Her second, deep breath brought back John Henry and the white smoke that had streamed from her father's lips between sips from his Saturday night glass of Jack Daniel's on the rocks. He had doled out advice on life while she tried to figure out racism or Catholicism or problems as simple as boys and dating; and later, how hard she had to fight for the life she wanted. "What the hell did you expect, Lena Inez?" John Henry fussed one night. "You want the life, you got to pay the price."

"Maybe *we* could get away when you come home."

"I'm not going anywhere any time soon. Unless I have to." If punctuation marks could be heard, Lena thinks, exclamation points would have banged like a firecracker at the end of Randall's sentence. Fatigue and irritation slip from his voice. "As a matter of fact, right now, I'm sick of hotels, of people who don't look or sound like me. I'm sick of the stares. I need a dose of black people. I want a party when I get home. Ten, maybe twelve people, that standing rib roast you make." At their last party months ago, their guests refused to leave until well after three in the morning. Reluctant to let go of the good feeling, Randall opened another bottle of wine. Lena retrieved the remains of dessert, and they stayed up until the rising sun tinted the sky pinkish yellow.

"I'd really like to wait until the situation is. . . smoother between us?" Or, she thinks, until her funk moves on.

"Make sure you invite Candace. I get a kick out of her theatrics."

"I saw her the other day. She had some sad news."

"Don't tell me: she needs more jewelry."

Lena cannot read the signs of his strong voice. There is no strain, although she can't deny its edginess. "It's not always about what you can buy, Randall. Dana and Carl are getting divorced."

"Well, scratch them off the list. It'll be good to see our friends."

"Please, Randall, can we decide about the party when you come home?" Three. Lena counts on her fingers, three more days.

"Nothing to decide. Just handle it."

Almost as soon as Lena presses the seventh digit of the number written on the bottom of the enrollment slip, a man answers the phone. The instructor's voice is twangy and aged when he answers with his full name instead of hello. She offers an explanation for missing the first class with a very adult excuse: "For personal reasons."

"Are you a serious photographer?"

The instructor listens without comment while Lena takes five minutes to summarize why she wants to hone her rusty skills.

"There are Saturday labs. You can develop your film at home. I'm not interested in people who need to fill their empty schedules."

If she thought he would care, Lena would tell the cranky instructor that she has plenty to fill her schedule; it's the hole in her spirit she needs to fill. "I'm serious. I'll do whatever I have to, but I won't be able to make the second class either. Can you give me your notes and the assignment so that I can keep up?"

"My policy's simple: skip one class, you're okay. Skip class twice, you gotta problem." He presses on with more terse words about dedication and continuity that Lena tunes out. "It's up to you, but the more you miss, the more behind you get."

The phone clicks off before she can tell him anything more. Sinking back into the bed, Lena lets sleep take over. Snakes and water. A man's hand beckons her into a gently breaking black surf, and she slips below. Her fishlike mouth opens to swallow people-plankton drifting by: Randall entwined in a headless woman's arms, a baby Kendrick morphing into a man, Camille crowned with stars, Candace's hand covered with pinky rings. Lena twirls, the reverse of falling into the sucking liquid, yet able to watch herself, hair swirling in slow motion, shrunk to its beloved nap. Diamond earrings glimmer in shrinking lobes, vibrant red fingernails. Wedding bands float past like dazzling schools of fish.

Beside an open coffin Tina Turner wears a zoot suit. Lena

belches bubbles full of a merry Randall, Kendrick, and Camille. Each bubble rises past schools of silver fish, past coral and seaweed and thrusts her up, up, up. Lena rises to the surface, naked before God's bluest sky and Tina Turner's outstretched arms.

The sheets are soaked when Lena awakens. The room is neither hot nor cold, yet she shivers as if it is the middle of winter and tries to understand her dream. Listen to Tina. Be the good girl—a girl at fifty-four. Follow the rules. Consider the blessings. Randall wants a party. He's tired. What's a little attitude in exchange for the life he has given her? And she has more than enough: this house, clothes, no worries, and diamonds on her fingers, neck, and ears.

The pictures, the memories spill from the planner when Lena picks it up. How innocent Kendrick looked in his Halloween costume, his first one. He was a puppy. When Lena explained that animals didn't make good costumes, he looked at her with a serious face and insisted. Camille liked ballet, liked dressing up and being the center of attention. She posed for hours in the mirror practicing pirouettes and pliés.

The account withdrawal slip is thin and narrow. Randall and Lena's full names are imprinted in block letters in the upper left-hand corner. On the photography enrollment paperwork her name is written in the same way and, looking from one piece of paper to the other, it seems odd to see hers by itself. Taking the two pieces of paper in her hands, Lena tears and tears until they blend into an unrecognizable heap atop the sheets.

Chapter 5

Ten after eight. Step fast, faster. Randall hates waiting, especially after a long trip. This afternoon Lena cleaned the house from top to bottom, right alongside the housekeeper. She cancelled Randall's car service and decided to pick him up like she did when his business trips first began to take him around the world. The Drambuie is back in the liquor cabinet; fresh linens envelop the bed. Run, Lena, run. Past people speaking in French, Spanish, and a myriad of Asian languages all intoned with joyous inflections that need no translation. Past a smattering of kohl-eyed Indian women swathed in silk saris, Filipino men in embroidered linen barong shirts, and Asian businessmen in conservative sharkskin suits.

Run, Lena, run. Passengers exit customs through two cordoned-off hallways. TV monitors flash weary and preoccupied faces to watchful loved ones and chauffeurs with handwritten signs. Randall's image crosses the screen. His trademark heavy-heeled gait is slow. Lena giggles; a surprise to herself and the man next to her.

Nearly fifty-eight, Randall is handsome in a way Lena knows women envy men for, the good looks that seem to get better with age. His head bobs to a rhythm only he can hear; maybe Miles or Charlie Parker or one of the little-known jazz artists he loves to discover. Scrunched forehead, heavy eyelids and tight lips; yet clean-shaven and crisp. How he manages to keep his clothes wrinkle free after long drives and even longer flights is a mystery that Lena appreciates but cannot understand. Thirty-four days of meals in fancy restaurants have left his stomach with a slight paunch that Lena knows he'll work off with his trainer. He looks good, as good as he did all those years ago when she spotted him on the dance floor, and her heart commanded him to look her way.

Lena was twenty, and Randall just turned twenty-four, that summer she walked into the party and noticed him. It was the cock of his head, the bass in his voice, and the confidence in his hands as he gave the high sign to his buddy, Charles, that first attracted her. She walked to his side of the room, lingered close to where he stood, and popped her fingers to the music. She figured he was bright, or she obvious, when he turned to talk to her and flaunted his credentials like an Easter litany: almost done with his MBA at Wharton, new GTO, the only summer intern in an all-white corporate communications firm, just shy of being a token, because he was smart. His stance, his articulation, assumed she would swoon over his budding potential.

Instead she told him a joke. A stupid joke. "Knock, knock." She tapped on his arm and made him ask who's there. "Orange," she answered. "Orange you glad I came over here?"

Lena sashays to the end of the customs exit corridor and lifts onto her toes to meet Randall's face four inches above her five-eight frame. "Welcome home!" She sniffs: pepper, cinnamon, and a hint of the fifteen-hour plane ride. He is her first love. Her love is centered in that place of emotion, not words; she will always love him. At this moment, she longs for that old heart-to-stomach-to-toes tingle she used to feel with the very thought of him. She angles her head in what she hopes is a seductive tilt and stretches her arms around his neck.

"Well, this is a surprise." Randall makes a smacking *mmm-wha* sound as he brushes her lips. "What got into you?"

"You!" Lena grins and lowers herself, but not her expectations, for there is a bottle of Duckhorn merlot in a sterling silver wine bucket at the foot of the six-foot bathtub at home. *The Gentle Side of Coltrane*, one of Randall's beloved albums—a compilation much like the one that played after the memories of the Tina Turner concert faded, and he seduced her—is on the stereo queued and ready to play.

That night was romantic, one of a kind. There was a shadow of beard on his chin then, like the one there now, but that was the silky shadow of a young man not in need of the daily use of a razor. Lena slides her fingers down Randall's cheek and over his prickly overnight stubble. "Tired?"

"Bushed." He stretches his empty hand and wavers momentarily; his hand stuck between handshake and hug, between peace offering and affection. His lips form a tight smile; fatigue or disinterest Lena cannot tell. Her hand goes up while his goes down, brushing only at that point, that fulcrum of mismatched timing, capturing only electricity and knobby knuckles.

Sadness and sameness run from her heart to her stomach to her toes. She picks up the lighter of his two bags, a leather duffle she gave to him one Christmas, and heads for the parking lot. "That's all?"

"If I said anything more, I'd have to sing, and I thought you said I should leave the falsetto to Smokey." He chuckles and stretches his arm around her shoulder; the airport, the exiting passengers, the gigantic monitors and patrolling security guards, anything but her eyes the focus of his attention.

At the exit of the crowded parking lot, Lena pulls onto the freeway and floors the accelerator until the speedometer twitches close to ninety and the gray marble facade of San Francisco International Airport looms far behind them. The last time she dropped Randall off, he chided her, all the way to the airport, for her racecar antics and the three or four hundred dollar moving violation that the highway patrol would issue to a black woman in a very expensive, very red convertible.

This evening, silence is a third passenger in the car. Lena rehearsed the scene, this ride home, in her head: she would say she missed him, he would say he missed her, too, and that he wants her to have the sense of self-reliance she seeks. No decision necessary.

Tina's voice rings out from the radio's speakers. Like the lyrics that slipped off the printer, this song is perfectly timed. Tina sings what Lena wants to say:

Two people gotta stick together
And love one another, save it for a rainy day

Lena looks from the road to her husband's profile; his broad nose and full lips—the thick salt-and-pepper mustache above them—are fixed in a stern pout. The car is a finely tuned instrument, as controlled and syncopated as the melody. The gears switch to the music's beat, and Lena steers in and out of the choppy Highway 101 traffic, back to the Bay Bridge and to Oakland.

"I missed you."

"It's been a long time." Randall turns off the radio and pats her thigh. "The woman next to me on the plane wouldn't shut up. The quiet suits me just fine."

They pass San Francisco's skyline to the west—the thin pyramid skyscraper and its stair-step sisters compete with one another in their stretch to the sky—the blue-black waters of the bay to the east. New York, Rome, Barcelona, Lena thinks—no matter where she goes in the world, this view of tall buildings and twinkling lights, stars under stars, is as beautiful as any place else she has ever seen.

Their house perches on a low knoll fifty feet back from the sidewalk. It is not the biggest house on the block, but it has the most curb appeal. There is no moon this evening to light the wide front porch, the square edges of its overhang, and the well-groomed lawn. Headlights cast a halogen glow on the white petunias bordering the curb. Clusters of redwood and oak trees on either side of the house form immense shadows around the yard.

"Frank does a great job with the lawn." Randall unbuckles his seat belt as Lena eases into the garage beside their stucco house.

Lena points out the tree drooping beside the garage. "He says the lemon tree is dead, and we have to decide what to replace it with." She will make this decision without Randall. The gardener will bow deferentially to Lena, as he has on other occasions, when she tells him to replace the forty-year-old tree with a younger, healthier one. It will take the sapling years to develop before the sweet fragrance of a mature tree can once again perfume a summer's night.

Loud music blasts from the house—more bass than words. Kendrick's stereo booms a rapper's version of a tough life their son has never known and connects Randall and Lena where their airport reunion did not. Together their heads shake in disapproval of the hard-edged music. Lena tolerates rap, at least those songs whose lyrics she can understand. Randall has said repeatedly that it's a waste of time, and his face says so now. But his face also says he's happy to hear the familiar sounds that confirm all is normal.

"Well, it's this way," Randall says, his version of prayer, his thanks for a safe trip home. Early in their marriage he explained his appreciation for shortened prayers: too much of his youth spent in all-day Sunday school. With the exception of funerals—his mother, John Henry, and a college classmate—he avoids church. For now these four words are as close to prayer as he gets. Luggage in hand, he wanders past green granite countertops, a sleek stainless steel refrigerator, and a three hundred dollar toaster to hallway to living room to sunroom to his office. Once there, he rifles through his mail and grabs the latest issue of *Audiophile Quarterly.*

Less than a minute later, he raps on Kendrick's door and hugs him when the door swings wide open.

"Looking good, Junior."

"What's with the Junior, Senior? That stopped in eighth grade. Not getting that over-the-hill disease are you?"

There it is. Lena pauses on the stairs to listen—the sound of harmony. Family. Home.

They prop themselves against the doorframe, father to the left, son to the right. Kendrick's smooth face echoes Randall's. They are similar in many ways: their legs cross left over right, the intensity in their eyes and language, words emphasized with their hands.

"Not much to report, Dad. Therapy. Looking for part-time work. Ready to go back to school. Still not driving—boring."

Randall fakes a cuff to Kendrick's chin and motions to him to follow down the hall. "I think we may be able to do something about that."

"Camille!" Kimchee meows as if Randall is calling him; a loud salutation, Lena knows, to its second master. Forever and a day she will despise cats. If Kimchee were human, Lena would tell the cat not to take it personally. Camille skips down the hall, Kimchee cuddled in her arms. The open door behind her releases the smell of the sour litterbox.

"Hello, kitty," Randall smoothes the scruff of Kimchee's neck. "Hey, Camille, how's my big girl?"

"Starless, Dad, Starless. And I've been a 'big girl' for a long time."

"Two things: one, I named you Camille, and that's what I'll call you." Randall busses Camille's cheek. "And two, I'm sad to report that I know you're a big girl—the reminder's for me, not you, Miz Smart-aleck."

"Then I guess I can make an exception. This time." Like the little girl she once was, Camille leans into her father's open arms and thrusts an oversized envelope into his hands. "Columbia, Dad!

The letter came yesterday." Her hands punctuate her words, too, and Randall embraces her again.

Lena halts mid-step on the staircase's last step. "Congratulations, honey!" She shouts the only response she can. This news is new to her. Though she should have known weeks ago that Camille would keep her acceptance to herself when, nervous to hear from colleges, she demanded her right to pick up the daily mail without having to compete with Lena. She was tired of Lena's over-mothering, her nagging to wear practical clothes, to stick to deadlines, to help with the mountain of essays and paperwork throughout the whole college application process. She wanted to get the acceptance—or rejection—letters first.

"And what about your brother here?" Randall asks. "Is it time to give him back the keys to his car? Have you kept an eye on him?"

"Kendrick's doing really great, Dad! He's ready." Camille slaps Kendrick high five. "And what little goodies did you bring your wonderful offspring this time, hmmmm?" The two follow their father down the hallway past Lena's framed photos of the family in various stages of life—baptism, kindergarten, chicken pox—their faces as full of anticipation as they were when he first began to travel. A younger Kendrick and Camille fought to carry Randall's suitcase, fought to open it. Now they stroll behind their father with the presumption of gifts in their stride.

"Didn't have time to shop. Too busy closing my deal." Randall turns both thumbs upward. "Your old man kicked ass, if I do say so myself." Kendrick extends a fist to give his dad the secret handshake they invented when he was nine—Randall's salute to the good old days, Kendrick's to a newly found discovery of Black Power. Fist. Palm. Black side. Fist.

Camille perches on the bed. Kendrick plops onto the chaise near the windows. To Lena, the large room seems crowded with the four of them in it; everyone seems adult and oversized; funny, the way time changes everything. So different from the Saturday mornings Kendrick and toddler Camille tiptoed into this bedroom and begged to watch cartoons, while she and Randall pretended to complain about the invasion of their privacy.

"Tell us about your trip." Lena motions to Randall to hold off his answer while she ducks into the bathroom to adjust the faucets so that the hot water will slowly fill the oversized tub and cool to a comfortable temperature by the time she and Randall get in.

Randall opens his suitcase and waits for Lena to return. The first layer is organized into sections: toiletries, clothes cleaned and laundered before he left the hotel. When Lena reenters the bedroom, Randall condenses three days into one concise description. In Bali, he and Charles saw buildings unlike any in Western architecture: stone temples nestled in mountain crevices or perched above a roiling sea, bald-headed monks draped in yards of orange cloth who tended to the grounds and prayed for the world.

He pulls packages out of the suitcase one at a time and with practiced flourish. "In a few of the temples, men could wear orange wraps like the monks. I thought I'd spare you that." He tosses a plastic bag to Kendrick, who catches it with one hand, and waits for Kendrick to open his bag of designer-rip-off shirts.

"Hella cool. Thanks, Dad."

"And you, Camille, should know that some people consider dance and drama the very essence of culture in Bali. Since we all know what a drama queen you can be . . ." Camille feigns offense with a look half smile, half pout. Randall grabs her hand, dances a one, two cha-cha-cha, like they did at the cotillion months earlier, and hands Camille a pouch. "I bought these to help."

Camille pulls the plastic apart and slips bangles onto one arm then her other until the bag is empty. "Thanks, Dad. I love this stuff." There are at least a hundred of them: silver and gold, colored rhinestones glitter from some, others are painted in vibrant blues, reds, and yellows; they ping and clink when she shakes her arm. The bangles complete her outfit; a long, ruffled skirt, homespun scarf around her head, her bare feet.

"I bought traditional outfits—one for Sharon and one for my secretary." Randall removes two flattened, white paper bags tied with rough string from his suitcase and stuffs them into his leather bag. "They worked hard for me on this end. They kept me on track and the local wolves at bay. I couldn't have gotten my work done without them."

"Where's Mom's gift?" Camille rummages through Randall's suitcase.

"If I recall, you're not into material things anymore." Randall stretches and saunters to the bedroom window. He yawns and looks directly at Lena without a hint of a smile or grin or taunt of possibilities to come. "You have everything you need. Right?"

The smile on Lena's face is telltale; her jewelry box is crowded with expensive trinkets and intricate charms from every trip that Randall has ever taken. She gets Randall's mockery and understands his message. "That's right. I am truly blessed."

"Aw, he's kidding." Kendrick gives Randall an all-knowing wink. "Give her the goods, Pops."

Camille looks from her father to mother and back to her father's face for a sign that Randall is indeed teasing, is indeed about to pull some shiny bauble from one of his pockets. "Have these, Mom." Camille tugs a few bracelets from her wrists and slides them on to Lena's arm. "Give her the outfit you said was for Sharon, Dad."

"It's just a token, not something your mom would like." Randall's short, urgent sigh, Lena tells herself, is exasperation not exhaustion. "But, I can always treat Sharon to an expensive meal."

Whenever Randall comes home from his trips, Lena unpacks his suitcase. A habit turned expectation that grew into its own ritual over the years and gave them time alone; like picking him up from the airport before he became a bigwig. Sometimes he sat on the side of the bed or in the chaise and regaled her with road gossip. Sometimes he waited for Camille and Kendrick to leave their room to tell her how much he missed her, or shut the door and showed her.

Now Lena takes *I, Tina* from the nightstand and walks past their king-sized bed, the rectangle of his open suitcase, and into her office. He is punishing her, she knows, punishing her for questioning the life he wants for her: be the good girl, follow the rules. She reads her email, goes onto the official Tina Turner site and resists the temptation to rush to the stereo, to turn off Coltrane's saxophone just now beginning to drift through the house and exchange it for Tina's music as loud as the speakers will permit.

Near the end of her time with Ike, Tina visited a friend who practiced Buddhism. The visual of the woman, though not her name, is still in Lena's head: the woman, and soon afterward Tina, made a small altar before which they could sit and chant and mold a ritual to soothe their spirits and make them strong.

Two stubby candles still sit on her desk. With a candle on either side, and a stack of Tina's CDs atop the paperback, Lena reminds herself to pick up incense and a holder, perhaps a crystal, tomorrow. Her ritual, she thinks, does not have to be elaborate. The process of lighting the candles, of slowing down her thoughts, of scanning random passages from *I, Tina* helps her to gather, little by little, the sum of all the parts—good and not—to help her to press on.

By the time she steps into the bathroom, Randall is already soaking in the tub. Two glasses of wine, his nearly empty, sit on the marble-tiled ledge. He slurps his wine and, eyes closed, rests his head against the tiled wall behind him. "Ahhhh. I needed this. Thanks, hon."

Lena kneels beside the tub so that her face looks directly at his and drags her hand through the scented water, forcing steam and the odor of musk to drift in the air between them. "I can't help but wonder, Randall, how keeping you on track makes your secretary and your assistant more worthy of your thoughtfulness than your wife."

"It's no big deal, Lena. You don't like cheap stuff anyway. I'll take you to San Francisco next week. You can pick up something then."

"That's not the point, Randall."

"The point is I'm home, not with them, and I'm tired."

Her boots come off slowly, as do her cashmere sweater and tight jeans. She tosses them next to the four pairs left on the floor from earlier this evening before she settled on the French ones, to show off her hips. Randall did not notice her hips or the jeans at the airport, just as at this minute, eyes closed in a trance of concentration, he doesn't notice her nakedness.

The water sloshes against the sides of the long tub when Lena stirs it with her foot. When she steps in, Randall opens his eyes and leans forward. He cups her breasts and massages them in that way that always makes her moan. Lena pulls away before she does, before she starts something even her momentary meditation has left her still too upset to finish.

"I'm already feeling the jet lag." Randall scoops hot water over his chest and head and repeats this motion two more times. Wrinkled eyebrows keep the rivulets from his eyes. "I'm ready to sleep in my own bed." He swallows the rest of his wine with one quick swig, steps out of the tub, and dries himself roughly before going off to bed.

The rasp of Randall's snores matches the sawing sounds of the final minutes of a movie on TV. Sleep is the only time that anyone would label Randall peaceful. If she is awake, when he lies motionless in the middle of the night like this, Lena often pokes his shoulder, his neck, his thigh in anticipation of the slightest movement: proof he is still alive and well. Half-open eyes tell Lena he is somewhere between dream and arousal.

Randall tugs her close, tickles her with his tongue in a new place, and she gasps from the sensation. They blend together in their familiar way. She surrenders to his touch, the bristle of his mustache, a hint of musk oil. There is no urgency to his movement, yet he comes swiftly, leaving Lena wanting more.

Chapter 6

Lulu and John Henry's dream house looks the same as the day they bought it in 1965. The house is painted a pale color somewhere between beige and rust; a lamp that switches on at 4:30 p.m. and off at 7:30 a.m. every spring, summer, winter, and fall. Year round Christmas lights, more fragments than bulbs, loop under the eaves and around the three-sided bay window that dominates the front of the house.

Whenever Bobbie and Lena complained of how embarrassed they were by the lights and the hideous, old-fashioned paint, John Henry told them he didn't have a problem with change as long as it stayed away from him. The biggest change he'd made in his life, he told his daughters every time, was coming to California, and, since he wasn't a risk taker, he saw no need to push his luck.

"Lulu? You in the backyard?" Lena ducks around the low branches of the California oak where she and Bobbie always wanted John Henry to build a tree house. The limbs of snowball hydrangeas straggle over the path; low pink azaleas, in ironic harmony with the painted red cement, ramble below. Two garbage cans filled with dead leaves sit in the middle of the path. This Wednesday, like every Wednesday of the eighteen months since John Henry passed, Lena feels like she has become her father. She lugs the trash to the curb where neighbors' cans jaggedly line the street up one side and down the other like whole notes in a measure of music.

Once done, she heads for the backyard. The yard that used to be John Henry's pride and joy is unkempt in a way that shocks this daughter of parents once so fastidious: overgrown hedges, scraggly lawn, brown spots on camellia leaves, wiry rose bushes; an apple tree branch hangs doggedly parallel to its trunk.

Lulu's posture is effortlessly straight-backed. She holds a tarnished brass nozzle attached to a green-striped garden hose in her left hand and listens intently to someone's conversation on the other end of the cell phone squeezed between her right ear and shoulder. The bluish rinse that Lulu tints her thin, curly afro with glistens in the sun. Not one hair on her head is out of place, no wrinkles in her blouse, not a drop of water on her pants. Lena can't help but smile at how beautiful her mother still is, how the color of her clothes warms her skin.

Phone still in place, Lulu holds two conversations at the same time. "Tell me your *husband* didn't see you looking like that? At least you could've put on lipstick." Lulu never goes without her trademark lipstick. Today, her fuchsia lips match the budding azaleas, her cardigan, and her loose ankle-length pants. "He back yet?"

Lulu is a petite woman; her frame frail and shrinking with each passing year. Lena bends, touching her lips to Lulu's cheek, and sniffs. Floral perfume is Lulu's trademark, too; its fragrance comfortable and reassuring; her forgetfulness is not. Three times over the last month, Lena has had to remind Lulu of details she should know—Randall is out of town, Kendrick is home and not away at college, Camille is about to graduate from high school, Bobbie lives in New York.

"Randall came home yesterday. Remember?"

"That son-in-law of mine is always off somewhere—China, Paris, New York—making big-time deals." Lulu shouts into the phone in the way octogenarians often do, forgetting the sophistication of cell phone technology. The hose falls to the ground and snakes beneath her folding chair. "He's the executive vice president at TIDA, you know. The only black that high up. I'm surprised

Lena didn't go with him and stay in one of those nine-hundred-dollar-a-night hotels he loves."

Lulu is Randall's biggest fan, and, on some level, Lena is both proud and bored with Lulu's exaggerations. Lulu winks, covers the handset, and mouths words that Lena cannot decipher because, despite this habit her mother has had for all of Lena's life—in church, behind John Henry's back, in rooms full of noisy relatives—Lena is not good at lip-reading. Lulu tells whomever is on the other end of the line she has to go and clamps the phone shut.

"You need a gardener, Lulu. What if I can't come over every Wednesday?"

"I'm not helpless." Lulu's knuckles are knotted with arthritis. She flexes her fingers and lays her hands on Lena's. "How's my baby girl doin' on this glorious day?"

Lulu presses her hands to Lena's temples. No need, Lena believes, to bother Lulu. John Henry and Lulu's marriage was different, maybe exceptional. They grew up in a Mississippi town with only a postal route number and no name. The day John Henry came home from World War II, he asked for Lulu's hand in marriage. The two of them worked hard, raised their girls, and spoiled them as rotten as they could on their government salaries.

John Henry took care of everything. He doted on his wife. He drove Lulu to work, to church, the grocery store, and shopping and brought his check home every Friday. In return, Lulu took care of him, served his dinner every evening at six sharp—a saucer of finely chopped onions beside his plate no matter what she cooked. She ironed his clothes and let him play poker with his buddies once a month.

"Did you ever feel like you were . . . losing yourself?" Once Lena believed her attachment to a powerful mate completed her. Power shifted their relationship, hers and Randall's, bifurcated their growth, like a tree, into independent directions ignoring the trunk that made it one; forgetting to meet at a glorious crown, joined and whole. Now she knows she cannot tell when her husband of twenty-three years lost his respect for her. But that loss has weakened her.

"Honey, that losing yourself thing is strictly for your generation. I knew where I was all of the time." Lulu chuckles. Picking up the nozzle, she takes a bottle of aspirin from her pocket. The cap is one of those now old-fashioned, no-childproof tops.

"I need to make some changes. And Randall is a little . . . impatient."

"I hope you're not thinking about that photography business again." The day Lena completed her acceptance paperwork for UCLA, John Henry, checkbook in hand, and Lulu stood beside her prepared to pay her tuition on one condition: no photography. They weren't about to waste their hard-earned money on frivolity: college was about getting a good job, a nine-to-five-with-an-hour-for-lunch job, a government job, a GS 12 or 15 job with a pension, vacation, and benefits.

"I *always* took care of my family first." Lulu jiggles pills straight from the bottle into her mouth, then sips from the nozzle. "Women have to put up with a man's moodiness until it runs its course."

"Maybe Bobbie should get her butt out here and benefit from some of this advice." Her big sister always says Lena tells their mother too much.

"It doesn't apply . . . and, Bobbie thinks her books are more important than . . . anything else. Maybe if she listened, she could have a husband, too." Lulu holds on to the chair to stand fully upright. "You forget how lucky you are. You're living the life I dreamed for you . . ."

"What can I help you with today? I won't be able to stay as long as usual, I've got to get ready for Saturday. Randall wants friends over for dinner."

"That's nice, baby girl. That should make Randall happy." Holding her right elbow with her left hand, Lulu opens then shuts the sliding glass door to the sparsely furnished family room behind them. After John Henry dropped dead of a heart attack on the eve of their fifty-ninth wedding anniversary, Lulu went into a frenzy. She threw away John Henry's yellowed, fake-leather recliner, years of past issues of *Life* and *National Geographic,* unopened liquor bottles, except for the now forty-year-old bottle of twenty-year-old blended scotch whiskey Bobbie gave them years ago as an anniversary present, the old TV, the broken hi-fi and the treadmill John Henry used every other day until it broke.

After Lulu forces the metal latches—top, bottom, and two above the handle—closed to the accompaniment of small grunts, Lena heads for John Henry's tool room, the one room Lulu left untouched, and grabs a can of WD-40. At the sliding door, she sprays each of the four latches and the metal runner tracks. She works the latches and the door back and forth until they roll without effort.

Lulu pushes at Lena's arm. "You get on home. Get ready for your party. Fix yourself up. You have a good life, Lena—I know I'm repeating, but it's the truth."

"What if that isn't enough?"

"Then *make* it enough. Make it enough to last until death do you part. I hope you're not thinking about doing something foolish. There's no way you could live like you do without Randall."

"You . . . you sound like a page from a black-mama manual: if you got a man, then you got to be happy." Mother and daughter stand opposite one another, two sets of hands perched on their own hips just like they did when Lena was a teenager, eager to get from under her mother's old-timey ways.

The locks glide open when Lulu opens the glass door, and Lena knows she is being ordered to leave, as Lulu's superstitions demand, the same way she came in.

"I'll get somebody—at least to cut the lawn and trim the roses, there are so many." Lulu sighs with resignation, as if this decision is her punishment for growing old without a man, and heads toward a full white rose bush. She nips three blossoms with her shears. "This is an Austin tea rose. Your father gave it to me for our fortieth anniversary. It stands for happy love." She dribbles water from the hose onto a paper towel then wraps it around the thorny stems and hands the bouquet to Lena. When Lulu starts to water the lawn again, it occurs to Lena that Lulu has been watering the same spot since she arrived. She is either methodical or more forgetful than Lena cares to ponder.

"How are you feeling, Lulu?"

"Don't worry about me; I'm fine. Your father would take care of the yard, if he were here. Your father was the man." Her words are practiced like the rosary she recites every Friday morning. "Your Uncle Joe was busy all of the time. He was a big shot, like Randall. Worked day and night on his real estate business so his family could have a big house—not as big as yours—and a new Cadillac every year. Inez liked to decorate, but she had to ask your uncle for the money." Lulu's face is serious, her eyelids close.

"What does this have to do with me?"

"Well, when Inez wanted new wallpaper in her bathroom, she peeled pieces from around the bathtub, the sink, places she knew Joe would notice, and she flushed them, and a few women's items, down the toilet. When the toilet backed up, Joe told Inez to call the plumber and while she was at it, she might as well get somebody to replace the wallpaper as well." The wind sprays dirt onto Lulu's face. She wipes her eyes with a lacy handkerchief peeking from her pant pocket and aims the water at the wilted juniper bushes beyond.

"I can't believe Uncle Joe was that stupid."

Lulu ignores the metered patter of Lena's foot intended to get Lulu to make her point. She pauses, her smile the best indication of how much she is enjoying her story and her daughter's undivided attention.

"Men need to *see* things to understand them. They don't like to *hear* about women's problems. If a woman understands the man, the man will understand the woman."

"I think you're never on my side."

"I know you don't like what I'm saying, Lena. You probably think it's old-fashioned, but that little piece of advice kept my man by my side for one day short of fifty-nine years. Figure out how to handle your husband while you *think* on that."

Chapter 7

Shoppers stare at Lena's tear-smudged eyes; a toddler points a chubby finger; his mother shushes and whisks the child away.

"Why did you talk to Lulu about you and Randall?" Bobbie asks. The sister Tina loved, Lena recalls, was not around when life turned bad. Growing up, Lena went to Bobbie when she wanted to know about life, bribing her first with hot cocoa and extra marshmallows before Bobbie would talk to her little sister. Lulu's advice was most thorough when it came to etiquette and politics. She told her daughters how to vote (Democrat) and why (hundreds of Negroes beaten with hoses, arrested, suffered, some killed so that every Negro in America could), but not how to handle a man; just that they needed one. Lena knows that Bobbie, miles away in New York, is more than willing to tell her what to do.

The courtesy clerk crams the last grocery bag into the trunk. Lena tips him five dollars and paces, phone crunched between shoulder and ear in the same way Lulu held hers. The converted warehouse in front of the parking lot is shaped more like an apartment building than a grocery store.

"At least I include her in what's going on in my life." And you never do, Lena wants to say, but then Bobbie would hang up like she always threatens to do whenever the conversation comes close to the intimate details of her life. "I'm all discombobulated. Why Randall wants a party so soon after coming home—"

"Because he knows he can." Bobbie taps a pencil against the receiver, and Lena wonders why both Bobbie and her mother like to make noises when they talk on the phone. "How's Lulu?"

"She seems a bit discombobulated, too. I think I might go with her to her next doctor's appointment. But if you must know, I was getting . . . perspective."

"You wanted 'perspective' from the woman who ate, slept, and dreamt John Henry Harrison?" Bobbie laughs.

"What do you know?"

"I don't have to be heterosexual, or married, to know that you let your husband get to you. You're too hard on yourself."

"It's what I do." Lena sighs like her eight-year-old self under fire from her big sister. "And why don't you call Lulu more often? You haven't been home in a year."

"Lulu doesn't know how to have a regular conversation without implying that religion and a good man can cure all she believes is wrong with me. I love her, and I forgive you for being rude, but don't change the subject. This is about you, not me. You love being married. You love Randall. I simply tolerate him because he's the father of my niece and nephew." Randall and Bobbie argue whenever they are together. The last time Bobbie was home, it was over music: easy-listening jazz versus bebop. "He would not be where he is without you. And that's a fact." Lena imagines her sister wagging her finger on the other end of the phone.

"What difference does it make?" Lena groans at the sight of Dr. Miller's stocky frame between cars one aisle over. She ducks and rattles her purse. "God, where are my keys? Kendrick's therapist is headed this way. Dammit, I don't want him to see me."

"Tell him to go fuck himself. Hand him the phone—I'll say it if you won't."

At the end of his first session, Kendrick stepped into the waiting room and told Lena that Dr. Miller wanted to see her. Lena assumed he wanted a payment and stepped into the tiny office, checkbook in hand. Once inside, she was surprised by the kitschy coziness of the middle-aged doctor's office. Flowered cushions on a slouchy sofa. Masks smeared with white ash, African spears, and fertility goddesses with swollen bellies and distended breasts. Their shared heritage seemed all the more reason to like him.

"My grasp of family dynamics will constitute a critical area of Kendrick's therapy." Dr. Miller settled into his recliner, his stubby legs struggled to reach the ottoman. "Kendrick has given me permission to discuss our conversation with you. While I will not breach doctor-patient confidentiality, I do sense that there are other issues, as they relate to you, specifically, that cause Kendrick to question your . . . value."

"As opposed to his father's? And measured by what? His income as opposed to my . . . non-income?" Lena focused on the cable-stitched afghan folded over Dr. Miller's armrest. The stitches were uneven and lumpy: a gift from a feeble-handed grandmother for her adored grandchild. "What does that have to do with why he took drugs?"

"There may be clinical depression. I'm not certain, of course, we've only spoken once. It's like a puzzle, and I have to fit all of the pieces together to assess the reasons Kendrick chose to use drugs so heavily. What *you* have to consider is the impression you've created and how it will affect his relationships with women and his view of women in general. Especially if the woman appears to be . . . weak." Nothing moved on Dr. Miller's body, not his eyelids nor a finger chilled from the air conditioner's breeze.

Lena pushed off the sofa like a baby and stumbled to the door. She glowered at the therapist and did not bother to ask how he could make such a snaky assumption after only fifty-five minutes with her son.

Now, Dr. Miller stands in the middle of the parking lot, four plastic grocery bags in one hand, and pats his jacket and pants pockets with absent-minded vigor. Lena pretends to search underneath the car while Bobbie yells, "Give it to him! Give the phone to him!"

Lena shakes her head no and stays lowered until she hears a car engine start. The doctor, his head swiveled in the opposite direction to monitor the parking lot traffic, drives away when she peeks over the hood. In the car, Lena pulls *I, Tina* out of her purse and riffles the edges with her thumb to let Tina provide inspiration, this time for how to keep away from people she doesn't like. "Don't laugh. I'm reading Tina Turner's autobiography. I like her guts."

"She has more than guts—surprise, I read the book. I own bookstores, remember? And she left without fear and without money."

"I haven't been on my own since I was thirty-one. I could never make as much money as Randall does. Maybe Lulu is right." Like John Henry, Lena is not much of a risk taker.

"Sell yourself short if you want to, but all you have to do is want it bad enough." Bobbie puffs on a cigarette and yells to a distant voice in the background that she can't help right now, that she's unavailable for a while so would they please close her door. Papers rustle, and Lena imagines stacks and to-do lists atop her sister's antique desk. "Once she left, Tina only looked forward and took every opportunity that came her way. She even cleaned houses, for a minute, until she got a break."

"Stop smoking. I can hear you puffing all the way from here." Lena swerves out of the parking lot and steers through the streets. "I want my life to be the way it was. And I don't know how to get it back."

"You wouldn't be so into Tina if that was your intention. And slow down, I can hear you gunning the engine *all the way from here*."

"It's not so easy to give up your dreams."

"You don't have to give up anything, and you don't have to meet any of Randall's stupid ultimatums. This is *not* a corporate takeover. Tell *him* to go fuck himself. If you don't want to have a goddammed party, don't."

"It's too late. I've already called everybody and shopped at three different stores."

Lena senses Bobbie shaking her head on the other side of the line. Unh. Unh. Unh. Exit, stick to the twisty road, left at the stoplight, one right, another couple of lefts, and she is almost home. From a half block away, Lena watches exhaust sputter from Kendrick's nearly new, lemon-colored Mustang. A brown delivery truck blocks his car. She extends her hand out of the open window and waves to Kendrick and the deliveryman.

"Stop waiting for Randall's permission. Let's see, when you were seventeen you waited for Leonard Templeton to ask you to the Senior Ball. As I recall, you never went. You waited for Randall to tell you when you could go back to work. And you still don't work."

The second time she asked, they sat on the couch in Randall's home office working on a speech he was about to give at the annual board of directors' meeting. He read it through, noting changes, words, phrases, commas, and periods that gave him time to breathe or the audience to ponder. Lena suggested memorizing the first paragraph to make immediate contact with the audience and gain acceptance and interest right away.

"I went to the bank today," she said.

Whether he heard her or not, she couldn't tell. He recited the first paragraph, experimented with his delivery—serious, with humor, smiling, not smiling, hands, no hands. "When I gave my father his first cell phone last year, he was astonished at the power of such a small device. 'Dad,' I said, 'you ain't seen nothing yet.' As I stand before you, on the cusp of a new century, ready to introduce the future of telecommunications, I speak those same words to you as I did to my father: ladies and gentlemen, you ain't seen nothing yet!"

As soon as he finished, her thumbs lifted in approval, Lena started again. "I talked to the manager about my photography business. It's been two years, and I'm ready." She smiled at the end of her sentence, hoping her declaration was light enough to encourage Randall's agreement.

"You're happy aren't you? The kids are happy. I'm happy." He took her hand and didn't wait for her reply. "I know I promised, and I mean to keep that promise." Randall stood and paced the length of his office, delivering his words in the same way he had practiced his speech: her expertise, her willingness to polish his speeches, not to mention her first-rate entertaining had become critical to his success.

"Bottom line, the next couple of years are key. I know we can make this work." He knelt in front of her, his eyes willing her to agree. "C'mon, Lena, it hasn't been that bad, has it? You help me, and I'll help you. I'm not breaking my promise, just asking for an extension."

Hadn't she known it would come to this moment all along? Lena swore she could handle all of that, take a few classes, develop a signature style, and check out galleries. How many extensions would it take to get to her dream? She reminded Randall that she had multitasked her way through kids and work and entertaining and managing the household for years. It would work, she reasoned, until she heard him say his goal was to be CEO. The sensation, like vertigo, went from head past stomach to knees easier than she thought it would. Like falling into a cushy ball of fluff. Surrender. Without fight, without words, just the certainty that the loyalty Randall valued would cost her her soul.

"Okay! I get it. There's a delivery truck in my driveway. I won't *wait* for him." The gloved driver jumps out of the van, opens its double doors, and shoves three boxes onto a handcart. Lena points to the front porch and a white envelope taped to the wrought iron railing. The driver tips his baseball cap and heads in that direction.

"See? The universe has just sent you a message. Make things

happen. And why don't you call Cheryl. Your old buddy always could knock sense into you."

"I haven't talked to Cheryl since Daddy's funeral. Too much time has passed to cry on her shoulder. Especially about Randall."

"Promise me you'll call her. If you don't, I will."

"Where do you think you're off to?" Lena opens the trunk and sets the grocery bags on the ground.

"I'm late for Dr. Miller," Kendrick says. Teenage girls suck their teeth, boys newly out of their teens, or at least this one, Lena thinks, smirk. Is this what I've taught you? she wants to ask. Is this the way you'll look at your girlfriend, your wife, when things get tough? She walks to his car and lifts her hand to rub his cheek like she did when he was three, and they were full and round, but Kendrick bobs out of her reach.

"It's only two thirty. Your appointment isn't for an hour and a half." It takes no more than a glance for Lena to double-check her calculations on the dashboard clock. "I'll take you."

"I can drive myself." Kendrick throws up his hands, looking, Lena thinks, just like Randall. "I'm almost twenty-one, I don't need my mother to drive me around like I'm a kid in grammar school. Anyway, Dad says it's okay."

Six months ago, Kendrick's phone calls and emails became sporadic, unlike his first year at Northwestern, when he called with weekly updates. Lena and Randall assumed that the demands of his second year and his academic scholarship kept him busy. He was sulky and distant and had been that way at Thanksgiving. They blamed his moodiness on fatigue. A phone call from his roommate, upset with Kendrick's erratic behavior, set Lena in motion. Kendrick confessed that he dabbled, he called it, with uppers, downers, and sometimes cocaine to help with a bad case of the blues and the pressure of everybody's expectations. Randall gave him no options: no more money and treatment—at home or in a rehab center—within seventy-two hours.

The day Kendrick came home, Lena, Randall, and Camille unanimously decided to surprise him at the luggage rounder instead of circling the airport until he showed up at the Arrivals exit doors. When he appeared at the foot of the escalator, Randall flinched as if someone had delivered a one-two punch to his head. The couple next to them stared, not with a stranger's usual admiration of Kendrick's confidence, but repelled by his appearance. Nothing about Kendrick was the same. His pants sagged lower than usual, more from weight loss than trend, a dingy T-shirt hung from his almost skeletal shoulders, his matted hair was on the verge of accidental dreadlocks. The crinkle in the corners of his eyes that always made Lena think he was up to devilment, even when he wasn't, was gone.

At home, Randall set rules for Kendrick and left them for Lena to enforce. He cut Kendrick's driving privileges and imposed a ten o'clock curfew and mandatory visits to a therapist.

Arms crossed against his chest, Kendrick frowns as if Lena is wrong. Lena wonders how much Kendrick values her right now.

"I love you, son, and I know these restrictions are tough, but you knew the rules when you opted for home treatment. Only a few weeks to go."

"Why are you being such a—" Kendrick catches himself and rolls his eyes. "I don't know what to tell you except, Dad says it's okay."

"Your father said nothing to me, and you're not driving anywhere until he does." Lena takes two bags full of groceries into her arms. "Come help me."

"It's been four months." Kendrick guns his engine. "I'm ready to go back to school and no curfew. I miss my friends. I want my privacy back. Dad said it, and I'm outta here."

"I can't apologize for something I haven't done, Kendrick. There's a reason why you abused drugs. I want to make sure that you take your time and get all the help you need so that it never happens again."

"Jesus Christ!" His words snap from his lips. "Are you ever going to forget, or do I have to spend the rest of my life making up for it? I'm not an addict, Mom. I just made a mistake."

"Yes, you did, Kendrick." Lena's words sail into the air as Kendrick puts the car in reverse and races down the driveway. "But you don't have to take it out on me."

Lena tosses her car keys and oversized handbag onto the kitchen counter and trips, not for the first time, over Kendrick's size 12 Nikes. If it's true that feet never stop growing, Lena thinks, her son's shoes will be two sizes bigger in no time. Adrenaline helps her to unload the rest of the groceries, to shove butter, vegetables, and the fifteen-pound roast into the refrigerator and hurry to the front door. It helps her lift the boxes, one by one, into the living room as carefully as if they are full of Steuben crystal and to strip away the clear tape of each box in one long piece.

She checks the invoice against the thirty-eight CDs and resists the urge to run to the computer, type each song into a spreadsheet, and alphabetize them. Instead, CD in hand, she scours the front of the complex stereo system for the simplest buttons: power, load, play. Randall has, they have, the best, most convoluted music equipment his money can buy. He once told Lena that even if they couldn't afford the amplifiers, concert-quality sound of the six-foot speakers with super-sensitive tweeters, woofers, and other components she doesn't understand, that he would have bought them anyway. After their children, music is their strongest common denominator.

The volume knob is obvious, and one exaggerated twist fills the room with music. Tina's voice bellows from the speakers, and the infectious melody cloaks Lena. For now, it is the beat she needs—steady, strong, funky. So, Kendrick can drive; can do whatever he wants without the need of his mother's consent. He values his father. His father values him. Who values her?

Tina knows it, sings it, summarizes it as clearly as the pain, the ache that works its way to Lena's heart: *And I don't understand what's your plan that you can't be good to me.*

Tina's question is Lena's: "Who will be good to me?" Her question is for Randall, for Camille, for Kendrick.

Through the living room, the hallway, up the stairs and down again. Head and hips shake to the beat. The handmade sofas, the wall-sized art, the spindly Venetian vases—they say Randall has been good to her. Fingers snap and feet dance. Let the tears stream.

The day after Randall gave her the yellow diamond, Lena put her camera into the armoire; a memento of who she was and her value. She stops in front of a black-and-white picture taken with her 35mm the year before she married: Lulu and John Henry on their thirty-sixth anniversary. The award-winning photo was published by the *Oakland Tribune* for all her world to see. Years later, it was supposed to be submitted along with her business plan. The contrast is high and sharp; the focus on their eyes. They look straight into the camera, and the lens captures their love for each other and the photographer.

Chapter 8

Randall flips through the rows of CDs hidden behind the doors of a built-in cabinet that also houses the stereo. He once told Lena that he wanted to own all of the most important jazz albums of the twentieth century. The first time he mentioned his goal, he and Lena had been sharing their stories. Like Lena wanted to study photography, Randall wanted to major in music even though he played no instrument. He chose to major in business—his father didn't care, Randall said—so that, unlike his father, his future family would be well cared for. Between the faux-painted cabinet, the shelves of his study, and his vinyl collection carefully stored in the temperature-controlled crawlspace under the house, he has, like every other part of his life, overachieved this goal. He loads six CDs into the player and waits for the first track to start. His head jerks with each click of the volume dial, like a bird attentive to its young; his hands adjust for the perfect balance of bass and treble.

On the opposite end of the rectangular living room, Lena drags her forefinger across the mantel and moves last year's family portrait one inch to the left. Randall passes two oversized chairs and the fireplace on his way to Lena's side of the room. Tonight, Lena feels like a trophy wife on display in the burnt yellow pants and top Randall insisted she put on. She wears it to please him; it is not her style. He fiddles with the sabuk around her waist—a cummerbund he calls it—and rubs his thumbs on the small of her back in a circular motion. She relaxes into Randall's mini-massage, her head falling against his chest, and wills him to recall his promise to make one more counseling session.

Three and a half days, the numbers going up instead of down, mark the time Randall has been home, and they have not spoken of serious matters. Lena wishes this respite signified the desire to move on. No spontaneous touches, no suggestive double-talk, no teasing as foreplay to time alone. Randall has occupied himself less with thinking or work and more with sweating: hours of racquetball, hoops with Kendrick beating him only once out of the five times they played, hiking the hills around their home with and without Camille, jumping rope, and shadowboxing. He has spent quiet time in the living room listening to music and sorting through his CDs. The coffee table becomes the focus of her attention: a dead leaf pinched from the bouquet of peonies, hydrangeas, and, her favorite, rubrum lilies; books poked into a perfect pile.

"Are you happy?" Lena asked Randall if he was happy before their first counseling session ended. His deep breathing had more than physical purpose: thought gathering, a careful delivery of words. Different from the breaths taken the first time he'd said "I love you." During the session, his finger thumped against the wing chair's arm and he said that she should be "fucking ecstatic, judging by what you have and the life you live."

"Every day at TIDA, the white boys measure my words and my work for potential mistakes. Work is not about happy. Work is about beating the odds and kicking ass." He closes his eyes like she's seen him do a thousand times—a trick learned in a year's worth of biofeedback sessions. "I'd be happy if we could table this."

"Not work. Like Tina says—whether times are happy or sad."

"That was Al Green. Tina Turner was singing, Lena, not espousing a philosophy." Randall's heavy voice is sarcastically chipper. "With the money Tina Turner makes, she's found happiness, trust me."

The singsong doorbell chimes, and Lena rushes to the dining room for one last survey of the table. She swaps two place cards, corrects the alignment of a spoon and fork to exactly two inches from the table's edge, and motions to the housekeeper in the kitchen to turn the oven off.

Randall steps into the entryway and spins on the doorbell's last note—his silk shirt flutters from his broad shoulders to its loose hem. He raises his thumbs: all systems go. "Look around, Lena. What do you have to be sad about?"

From her end of the table, Lena feels like a minor character in her hundredth performance of play: a vital prop, without dialogue and unnoticed. She is unable to figure out if she has grown away from her friends or too much into herself.

Lynne, who worries more about pedigree than personality, blathers on about a couple she recently met: the husband's father was the first black appellate court judge in his state and the wife is a third generation AKA. Charles's fear of Bali street food. Candace prattles on about her children: X is getting a PhD, Y is pregnant by her doctor husband again, Z is up for partner at his law firm.

Lena takes in the room—gilded mirror over the buffet, the crystal chandelier, the curved arches cut into the Oriental rug's thick wool pile. What does she have to be sad about?

"How's your dinner, Charles?" Lena asks Randall's best friend.

"Perfect, as usual," Charles volunteers through a mouthful of roast and reaches for another slice.

"And these cut veggies . . . what are they?" Charles's bimbette girlfriend asks Randall. As if he knows, Lena thinks. Randall makes suggestions, like executive overviews, and leaves the details to his wife. The young woman, sultry and innocent at the same time, refocuses her attention on Randall before Lena finishes her description of the sharp mandoline and its precision cuts of yellow and red beets, jicama, and carrot tied with softened strands of chive. The bimbette sits on Randall's left, Charles on his right. Randall chitchats with the two of them and flashes his even-toothed smile. Watching the three of them, Lena wonders if Charles brings these air-headed, busty women to their home more for Randall's entertainment than his own.

"This is why I adore your parties, Lena." Lynne nudges her husband, who is almost done before the others have barely started. He shoves food in his mouth and tells them he can't stop this habit—six sisters and brothers who all ate fast in order to get seconds—even though it's been forty years since he sat with them at his parents' table.

Lynne dismisses him with a wave of her hand. "Your food is so creative, like one of those TV shows. Artsy."

The dark wood is the perfect backdrop for the food arranged in the middle of the round African mahogany table Lena commissioned for the square dining room. The rich wood is striated with tiny rings that testify to its age. Frilly paper caps on the standing rib roast, garnishes of purple cabbage, parsley, and finger-sized fruits; presentation and taste are important to her. She cannot brag about well-earned promotions or increased corporate profits or the next big takeover like Randall, but she can outdo most with her food.

Candace, her politically incorrect, six-carat diamond, and her dimpled husband, Byron, sit to Lena's right and left. Candace catches his eye as her tongue drags creamy potatoes across her fork.

The bimbette joins in. "Oh, everybody's life seems much more exciting than Charles's." She bats her obviously false eyelashes in Randall's face.

"I make money, baby," Charles says through his second helping of garlic mashed potatoes. "That's exciting enough."

Randall slaps his buddy's back and winks at Lena: I told you so. The bimbette hasn't been and probably won't be around long enough to understand she should keep her mouth shut. Or perhaps, Lena muses, this one gets a "get out of jail free" card, because she is young enough to be the daughter of any one of them or, as her neckline creeps farther down between her full, taut breasts, no man pays attention to what she says.

The housekeeper brings in a silver tray with two dessert choices—a thinly slivered chocolate ganache cake and an orange-scented brioche bread pudding with amaretto cream—paired with Dolce, Randall's most expensive dessert wine. Every man, save for Byron, whose mouth twitches in anticipation of Candace's next suggestive move, engages in a segregated conversation with Randall. They natter raucously over sports and bullshit in that way men do: disjointed hyperbolic statements that mean nothing, but their laughter says they're having fun.

"Why is it . . . ?" Lena straightens so that her voice projects across the table. "That the men talk. The women talk. But we never talk together?"

The beads of the crystal chandelier tinkle from laughter's vibration, Randall's being the loudest. "Because we men never have time to get together." To a person, except for Lena, all heads dip in agreement as if Randall is their leader and it is his right to voice the group's opinion. Lena is unsure if this is because he is or because they're in his house, eating his wife's good food, drinking his expensive wine. "We work hard to support your habits." All eyes follow Randall's finger as he thumps it against his chest on the spot where the yellow diamond rests on Lena's.

"Whatever happened to what attracted you to us in the first place: politics, race, music, art, last summer's bestseller . . . fucking?" Lena snaps and watches Randall's eyebrows arc in dismay at the same time that the doorbell chimes.

"That must be Sharon." Randall grimaces and shoves his chair back from the table. "I told her to drop by for dessert."

"Why?" Lena asks.

He looks at Charles. "You'll get a kick out of her. She's sharp."

Lena brushes crumbs from her now crumpled outfit and watches

Randall guide Sharon into the dining room by the elbow and make introductions. Randall has told Lena on more than one occasion that in corporate America, like other places, black folks have to look out for one another—Sharon needs a mentor, and he needs someone to keep him abreast of what goes on in middle management. The not so subtle hints that Lena has watched Sharon toss in his direction for the three years she has been with TIDA are not the kind of loyalty Lena appreciates.

"Why, don't you look cute." Sharon bends to greet Lena with a hug. The skinny spaghetti straps of her sleek black cocktail dress have fallen off her angular shoulders and she looks Lena over again. "That's the same get-up Randall gave his secretary. I told him I'd have to teach him a thing or two about presents. Don't you agree?"

"Oh, I think he does quite well." Lena fingers her diamond. "When he sets his mind to it."

Randall squeezes an extra chair in the space between him and Charles and immediately launches into a recap of how he fired his associate. Sharon chimes in. Together, the two make the dismissal seem like a lively event.

"You should have seen Thompson's face." Sharon pantomimes a dejected look. "When he came to clean out his office, he never looked me in the eye. He was in and out so fast that he left a picture of his kids and dog on his desk."

"Mess with me once you're on my shit list," Randall says. "Twice, and you're out. You were great, Sharon. I won't forget that." Randall lifts his glass. "To Sharon."

"And thank you for letting me barge in." Sharon clinks her glass against Randall's.

"I bought three chunks each of Novo, Quadra, and IntelligNT." Randall changes the subject. "Got them all for a steal when they split." His voice drops when he reveals the stiff three-figure price per share. Lena watches Sharon's eyes grow wider every time his chest puffs higher and higher with each stock description. Lena has told him a thousand times that the men don't like to hear him brag. They suffer from financial penis envy, his portfolio is bigger than theirs, but right now she is unsure for whose benefit the boasts are.

For the second time in less than ten days, Lena has an attack of fantasy violence. This time Sharon is the object of her desire, only unlike Candace's comical recovery, Lena imagines Randall would push her away and gallantly rush to Sharon's side. If she had the guts to be a bad girl, Lena thinks, she might loosen this damn, scratchy tunic, drop the baggy pants to the floor, unhook her bra with one hand, and push her lacy bikinis down her legs to get her husband's attention. She could sidle up to Randall, press herself against him, moan until he apologized for inviting Sharon.

"You're a better woman than I am. I wouldn't have let her in my house." Candace's look says you better show that woman whose man Randall is. "What's the matter with you? Why did Randall invite her? What was he thinking when he gave you that outfit?"

"He meant for her to have it." Lena wonders if this is the expensive meal he promised Sharon.

"Randall says you're quite the decorator, Lena." Sharon redirects sections of her chocolate dessert to the edge of her plate. "I'd love a tour of the house. Maybe you can give me a few pointers. I don't have an eye for that sort of thing." She pats Randall's arm. "And this one keeps me busy."

"Show her my office and the master bedroom. Take the ladies with you. She just finished redecorating." Randall rises from the table and holds an invisible cigar to his mouth—his signal for a smoke on the front porch.

"I think we'll skip the tour and go into the sunroom. Upstairs is a mess," Lena lies.

"In that case, I think I'll join the boys on the porch. I'm sure Randall won't mind." Sharon glances at the front door, and her smile conveys more than friendliness or amusement.

"I'm sure I have a cigarillo you could handle," Randall says.

"Oh, I can handle that, and more," Sharon says, standing to follow Randall to the porch.

Lena knows Sharon isn't the first woman at TIDA to hit on Randall. The CFO's second wife cornered him at last year's Christmas party and told him in no uncertain terms, which Lena could plainly hear, that she always wanted to fuck a powerful, sexy black man. That woman was not this determined.

With two measured steps, Candace puts herself between Randall and Sharon, separating them with her wide designer skirt and the woody-amber scent of Hermès perfume. Lena watches her take Sharon's arm in a firm girlfriend grip, and with that one motion she forgives Candace for each and every bragging word, for each and every bit of raunchy gossip; this one action endears Candace to Lena forever.

"Let the boys tell their dirty jokes and smoke their stinky cigars. It's the one vice we wives allow." Candace steers Sharon to the sunroom, leaving Lena and Charles alone beside the table.

"Is she fucking him?"

"Ask him. But Randall's no fool. You don't mess around in your own backyard, especially when you're trying to be the head of your company." Charles feigns a slight bow. "I, on the other hand, wouldn't let my head be turned by some overambitious twit. If you weren't married to my best friend, I'd seduce you into having a torrid affair with me and fuck you all over the kitchen between all the lovely meals you'd cook for me."

"Drop dead, Charles. If Randall is your best friend, why do you say things like that to his wife?" Lena empties the last of a bottle of aged cabernet into her glass. "Why don't you go fuck Sharon? She seems to want to give it up pretty badly, and you've got enough money."

"Because you know I'm not serious. Because she's not my type. Because everyone knows you'd never leave the son of a bitch." Charles winks and saunters to the porch.

The hint of cigar smoke wafts between the threshold and the

door as Lena walks past. Tonight the smell does not remind her of John Henry or the night Randall gave her the yellow diamond. It reminds her that Randall has his own agenda. That once she shared that agenda with him. As she nears the sunroom the bimbette's shrill voice reaches Lena before she sets foot there.

"Does she always go to this much trouble? I mean, that meal was fabulous."

"For what you ate of it, dear," Lynne says, her back to the sunroom's double doors. "We call Lena the black Martha Stewart. She got away with that off-the-wall comment, though. I thought Randall was going to lose it."

"Randall? He's a big, cuddly bear," Sharon says.

"Yeah, a grizzly," Lynne retorts.

"Got to give the girl credit," Candace says. "She *is* talented."

"Would Lena be nearly as inspired without Randall's . . . resources?" Sharon asks.

"Look at these orchids. And who uses their best dishes and silverware, and those tiny veggie dealies, for a casual 'get together'? Please." In one soundless step, Lena traverses the sunroom's threshold before Lynne realizes her hostess is in the room. "She's such a hypocrite. You see that diamond? For all she complains about being tired of material stuff, she flaunts the hell out of it and everything else. Lena married well."

"And what the hell does that mean?" Lena's voice is hard, her enunciation perfect. She knows that Randall can take down a company, make managers tremble with a simple request, control millions of dollars; he reeks of power—apparently, she is just the woman attached to the powerful man. "If this is what you say when you *think* I'm not around, what do you say when I'm not?"

The bimbette slinks through the side door. Lena gives the young woman credit for having more smarts than she thought. Unlike Sharon, who approaches Lena, arms extended, with concern that her face does not show.

"And you. I have no idea why you're here." Lena sways—from

wine or words, it makes no difference to her—the wineglass slips from her hand, sending teardrops of red wine onto the now wrinkled sabuk and across the tiled floor.

"I'm here because Randall asked me, Lena. I had no idea you'd object."

"You need to leave. Now." Lena points to the door through which Lynne and the bimbette exited seconds before and watches Sharon take her time to collect her purse and pashmina and strut out of the room.

"Don't mind her," Candace says. Lena is unsure which *her* she refers to. "And don't be a fool. Follow her, and I mean Sharon, and act like nothing happened. I'm telling you." Candace pushes a lacy handkerchief into Lena's balled fist. "She'll tell Randall that you asked her to leave. If you stay here, she wins."

The "everything is okay" smile disappears from Lena's lips after she pays the housekeeper and turns off the lights. Within five minutes of closing the door on their last guest, Randall lounges on the cushy chaise beyond their bed. He takes up the entire space wide and deep enough for two. One leg stretches onto the dark hardwood floor and the Persian rug with a provenance. He pokes between the cushions for the remote control while Lena paces, full of the energy she needed earlier.

"I told you I didn't want to have a stupid party."

"Lynne is too dense to have been serious. She's jealous. More importantly, you embarrassed me in front of our friends and my colleague."

"I embarrassed you, Randall? You invite that . . . woman to my home. You don't bother to tell me. She shows up looking like she's ready to eat you while I'm dressed in this"—Lena waves her hands up and down her body—"this clown suit, and you're embarrassed?"

"You were crude. You told Sharon to leave. You owe her an apology." Randall's expression is somber and without a hint of sympathy. He curls his fingers beneath his chin and looks at her in a way that says no further discussion is necessary.

"You get Charles drunk. I have to put up with his lechery. You toast someone I suspect you're having an affair with, and you want *me* to apologize?" Lena stands in front of Randall, looking at him looking at her like she is crazy. His eyes say he doesn't get it, doesn't get her.

The only way Lena had been able to fend off her tears was with the handkerchief Candace thrust into her hand. Now, Lena twists that handkerchief into a tight, skinny spiral and marches into the walk-in closet big enough to be another bedroom. Gucci, Vuitton, Prada, Armani, and more surround her. She grabs on to the built-in dresser to balance herself and gasps for air. Left foot then right, she kicks off her high heels and slips into her fuzzy slippers. Eyes blurry, she feels for the corner shelf full of carry-on totes and yanks at a black travel bag. She needs panties; one pair goes in. She needs a bra; five go in. The charger for her cell phone, a candle, jogging bra, sweats, jasmine perfume, a sweater, a cocktail dress Randall gave her two years ago.

Lena emerges from the closet wrapped in a wool coat better suited to a winter freeze than this spring night. Her lipstick is smeared, her face wrenched as tightly as the handkerchief she still holds on to. "I would expect that my husband would side with me, not with his *colleague*." She avoids Randall's eyes, his seeming nonchalance when she crosses in front of him and snatches Tina's book from the nightstand drawer. "How can I sleep beside someone who won't stand up for me? Who gives me an ultimatum that could change my life but doesn't even bother to ask what I decided?"

"I take it the fancy gym bag means you've decided." This is the icy tone that makes Randall the great businessman sought after by corporations looking for more than just a black face to fill some arbitrary affirmative action slot. Lena shivers in the doorway, her back to Randall. Stay. That is all he has to say, and she will put down her bag. Get up from the chair and hold her tight is all he has to do, and she will stay.

"I'd think twice if I were you, Lena. You're the one who's got everything to lose."

"Maybe it all stops here."

"Maybe it all stops. Period."

Lena prays that her keys are in her purse, her purse in the kitchen so that she does not have to go back into that room or look at Randall. She pauses, then sets one foot ahead of the other in the same thoughtful way she did when John Henry walked her down the aisle, all the way down the stairs and to the garage to give Randall time to act. Night camouflages her car while she watches her bedroom window from the driveway. After ten minutes the bedroom lights darken, and Lena drives away.

Chapter 9

At the grand hotel on the Oakland-Berkeley border a rosemary bush hedges the front of the building and releases its savory fragrance when Lena brushes up against it. Fresh rosemary is the herb she loves most, a pleasure for the tongue and the nose. Sure she looks like a hooker, all dolled up with no place to go, she hands the night clerk her platinum credit card and demands a room. He examines her from head to toe, this young man ensconced behind the well-oiled, wood-paneled counter in a pinstriped suit and gold badge, his name and place of birth engraved on it in two lines: Ali from Kenya. His eyes are shadowed by a furrowed brow as if she should be ashamed of checking in to his high-ceilinged, Oriental-carpeted hotel by herself at midnight, as if she should be ashamed of her fuzzy slippers, the pooled mascara under her light brown eyes, and her thousand-dollar designer tote.

Lena grunts from the doubt that cramps her insides; she has no place to go. She has no plan—her tote is evidence of that. Whether she charges this hotel for one night or a thousand, she cannot pay the bill. She has no real money. Snatching her upscale credit card back from Ali, Lena turns around and stalks out the lobby; her back dares him to say one more word to her so that she can scream, "Fuck you and Randall, too."

When the valet hands Lena her keys, she sits in the car under the poorly lit portico until he goes back into his little booth. Lena picks through her bag and pulls out her book and lets it fall open to a random page for guidance.

"*Some of these people read cards, some read the stars . . . Some of them weren't for real but others gave me something to hold on to, some insight into what was going on in my life.*"

Tina visited readers, psychics, for a hint that a better life was in her future. Images crowd into Lena's head of places she has seen without seeing when she is out and about. There is a reader on Piedmont Avenue, a familiar street where Lena gets her nails done, does her banking, and lunches on Kung Pao beef. The words *Psychic Healer & Palm Reader Always Open* are pasted in careful strips of preformed block letters on the sandwich board in front of the small house. She has walked by the sign a hundred times, more fearful than curious to drop in.

By the time she gets to Piedmont Avenue, the streets are still crowded. Who are the rest of these night-owl drivers, she wonders? Nurses on late-night duty, philanderers and bar-hoppers, singles on their way back home reluctant to spend the night in a lover's messy bed? Other wishy-washy women who cannot make up their minds what to do with their lives?

She swerves into the short driveway beside the clapboard house. Clay pots full of red and white geraniums line the four stairs and lead to the glow-in-the-dark stripes painted on the wooden porch. Tiny moths dance around the pale overhead light, drunk, perhaps, on the geraniums' grassy perfume. Lena presses the doorbell; the scratch of soft soles against a hardwood floor follows the strident buzz. A short, bald man opens the door; his complexion is swarthy, but clear. The line between the top of his upper lip and his neatly clipped mustache reminds her of old military pictures of her father. Lena steps away from the door.

"Come on in; I won't bite." His husky voice reassures. The older man extends a sunburned hand and introduces himself as Vernon Withers. Like the southern gentleman his drawl makes him out to be, Vernon leaves the front door open as if the geraniums, crickets, and fluttering moths could offer help, if she needed any.

"I'm Lena." Her mind hesitates where her feet do not as she approaches the front room where low flames crackle in the sooty fireplace.

"Chamomile tea, Lena?"

Her left, then right eyebrow arches at this first hint of Vernon's insight. Chamomile is the tea she loves to drink when she is tired or stressed.

"I know, you're wondering, 'Now how in the hell does he know that's the tea I like?'" Vernon winks at Lena and waddles toward the kitchen looking more like a rascally elf than a man who is supposed to know about the future. "No need to answer, dahlin', just accept."

Unsure of the psychic process, Lena accepts Vernon's offer of tea and walks to a small wood-paneled area beyond the living room where two brocade-covered chairs face one another, a small round table between them. The room's walls are the soft yellow of fading daffodils; the house smells like lavender sachet and old people. Water splashes, the microwave beeps.

"You have questions?" Vernon sets a cup and saucer painted with red-lipped geishas by her left hand. "Ask the first thing that comes into your head."

"I'm only here because . . ." Lena figures if Vernon is true to his title he should know why she's here and what her questions are. "I'm here because a friend recommended I see a reader."

"*Reader* is confusing. I prefer *psychic,* like my sign outside says, it's more . . . specific. So?"

Questions are not her problem; they frolic like curious monkeys in her head. It's answers that have her stuck. When she entered the house, she didn't bother to check it out or ask if there was anyone else present. Lena squirms under Vernon's expectant stare and glances back at the door. He spreads her palms open, then rests his on hers. His touch fills her with a peace she hasn't felt in a long time. He stares at her eyes, in almost the same way John Henry did when she misbehaved as a child, then examines the jagged, interlaced lines across her palms.

"The palm, my dear, is simply a reflection of our lives. Yours are beautiful. Youthful." He stares at her left hand, pushes and presses the Mount of Venus beneath her thumb. "The lines on the dominant hand vary across the span of one's life, because of the changes in life's path. This section of your hand tracks midlife. See? A Y. The Y represents choice and change."

"Everybody has that." Lena wonders if this is what the psychics saw in Tina's hands.

"But, *everybody* isn't here." Vernon opens his hands. His right hand is without a little finger. Any other time she would have asked the story of this missing digit. Better to see this odd injury instead of something, like a sixth finger, he claims enables second sight. She searches for the Y. Nothing on his palm resembles that letter.

"Say what you want, dahlin', but you're the one willin' to plop down your husband's hard-earned money in the middle of the night, fuzzy slippers and all, for me to tell your future. You rang my doorbell. This isn't the time to be indecisive. Look where that got you this evening."

Lena jerks her hands away from Vernon and pushes back from the table. "What would you know?"

"It's not what I know, but what I sense: you can't keep letting people push you around. Sit still and let me have your hands so you can get your money's worth." Vernon sips his tea and peers around the room as if to search for scones and crumpets. His face is playful and serious. He pulls a gold watch on a chain from his pocket and sets it on the table. "Now, take your watch and set it beside mine."

"*You're* pushing me around just like everybody else."

"Like I said, Lena, you rang my doorbell. Don't fight me; I'm not the one you need to show your strength to. Trust."

Lena looks around the room and through the open kitchen door. The house is quiet; the chirring of night insects outside the door is the only other sound she hears. She stares at her watch, another gift from Randall, another expensive gift from Randall.

The night he gave her the watch, he insisted that she stretch out her arms and look away. She flinched when the cold metal touched her skin but kept her eyes averted from her wrist. It was the same night she discovered she was pregnant with Kendrick, but not ready for a baby. He hugged her, held her there in the middle of their bathroom; convinced her she would be a wonderful mother. They would be wonderful parents. Trust.

"Dahlin'," Vernon's is a voice reserved for church. "If I was gonna steal from you, I'd'a conked you on the head by now, taken your watch, and that big ole diamond 'round your neck, and tossed you down the front steps. Give me your hands."

Lena picks at the double-locked clasp and puts her wristwatch next to his, then her palms in his hands again while Vernon explains that the metals throw off their magnetic fields. The dimple in his chin—an uncanny resemblance to John Henry's, along with the same soft edge to his words—sinks deeper into itself when he laughs.

"I feel an energy surge coming from your watch. What's your husband's name?" Vernon reaches for a thick green book that resembles a Bible, a ribbon bookmark sewn into its gilded binding. "And his date of birth?"

"Randall's name is Randall. Birthdate: July 24, 1945."

Vernon shuffles through the pages. The gray hairs at the top of his head wiggle as he scans a lengthy paragraph. "Your husband is a dogmatic Leo. He is pragmatic. Is that the word? This is his approach to life. He doesn't understand any other way."

Lena shudders at Vernon's truth and inches to the edge of her seat. Pictures, books, furniture, and Vernon spin around her, a blurry montage of color and light.

The pitch of Vernon's voice raises for the first time since she arrived; he folds his stubby hands over Lena's palms and pauses, looking more through her than at her. Lena feels the emptiness of his absent finger. "These intertwined lines, see? Independence and forward progression. These movements clash with his. But, forget him. You're not a delicate woman, but convenience makes it easy to pretend. You are meant to be powerful. Follow your creativity."

Lena focuses on the small blood spot beside the iris of Vernon's right eye. She shuts her eyes and processes Vernon's words. His stare says that he is waiting for her; he will only guide not lead. Tina's psychics gave her a direct notion—that she would be successful; they offered direction and promise. "Tell me what to do."

"You have found the star who shines for you; she leads the way. Begin your journey with her. Reconnect with the past. Someone you closed yourself off from is waiting for you." Vernon beams and points to a bold line in her right hand. "As for me telling you what to do: you already know."

"Yep, I'm a fool in love." Lena leans back in the chair. "And I need to accept my life or move on."

"Don't indulge in what might have been. Delight in what can be." Vernon squeezes her hands; his grip is tingly and rough. "You're stubborn, and you don't always listen to advice: even your mother has something to offer. Just like the silver ball in a pinball machine spins, moves at the whim of someone else, you move backwards before you understand how far you can go with just a little push."

"Go ahead. Push me."

"You don't need me." Vernon releases her hands, pulls a monogrammed handkerchief from his shirt pocket, and pats his forehead where perspiration threatens to fall into his eyes. "Step into your power."

Chapter 10

"What smells so good?" Camille plucks a strip of sautéed chicken from a bowl and dips it in the peanut sauce beside it. She is a nibbler, like her mother, though the empty soda cans and candy wrappers in her room attest to her unhealthy choices. "And low lights, too? Hmm."

"Take this." Lena feigns a blush and hands fifty dollars to Camille. If only she could send the kids to bed early after a fast food treat of hamburgers and pasty french fries. Compromise with Randall was less complicated when the kids were young. "Dinner and a movie. And where's your brother?"

Camille tickles Lena's shoulder. "Glad you and Dad are getting back to normal."

"Out!" Lena flushes at her daughter's insight, shooing her out of the kitchen, even as Kendrick walks in to meet them. Lena doesn't have the slightest idea whether or not her son shares his sister's insight. Silent meals, Randall's late hours, her clothing piled in the guestroom for three days—her kids are no fools.

The tension between mother and son is palpable. She fans herself with both hands, a gesture meant to clear the air, and hopes that Kendrick gets her hint. "I do trust you, Kendrick, I hope you know that." She speaks as if their confrontation was moments instead of days ago and points to his keys on the counter with a wide smile.

"Thanks, Mom." Kendrick ruffles Lena's hair and then juggles his keys between both hands, like the metal Slinky he had as a kid. As nosy as his sister, he heads to the stove, lifts a lid from a saucepan, and dips a finger into the curry. "Food works for us, too, Mom, in case you forgot."

With one swift turn, Kendrick and Camille connect palms with a loud high five and slap a second one with Lena. "What's that corny old-school saying? Something about a man's heart?" he asks. Lena offers a thumbs-up to her son's obvious hint, knowing that if the timing were different—or more full of the happiness of the old days—that would have been her only intention.

Lena places small, square white bowls filled with curried carrots topped with fresh basil—for color and contrast—and strips of sautéed chicken fillets on the kitchen table. Mixed green salad and jasmine rice balance the Thai food; the proper mix of carbs, protein, and veggies. She stirs passion and love into the tangy coconut soup in the hope that Randall will taste those emotions and daydreams of contentment while the lemongrass stems soak in cool water.

The first time Lena cooked for Randall, it was a disaster. She called the New Orleans hole in the wall they had visited and begged the cook for his shrimp Creole recipe, then labored hours more than she should have, given how simple the recipe read. Once they sat down to eat, the shrimp were tough, the sauce salty, and the rice mushy. After two mouthfuls, Randall told Lena to get her coat. "I'm not the kind of man who'll suffer through his woman's bad cooking." He chuckled when she playfully twisted his arm. "You just remember those words when *you* cook for me." She wanted to tell him that her feelings were hurt, that if the tables were turned she would have eaten his salty food. That was the first time she held her tongue with Randall. In that moment she learned his intolerance for error, and it bothered her, but not enough to stop seeing him. That was the first and only time he left her food on the table. In the end, her cooking snared him.

Surely, she thinks, it will help her keep him.

At five minutes after eight Randall opens the kitchen door, his tie loosened from his collar. His lips are tight; his moves calculated like a boxer considering which corner is neutral territory.

"Truce." Lena helps Randall slip out of his jacket and leans close.

This night her neck and the dip between her breasts, behind her ears and knees are covered with jasmine. Jasmine is the scent that mixes best with Lena's own. Randall gifts her with bottles, bars, and creams of the lavish fragrance every other Valentine's Day, though Lena cannot remember the last time she wore the perfume. Perhaps when malaise overtook her long before Randall's nearly month-long departure? Or after the Christmas holiday party and the argument, in front of Candace and Byron, over the best route to take home? Or last summer when she asked him not to take her car to the horrid, lecherous man at the flatlands automated carwash and he did anyway? Randall sniffs. The jasmine will do its work; help them to recall that first year of marriage, that first serious argument, and making up.

"Truce." He gave her a bottle of jasmine oil, and later, massaged it all over her. All those years, it stood for apology, if needed—his or hers—for romance and good loving. Now, a hint of prim satisfaction stretches across Randall's face, and Lena wonders if he remembers that first time she wore the perfume, much less expensive then, the scent still the same. Randall looks from the food to Lena and slides onto the upholstered bench. He sniffs. At the food. "Smells good." At Lena. "You, too."

Lena scoops a healthy portion of the made-from-scratch green curry sauce over his rice. This food comes close to what she thinks he experienced in Bali: spicy, thick, and rich. Once she settles in beside him, she takes his left hand in her right. They sit that way for a time that she does not count, the smell of her jasmine mixing with the curry, until he reaches for the remote control on the bench. When she grabs it first, he tickles her arm until the remote falls loose so that his fingers can now dance on its pad. The TV screen explodes like lightning in the darkened room. Even as she scrutinizes him, his eyes puffy from concentration and the long day, Lena knows he seeks solace in the inanity of TV.

"I'd like to talk about the party and about us. We need to clear the air and make a fresh start, and we can't talk if the TV's on." Lena catches herself and the sigh about to escape her lips. One. Two. Three. It took all day to concoct this exotic meal, to gather the ingredients, to select the right tiny red chilies to heat up their food and their marriage. "I worked hard today to make this evening . . . special."

"And I worked hard today so you can make fancy food. Are you ready to apologize?"

"I think we need to apologize to one another." Lena uncovers the tureen and hastily ladles chunky soup into Randall's empty bowl.

"I don't see it that way."

With exacting synchronicity, Lena's jaw twitches at each abrupt change of channel—the staccato of newscasters, commercials, random dialogue—and his casual acceptance, his expectation that all of his meals will be this grand, this tasty.

"Let's make a deal. A little food. We'll talk." Lena presses her hand to the back of his neck, and the spot at the base of his ear that usually makes him melt. "Then we'll watch the last quarter. Upstairs. In bed. That is, if you feel up to it." For Lena and Randall, makeup sex has always been their best.

"But . . . the Warriors play the Lakers tonight." Randall grins like a mischievous boy. "Last game before the playoffs."

Lena pushes thumb against the Y, Vernon's Y for change, on

her palm while the basketball players on TV run up and down the court. Run, run, run as fast as you can, you can't catch me, I'm the gingerbread man. The urge to scrape scrape scrape the fragrant food down the garbage disposal, to flip the on/off switch again and again until the whirring is smooth and food, ground to pulp, washes down the drain, is strong. As are Kendrick's last words. She yanks away the remote from Randall's hand and turns the TV off. Wineglass in hand, Lena pushes away from the table and goes to the sink full of the pots and pans and skillets she used to prepare the special dishes.

"You're acting like a spoiled brat." Randall clicks the TV on again.

"I'm sorry." Anxiety rushes to Lena's tongue, mixes with her spit, and swims over her taste buds. Maybe I am, she wants to shout, a spoiled, frustrated midlife woman unable to get her husband to accept her apology, her food, her sweet jasmine perfume, to understand she seeks change for the benefit of the both of them. In the instant she hurls her glass across the floor, Lena both intends and regrets the action. The glass shatters, scattering wet shards from the sink where Lena stands all the way to the table at the opposite end. Only the stem remains intact. The odor of wine mingles with the basil and curry, and the kitchen smells more like a cheap bar than home.

"Look, Lena. I don't know what more you want." Randall stands, a man on the verge of action, looking from Lena to the shattered glass to the louvered door that separates the kitchen from the hallway. The long, low sigh he releases is like, Lena supposes, the tears she fights with a barrage of rapid blinks. "I'm tired. And you're obviously irrational."

"Don't leave, Randall, we've got to do this sooner or later."

"I've done all I'm going to do tonight, Lena." The door swings hard and wide as he passes through it.

If she were taller and huskier, if she were a man, Lena knows she would punch Randall, punch him hard until he fell, until he understood. She tiptoes around the pieces of glass and through the swinging door. Keeping a healthy distance between his body and hers, she points a trembling finger in his face. Randall backs away, hands clenched at his sides. He watches her hands, keeps his distance.

"I don't have time for tantrums. You're only pissed because you think I'm having an affair with Sharon. Charles told me what you said."

"I don't doubt it, but this is about more than who you're fucking. This is about our life."

"I don't need drama at work *and* at home."

"No, you're the drama king, lover man. Like that little trick you did with your tongue the night you came home?"

Randall's face is motionless except for his pulsing, left eyebrow. "Stop." He grabs Lena's wrists. She yanks them away with a force that startles them both. The TV blares with the announcer's scream and the crowd's roar. He walks past the photos that mark their years together: wedding day, chubby Camille at six, Kendrick's senior prom, their first time in Paris. The frames rattle with the weight of his footsteps. Lena steps to the opposite side of the hallway. Is this how it begins?

"Is that why you're offering me ultimatums, Randall? Answer me!"

"What do you want me to say?" He holds up his hands in a gesture of surrender. Once at the stairs, he takes them two at a time.

"Is this one of those decisions, like the lemon tree or what restaurant we'll eat in, what movie we'll see, that don't mean anything to you so it's left to me?" She wonders why what she thinks is not what she says. Power is powerful.

"I'm a businessman, Lena. I have to consider the pros and cons." Randall shrugs.

Footsteps clamber outside. Randall and Lena used to confine their occasional fights to their bedroom, used to close their door and muffle their words, used to make up and apologize ignoring who may have been right or wrong. They stand stock-still while Lena searches for the right words, the most expedient way to say what's on her mind in the seconds before Kendrick and Camille come in and shatter this moment as cleanly as the wineglass strewn across the floor. Lena loves her kids; lately, though, they appear at the most inconvenient times. It didn't matter when they were toddlers and they walked in on her naked or on the toilet. Now, she wishes fifty dollars bought more time.

"I won't go on like this. I have to consider my pros and cons, too."

"Don't threaten me, Lena." Randall heads for their bedroom and reappears within minutes, overnight bag in hand. "I was thinking about doing this anyway. I need a head start on tomorrow's work, and you need time to cool off. I'm going to the corporate apartment."

This is not the Randall she knows. Not the man who talks loyalty. She wasn't his first girlfriend, or his first wife, but he said she would be his last, that he would be faithful, take care of her, the opposite of what his old man had done with his mother.

Now, Randall's eyebrows are lumpy with frustration; Lena's emulate his—proof that married couples look and act alike after so many years together. In better times, if they were to see themselves in one of the many gilt mirrors Lena has placed around the house, they would tease one another over who was the original and who the copy.

"Hey, parents," Camille calls out. "What's up with the glass all over the floor?"

Camille and Kendrick suck in air at the same time as if they can breathe the tension they have encountered. Kendrick stoops to pick up the largest pieces and signals Camille to wait. Camille bolts straight into the front entryway, where their father stands near the top and their mother stands in the middle of the stairs. When Kendrick joins them, daughter and son rib their father about his very real need for a haircut. Randall breaks into a smile, leaving Lena flattened against the wall, shocked at his swift transition.

"Where are you off to, Dad?" Camille asks.

"Please give us a few minutes," Lena prays that Camille and Kendrick are smart enough to recognize her request is really a plea.

"We're done." Randall tousles Kendrick's woolly head when he reaches the bottom of the stairs. "If you think I need a haircut, man, you should check out your wild 'fro." Father, son, and daughter's laughter reverberates throughout the house. "I've got to be in the Novato office before dawn tomorrow morning. I'm going to stay at the corporate apartment."

From the living room window, Lena watches Randall's long car pull out of the garage. Twenty-five years ago, Lena discovered that Randall had returned from the East Coast the summer day she drove down Highway 580. From a distance, she watched a man trying to talk a highway patrolman out of a ticket. His distinct hand movements tipped her off: Randall.

Lena sped across two lanes and parked her sports car on the embankment. When the CHP drove off, she jumped out of her car and waited for Randall to look her way; a different version of their first meeting. They hugged for five minutes while cars honked their appreciation for such a public display of affection.

Now, anger fuels Randall's swift descent down the driveway, morphs his taillights from red dots to snaking stream. His car disappears down the hill and around the corner. Lena loved the way she felt that day long ago: protective and powerful. Powerful enough to slow traffic, to keep Randall from speeding away, to control her destiny. For all of the years she has loved him and more, she has cared for him, worried about him, prayed for his safety. In this instant, she doesn't care what he does, how fast he drives, or where he goes. But never, never in a million years, did she ever think she would wish he would go to hell.

Chapter 11

Three days.

The first day, Lena retreats to her bed, a bottle of water under the sheets, the bottle of Drambuie on her nightstand. Calls ring through to the answering machine. She listens while Lulu asks, "Why haven't you come over?" The light bulb in the bathroom, she insists, needs to be changed right away because the new energy-efficient bulbs make her look old and green. She listens when Bobbie insists, "Pick up and tell me what's going on, Lena-Bena." She listens to Candace: "I hope you gave Randall a piece of your mind. Let me know if you want to talk."

The second day Randall calls late in the afternoon, Lena answers when his number flashes on the caller ID screen. She lays the phone on his pillow instead of using her hands and listens to Randall ask about Camille and Kendrick and what bills have come in the mail.

This third day falls into night, and feathered, dark clouds gather in the sky with the threat of rain. She cannot move in her bed, cannot talk to her children, cannot stop thinking of the vials of pills in the medicine cabinet. The lyrics Lena printed out, what seems like years instead of three weeks ago, are piled on the bed. Of all of Tina's songs, "On Silent Wings"—the words more than the melancholy music—brings tears. She does not have the mental ability this night to understand if it is good or bad to be so average, to live life, or lose love in such an ordinary way that it can be generalized in lyrics that could, and probably do, apply to many. But the songwriter has captured what she believed: the willingness to share a life, the strength of a love that held when times were tough. Someone to hold on to. Randall. They read like her story:

I always thought our love was strong enough
One you could hold on to

Lena climbs out of bed and pulls sweats over her pajamas. Tina gained strength with the help of Buddhist chanting, but it took courage for her to step out on her own. A moan is Lena's chant. She releases it and lets this depression that runs deep in her bones render her passive for the last time. She stands over Randall's dresser. Sunglasses, cuff links, and a mound of change are lined neatly on top.

Winter waves crashed on the cliffs behind the restaurant in San Francisco when Randall put that one-carat, emerald cut diamond on her finger. She believed: wife as partner, wife as friend. She believed when he replaced it with this larger stone. Each time he twisted her hand this way and that—like she does from time to time—the stone sparkled on her slim finger. The gold band accentuates the gold in her skin, the gold that comes shining through whenever she sits too long in the sun.

Now she twists her ring—it slips easily from her finger—and tosses it onto his dresser in this bedroom soon to be for one. Wife in name only.

Lena drives fast and hard. If the two thousand pounds of steel encasing her could lead her to her death, she would not care. A bridge, an amusement park, hills sprinkled with trees. Forty-two miles in forty-two minutes. To do to him before he does it to her.

Not like sex: no sweet anticipation. No hunger for his touch, his broad shoulders sexy in the dark, his fingers and tongue working to please, not berate.

The rain pours like December instead of early May. Rain sheets on the windshield so hard that even the fast, swiping wipers cannot make the windshield clear enough to see more than twenty-five feet ahead. Headlights sweep in motion, cars blur midnight blue in the black of 9 p.m.

At the double doors of TIDA's executive suite, the carpet beneath her soaking-wet flip-flops is plush and thick. Framed posters of San Francisco and the sun setting behind the Golden Gate Bridge line the corridor's walls; glass sconces light the doors. Lena breathes in one, two and out one, two and tries to formulate her words. No more pretend. She will not ask Randall why he puts his wife last, work and grown children first. She fears his answer: wife like ice, distant as the moon, rose thorn in his side like the white man and the glass ceiling above his head.

It seems stupid, formal, to knock on the door when the corporate apartment key is in her left hand. Knock. It is a red key. She raises and lowers the key, then returns it to her pocket. With that one gesture she feels the change, the shift. Knock, knock—have they come full circle? Randall opens the door with the confidence of a big man who knows he can handle whatever awaits him beyond the threshold. There is no astonished look on his face. No smile or hug or happiness like the times when Lena visited this same suite for no reason except that she missed him, or surprised him in silk nighties and no panties beneath, for no reason except that she wanted him. He stands aside without concern for the wildness in her eyes, the intention in her step. The smell of burning wood reminds Lena of home: Irish coffees, music, conversation, Kendrick and Camille's fights over who could stoke the gamboling flames.

Lena scans the long hallway: two closed doors. She pushes open the door to the left, a closet, and the door to the right, a bedroom, and peers inside each one. Heat from a raised vent tickles the hair on her neck, but she is in no mood to laugh. From this end of the long hallway to the combined living and dining area Randall appears small and far away; a slight figure at the wrong end of a pair of binoculars. There is nothing small about Randall. She allows herself to be sidetracked by the pale green walls and the art she'd seen in a San Francisco gallery that would look perfect there so that she can gather her thoughts and slow her hammering heart. Lena wipes her wet hands on her sweats and sits on the angular sofa on the opposite end from Randall. She picks up the remote and clicks off the TV, and this time, he does not complain.

Randall waits and watches. His silence says, "You first."

Her words fall, like cards from a dealer's hand, easier than she thought they would. "I love you, but I can't be this way anymore."

"And, I love you, I always have." Randall's forehead creases so that little veins snake across it. "But, I don't feel loved. Why do you think I didn't ask you to come on this last trip? I needed a break. From the tension, from the anger." He rises from the couch and paces from the window to the small dining table and back, from the heavy coffee table to the fireplace in front of it.

Rain thrums against the sliding glass window. Its rhythm beats their message. Only when Kendrick and Camille were born, when Lena walked down the church aisle toward him, has she ever seen this kind of reaction on Randall's face. His eyes are tight, his lips fixed, his posture sloped in a way that only she would notice. Her hands tremble. They ache to reach out in a gesture all their own to take Randall's hand and make everything all right. She furls her hands tightly in her lap.

"Either we go back to counseling . . . or . . . separate." Lulu will say that separation never happens in their family, that Lena is inflexible, that she won't know how to make it without the man who's taken care of her for so long, that being single at fifty-four will make for a tough and lonely life. But courage itches in Lena's right ear, and she will not scratch it away.

Randall paces, diverts to the kitchen, splashes more wine into his glass. He sips, looking at Lena over the top of the clear rim. "I don't want some thirty-year-old therapist telling me how terrible I am."

The clock on the mantle intrudes on his words. *Tick. Tick. Tick.* No time. No time. Sixty ticks mark the minute, change their lives.

She wonders why he doesn't think the therapist would tell him how terrible *they* are. "Would it make a difference if he were older?"

"No." No tears, 'cause this man don't cry. But Randall's eyebrows fall down, and wrinkles gather on his brow and his mouth and the corners of his wide eyes. His answer resonates above the crackle of the fire, above the rain's patter, above the knock of Lena's heart. Lena wonders why so much now. It could have been put to better use when Camille screamed at her, when that damned cat stunk up the house, when Kendrick snipped at her for not being the same ole mom, when Lynne spoke like Lena was nothing in her own house, when Sharon flirted with him right in front of his wife.

Lena stands and tugs at the space where her ring used to be. She steps toward Randall, but his eyes are dull and flat and have shut her out. The last words of love that she wants to speak do not fall from her mouth. If she knew then—that he would never come home again—she would have stolen a last hug. One long kiss good-bye, so that her imagination would not have to fill the places he no longer is. So that her Thursday chores would have left old sheets on her bed, or towels in the bathroom, his shirts in the hamper so that his smell would stay with her, and she could breathe deep his cinnamon scent for just one more night.

The mistake she makes that night is leaving him in control, but old habits are hard to break: the prompt hers, the decision his. By the time she gets home, Randall will have called Kendrick and Camille. Daughter and son will call her traitor; cite her tough love, her insistence on rules, and recent inattention as reasons to side with their father. They will comfort themselves in their father's temporary attention, so that when she gets home, forty-two miles in forty-two minutes, and gazes upon her children's faces, they will no longer be hers. Kendrick will be a turtle hidden in the shell of his twenty-year-old body; Camille, like her cat, claws extended and ready to fight.

And from this day on nothing will be the same. She will clean for one, not four. And eat for one, not four, and cry for one, not four.

The freeway signs say exit.

And her heart is broken, too.

Chapter 12

Still woozy with the morning-after haze of sleeping pills, Lena busies herself in the kitchen: chop, mix, sauté. Despite the intentional clatter of pots and pans, Kendrick and Camille have not gotten the hint, not smelled the vanilla, melted butter, and thick chunks of milk- and cinnamon-soaked bread simmering on the griddle. Hope rises with the clomp of Kendrick's heavy shoes on the stairs; perhaps the smells have lured them after all. Kendrick bolts into the kitchen, his backpack sagging between his shoulder blades. Camille, dressed in flannel pajamas, thick leg-warmers, and a hooded sweater, strolls behind her big brother.

"I want to talk to you both about me and your dad." Lena sets a medium-sized platter with four slices of French toast on the table, then sprinkles them with confectioner's sugar. These thick, fluffy pieces of cooked bread are Camille and Kendrick's first choice for breakfast food. The memory of six-year-old Kendrick gobbling the spiced bread by the mouthful, syrup on his cheeks and greedy hands, and a much younger Camille dipping her pieces into the tangy berry compote Lena concocted flashes in her head. Lena nods toward the table and prays Kendrick and Camille understand: food as love.

"I can't be late. I'll grab a breakfast burrito from 7-Eleven." Kendrick leans against the back door, the eagerness to get to his part-time job obvious in his shuffling from one foot to the other.

He refuses to look at Lena. Camille edges, sinewy like Kimchee, toward the table.

"It won't take long. Please."

Kendrick picks up a piece of toast with his hands and folds it into a pizza-like wedge before swallowing it in two bites. Camille stabs the toast with her fork and drags it onto her plate. Even now Camille dips. She never pours gravy onto her mashed potatoes; she dips forkfuls of the creamy side dish into the gravy boat, or chunks of bread into melted butter. When Camille was eight, Lena decided not to stop the habit and bought her a tiny, bone-china dipping pot.

"I want you to understand that separating from your father doesn't mean that I don't love you or that life won't be the same." Lena looks from Kendrick to Camille. Two sets of eyes roam from food to table to each other; anywhere but their mother's eyes. "I don't know how to explain to you what has happened. I'm not sure I fully understand it myself."

"I don't know what's going on. All I know is that you haven't been Mom, Mom, in a while." Kendrick fidgets with his keys, sticking each of them into the lock on the door, even though only one fits. "And, I can't speak for Camille, but this is between you and Dad. I'm going back to Chicago as soon as summer school starts. Dad already agreed."

"I guess . . . I mean it's scary. You know? My life should be about college and prom and graduation, not my parents' problems," Camille mutters. "Dad told us he's in the middle of some crazy shit at work, and you don't do anything to help."

"I'm not going to argue with either one of you. You have no idea of how it is between married couples. You don't understand my sacrifices."

"Those were your choices, Mom." Kendrick opens the back door and steps out as if his abruptness will change her decision.

"Are you getting divorced?" Camille pushes food around her plate.

"Nothing is settled. No matter what happens, graduation will be the same. For now, I assume, your Dad will stay in TIDA's corporate apartment."

"Can I stay with him?"

"I'd like you to stay with me." At the sink, Lena runs water into the teakettle and sets it onto the burner. She angles her head so that Camille cannot see her face and the tears she tries hard to blink away. When steam hisses from the capped spout, she reaches into the glass cabinet behind her and pulls out two flowery teacups. A heaping dollop of honey, lemon, and chamomile tea go into the cups. Lena sets a cup in front of Camille.

When Camille was ten, Lena started a tradition similar to the one her Auntie Big Talker had with her seven nieces: they gathered once a month for a manners and vocabulary lesson and lemon- and honey-laden tea. While the cousins sipped their tea, Auntie Big Talker read to them: the encyclopedia, obscure English novels, the dictionary. She made them write the words they didn't understand on three-by-five cards and insisted the cousins memorize them. *Conundrum* irritates Lena's tongue now. There is a riddle, but no amusement; no pun in the answer to what mother and daughter can do to get along.

For her version of the ritual, Lena took Camille to a collectables store and together they selected teacups and matching saucers. At the bookstore, they searched the shelves until they came across a book about a gutsy little girl who braved her way through a country swamp. Then they sat at the table in front of the kitchen window, the three tall pine trees outside the sole witnesses to their closeness. They sipped tea, ate too many cookies and read aloud to each other. In the years that followed, the last Saturday of the month was theirs. They read the swamp girl's story more times than either of them could remember, all of Beverly Cleary's books—it was because of Ramona's cat, Socks, that Camille fell in love with cats—and *The Count of Monte Cristo.* They talked about the world and life and what Camille might be when she grew up.

"I'm late for school." Camille shoves the untouched tea across the table. She is upstairs and back out of the house before Lena can figure out what more to say.

Lena feels it; a barely perceptible rumble on her emotional Richter scale. She understands it: another shift. A shift from her cocoon, her warm fuzzy life, the lovely family she worked so hard for has a nasty crack and may soon rupture and split.

Upstairs in her office, Lena lights her candles, holds her book in her hands. It is hard to see through the tears that splash onto the yellowed pages. The thin threads of similarity between her life and Tina's are always in her head: their birthdays, a little insecurity, and deference to men. Creativity. For years Lena's art has been limited to the preservation of family posterity: anniversaries, birthdays, holidays, vacations. Time to step it up. If, she wonders, psychics gave Tina clues about her future, then shouldn't she consider the clues Vernon gave her?

The parking lot outside the camera store overflows with cars and the men and women who rush in and out of them. Lena sits inside her car watching people watch her rip the cellophane from the digital SLR camera she purchased minutes ago. Drizzle collects on her windshield, blurs the sharp edges of the megastore's grayish facade, the sky, and the people in a way she would like to capture in pictures.

The chunky silver camera hides between layers of molded styrofoam, cardboard, plastic wrapped cables, a laminated quick reference chart, a 1GB compact flash card, batteries, and quarter-inch-thick instruction booklets in Spanish, English, and Chinese, all of which Lena tosses back into the limp plastic bag. She slips four batteries into the chamber. The camera emits an electronic, susurrant whine. Lena rolls down the window and points to the huge electronics store. *Click.* Points to the sky. *Click.* Points to the little girl passing by pointing at her. *Click.* Turns the camera lens around to her own face. *Click.* Camera in hand like a newborn, she sets it back in its cardboard cradle on the passenger seat, turns on the ignition, and backs out of the lot.

The city of Emeryville used to be an obscure industrial city on the edge of the entrance to the Bay Bridge. In the sixties and seventies, the mudflats were blank canvases for artists and rebellious hippies from UC Berkeley to build wooden sculptures and Vietnam protest signs in the slushy marshes alongside the freeway. Now the steel factories are gone, replaced with biotechnology headquarters, a mall, and a movie complex; only the train tracks remain. Lena drives to an empty lot next to a new condo building where anise grows wild, and the air smells of licorice.

Out of the car, into the street and the lot beside it. She takes the camera and snaps picture after picture. *Click.* The rusted iron tracks, the rocks and gravel, the feathery weeds between the jagged stones and splintered wooden ties, the cracked brown beer bottle and discarded keychain beside it. *Click.* The back of an abandoned warehouse, its dock covered in graffiti, discarded grocery carts, the wrought iron gate of the condo complex. *Click.* She shoots at every angle she can imagine: upward looking down, downward looking up.

She wishes that she had someone to hug and to hug her back, because she is so filled with the thrill of creating, the thrill of knowing that this old love will be the foundation that roots her to herself, especially if Randall no longer will.

Chapter 13

This lake in the middle of Oakland is only odd because it is not in the middle of the city. But that's what Oaklanders say: Lake Merritt is a lake in the middle of the city. Actually, Lena thinks, it's kind of cool. Like the canals in Paris. Or Central Park, if there is a lake in Central Park.

A photographer focuses his camera on a bride and groom in front of a pillar covered with rambling ivy. That is not the picture she would shoot, Lena reflects, pleased that her old passion fulfills the possibilities of Vernon's prediction. She would pose the couple in front of one of the thick, gnarled trees near the western side of the lake to accentuate the opposites: the couple's loving intimacy and the bare-trunked tree's solitude.

With both arms extended above her head, she leans to her left and the bushy-haired man with seventies-style headphones coming her way. She prays he can't hear himself sing, knows that James Brown never sounded so bad. Arms to the right and away from the man who speed-walks in a kelly green Lycra bodysuit. If only her buns were that tight.

Most runners take the path to the right from this exact midpoint of the lake; there is the option of the higher cement sidewalk or the lower dirt path. A tree-lined grassy knoll between the two paths is filled with twenty or more elderly Chinese men and women in the midst of ancient Tai Chi moves. Lena begins a brisk trot behind a wizened couple holding hands. The gray-haired man and woman move solidly up the tamped dirt path and step to the side at the crunch of Lena's noisy gait. Today the lake is beautiful, odorless, and clear, with none of the slimy algae that often turns its water brackish.

"I guess this *isn't* the best time to get on your ass for not keeping in touch," a loud voice calls from behind.

"You're late." Lena waits for the body of the familiar voice to catch up. She has told Cheryl more than once, over the forty years they have known one another, that she will probably be late for her own funeral. "I guess this *is* the best time to say you haven't done much to keep in touch your damned self."

Lena rubs her hand over her friend's gray-streaked hair. "You cut all your hair off." Cheryl has been obsessed with her hair since their college days. She went to the beauty salon two, sometimes three, times a week, despite persistent complaints that she was short on cash. If Cheryl made special arrangements with their handsome hairdresser, Lena never asked what they were, Cheryl's hair—long, short, or in-between—always looked good.

"And you should do the same; it's liberating." Cheryl tugs at Lena's stubby ponytail. "Us mature women don't need all this hair anymore. Short hair sets us free."

"Leave it to you to fight for a fashion trend." Cheryl is the medicine Lena needs. She would have called her old friend sooner or later. Bobbie's pushing made it sooner. Lena makes the sign of the cross over her heart when they pass the Church of the Virgin Mary on the opposite side of the street.

"You don't work and let yourself get all Suzy Homemaker conservative. Stop. Let me look at you."

When she was in her twenties, Lena jogged the lake regularly. Her legs were her best asset then, and short shorts showed off her trim thighs and molded calves. Lena pulls her pants up to her knees and flashes a quick grin, proving to Cheryl and a chubby-cheeked man that they still are. "Looks are the least of my problems." Lena continues along the path and motions for Cheryl to follow.

"Let me guess. Mr. Spencer."

"Something like that." Lena picks up her pace as a light drizzle begins to fall; joggers speed past them. She pauses for Cheryl to catch up. Back in the day, Cheryl ran faster than Lena, socially and athletically. "I want to take pictures again."

"Photography is competitive. I'm not even sure how many black photographers are making money." Cheryl speaks with the knowledge and authority of fifteen years of representing emerging artists working in all kinds of mediums: acrylic, oil, organic and recycled material, metal, and indigenous stone.

"Art can't be subject to racial boundaries." Lena snaps. She knows the *business* world is underhandedly racist—Randall's battles, his struggle to get to the top, prove that.

Cheryl pokes a finger into Lena's taut bicep. "It's who, not what, you know that can keep some blacks from garnering the kind of success that makes them the big bucks." Cheryl lists the downside of photography: expensive equipment, darkroom time, or the latest digital software. Finding galleries. Rejection, rejection, rejection. "What do you want to work for anyway? You've got Randall."

"Randall may not always be around," Lena whispers.

"I knew it the minute you called." Cheryl's face reminds Lena of a person who has tasted something awful and wants desperately to spit it out. "I could hear it in your voice."

Lena points to a six-foot, multicolored sign and the giant heads of yellow and orange fantasy creatures visible through the trees. "Our parents took us to Fairyland when we were little."

"You didn't call to reminisce." Cheryl stops to retie her shoelaces and wipe sweat from her forehead with the terrycloth band on her wrist. "Talk."

It was Cheryl who listened when boyfriends dumped Lena, Cheryl who cried with her when Lena discovered she was pregnant with Kendrick. Cheryl took her to the hospital when she suffered false labor pains, comforted her after John Henry's first stroke, listened when she had no one else to talk to about Camille's temper tantrums. Cheryl knows most of the good and bad of Lena's life.

"Randall and I have separated."

Cheryl yanks at Lena's warm-up and embraces her friend. "You're going to be all right, you know that, don't you?"

Lena shakes her head no. "Oh, Cheryl, I'm so sorry for reconnecting like this. When I have a problem. I know I haven't been much of a friend. It's just that Randall . . ."

Cheryl and Randall tolerated each other for Lena's sake. Their common loyalty ended five years ago the evening Cheryl ran upstairs after dinner to say goodnight to Kendrick and Camille and returned to the kitchen in time to hear Randall: "I need more wine. This is the last time we entertain Cheryl. It takes three or four glasses just to put up with her loud clothes and louder mouth." Cheryl snatched her red cape and silver-studded handbag and told Randall, in a voice more earsplitting than the one he had complained about, that she wouldn't dignify his comment with a response, loud or otherwise.

"Good friends pick up where they left off without explanation. What do you need me to do?"

"We haven't talked or decided anything. I'm worried about Kendrick and Camille."

"I know you love them like they were still babies, but Kendrick and Camille are grown. You need to take care of yourself and get a lawyer, because I know Randall will."

"I don't think he'd do that without talking to me first."

"Ha! Randall didn't get to where he is today by being timid or indecisive."

On the dirt path in front of them, leggy, green-wing-tipped geese squawk exclamation points to their conversation. Lena speeds up a small incline, stomps her feet at the top, and yields the right of way to a gaggle of the ubiquitous geese on the graveled path. She sidesteps to her left and away from the bird droppings, and Cheryl steps with her. Any day, rows of downy ducklings will waddle across this same path to the water's edge. Spring has crept in; bougainvillea buds are fat and primed to burst in sprays of red. Already several new mothers, waists thick with baby fat, determinedly push their newborns in three-wheeled strollers to exercise away their pregnancy weight.

"I'll help any way I can, but you knew that when you called. You could have told me outright about you and Randall. You didn't have to make up any excuses."

"I'm embarrassed."

"Girl, I knew you when you were still a virgin. Please. Divorce is simply another phase of life."

"We're not getting divorced."

"You sure about that?"

Lena gives the only answer she can: a heavy-shouldered shrug.

Cheryl has had two husbands and no kids. Even though her marriages were short-lived—the first one twenty months, the second three years—she once told Lena that marital bliss was an ideal state. Lena thought so, too. She kicks stones from the path, stoops to pick one up, and tosses it at the geese, dispersing them in all directions. Don't blame us, their squawks seem to say, it's not our fault.

"I missed you. We can hang out again, even though . . ." Cheryl waves her hands around her and stops at the promenade where they started. "At our age you better think seriously before you step back into the single life."

"What's age got to do with it?"

"We've passed men, and not one of them has looked at us, said hello, or, God forbid, flirted. We're in our fifties. We're invisible. And while I don't give a damn about that, you might, if you were single."

"I'm not the kind of woman that men have ever fallen over themselves for." She snickers, her broad shoulders relax. Not fat. Not skinny. Breasts Randall still calls, called, perky, hands without dark spots or lines. "I don't care. Age is just a number, right? At least that's what you used to say when we were forty, and you hit on thirty-year-olds."

"Still do!" Cheryl grins. "Just like you say art ignores color, I have to *believe* art, and possibly thirty-year-olds, ignore age. That said, do you really want to be single and start over in photography or anything else at fifty-four? It's going to take hours and hours, maybe years of hustle." Cheryl looks Lena straight in the eye. "Bottom line: is he really all that bad?"

"If I believed he was bad then I would have to question why I've been with him all these years. He's not good or bad; he's Randall." From the arches Lena catches a glimpse of the older couple outlined in the distance, they walk arm in arm now, their pace steady and assured.

"Find another way to *find* yourself. I assume, unless he's got someone on the side, that he loves you. So what if he doesn't say it. He gives it, which ain't bad, sweetie. I could use a bit of loving like that myself. Go screw his brains out and tell him to come back home."

"I wouldn't do it because of the money."

"(a) It's your money, too. And (b) you'd better get a lawyer, because money, my dear friend, is what Randall is all about. Call me when you're ready; I've got tons of recommendations."

Chapter 14

The mail has collected in its metal box for six days. Camille stopped her daily trips to the mailbox after her early acceptance letter from Columbia arrived. Her agreement letter went back twenty-four hours later. An oversized envelope stands out among the business-sized ones, the catalogs, the magazines. TIDA's blue and white logo, the label clearly inscribed in her full name, Lena Harrison Spencer. After packs of coupons, credit card solicitations, and real estate brochures go straight into the recycle bin, Lena trudges back to the house.

She clutches the envelope in her hands, turns it over once, then once more for a clue to its contents. In the six days since she last saw Randall, they have not spoken. Through short, snippy emails, he told her that he would pick up the rest of his clothes and some furniture as soon as he finds a place. Kendrick has shuttled Randall's belongings and toiletries back and forth between home, the corporate condo, and a hotel suite that Randall has taken in San Francisco.

With one easy tug, Lena rips off the top of the TIDA envelope and yanks out the loose pages of typed correspondence. The cover letter is typed on TIDA's bold letterhead. Randall's secretary's initials are printed in a small font in the lower left-hand corner. He dictates his letters, he doesn't type, and Lena knows that he would not spend his precious time on a hunt-and-peck search around a keyboard to type a letter to her. If she wasn't a priority before, why would she be one now?

Ms. Lena Inez Harrison Spencer
3567 Rockhead Road
Oakland, CA 94602

Lena:

Enclosed are Dissolution of Marriage papers my attorney will file next week with the Alameda County Family Court. These documents require your acknowledgment and immediate action. I am not interested in any more drama. You need a lawyer. Please direct future communication on this matter to my attorney. His information is located on the petition.

The cost of divorce and attorney's fees can be ridiculously high. Stay in the house, and I'll find other lodging. Be prepared to sell the house within the next 90 days, unless you want to cut a deal before the lawyers get involved. It would be to your benefit to do this, since my expectation is that you start to provide for yourself immediately.

I propose that you keep the house and, with a few exceptions, its contents. The appreciation will offset my stock options, annual bonuses, and a reasonable portion of our joint portfolio. In return, I would expect your written agreement to release any other or future claims on my income, pensions, or IRA.

By waiting to file the dissolution paperwork, I have given you sufficient time to consider my proposal. This is a generous offer. I suggest you take it.

Cordially,
K. Randall Spencer

Cordially?

"Damn you, K. Randall Spencer," she yells, noting her husband of twenty-three years has signed the letter like he would any other legal document written to a stranger.

"Mom?" Camille bumps into Lena as she rushes into the kitchen. The house had been so quiet, she forgot her youngest was home. Camille's question is urgent, the tone she would use in an emergency. "Is everything okay?"

"Don't you have school?" Lena's voice is harsher than she intends.

"Relax. Teachers' meetings. No classes until after lunch."

Lena turns away from Camille. The distinctive pleadings paperwork, its margins lined and the sentences numbered, is scattered on the counter and the floor.

"What's wrong?" Camille pushes aside the envelope and scans the divorce documents. "Are you crying?"

Lena snatches the papers from Camille's hand. "This is not your business."

"So this is it, huh? My parents are getting divorced. Shit."

"Don't curse."

"Don't do this to me." Camille's eyes tighten.

When Lena reaches out for Camille's hands, her daughter steps away. "Know that this is not about you."

"Well, Dad already warned me and Kendrick anyway." Camille smacks her hands together.

Damn, Randall. Lena's hands shake with the adrenaline rush. She snatches the TV remote, throws it on the floor, and jams it with her foot into the counter's wooden toe kick until it breaks apart.

"Mom! Stop!" Camille dashes to the opposite side of the kitchen, waits for her mother's furor to pass, and covers her eyes with her hands. "He says you gave him no choice. What's up with that? Don't you care about our family? Don't you care about me or Kendrick?" Her voice booms across the room.

Lena laughs. A crazy laugh, like the mad wife in *Jane Eyre* whose barmy laughter echoed through Rochester's mansion. Her laughter is so loud, so hard, that fear widens Camille's eyes and nostrils.

Lena prays that daughter understands what mother finds so hard to understand: Randall won't talk to her, but he has the nerve to tell his daughter and son, before he tells his wife, what will happen to her life. Lena steps close, and Camille freezes when Lena embraces her. "I love you, Camille. Go to school. This is my fight, not yours."

Without a hug, a wave, a "see ya later," Camille slams the door. Lena hopes that one day Camille will understand how incapable and powerless her mother is at this moment. How she wants to kick and scream and hold her daughter tight, protect her, and show her how to be strong. When the time is right, when her head is right, Lena will sit Camille down and make sure she never ends up this way. There isn't one word she can think of that would have made these past ten minutes easier. Damn Randall for putting that on Camille, for putting her in the middle, for putting her on his side.

As clear as the view through the windows of this metal- and granite-filled kitchen, she tries to see the lesson in divorce, wants it to open out like the landscape before her: garden, trees, streets, sky, sun, clouds, stratosphere, heaven. Everything happens for a reason. She knows what Randall doesn't: she has to be free to fulfill her destiny. How could he explain that to Camille?

Beyond the windows, the day is brilliant. It feels like black inside Lena's head. Like midnight and death. Perhaps ninety minutes focused on her body; a release of her mind to its inner energy is what she needs. Stretch, downward facing dog, sun position, hands over heart, warrior pose; meditation for a restless mind that cannot stop. But the lethargy, the heavy weight of gloom, sends her one sluggish step at a time up the stairs.

Randall offers no option. Randall is not the option. Every single part of her body feels dead: her head lolls, her shoulders slump, her hands hang, her body sinks deeper into the bed until she feels that she is on the floor. Already, her body aches for the old days, the joy, the joking, sitting together without the need for words, body heat, the pride in her family and what she worked so hard to build: the promise of happily ever after.

She reaches for the telephone. It takes an eternity to lift it from nightstand to ear. She pushes eleven numbers. If she can hold on through the sales staff, the canned music, the minutes until her call is transferred to Bobbie's office, then she can cry.

"What's up?" The keys of Bobbie's computer keyboard click in the background.

"I got divorce papers." Lena explains Randall's proposal. She knows she's done the right thing. It is the anger at being spineless that hurts the most; the realization that, having given her all to marriage and family, the person she loves more than herself could let go as quickly as he did his ill-fated assistant. "Maybe I should call Randall—"

"Stop! Don't let him bully you into something you haven't thoroughly investigated. Run the numbers. Get a lawyer."

"A woman. Black."

"Divorce isn't about gender, color, or emotion. It's business."

"A black woman might understand how another black woman feels."

"Pain doesn't know color. Divorce is no more difficult emotionally for a black woman than it is for a white one. The difference is the shock on the lawyers' faces when they've spoken to you on the phone and heard your very white-sounding voice and then see what they didn't expect walk through their door. When they see your black face drive up in your gaudy Mercedes-Benz; when you list your assets—more than their own—and they want some explanation of why you've got it and they don't."

"So, how do I decide?"

"Pick the best, the sharpest. The most experienced lawyer will do what it takes to win." Bobbie's sigh is long. "There's a big difference between cynicism and racism. Understanding how much of either one you will take is how you decide who you'll work with and who you won't." The tap, tap of Bobbie's pencil or fingernail against the phone makes Lena feel like a poor student about to give a wrong answer to the teacher's question.

"I failed."

"You stood up for yourself. Did you think if you threw down the gauntlet Randall would sweep you off your feet, make passionate love to you, and promise to value you for what you do for him and your family? Please."

"This is the most thoughtless, thought-full decision I've ever made." Lena pulls the covers over her head to shut out the radiant sun and what was a wonderful view of the neighborhood trees and their speckled shadows, San Francisco, and two bridges before she opened that envelope. "I should have spoken up sooner."

"I can't hear you. Where are you, Lena?"

"I'm in hell. At least he could have given *us* more thought—it's only been six days. It's like I'm no good . . . something that needs to be gotten rid of quickly. Like the garbage or . . . a big black spider."

"Can you finish what you started?"

"I can't breathe." Tina started over at forty-five. Now she has to start over, too. "What will I do? I feel like something is stuck in my throat. I can't breathe." Under the weight of the covers Lena feels like a ten-year-old hiding from the bogeyman, waiting for her big sister to rescue her with a flashlight.

"The choice has been made—move on, sister."

In the bathroom, Lena stares at the cabinet shelves lined with amber vials of leftover prescriptions for the insomnia that comes from menopause and the aches that come with aging. She snatches seven amber vials from the mirrored cabinet and folds them carefully into the bottom of her pajama top. With her free hand, she rearranges what is left behind—aspirin, a box of cotton swabs, alcohol, peroxide, dry-eye solution, tea tree oil, and a box of estrogen patches—around the shelves, then walks back into the bedroom. What would Randall say if she did it? What would he do if she swallowed these pills? One by one, she empties the vials onto the bedspread; pills tumble, bead-like, left and right into piles. They should have held on to simple things, said I love you. Let's try.

Her pajamas are wet, her pillow is soaked, her glass filled with Drambuie. She sips and holds the liquid in her mouth. Would he be sorry that he didn't try to understand how much she loves him, how much she needs to be herself? Does he understand that she will never be able to get back what has been broken? She swallows hard and waits for the liquor to go down her throat and dissolve in her stomach juices. Stupid Randall. Stupid Lena.

Lena rolls the caplets between her fingers, watches them crumble with the heat of her hand. She gulps more Drambuie, lets it take its last slow ride down her throat. Sleep used to be sweet. If only she could sleep. Forever. If she had taped that Tina Turner interview she would watch it now. Lena reaches for her book and settles for Tina's image on the cover.

There is hope in Tina's eyes and the knowledge that life goes on, and it is good. Tina looks into the camera, looks straight into Lena's soul. The book falls open, the words are underlined: *I knew that change had to come from the inside out—that I had to understand myself, and accept myself before anything else could be accomplished.*

Tina reinvented herself.

Tina survived.

Chapter 15

Lena swerves into the underground parking lot of the new apartment building on the western side of Lake Merritt. She has watched its skeleton rise above the lake from the hill her house sits on and passed it more than once on her walks. Its multistory reflection on the water makes the structure look taller and whiter than it is. Signs posted on the building's windows boast great views of San Francisco and the hills, a gym, a swimming pool, and enticing leases.

The marbled entryway is high-ceilinged and full of tall palm trees. The lobby resembles a five-star hotel—luxurious, comfortable, and welcoming. The advantage, Lena thinks, as she strolls toward the reception desk, of being married for twenty-three years is the knowledge the spouses have: they know one another. What Lena knows about Randall is this: whenever he cuts a deal he makes sure he is on the winning end. Years of watching him barter with humble vendors, cut business deals over dinner, and recap his victories have shown Lena what her soon to be ex-husband is capable of when he wants something. She assumes that if Randall wants her to keep the house, he—no they—must be worth more than he has let on.

Today everything is different. She knows it is better to be less controlled by Randall, to be out of the place that no longer feels like home. Even though, physically, Camille and Kendrick are around, the house has lost its soul.

"I'd like to see a three-bedroom apartment." Lena stands before the guard at the desk, impressive in his black uniform, as he dials the leasing office.

A gawky agent steps into the lobby from behind a door with a sign that reads: STAFF ONLY. The young man begins with a tour of the lobby, the workout room, and a small library area for the use of all the tenants.

Lena waves off his canned spiel and presses her hand to his arm—the same calming gesture she would have made to Kendrick or Camille. "All I want to see are the available units. I can't take a sales pitch today. Sorry."

They head for the two banks of elevators and tour several vacant units until she sees the apartment she wants: one with a view of the lake and the hills so that she can see where she lived from where she will live.

The apartment will do fine for her and Camille, and hopefully Kendrick, until Lena decides on a permanent place to call home. She will miss her house: scrub jays trilling at five in the morning, rock doves cooing, rain pelting against the tiled roof; chirping crickets and dancing butterflies; the full moon through the bedroom window—luminous and mysterious; the crunch of autumn leaves, winter wind singing through the trees; the secret compartment behind the fuse box where a four-year-old Kendrick stored his rubber dinosaurs; a six-burner gas stove, blueberry pancakes on Sunday mornings.

In this kitchen, three times smaller than the one she has now, she thinks of how she will manage Thanksgiving dinner and Christmas, too, if she is lucky, and in a few weeks a cake for Camille's graduation. Lena will do whatever she must to make Camille's celebration normal. Let Randall do it. There's more to raising a child than signing checks. Let him hire a caterer, handle the details of the graduation party. Ha! Let him make sure Camille roams among family and old friends, collects envelopes of money and gift certificates, and pretends, if only for one day, that nothing in her life has changed. Let Lena be a guest in what was her own home.

"Ma'am?" The agent is tentative, but Lena does not need to be sold. "Excuse me, but this is the last apartment I have to show you."

"Where do I sign?" With no thought to where the money will come from, Lena decides a six-month lease makes the most sense, requires the least obligation for such a tenuous situation. The last time she rented an apartment she was twenty-five and three years away from buying the stucco house—a half-mile from Lulu and John Henry—that she lived in until her marriage.

While the gleeful agent completes the paperwork, Lena returns to the place she will call home. The apartment is simple: the ceiling meets white walls in sharp angles without the crown molding in every room of her house, a gas fireplace, wall-to-wall carpeting. This new place fourteen floors above street level is lovely but sterile.

"Hello, hello," she calls out, waiting for her echo to repeat her words like children do in empty rooms. When she moved into her first apartment, there were friends there to help. It was a party: a celebration of independence, a joyful adjustment to living without parents, sister, or roommates. The process begins again. Same but different. The period of adjustment. The vocabulary change from *we* to *I*. She walks from the open kitchen to the bedrooms and the small balcony. Who will greet her but these walls when she comes home? Who will she ask about their day? Who will say goodnight?

Twenty-three years of hard work: for her children, her husband, her marriage. Twenty-three years of sowing the seeds for a good life. Lena crosses her heart and whispers, "Dear God, I know my life will never be the same again. Please bless me and let new seeds sow themselves here."

"This is the easiest commission I've ever made." The agent is excited when she returns. Lena imagines that he has spent part of that time computing, if the calculator next to her paperwork is any indication, his commission.

Up to the time she rented that first apartment years ago, the biggest check she had written was for her car. That check for five hundred dollars was small compared to the one for the security deposit and first and last month's rent she will write today. Her hand trembled when she signed that lease and handed over her check. Her hand trembles now; this time, she understands, for a different reason. The checkbook inside her Louis Vuitton is the one for their joint equity cash fund. The one she supposes she can still draw funds from. It has not dawned on her until this moment, in front of this nervous young man, that, like a husband from the movies, Randall may have cut off her access to their joint accounts or, worse yet, taken all of their money. She has no idea of how this divorce thing works. But she knows that she better find out soon. If he has a lawyer, then he has one up on her. Up his.

If Randall has dared to pull out all of their money, she will make a few phone calls, the first to Candace, to assure that the whole world knows. If the balances have not been touched—what an odd salute to her trustworthiness—Lena cannot help but think how funny, for all his formality, that Randall still leaves managing the household funds to her.

If her change, like Tina's change, means taking the best from who she was to form who she wants to be, then Lena must accept and move on. She signs the new lease, effortlessly writes a check, and reminds herself to transfer funds to a separate bank account in her name.

"You really know what you want." The agent grabs Lena's hand and pumps enthusiastically, and she hopes, from the look of his frayed cuffs, that his commission will be spent on a new shirt. Let Randall worry about the cable bill, the PGE, the crack in the living room's bay window, the ashes in the fireplace, weeds in the patio cement, the cedar armoire, Kendrick's baptismal gown, Camille's first Easter dress, his great-grandmother's Bible.

She will move into this apartment and live here until the divorce is over and done done done.

In the car, Lena dials Bobbie's home number and listens to the latest greeting on her sister's voicemail: "You know what the deal is, and you know what to do. So, unless this is an emergency, leave a quick one."

"I've told you about that message, Bobbie. What if Lulu calls, what kind of message is she supposed to leave?" Lena is tired of being ombudsman between the two women she loves most in the world. She sighs and tries not to let out all the sadness her stomach is having a hard time keeping down. "I'm glad you're out. You need to do that more often anyway." Lena pauses long enough to compose herself but not long enough for the machine to turn off automatically. "I signed a lease for an apartment. I feel like shit—but good shit. If you have any suggestions for telling our mother, let me know or, better yet, I don't suppose you'd do that for me? Would you?" She can hear Bobbie's voice in her head as clearly as if she had picked up the phone: no way.

Cell phone pressed to her ear, Lena peers through a crack in the curtains. Her mother sits at the table, a cup in front of her and a book in her hand. The television set is on, but Lena can't hear it, and she guesses the volume is probably muted. Sometimes, Lulu keeps the TV on for the company the images, not the sound, offer. "I'm outside the back door, Lulu. Open up."

Lulu flips back the flowery curtain from the kitchen door window before opening it. Her hair is covered with a blue slumber bonnet, her cheeks and lips are bare, her housedress is faded and worn at the elbows. The kitchen sink is full of dishes and pots. At the sink, Lena runs water into the rubberized dishpan. She searches under the cabinet for dishwashing soap hidden between assorted half-full bottles of cleansers and squeezes the blue liquid over the dishes.

The running hot water steams up the window above the sink while she washes the dishes and rinses them one by one. Lulu picks up a dishtowel and dries the plates and bowls and places them on the counter instead of onto their shelves because she likes them air-dry not just towel-dry. "Randall served me with divorce papers, and I've decided to move out." Lena says matter-of-factly, surprised at how even her voice is.

"Oh, my God, look what you've gone and done. I told you not to bother Randall with your problems." The soft scent of her dusky perfume floats between mother and daughter. Lulu backs into the kitchen table and lowers herself into her chair. "You never listen, do you, Lena?"

"Oh, Lulu . . . I feel bad enough as it is." Lena scans the kitchen. It is messier than normal: five soda cans and three empty gallon water containers sit, along with newspapers, beside the refrigerator. She pulls a folded grocery bag from underneath the sink, snaps it open, then drops the cans, papers, and containers into the bag.

"You better keep yourself in that house. Don't let him take it away from you."

What, she thinks, is the point of telling Lulu about Randall's manipulative offer? "I'll feel better in neutral territory."

"I hope you put some money away." Lulu purses her lips and sips from a cup she has had since Lena and Bobbie were little girls.

"I'll sell my car if I have to." Lena pulls the broom and the dustpan from the tall cabinet beside the stove and begins to sweep the floor in hurried, choppy strokes. "I'm sure he has to pay me alimony or something . . ."

"Even *I* kept a secret stash, baby girl."

Whenever Lena joked that Lulu encouraged her to hide a little something on the side, Randall chortled and told Lena that if she was, he hoped it was a lot of something because, with her expensive tastes, there was no way a little would ever do.

"These things don't happen in my family." The volume rises suddenly on the TV as if Lulu senses her daughter's breakup can be masked by the sound.

Standing on the other side of the kitchen, Lena thinks of at least two of her aunts and a cousin who should let it happen to them. Divorce or separation, that is. She sweeps the dust and dirt into the dustpan and empties it into the trash. Lulu points at a corner underneath the cabinet, and Lena sweeps there as well.

"I'm sure Randall still wants you, Lena. He's a good man. He just works too much." Lulu fumbles with the slumber cap and pushes the lacy edges behind her ears. "What can you do without him? How will you take care of yourself?"

"I don't know why I'm here. I didn't want you to have a heart attack if I told you over the phone." Lena shoves the broom and dustpan back into the little closet and reminds herself to buy Lulu one of those handheld vacuums for spot-dusting and spills. Lulu believes in forever and so did Lena until almost twenty-four hours ago. Tina believed in herself, and Lena has to hold on, too, or she will wilt like one of Lulu's short-blooming azaleas. She steps past Lulu to the back door and pulls it wide open, letting a chilly breeze into the overheated house.

Lulu hobbles to Lena and yanks at the elbow of her sweatshirt just like Camille and Kendrick did when they were kids and wanted her full attention. "Your Aunt Fanny left your Uncle Johnny two or three times before he finally straightened up. They made it through forty years of marriage before she died." A rare stern look crosses Lulu's face, the kind that would have stopped Lena in her tracks if she were thirty years younger. "Get yourself together, and don't leave that house. Make Randall take you back before he finds another woman to take your place."

Chapter 16

Time to do it. Time to pick up the phone and call that stupid Randall. She tried to erase him from her thoughts during the purgatory of hours since she signed her lease. When Lena picked up his shirts—wishing she had the guts to burn them—she lied to the two chatty proprietors behind the counter that she would no longer bring in Randall's shirts because they were relocating to another state. The state of no-longer-married. Randall's absence is an ache that deepens when she least expects: while she balances the checkbook, completes change of address forms, changes the bed linens.

Lena lights the candles on the corner of her desk. Music, music, music will help. She scrolls through 173 Tina Turner songs on her MP3 player and stops wherever there is inspiration. She searches for the tunes she imagines Tina, onstage, strutting her stuff to and dials.

"Randall. This is Lena." She knows he knows who it is. She needs to distance herself from him this way. This is business. "I leased an apartment. I'm moving out."

"My offer is reasonable. I gave you enough time to evaluate it."

"Well, it's this way," Lena mutters Randall's prayer. A false cough covers her unsteadiness. She doesn't want Randall to know how off balance she is. "I'm thinking there might be more to it than you've let on."

"Think what you want, but you'd better get a job. I won't pay for an apartment when you should stay in the house."

"Oh, but you *will* pay for one for yourself? I have that right?" Had she planned better Lena would have taken money out of the bank—no, taken money out of the household funds, ignored monthly bills; if needed, hidden a ton of money so that she wouldn't have to deal with Randall.

"Stay in the house, Lena. Don't make it any harder on Kendrick and Camille than it already is."

If the blame-game gauntlet were something she could see, touch, or feel, it would be coming at her hard and heavy like a brick through a glass window of this lovely house; she would take it and throw it back. "It already is, Randall, and that's not all my fault." Breathing brings Lena back to her business mind-set. One. Two. Three. "I have room for them, and I'll make sure they understand that wherever I am is home. You make sure there's money in the bank."

Like a dancer, Lena moves around the kitchen at a frenzied pace grabbing plates, silverware, and napkins, ignoring the flush of perspiration across her forehead. The table is set as it was for the last meal Lena prepared now more than two weeks ago. That day marked an end. Tonight has to be peaceful. A time to savor and enjoy.

The back door opens with Kendrick's familiar entrance; a couple of inches at first, as if he needs to peek in, then a full swing. His profile is trim and still borders on skinny. He is not close to his normal weight, though his arms look muscular through the long sleeves of his shirt. His brown-red complexion is finally clear and free of the acne brought about by drugs or his final bout with adolescence.

"Wassup, Moms?" Kendrick's greeting is a gift. Conversations over the past few days have been brief, as if he has been hiding his life from her. Lena leans against Kendrick's chest and rests her head against the flat ridge of his sternum. His backpack makes a soft thud when he lowers it to the floor. "Smells good in here. Camille," he shouts, pulling away from Lena to sit at the table. "Get your butt down here!"

Any other day, Lena would have fussed over what she considers impolite shouting. Camille's reply is equally loud. Their voices are welcome: a call and response, a kind of jazz breaking the silence that has permeated the house since the separation.

"I emailed my scholarship paperwork. They renewed starting fall semester."

"Yea, Kendrick! I knew you could do it. We should celebrate."

"We're celebrating?" Camille distracts Kendrick from the details Lena wants to hear. Sister slaps brother's back. Kendrick raps Camille's shoulder, and she yelps with fake pain at what she describes as a hard knuckle-hit, not brotherly affection. They are their old selves: kids who know they are loved. Lena crosses her heart, thankful for this one second that makes her world seem like nothing has changed.

The house feels warmer with their banter; it feels like home. They eat and gossip about friends, as if Lena is not within earshot, while she dishes hearty portions of food onto their plates. Tonight, she feels like an observer. She leans against the upholstered bench, picking at the cherry tomatoes in the salad, nibbling on the crunchy corners of the macaroni-and-cheese casserole, hearing without listening until they bring up the subject of their father. Kendrick went with Randall to look at condominiums in San Francisco. He's pushing for the unit with eighteen-foot ceilings, a view of the East Bay, and bedrooms for him and Camille complete with flat-panel televisions.

Because the sound of their laughter is so sweet, because she learned from that last meal with Randall, Lena holds her tongue. She wants to shout from the ceiling that their father is manipulating them, but she waits until Kendrick's and Camille's plates are empty and they seem to have run out of friends and TV reality shows to talk about. "I have something to tell you."

This same phrase was once a signal for good news or good times: anything from going to Lulu's to flying kites near the estuary or taking a trip to a warm place where the whole family could romp in the ocean. Kendrick's smile turns somber. Camille's knees shake underneath the table; a new habit. Their expressions ask the same question: what is our crazy mother up to now? Or worse: can't we pretend that everything is the same for a while longer?

"I love both of you, and I want you to be a part of this different life I'm beginning. I rented an apartment near the lake. It's small, and there aren't any fancy TVs, but there's a bedroom for each of you."

"I knew it. I knew it when I saw the food. This is bullshit." Kendrick's voice cracks like it used to when it first began to deepen.

"Your timing sucks." Camille's dimples disappear, just as tears begin to fall down her cheeks.

"Why is it always about you, Mom? You could've waited until later. We were having a good time."

What does a mother do when she is responsible for her children's tears? When their hearts are broken, when the decision to save herself is as hurtful for them as it is for her? The urge, the need to grab both of her children and shake sense into their heads, is strong. The closest she can get is their hands—one hand on each of theirs, and she holds them in a tight grip so they cannot pull away. "How can you in one breath be so happy for your father's move and criticize me in the next for doing the same thing?"

Now their words fly like arrows all aimed at her so fast and hard that Lena ducks at the imaginary points coming her way.

"You're our mother." Kendrick wrenches his hand from Lena's grasp and rises from the table. "I can't believe you, Mom. You've fucked everything up for all of us."

"You're supposed to take care of us, take care of Dad, take care of our house. What's the matter with you, Mommy? I hate you."

Camille's best friend's mother called days ago. After apologizing for being the one to break the news, the woman told Lena that Camille had posted bitter poetry that blamed Lena for the separation on a teen blog. Posted what the best friend's mother would only say used words no mother would want her child to write in the same sentence with her name: *selfish, hate, dead, fucking bitch.*

"Trust me. Please." Now Lena's legs, too, shake beneath the table. How can a child understand the need for a mother to make it on her own? She pushes her hand against her eyes, knowing that tears will accomplish nothing. "Kendrick, you're settled for the summer, but I want you with me, at least some of the time, before you go back to Chicago. Camille, I'd like you to stay with me."

"You're trying to take away everything Dad has worked for," Kendrick says.

The words, Lena knows, are not his. The hard look on his face, a copy of his father's, clearly indicates he has more to say. Her left eyebrow arcs at his nerve, and he backs off. "I don't know what your father says, but shame on him for it. I don't want the two of you to be involved."

"At least Dad tells us what's going on," Camille says.

Her raised finger stops Camille from adding anything more. "Don't let him brainwash you. Kendrick, you may have a wife someday, and one day, Camille, you may *be* a wife in this very same position. So, check your attitudes about women who choose family over career."

"Well, what about Kimchee? Do I have to decide who I'm going to live with right now?"

"No, sweetie. Yes, Kimchee can come, too." She extends her hand to Camille's cheek, and Camille shoves it away. "I hope one day you'll both understand."

"Summer school starts in three weeks." Kendrick stands and hugs Camille. There are no tears in his eyes, but the strain of his parents' decision is back. "I'm staying with Dad until then."

"I love you. Don't forget that." Lena promises herself that whatever comes next in her life will show them this pain—hers and theirs—has been worth it.

"If you loved us, you wouldn't do this to us," Camille says; tears stream down her face. "Or to Dad."

"I'm sorry. I'm so sorry. . . . If I could make it hurt less, for all of us, I would."

"Then I'm going to stay with Dad, too. You kicked him out of the house. He goes to all of the trouble of looking for a new place, and now you're leaving? It's not fair."

When Lena went online and read Camille's poetry, the words, their meaning, were clear but seemingly not directed at her. Now hearing her children's words and the force of their anger is hard to take, but the sentiments were easier to handle delivered from the protective distance of cyberspace.

Chapter 17

On this fourteenth day since that rainy night, Lena awakens to the music of her neighborhood: children shriek through a game of tag, a lone bird chirps; a sprinkler head sputters, a gardener's blower buzzes. It's been a long time since she's paid attention to these early morning noises, and now her ears perk up because she is listening to them for the last time.

Pulling on jeans and a sweater in the haphazard fashion that is now her style, she wanders toward Kendrick's and Camille's rooms to crack their doors open and check their breathing, as if they were still toddlers, underneath their muddled covers. She stops in the middle of the hallway. Kendrick and Camille are not home. They left last night with barely a smile or a tilted eyebrow or a mischievous wink and headed to wherever Randall lives these days.

Outside, gears grind in the driveway. This truck announces their separation to the neighbors. Lena storms down the stairs and opens the front door. Two burly men with huge moving pads slung across their shoulders ask where she wants to begin. She looks back at them and waits for them to answer their own question.

Their first home was a mishmash of her furniture and Randall's bachelor trimmings. Lena decorated this house on her own. There were days spent in cold, dusty warehouses to find pristine bathroom tiles; she scoured through racks of granite slabs, as long as they were wide, in search of the right one for the kitchen. She hunted through the crowded aisles of the Everyman's Bazaar for antiques and sterling silver whatnots. The veneer plastered walls, the coffee table, the dining room table, and several handcrafted lamps are her designs. The corners filled with unobtrusive objects from their travels. Her mark is on everything.

The movers ask again, quieter this time. Lena points out what she wants: half of the pots and pans, the mixer, the toaster, the couch, the coffee table and the photography books on top of it, the jade lion from Hong Kong, the red Chinese armoire, the Persian rugs, the fine china with cobalt blue bands, silverware, picture albums, all of her clothes. The art she loves and her photographs.

With a final glance in the dresser's mirror, Lena examines the gray strands scattered in her reddish brown hair, the puffs that have replaced the smooth skin under her eyes. She points to the dresser, but not the matching bed where Kendrick and Camille were conceived, where she and Randall swore to be together till death did them part, where they made love, ate popcorn and ice cream, slept in each other's arms. The thought of sleeping in that bed alone, though she has many times over the years, always eager for Randall's return, is enough to make her double over in pain.

No. The bed holds too many memories. The last time she and Randall made love, really made love—not just gotten off because he needed to—must have been months before he left on this last trip. She gasped and held her breath, while he moved in and out, out and in. He called her name, and she called his from the back of her throat in a moan she can hear right now. She cannot bear the thought of him making love to another woman in that same space.

At last, the movers signal to Lena that they are done. She wanders around the house. In the hallway, faded squares outline the rectangles of pictures that once decorated those walls: the concentration on Kendrick's face during his first piano concert, Camille's first recital, Kendrick and Camille at Disneyland, Lena and Randall on their honeymoon in Puerto Vallarta. Short hair, long hair, mustache, no mustache; infants, toddlers, teens. The story of their lives is in those pictures. She beckons to the only trim mover of the crew and points to one of the whole family: a black-and-white photograph, Randall's arm around her shoulder, she leaning into his, Kendrick and Camille seated in front of them. All dressed in jeans and turtleneck sweaters. Christmas 1999. The photographer told them they looked perfect enough to model, perfect enough to be the all-American family, and he'd snapped their picture as they laughed.

Lena is not picture-perfect today. Has not been in a long time. Cannot get back into the groove of designer clothes and perfectly coiffed hair. Through her loose top, the shoulders of her five-eight frame have not slumped, but she feels bent over and aged. Feels like punching herself, even though the fingers of her right hand do not fully bend, shaving her eyebrows, eating herself into obesity. Punishment for what she believes is failure. Her failure.

She works her way through the house past reminders of Randall: *Sports Illustrated, Fortune*, Mentadent toothpaste, Tabasco sauce, Uncle Ben's long-grain rice, mayonnaise, little-eared pasta shells, and red felt-tipped markers. She stuffs odd mementos in her tote: his lucky plaid pants, the ones he wore when he won the 10k Race for Race around Lake Merritt, a can of shaving cream, the blue rubber bulb he uses to clean his ears. She hopes his ears stay dirty and hairy and full of middle-aged earwax.

At the front door, she pauses then locks it and strides past the movers smoking on the lawn awaiting her next order. An unintentional wave—a small fluttering hand movement that in another time would have greeted her children, her husband, welcomed friends and family to her home—lets them know she is ready to leave. She opens the garage door and tosses the opener and all the house keys onto the floor. Pulling out of the garage, she reminds herself to tell the gardener that it is time to trim the magnolia tree. But no, she doesn't have to do that anymore. It is only when she reaches the bottom and looks back at the yellowish house seated above and away from others that her tears begin to roll. It is only when she looks at the van in the driveway that she understands that the house is neither Randall's nor hers—it is just where she used to live.

The sky outside is bright even though Lena's watch shows eight o'clock: almost the end of the longest day of her life. She sits crossed-legged in the middle of the living room floor of the place she will call home for a while. Lighted candles cover the coffee table, the kitchen counter, the wide windowsills. Tina booms through the perfection of the MP3's tiny earphones and sings of universal heartache in a tune written back when Lena was happy. When she would not have felt what Tina sings of those wings and the unhappiness—soundless, surprising, invisible—they bring.

I will never be the same again . . .

The room darkens, a sign that—though she cannot see it from this side of the building—the sun is toppling behind San Francisco. In the hours that Lena has been in her new space she has scrubbed, dusted high corner ceilings, sponged fingerprints from switch plates, disinfected toilets and sinks, bleached the insides of the refrigerator and dishwasher. Signs of whomever lived in the apartment before are gone, and she wonders if she had smiled and fucked Randall every night and more like he thought a good wife should, would she be here now?

Once she believed that when they were empty-nesters, she and Randall would move into a smaller place, maybe an apartment in San Francisco. Once she relished the idea of wearing the sexy nightgowns she rarely wore because of the kids, or making love instead of dinner on the kitchen counters. That was the way life was supposed to be for her and Randall. What else had she worked so hard for? Not this loneliness she can already feel sinking into her bones.

"I have to get out of here."

There are few customers in the video store: a weary-eyed man—an insomniac Lena guesses from the drawn look of his face—two teens with popcorn and sodas, an old couple tittering in front of the adult movie section, and a bedraggled woman in pink terrycloth house slippers and a floor-length trench coat. Lena peers at her own fuzzy-covered feet and wonders if this woman is fighting the blues, too. She follows her down the aisle and pretends to scan the shelves. "I'm getting a divorce, and it's so hard to sleep."

"Me, too. I do nothing but cry. All of the time. And look at me . . ." The woman's voice is edged with controlled hysteria. Her hair and dingy outfit give the impression that no one who cares has looked at her in a long time.

A bleach-stained sweatshirt and Randall's good-luck shorts hang from Lena's hips, slimmer now from the stress of separation. "I came looking for a little inspiration. Have you ever seen this?" She points to *What's Love Got to Do with It* on the last row of the wall-to-wall shelving. "If you can get past the violence, there's a message."

Pink Slippers shivers and stares like Lena is crazy.

"Think about it. She found her inner strength and left a terrible relationship. In her forties. With nothing but her name and her talent."

A light of recognition brightens the woman's reddened, blue eyes. "And then she turned into a superstar, and he was never heard of again."

"Maybe there are other movies like this one." Lena walks up

the aisle, her new friend behind her, to the clerk barely awake behind the counter. The woman appears to be over fifty, if the lines in the corner of her eyes and mouth mean anything. "We're looking for movies to inspire us. We're getting divorced."

"From our *husbands*," Pink Slippers chimes in.

The clerk points to her unadorned ring finger and scribbles titles on a tablet.

"Oh, look! *Waiting to Exhale*." Pink Slippers shouts.

If a café were open they could collect their movies and go there to guzzle gallons of coffee and cry. She would have told Pink Slippers that if she had watched that movie sooner she would have slit Randall's tires or burned his clothes or sold all of his stuff and that he probably would have had her arrested.

"Mostly, I want to watch Tina's movie," Lena says. "That's all I need right now."

Outside, Pink Slippers digs in her pockets and pulls out a cigarette. She opens what appears to be, in the brightness of the white neon sign, an expensive lacquered lighter. "I don't know about you, but this is the most fun I've had in a hell of a long time." She sucks in a long drag and extends the cigarette to Lena, who takes it, coughing as she, too, inhales deeply.

"Thanks." Lena snickers. "I hope it was as good for you as it was for me."

Chapter 18

With a scone and her purse in her right hand, her extra-large latte in her left, and a speckled notebook under her arm, Lena heads for the counter in front of the window. The window bar of the Magical Café is empty save for the freckled man next to Cheryl who sips his coffee from a stainless steel mug. Cheryl is short, and her cowboy-booted feet dangle under the high, granite-topped coffee bar. She measures three teaspoons of sugar into her cappuccino and stirs the creamy brew while Lena gulps from her hot drink without hesitation.

"Let's get to it, Lena." Cheryl's tone is like that of a mother to a child. "I won't let you belabor this decision or turn it into a different kind of discussion."

Lena picks at the crumbs that tumble around her scone in the way that she wishes to pick away at time and slow it down. She rests her face in her hands and sobs inaudibly. The two women sit that way for a moment: silent against the hiss of the espresso, the clatter of coins against the granite counter, the orders for new beverages with and without foam. The freckled man's eyes follow Cheryl's hand into her red handbag. She pulls out her address book and begins.

"First, here are the names of three gallery owners. I've spoken to them, and they're waiting for your call. All of them are looking for help. They may not pay much, but something is better than nothing."

Lena opens her notebook. DIVORCE is written in block letters on the front. She writes down the names and numbers and promises to call as soon as she gets home. Until she understands family law better, and the Internet has helped, she knows there's no harm in having extra money.

"Lawyers. I have at least ten." Over the years, Cheryl has given Lena the names of florists, cleaning ladies, caterers, restaurants, stockbrokers, and window cleaners. When Lena once asked how Cheryl gathered all of this info, she explained that it was a habit she'd picked up from her mother, who was raised in a small town without access to a phone directory and kept the names of people she knew she could count on close at hand. "Elizabeth Silvermann is more your style. She's sharp and a bit egotistical, but she knows what she's doing.

"Now, I want you to memorize these four rules—they'll help you deal with your lawyer and with Randall. They worked for me, and the least I can do is pass them on."

Lena holds her pen tightly in her hand, poised and ready to write.

"Lesson number one: time is money. If your lawyer won't give you her time, then she won't get your money. Lesson number two: even if muscle remembers, the heart must forget. You understand?"

The man boldly looks over Cheryl's shoulder. She gives him a cold MYOB smile. "Do you need a lawyer, too?"

"Oh, no, ma'am. Been there, done that."

Cheryl whispers. "He's fascinated that a black woman knows this stuff. Happens all the time. Lesson number three: the only color that matters is green. Our friend here just proved that. And lesson number four—this one may be hard for you, Lena—let Randall *think* he has the upper hand. Let his ego get him in trouble. Now, questions for the lawyer."

"You're no fun today."

"Work now, lots of fun later. I've got plans!"

Lena turns the page and writes her questions in outline form: what am I entitled to, lawyer fees, options, support—who pays for the apartment once we have separate accounts, the house, art and furniture she still wants but had to leave behind, how long does it take, next steps.

The freckled man chimes in again in that effortless way Californians have of butting into strangers' conversations. "If you haven't acknowledged receipt of your divorce notice you should take money from joint accounts."

"Now that," Lena says, extending her hand to the man, "is good advice."

"Timing," he finishes, beaming at the flattery. "It's all a matter of timing."

Lena let go of her white voice when she gave Elizabeth Silvermann all the details on the phone—she a homemaker, Randall the successful businessman—so that Elizabeth could occupy herself with the facts and not the mystery of how two black people got to be where they are. Still, the lawyer's eyes widen briefly when Lena walks into her office, and Lena can tell by Elizabeth's quick double-take that she is not what the lawyer thought she would be either. On the phone Elizabeth's voice was forceful, and Lena imagined the lawyer would be masculine and broad shouldered. Not that it matters, Lena thinks. The white lawyer is lithe, skinny as a rail with full head of black hair. Her exaggerated stride and firm handshake hint that she will do well by Lena.

Lesson number three: the only color that counts is green.

Elizabeth's confidence oozes across her massive wooden desk as she brags about her successes for fifteen minutes nonstop: how many cases she has won, how many clients she has, the settlements. Her voice is full of ego, self-assurance, and challenge. Slowly it becomes clear to Lena that this is the lawyer's prologue, her curriculum vitae to back up one of the most important pieces of advice Lena has ever received.

"I have no doubt that this is a painful time for you." Elizabeth stops to call to the outer office, where an aide shuffles papers, to hold her calls for twenty more minutes. "Divorce may not be what you want, may not be what you end up with, but you have to decide. This could be the best thing that happened to you, or the worst. Do you want to be a victim or do you want to make this an opportunity for a fresh start? Your chance to rediscover yourself and what you want out of the rest of your life."

This, Lena thinks, is undirected direction. "So what you're saying is that I should take advantage of change?" Elizabeth's concept or Vernon's foresight? "Divorce as a second chance?"

"It's the only way to look at your situation, and I don't represent victims."

Lena nods her agreement.

"Do you have a plan?"

Elizabeth listens carefully while Lena explains the details of Randall's proposal. The lawyer takes his note and chuckles. "He may know his way around a corporation, but he doesn't have a damn idea of how family law works. I hope you didn't say yes."

"I moved into an apartment. Randall says he won't pay for it."

"Moving was probably not the wisest choice, especially if you have to worry about money, but we can fix that." Elizabeth pauses to read the rest of the letter. "Oh, he's in for a surprise. A few surprises, I'd say. What's the rest of your plan?"

"A friend is helping me look for work at a few art galleries. My photography. Other than that, I have no plan."

"Are you waiting for your husband to tell you what to do? You *do* understand that he relinquished that privilege when he served you with divorce papers, don't you?" Elizabeth's chunky tortoiseshell eyeglasses slip down her thin nose. She pushes them back with the heel of her hand—something she will do every five minutes or so this and every time they meet—and washes down bite-sized chocolates with diet soda. "If your husband is as savvy as you say, then you better make sure you retain representation that can help you put a good plan together."

Lena considers Cheryl's rules. She chooses to stop counting the days since Randall's been gone. Yanking her checkbook from her purse, she reminds herself of the most important rule: let Randall think he has the upper hand.

"I may have been some kind of victim before this," Lena slaps a ten thousand dollar retainer check on Elizabeth's desk. "But I'll be damned if that's what I'll be from now on."

Hours after meeting with her new lawyer, Lena sits at her desk ready to follow Elizabeth's suggestion. Her business plan, loose family photos, scissors, and magazines are stacked in front of her. Tina's book lies open, once again: *I was looking,* Tina wrote, *for a truth of a future that I could feel inside of me.*

Lena writes those words in broad letters across the top of a sixteen-inch square board. She picks up the scissors and begins: a camera, a bouquet of white rubrum lilies, the word MOM, a snapshot of Bobbie, Columbia's campus from one of Camille's brochures, Kendrick at five displaying his kindergarten diploma, his high school graduation picture, and a printout of a postcard with a scrub of bushes high on a hill encircled with the words *Tina Lives Here*; a ski lodge in Switzerland, Agra, and the Taj Mahal. She pastes the letters S-T-R-E-N-G-T-H across the bottom. This reminder shapes her plan and, she figures out, as she pastes on the last touch—a picture of Tina performing—that somewhere, somehow Tina Turner will be part of it.

When the first tingle of discontent began to nag at her, perhaps two years ago or more, Lena hired a feng shui consultant—an energy cleaner. The consultant emphasized the importance of keeping a living space positive regardless of negative interactions. In this new space, the only negativity is in whatever she has brought with her. Lena steps into the hallway, flexing her fingers all the while, and practices the motion she forgot to use when her relationship with Camille soured, when Randall began to favor early sleep over conversation, when Kendrick avoided her.

Standing in the middle of the living room, boxes still piled high against the walls, Lena rests her thumbs on the tips of the middle fingers of her left and right hands and considers the gesture she is about to make. The motion symbolizes a casting-off: doubt, fear, insecurity, disrespect—all those forces that threaten her well-being. Lena flicks those fingers, gently at first. Over the boxes, the couch, the few pieces of furniture haphazardly arranged around the room.

Through the entryway, the kitchen and bedrooms. To Kendrick's new room, then Camille's to banish their pain. Are they asking their father why?

Flick. Faster. Through the master bedroom. She can make it on her own.

Flick. Flick. Harder. To her desk and into every nook, every corner where frustration might hide. Lena blows out a long sigh and snaps to attention. Energy shifts. She is ready to fight.

Chapter 19

The waiting room is plain and without a distinct personality. There are no knickknacks, no university diplomas or certificates of merit, no assembly line or mass-produced landscape art. Randall enters the small area, sits on the chair perpendicular to Lena's, and utters a terse "Good morning." He scans a magazine while Lena stares at the words she wrote when Elizabeth spoke them this morning: victims *let* things happen; victors *make* things happen—you are a victor, Lena.

A husky, dimpled man steps from an inner office and introduces himself as Harry C. Meyers. His face, straight and serious, indicates his neutrality. He gestures toward a conference room and the two follow him into it. Reflex courtesy takes over as Randall signals that Lena should enter first. They choose the same sides of the table as the bed they used to sleep in together: Lena to the left, Randall to the right.

Mr. Meyers is a piler. His hands rest on top of the evidence of his obsession before him at the head of the table: two reams of 8 ½ x 11 paper, five 8 ½ x 14 yellow legal pads, two boxes of paper clips, two pads of forms, cell phone atop electronic planner atop calculator, and two containers of breath mints—the kind that rattle when they shake free of their plastic container.

Under the table Lena crosses and uncrosses her legs, wipes the palms of her hands against her black dress, and wonders if it's too early to ask for a bathroom break. Instead, she opens her speckled notebook to the page where her rules are written and reads rule number four—let Randall think he has the upper hand.

Randall sets the leather briefcase Lena gave him when he started at TIDA on the table. The inside of the briefcase is inscribed: *I'm with you through thick and thin. Congrats on the thick. Love, Lena.* The gold latches spring open with one touch of Randall's thumbs. He pauses, looks at Mr. Meyers and then his watch, and pulls out three clipped sets of papers. If asked, Lena would swear there is a Cheshire cat grin on his face. "Since Kendrick and Camille are of age, their support and tuition will not be an issue. We put away enough to cover their education, so this should be a fairly straightforward transaction." Randall pushes papers to the mediator and Lena. "I've outlined what I think is a reasonable and equitable division of property."

"Your papers may be useful later, Mr. Spencer." Mr. Meyers cuts Randall off before he can respond with a hand gesture that says stop and pops a couple of breath mints. Lena watches the mints go from his hand to his mouth. He pops one red, one yellow, one white.

"However, in these sessions *both* parties will determine the division of all community assets to include personal and real property. With the statutory guidelines mandated by the state of California in mind, my job is to assure that the settlement is fair and equitable for both parties and, if necessary, to propose alternatives if it appears the two parties have difficulty reaching agreement."

Lena listens closely to Mr. Meyers, rests her hands in her lap, and wipes them on her dress. She steadies her eyes on the evenness of the gold bands on the ochre law books behind him so that her gaze doesn't move to Randall's. She doesn't want to look at him, doesn't want to acknowledge the anger she sees in the small jerky motions of his right hand.

"You've chosen mediation, I assume, because it avoids the costliness of a court case. In mediation, both parties will come to a mutually acceptable resolution. Neither party may end up with all that he or she has requested. In this room, compromise is the operative word. Typically, the process takes five to six sessions." Mr. Meyers reads from a document atop the pile, in a clear and practiced manner, what they will accomplish in the sessions. He explains the rules and tells them their lawyers may be present but can only advise, not advocate for them.

"In this case, because the wife is not currently employed, temporary spousal support must be set. That is what we will determine today. How much the supporting spouse—in this case you, Mr. Spencer—pays the non-working spouse on a monthly basis is defined by California Family Code and a computer formula. And, by each party's income and expense declaration supplied by both of you prior to today."

Mr. Meyers turns to his laptop and types. He tabulates numbers on an old-fashioned calculator with one hand. The calculator shakes like a miniature locomotive; paper billows from the top like steam. When he is done, the mediator writes a five-figure number on two separate yellow pads and passes them to Lena and Randall at the same time.

Just as Lena has a new mantra, so, she thinks, does Randall.

"Shit," he whispers under his breath.

Lena hears him loud and clear. He snatches a red pen from the mediator's pile and strikes a bold line through the figure that will be the above-the-line, tax-deductible amount of spousal support the state of California requires he pay.

"This is a non-negotiable number," Mr. Meyers insists.

"I see no reason why I have to pay for her apartment. I told her to stay in the house. This was her choice."

"By law, Mr. Spencer, regardless of where Mrs. Spencer has chosen to live, this," the mediator says, rewriting the number on Randall's pad, "is what you're required to pay until you and Mrs. Spencer reach your final agreement."

"Then we better get done quickly, because I'll be damned if I'm going to pay for her life of leisure."

For the rest of dinner the night those years ago that Randall gave her the diamond, Lena was in a fog. Between the wine, the food, and his surprise, he'd caught her off guard. At home, in bed, she climbed on top of him, a bottle of almond oil in her hand.

"I'll do everything I can to support you. I believe in your dream."

"It's not just *my* dream." Randall sucked in a deep breath and tried to hold on to his train of thought while Lena's fingers massaged his legs and thighs. "It's *our* future."

She rubbed him, stroked him, tasted him until he moaned. "But," she said, letting her hair drop over her face and onto his shoulders, "I don't want to lose *my* dream." Before he lost his concentration, she quieted and let him release, let the feel of him run from her thighs to her breasts, let it sing in her head.

Afterward, she cuddled into him. "I don't want to be a stereotype. The man makes the money, while the little woman takes care of the house and the kids." They had had this discussion before: black people changing stereotypes, breaking the barriers, creating a new norm. "So, I'll accept the diamond; *if* you agree that I'll get back to my plan after one year."

He admitted with all of the changes he wanted to implement at TIDA, it would take at least eighteen months to two years to gain full acceptance. "Two. For me."

Lena thought of partnership and sacrifice, the two words John Henry had stressed before he walked her down the aisle. The biggest question in her mind as Randall ran his fingers over her body, the diamond above her breasts, was what would stop Randall, once the two years were over, from another promotion, another big deal, another giant career step to becoming the black king of the world.

What would his sacrifice be in this partnership? She pressed two fingers to his mouth.

"Deal."

His smile was easy to hear in the dark. He took her fingers into his mouth and sucked. Lena pointed to her diamond with her free hand. "Then, we'll renegotiate."

The allure of Randall's promise was seductive. Lena substituted being the successful woman for being the supportive woman behind the successful man. By the end of Randall's second year at TIDA he'd been given more responsibility, and she slipped deeper into her cashmere cocoon.

Randall whips out his PDA and punches the screen with the metal stylus. "Let's schedule all of the sessions now." Every one will be the same: a single step forward, two or three back.

"You are not in charge here." Lena snaps. "And don't use that tone with me." In this instant, she leers at Randall and assumes his expression mirrors hers. They are, after all, an old married couple. No stranger, not even Mr. Meyers, knowing full well their circumstances, would ever have guessed these two people had once been giddy lovers or shared a bed or parented two children or lived together for twenty-three years.

"Mr. and Mrs. Spencer! Please leave the hostility outside." In every meeting from this first one to their ninth, Lena and Randall will pout and argue unconcerned about the mediator's cautions and his piling, un-piling and re-piling of the items around him, until their lawyers attend the sessions and assist in settling who gets what and the amount of permanent spousal support that Randall will pay Lena until she remarries, cohabitates, or dies.

Mr. Meyers presses a finger to a lone droplet on his left temple. He glances at his watch and suggests they stop here. Lena sympathizes with the man; her own armpits are damp. She stares at Randall and wonders if, underneath what looks like a cool, poker face, he is straining to hold back his own sweat. She wonders if he has another compartment, called cool, that helps him maintain this demeanor. Probably. Someday, if they can ever sit together calmly again, she will ask him about that ability and perhaps he will teach her how to do the same.

"We will begin the division of assets in our next session," the mediator says.

There is a clue, Lena thinks, an intimation in his tone that suggests that Mr. Meyers is no more looking forward to it than she is.

Angela Bassett spins and lip-synchs on TV. Pink Slippers is right: the violence is hard to take. Lena concentrates on Angela Bassett's biceps, her forceful performance—her angst, the slow trust in self, a Buddhist chant: *nam myo ho renge kyo.* Bottom line, the movie is depressing. Every time Larry Fishburne fake-pops Angela, Lena cringes. But thankfully, with one click of the remote she can skip those scenes and focus on the message, not the violence.

Tina's message is about getting away. Anywhere. Far. Fast.

Lena picks up the autobiography, leaves where it opens to fate: *. . . that trip changed my whole life. I felt like I had come home—like I had never known my real home . . . I loved France—loved the ambience of it . . . on that first trip to France, that's when I began to feel, deep down inside, that maybe I was French, too.*

France!

Lena skips to the computer. Connects to the official Tina Turner website. Tina lives in the south of France. It was one of those places that Randall and Lena planned to visit when they talked about the world and seeing as much of it as they could. They promised to lie nude on the beach, to learn French, to extend their trip westward and sip Bordeaux in Bordeaux.

A performance schedule for this year and the next is imposed over pictures of Tina and international celebrities. Lena selects "concerts" from the top left margin. One, two, three clicks. Lena scrolls through dates and places and stops on the final entry: October 8th. Nice, France.

Moving to the computer once again, she selects a travel website and dials Bobbie.

"I have to meet Tina!" Lena shouts, happy that her sister can pick up a conversation in the middle of her slumber. One day she will thank Bobbie with more than words for talking to her, listening to her any time of the day or night.

"Go for it."

"Tina loves France. She lives in the south of France. We . . ." Lena swallows hard. "I mean *I* always wanted to go to the south of France."

"As long as you're going for the right reasons. Seeking, not running away."

"I want to meet Tina. I want her to sign my book." Yes, that's what she wants. She thumbs the pages of Tina's story like a deck of cards. "And I'm going to take pictures, hundreds of pictures."

"Then what are you waiting for?"

"Randall demanded, and the mediator acceded, that I find work. Which I'll do, with Cheryl's help. But, he has approval over any large expenditures I make until the final division of property." Lena accepted the condition with an exception to the furniture she needs for her apartment. ". . . And what about Lulu?"

"Why does he get to call the shots?"

Lesson number four: let Randall *think* he has the upper hand.

Bobbie puffs on her cigarette. "As for Lulu . . ."

Lena holds her breath and waits for Bobbie to say she'll take care of Lulu, to say she'll come home and change light bulbs, lift the heavy packages from Lulu's car to the house, balance her checkbook, drag the trash to the curb, say she'll listen to Lulu's endless parables.

"You've got to live your life . . . that's what I'm doing. Lulu and

I are fine on the phone," Bobbie says. "In person, that's a different story. She can't cope with my life . . . and I'm not going to keep trying to explain it away. Anyway this is about you, not Lulu."

Lena gets out of the bed and heads for the window. An airplane, well on its route to a faraway destination, blinks the only illumination in the dark sky. She presses her ear to the glass, straining to hear the engine's distant rumble. "I listened to Tina all evening long. I forgot how much I used to like her."

"It's like you're obsessed with an assignment: write an essay on why you like Tina Turner," Bobbie says.

"We have intersecting emotional points. Her birthday is November twenty-sixth, too."

"Is this why you woke me up?"

Lena knows that it doesn't matter what time it is or what day, her sister will always stop, listen, and love.

"When you were eleven you thought you had something in common with aliens. You spent hours at the library researching life on Venus." Bobbie chuckles.

"This is not the same. She got past her fear, and this is what I know: there's a little Tina Turner in all of us. Call it pep, audacity, or a look that camouflages the pain. We do what we have to do—be on stage or be who everyone else wants us to be—and finally come to the conclusion that nothing will work, unless we're true to self." Lena stops, breathes in and out slowly. "I'm just searching for the Tina in me."

"Well, don't wear your hair like Tina's." Bobbie's wit is sharp even at this hour. "I don't think blond is your color."

Chapter 20

The months since Lena walked out of that corporate apartment, the door refusing to close behind her, have flown much like summer does for a school-bound youngster—with speed and the inability to distinguish one day from the next. Mediation sessions. Body-numbing depression. Drizzling spring rain. Camille's graduation celebration; Lena entering through the front door feeling like a stranger in the house she made a home; mother and children like strangers until she gathered them both in her arms. Juicy peaches have given way to bushels of tart green apples at the farmers' market, where now she looks, but doesn't buy. Foggy mornings, the threat of drought. September breezes blow warm across Oakland and the Bay Area even as New England leaves redden and the Midwest prepares for winter's blanket of snow. Awake at six, Lena sports a light jacket this cool morning ready, like everyone else in the Bay Area, for Indian summer—another round of flip-flops, shorts, and weekends of sunshine.

This morning's exercise around the 3.5-mile perimeter of Lake Merritt is her march of tears: because Kendrick is back in Chicago and rarely responds to her emails or phone calls, because Camille lives with Randall and chooses to have him drop her off at Columbia—a decision made a day after her eighteenth birthday one month ago. When Camille visited two days after graduation—and what turned out to be a civil and joyous celebration—she slumped onto the couch and absentmindedly jangled the extra set of keys Lena gave her. "All my stuff is at home."

Lena sat, holding herself, and her tongue, in hopes that Camille would recognize her disappointment by her body language. Then Camille came up with what Lena supposed was a peace offering.

"Come to New York for Thanksgiving."

"Well, Camille," Lena said, not bothering to argue with her daughter's decision or fight back the tears at her offhanded dismissal. "That's not quite the holiday I envisioned, but Bobbie will be excited, and maybe I can get Lulu to come, too." Only four at the dinner table for Thanksgiving, not the twenty or so—cousins, Lulu, Randall's father, friends without local family—she always included. No days and days of planning, shopping, cooking. No thrill of turning disconnected items into mouthwatering dishes everyone stuffs themselves with. That thought hurt then. It hurts now past her heart, and if asked her, she could not describe the pain.

After today she will no longer cry.

Mr. Meyers prefaced each of their sessions with a rolling summary: credit card debt divided 70 percent him, 30 percent her; equal division of savings and stocks; Randall kept his beloved Raiders sky box; Lena the Berkeley Repertory Theater seats; fifty-fifty split of the SF Jazz season tickets.

At the end of the ninth, and final, session and with the help of their lawyers, they reached final agreement. Randall insisted—if Lena wanted Camille and Kendrick to stay with her—that she had to keep the house.

"Or else what?"

Elizabeth warned that Randall would more than likely use the house as a bargaining tool. Lena stopped his momentum with a deliberate bathroom break and collected herself in the cold lavatory. She stood in one of the three stalls and blew her nose, wiped her tears on the coarse toilet paper, then returned to the conference room twenty minutes later as if nothing more than her biological urge had been taken care of. Randall picked up the conversation as if she never left the room.

"I've worked hard for what I have," he said.

"So now it's all yours, huh?" Lena leaned against her leather-backed chair, looked straight into Randall's tight, brown eyes, and reminded him: "I worked hard, too. For *us*. You. Keep. The house." She gathered her papers and stuffed them into her portfolio. Her hands trembled. The papers shook, and she didn't hide them. She slipped her purse onto her shoulder, left it to the lawyers to balance the house's appreciation with Randall's retirement fund, bonuses, the TIDA stock options, and walked out of the office, into the elevator, and held her tears until she got to her car.

Her tears flow freely now and wash away all emotion, so that by the time she faces Randall later this morning to sign their finalized agreement, she will not cry at all. His face has been so stern, the crease in his forehead so deep through each of the mediation sessions and the nasty correspondence in between. She cannot help but question his motives when his behavior is so aloof. Which compartment has she been relegated to? Where did he put that man who could never remember the punch line to a joke but made up his own, who held her when John Henry died and worried about how Lulu would get along, who cradled each of their children on the day of their birth and marveled at the miracle of their perfect fingers and toes, who rode with her in that fancy new car as excited as she was?

Back in her apartment, Lena steps into the living room and beams. It has taken three months to make this apartment feel like home. Furniture and flowers, walls covered with her photographs—rusty wrought iron fences entwined with weeds, aged doors from the decaying West Oakland train station, junkyard capitals atop Corinthian columns, abandoned cars, and a homeless man preaching to a garbage can. She cannot deny that the absence of playful shouting, the smell of food in the oven, hugs, and no one to say good morning or good night makes her feel sad.

The phone rings as Lena strips off her sweaty clothes.

"That Randall. I'm so disappointed." Through the phone Lulu's noisy slurping reassures Lena that the world is normal.

Lena snickers. If only Lulu knew. If only Lena had a dollar for each time Randall has scratched a red marker across Mr. Meyers's drafts or told Lena she couldn't, couldn't, couldn't do one thing or another with *his* money, *his* kids, *his* house, *his* season tickets, *his* schedule, *his* job, *his* friends, *his* life.

"Want me to come with you?"

The thought of Lulu at her side—outfitted in fuchsia or sunflower yellow, complete with coordinating fingernails and toenails—in the mediator's office with Randall and their very proper lawyers is enough to make her chuckle.

"I love you, Lulu." Outside the window and fourteen floors below, a single rowboat, its crewmembers tiny dots, skids across the lake's glassy surface. Sections of the path she walked this morning, will walk again for many days to come, are easy to see. "After all these weeks, I believe I can handle it on my own."

"I love you, Lena. You get your strength from my side of the family, you know." From the shallow sound of her sips, Lena can tell that Lulu's coffee cup is almost empty. "Dress sexy, and do whatever it takes to soften him up."

"Sexy," Lena says, "won't do me any good anymore with *this* man. I'm invisible to him; a parasitic harpy he believes wants to bleed him dry." She settles on the bed and laughs until more tears come into her eyes. Flick.

"That's my baby girl!" Lulu laughs, too. "Always the drama queen."

In the shower, the hard, hot water blends with the last of Lena's tears, sprays over her cheeks, back, and thighs. If, all those years ago, Randall could go back to his first ex, the gold digger, could he come back to her, and would she want him if he did? Could the lilt of her laugh make Randall regret this decision, make him change his mind? Months of sitting across from him at the mediator's table have changed hers. He no longer looks familiar. Lena is amazed at how callous Randall has been. Is he surprised by how tough and prepared she has been?

Lena takes her time to dress in a conservative, body-hugging, taupe pantsuit (that's just a bit sexy) and admires herself in the mirror above the sink. The whites of her light brown eyes are clear, the stress acne is gone, the hair is growing back in the tiny worry-patch above her right temple.

The glass top of the small bottle of jasmine essence on the bathroom counter is shaped like a flower. Randall never told her how much it cost, preferring to keep her supplied himself, but the cut crystal bottle and the gold filigree hint at its price. This bottle is nearly full of the delicate perfume. She rubs jasmine on her neck and wrists and behind her knees, then turns the bottle upside down and lets the rest run into the sink and down the drain. In this new place there is no room for old memories.

She stuffs *I, Tina* into her purse like she has before every other session. Out the door, down the elevator, and into the car. Ready. Set. Go.

Mr. Meyers pats the papers stacked before him and explains that both parties will sign this master document, copies to be distributed once it is filed with the court and finalized at the beginning of next year. The document is a half inch thick. For all the time, arguments, and concessions, the fluorescent light makes the black marks on the crisp white paper appear insignificant.

Across the table, Randall's broad face avoids hers. He is Kendrick Randall Spencer now. Businessman. Formal and distant. Some other woman will soon be the beneficiary of his attention. The grin she loved, loves, hides behind his tight lips, nevermore to expose itself to her. Randall's smile has been removed from community property, not included in the division of their assets.

"And so it is done," Lena says, her tone so formal it surprises her, and she glances around as if someone else speaks with her singsong voice. She wants to tell a joke, maybe a parable like Lulu would if she were here: A man and woman find each other again after many years apart, many loves in between. They get married and live in a lovely house with a picket fence and tulips that bloom in the spring. Their son is handsome, their daughter beautiful; both kids are smart. They are blessed. One day, they lose themselves in the fantasy of it all and let it go without really understanding why, without taking the time to make it work when the going got rough.

Punch line: life is too short. Ha. Ha.

"Page two sign and initial here." Mr. Meyers is gruff with them today, tired, Lena supposes, of their bickering. "This paragraph outlines the purpose of the agreement and commences the specifics of the division of property."

L. Harrison Spencer

K. Randall Spencer

"What God has joined together, let no man tear asunder," the diminutive, white minister said on their wedding day in that beautiful cathedral where candles twinkled and the scent of so many lilies made Lena sneeze just as she said, "I do."

Page 15 covers spousal support and stipulates the amount Randall will pay to Lena until her death, remarriage, or legal domestic partnership. Today, the thought of another man in her life makes Lena laugh out loud. None of these things matters as her Mont Blanc pen holds steadfast to its path across the papers. Randall slides each page to her side of the table after he signs them.

L. Harrison Spencer

K. Randall Spencer

Funny, Lena thinks, what she will remember about this moment. The thin red stripes on Randall's black suit and matching tiny dots on his tie, how it skews ever so slightly to the right, the absence of his wedding ring. The feel of him pulsing inside her, her body close to his, the smell of their mingled sweat. Her pressing urge—psychological, not physical—to pee. The mediator's rubber-tipped finger flipping through fifty-two pages. Fifty-two sets of initials. Six signatures. Rows of legal code shelved around the room: dull brown books, gold horizontal stripes—California Family Law, Division of Property. Stipulation, petitioner, and irreconcilable differences. Dissolution of God's law. The piles. The piles. The piles.

Ain't nothing guaranteed but death, John Henry used to say. Divorce is a death. She wants a funeral, a farewell to what was. Where is the champagne to toast this freedom?

"By placing your final signatures here, you both agree to the terms and conditions of this Marital Support Agreement. This is a legally binding document and any diversion from it, without the written consent of both parties, is considered breach." Mr. Meyers glances from Lena to Randall to Lena, then passes the last page to both of them.

Lena looks across the table to Randall's smile-less face and considers extending her hand to touch him one last time. Their eyes lock in one swift, never-to-be-forgotten millisecond, and Lena will never know if it was reality or imagination that his hand almost extends, too. That love is flat. Gone like a helium balloon slipped from a child's hand floating up to the atmosphere, to heaven, to God. *Pop.*

Before they married, Lena practiced signing versions of her new name, like most brides-to-be: Lena Harrison Spencer. Lena Spencer. L. H. Spencer. She decided on L. Harrison Spencer. Now, she uses that signature for the last time.

L. Harrison Spencer

K. Randall Spencer

"And so it is done," she says, knowing full well she is speaking.

“I know you’re in bed,” Bobbie says when Lena answers the phone. “You okay?”

“No.” Lena yawns into the phone. Outside, the afternoon sun beams through the window and creates a crisp parallelogram of light on the rug. “It’s been three days—I’ve broken the blue-funk rule, and I don’t care.”

The sisters created the blue-funk rule for themselves years ago to handle heartbreak or disappointment: one, and one day only, to cry, hibernate, stuff themselves with their favorite food—chocolate ice cream with nuts. An empty cardboard pint once full of chocolate ice cream with nuts and chunks of white and dark chocolate sits beside Tina’s autobiography on the long table doubling as a nightstand.

“I have good days and bad ones, Bobbie. This is a bad day. A very bad day. The worst.” Time to get back to the rule, and her time is overextended. “But, it’s my last one. I start work at the Oakland Museum in two weeks, and I signed up for another photography class in the winter quarter.”

“The hardest part is over. I’m glad you’re moving on. Compared to some people, you don’t have anything to worry about.”

More than once during the mediation process Lena has thought about other divorced women less fortunate than her with children to feed, no money, and a real fear of what comes next. She makes a double sign of the cross over her heart, thanks God for her blessings, and promises to donate a little extra to a shelter.

“Leave me alone.”

“You don’t need to be alone. You need to get your ass out of the bed. Look at it this way. At least when the final divorce papers are filed you won’t have to see him.”

Bobbie talks tough. Lena is unsure if Bobbie could take her own medicine if the tables were turned, having kept most details of her love life confidential throughout the years. They were not born into a family prone to share their business with outsiders. Who, she wonders, not for the first time, does her sister talk to when her emotional life gets jumbled and messy? This will be the way she pays Bobbie back: she will pick up the little hints Bobbie infrequently drops and be a better listener.

"I'm hanging up."

"Time to get back to you. What about Tina Turner? Have you finalized your plans? Have you *made* plans?" Bobbie's pen or fingernail taps against the phone, and Lena wonders when a little sister stops feeling like a little sister and begins to feel simply like a sister. She straightens, taps her fingernail against the phone, and tells her sister that she'll get around to finalizing the arrangements when she gets around to finalizing the arrangements. There is still time to buy a ticket.

"Get up right now."

Lena picks up the empty ice cream carton and licks the sides for what is left of the melted treat. "Let me have this last moment to sulk, please."

"Just do it. For me."

"That's what Randall used to say."

On the stereo Tina croons music meant for scrunching and slow dancing, for making love. A new loneliness tugs at Lena's insides in a way that makes her draw her body into a fetal pose atop her bed.

Two weeks ago a forwarded invitation showed up in the mailbox alongside invitations to open new credit card accounts. It was the first time she'd been out after sitting in the new apartment for six weeks. Two weeks ago, the effort to pull herself together had been great, but she did, and she looked good in a sleeveless blue dress she hadn't been able to wear in over a year. Lena left that party within twenty minutes of her arrival after a gentle-eyed, very short man caught her off guard with his oddball question: what kind of fool was the man who could leave someone as good-looking as you?

If Lulu is right—about Lena never following anyone's advice, maybe, she thinks after Bobbie's suggestion, she should start. Now. Cheryl would be delighted to get her out of the apartment, but Lena is not ready to take the plunge into her friend's frenzied social life. Too bad she didn't get Pink Slippers' phone number. Flipping through her address book, Lena finds the pickings slim in the names of women she once called friend. She understands the protocol: she is off-limits now, the almost-divorced woman Candace, if she holds true to her word, will spurn. Lena imagines Randall's social calendar is full: her old friends have probably paired him up already. Good catch. So is she.

Without brooding over her decision, Lena gathers her hair into a ponytail, dusts blush on the apples of her cheeks, layers mascara on her eyelashes. Jeans, heels, white blouse, orange leather jacket. Enough.

Vertigo, a neighborhood restaurant and bar, is within walking distance of her apartment and comfortable. In the old days, whenever Randall and Lena walked into a restaurant, she pitied the men and women seated alone at the bar and assumed they were single and sad. If someone cared enough to look closely, they would see that she is; but she doesn't want anyone's pity. Once the hostess establishes that she is alone, she points instead of escorts Lena in the direction of the bar. Couples dine at cozy marble-topped tables; singles eat at the bar, the hostess's taut finger seems to say.

When the muscular bartender glances her way, she asks twice for a seven and seven on the rocks with extra lime before the young man acknowledges her. The lime slips from the rim's edge and into the honey-colored drink when he sets the cocktail down. Never one to sit at a bar, nurse a drink or two, and chat with a stranger, Lena's mind is a blank as she searches for small talk. "Thanks," slips from her lips as the bartender turns away. She examines the menu more to busy her mind than select a late-night snack.

On her right, several young women watch the door in anticipation of a friend or perhaps their dates. They remind her of her single days, the first time around, and the occasional bar-hopping in packs; even on the infrequent business trip she avoided solo eating and drinking. On her left, a man, tie loosened from his unbuttoned collar, preoccupies himself with the newspaper while shoving large forkfuls of linguini into his mouth.

A cool breeze blows down the bar when the restaurant's huge glass door automatically opens for an amorous couple. The man's wide hand rubs the woman's—the much younger woman's—firm hips, and she does not seem flustered by the contact. When she glances at their faces, Lena blanches at the sight of Candace's husband and the bimbette from her dinner party. Snatching a section of newspaper from the man one seat over, Lena hunkers behind the pages. That same fear and anxiety that took over her when she ran into Candace at the bookstore now runs through her body again. What if they saw her? Poor Lena: no husband, no family; she's all alone. Alternating her attention between the paper and the door, Lena forgets that Byron is the one who should hide.

From behind the paper, the bimbette's infantile voice is exactly as annoying as Lena remembers from the night of the party. The night she remembers, too, that Candace confirmed her friendship. Lena drops the newspaper as Byron and the bimbette pass in front of her and the polished wood bar. "Heyyy, Byron." She exaggerates her greeting, makes it sweet and syrupy like she would for a long-lost friend, and stares right into Byron's eyes. If Lena ever tells anyone about the scene before her, she will describe it as a moment from a slapstick movie: the bimbette's face lights up with recognition and dims just as quickly; Byron's head swivels from left to right searching the bar for the possibility that his wife is there with Lena.

"Be sure to tell Candace I say hello."

"I'll do that," he says, stepping an arm's length from the bimbette. "Good to see you, Lena." Lena is positive that even if Byron were fifteen, maybe ten pounds lighter, he could not move out of the restaurant any faster. As for Candace, all of those women who think that she might be a threat to them, ha. It's the bimbettes of the world, she thinks, they better watch out for.

"That just made my night." She turns to the man from whom she grabbed the paper and pushes it back down the bar. He shrugs as if he has seen it all. Lena drops a ten-dollar bill on the counter. The bar has become more crowded with couples. The man with the newspaper is still more interested in reading than conversation. Perhaps some other time, she thinks. Then she will find new friends or a prospective lover or even a stranger with whom she will talk and drink and joke.

By the time she gets back to her building, the night guard is making his hourly rounds and the front desk is empty. Lena heads for the wall of silver rectangular mailboxes. She likes to pick up her mail late at night. No one sees her. No one cares.

The mailbox door creaks. Lena pulls out a wad of mail and weekly grocery store advertisements for foods she no longer eats or cares about. It must be four days since she last checked the mailbox. The small box is so full that she is surprised the postman hasn't complained. Standing in front of the marble-topped counter where the trash can is tactfully concealed behind a maple veneer door, Lena separates catalogs, credit card solicitations, and postcards sent by real estate agents looking for new clients. There are eighteen catalogs. Eighteen businesses that want her to buy furniture, linens, stationery, luggage, and cosmetics. She tears off the back page of each catalog, flips to the middle, and tears out the order page where her name and address are printed: Lena I. Harrison. Identity theft. Who cares?

A red envelope protrudes between bills and solicitations. Lena recognizes Bobbie's bold handwriting. She always uses a medium-blue felt pen. Royal blue. Inside the envelope, a black-and-white photograph is glued to the front of a note card: Lena and Bobbie, in matching dresses and ruffle-edged pinafores, sit atop the shiny hood of their uncle's pickup truck. Each of the sisters holds an ice cream cone in a gloved hand. Lena remembers the day the photograph was taken: Easter Sunday, 1956. Lena was almost seven and Bobbie ten. They'd begged to eat Auntie Big Talker's homemade ice cream before, not after, they changed their yellow and blue Sunday clothes, and for once, Lulu let them. Their grins are wide and toothy.

Lena recognizes the quote from one of Tina's songs written across the bottom of the photo in Bobbie's bold slanted hand: *There's something special about you*. Inside is a first-class airline ticket from San Francisco to Nice, France, imprinted with Lena's name.

"Tina said it, and I know it. Use this," Bobbie's bold handwriting commands. "Now!"

Chapter 21

Each stark white wall of this square room is covered with paintings from the baseboard along the cement floor to the top of the eighteen-foot ceiling. Red, bright turquoise, cerise, and purple. Bold strokes of gouache form thick paint waves. Black-and-white photographs—thick lips, kinky and straight hair, kneecaps, noses, crusty heels—are spread like collages between the canvases. Some of the paintings are words outlined underneath layers of color. None of the paintings clash; instead of creating a frenetic, jarring sensation, they are ordered in a way that imparts control.

"See, getting out is a good thing." Though Marcia is Cheryl's client and not a close friend, she hugs Lena warmly. "Make yourself comfortable, walk around, meet somebody, and take them home." Her invitation is throaty and sexy.

Randall and Lena first met Marcia on the wooden bench in front of a Diane Arbus photograph, "A Young Negro Boy," at the San Francisco Museum of Modern Art. Marcia squeezed onto the bench, uninvited, and talked about the photographer's work, her hands gesturing rapidly the whole time, without any signal from Randall or Lena.

"Diane Arbus once said or wrote that she believes that there were things nobody would see unless she photographed them." Marcia offered her interpretations of the artist's intentions—"She wanted to capture life and give meaning to everyday existence" —that continued over dinner at the restaurant next door.

When Marcia discovered that Lena was a long-time friend of Cheryl's, she insisted on paying the check. With Cheryl's help they bought two pieces of Marcia's art the following week. Marcia encouraged Lena to take a photography class with her on the one occasion they'd gone for coffee. The class, Marcia emphasized with her hands more than her words, was a way to stretch to the next level and, if Lena was really interested in taking pictures, the class would help to make her photography art.

"Your work is lovely, Marcia," Lena says.

If there had been a paintbrush in Marcia's hands for her dismissal of Lena's flattery, it would have feathered large circles around the room and touched every painting. "This is my home *and* my gallery."

"Thanks for remembering me," Lena calls to Marcia's back. There haven't been any invitations in Lena's mailbox for a long time, despite the change of address notices she sent to all of their friends. No dinners or movies, weddings, or parties. Marcia forgot —or Cheryl forgot to tell her—that Lena and Randall were no longer a couple: her metallic envelope was addressed to the two of them. The familiar unfamiliar sight of their two names together set off a sudden burst of tears. Lena promptly accepted Marcia's invitation, not so much out of fear that it might be retracted but with the knowledge that if she let it sit she would change her mind and Marcia might not think of her the next time around.

Lena breathes in the scent of cumin and curry and maybe nutmeg or mace. The house smells like home. Old home. She wanders around the condo. An artist, whose angular, steel sculptures she loves but can no longer afford, waves from across the room. A singer from a local jazz club Lena keeps intending to visit introduces herself and hands her a postcard with the date of her next show.

The living room and the smaller one across the entryway are full of men and women dressed in every type of clothes from holey designer jeans to African garb. Conversation and hilarity clash with the pianist who alternates between jazz and classical music on an upright piano in the corner. Where Marcia succeeded with the artwork, Lena thinks, she left a lot to make up for with the acoustics.

A thirty-something man dressed in paint-splattered coveralls approaches Lena. "You look thirsty." He offers her a flute of champagne from a red enameled tray.

"Flirtation or kindness?"

"Duty. Just a starving artist doing nowhere near as well as my friend. Marcia asked me to help out. And as for flirtation . . ." He leans into Lena just enough so that she can smell the peach scent of his twisted hair. "I'm Imara, bartender-artist, and I'm game if you are."

Funny, she thinks taking a glass, how women, famous and ordinary, talk about the confidence they've gained by the time they reach fifty. Lena feels none of that. She swallows the bubbly liquid in two gulps to calm the tightness nagging at her stomach and takes another. Being single makes her feel like a fifty-four-year-old virgin; her confidence is nonexistent. "Thank you, Imara-bartender-artist."

Imara is close enough so that Lena can see the tiny moles across his sandy-colored nose. She steps back and away from him. She is not afraid of men; she has simply forgotten what to do. At thirty, before walking into a party, bar, or an afternoon gathering, Lena sought security in the easy hand-to-mouth action of smoking. Even then she found small talk useless; men seem to want conversations in shades of gray. She speaks black and white.

"Well, look who got out of the house!" Cheryl's voice booms from behind the server.

Imara-bartender-artist slips his card into her hand. "Call me."

"Your taste in men is as good as ever, Lena. Barely separated and flirting with that delectable young thing?" Cheryl's clothes coordinate with Marcia's paintings. Her form-fitting lavender pantsuit might have been simple on anyone else. The long jacket is slit on both sides from the waist down, and the fuchsia and turquoise pashmina across her shoulder matches her earrings and bold jade and silver jewelry. She is at once sophisticated and ostentatious.

"The end of January." Lena resists her new habit of rubbing her third finger left hand and instead motions to Imara. "The settlement papers are signed, but the divorce won't be final for four and a half months. Hell of a way to start off the new year. It's one of the hottest pieces of gossip since that newscaster's wife caught him with his assistant on the floor of his office."

"I'm sorry, Lena. I know it's been tough."

"It's been a bitch, if I do say so myself." Lena avoids Cheryl's eyes.

Imara-bartender-artist hovers around the two women until Cheryl takes another glass of champagne from the tray and points a finger of her free hand at Lena. Together they head for the table that Marcia has covered with food. Cheryl loads her plate with curried shrimp, chicken, and rice pilaf. Lena puts a teaspoon of each of the same dishes on her plate along with a dab of mango chutney.

"Eat, ladies." Marcia unloads another platter of food on the table. "And when you're done, Cheryl, take Lena to look at that painting over the fireplace."

"Art, my dear, gifted client, is not on my mind." Cheryl looks around the room. Her eyes pause at every man who is not attached to a woman. "There aren't many men here, and tonight this girl is on the prowl. Except for the champagne-serving cutie, and I assume Lena's got dibs?"

Falling into their old she-said, she-said rhythm, Lena lets Cheryl know that it's too soon for her to think about men. "But even I have to admit the pickings seem slim."

"Girl, you better forget that Negro and have some fun! Randall was always too stuffy. You need to be like Tina Turner and move on."

"She didn't run out and get a man—she got her life and career together." Lena pauses to see if Cheryl's face shows more than a momentary interest in Tina Turner.

A tall, lean man steps up to the table. Cheryl beams and points to the shrimp. She puckers and tells him to watch his lips because the curry is spicy. When his wife, sister, or girlfriend steps beside him, Cheryl turns back to Lena. "Well, Tina has both now."

Lena tugs Cheryl past the couple and tells her in one long breath how Tina has inspired her. How she makes sure that each purse she carries, like the one hanging from her shoulder now, is wide and deep enough to hold her wallet, cosmetic bag, keys, and Tina's autobiography.

"Why didn't you tell me? I love Tina Turner!"

"Her last concert of the year is next month in Nice." Lena tells Cheryl about Tina's villa in the hillside city next to Nice. "Bobbie sent me a first-class ticket." Her voice is so low that Cheryl asks her to repeat what she said. Lena does and adds, "But I haven't finalized anything," understanding that the concept of postponement is completely foreign to Cheryl.

"Lena, Lena, Lena." Cheryl slaps Lena on the back so hard that she jumps. Neither one of them is fragile, but Cheryl is obviously the stronger of the two. "Don't tell me you've reverted to your timid thirty-year-old persona, have you?"

"I'm not used to taking trips alone. And, anyway"—Lena

downs the rest of her third glass of champagne—"my contract with the museum won't let me."

"Remember? It's *who* you know that gets you what you want." Cheryl winks in that way that means an idea is brewing behind her long eyelashes and clinks her glass against Lena's. Her face brightens as her lips form four words that lift a weight from Lena's shoulders. "Let's go to France!"

Chapter 22

Oleander—laurier-rose, the French call it—is a slender-leafed, bushy plant that bears cherry red or white flowers. In Northern California the deceptively beautiful plant lines freeway meridians and roadside pit stops from Oakland to Sacramento. In the south of France it is everywhere: near the beach, on the streets, in the park in the middle of Nice's downtown. The leaf of the oleander is poisonous and as dangerous as it is beautiful, and Lena wonders if this plant is another omen reminding her to be careful, to look closer before she judges.

The differences between Nice and Oakland, perhaps California, are mostly visual: Nice is old, centuries old. Nice is crammed with tourists. Signs and flags, all geared for tourist eyes, proclaim it as the fifth largest city in France. Nice is a winding city, flat and hilly; more complicated than it first appears. The cities smell the same: the air from the bay, the dampness, the hint of eucalyptus. The light is the same vague and wistful indescribable color that gives the skin a healthy glow and signals the beginning of the end of the day. Nice is red-tile roofs atop aged stucco buildings, small boutiques crammed one after another after another into ancient stone buildings, the singsong tones of a bundle of languages. "Bonjour," a florist calls out. "Bonjour." Lena mimics his greeting and stops at his window to marvel at the beauty and art of the floral arrangements, the rose petals intentionally scattered on the floor to please the eye and the nose. What is different is the absence of the familiar diversity of yellow, black, white, and brown faces; Lena hears it in language—French, Italian, Spanish, German.

Nothing is familiar. Not the yeasty smell of baking bread, nor the rapid movement of the small, two-door vehicles that resemble bug-eyed insects more than cars and scoot along the promenade, nor the endless stream of evening strollers, nor their full and throaty *R*'s. Lena allows this European reality to seep in and merges with the evening crowd. The guidebooks say that the French love the evenings as much as they do the days. Couples hold hands, toddlers waddle between their parents, teenagers roughhouse and tease. After two blocks she stops before an ancient portal, Latin words carved above its arch. *V*'s replace the letter *U*, making the words even more impossible to decipher. By the looks of the nineteenth-century dates, the arch has a history all its own. Like Lena.

Once through the portal, Lena stands before the back entrances of restaurants in a blind alley filled with trucks and garbage cans that could place her anywhere in the world: the scent of discarded vegetables, overripe fruit, bones, and uncooked meat; trucks grind leftovers to unrecognizable garbage; men in white smocks and dirt-smeared aprons yell to one another as they pile the wiggling carcasses of the morning's catch onto loading docks.

This alley reminds Lena of Randall's habit of taking her, wherever they traveled, through back streets to smell the real city. He would stop and talk to dockworkers and busboys, using his hands and face more than any foreign words he knew. "This is how you find out where the real people eat." She almost turns to look for Randall, to ask him to sit with her over a glass of wine. A glass of Beaujolais? She brushed wine on her lips the day he proposed. He said she tasted like violets and berries.

The alley leads to the corner and the wide Cours Saleya. Time to walk where Tina might walk, to smell what Tina might smell. Even though Nice is one city over from Villefranche, it is sophisticated and charming and, Lena speculates, a city that Tina might occasionally visit. The promenade of the famous Vieux Carré is crowded. Slender young men and women hand out sample menus to lure hungry tourists into overpriced and nondescript restaurants; people stroll everywhere—arm in arm, in tight packs, comfortable with brushing elbows. She inhales—there is a hint of mildew in the air—and sticks out her tongue to taste what she smells around her: salt, basil, garlic, lavender, and wine. She will come to know that Nice smells different each hour of the day and night.

A handsome maitre d' smiles. His badge is printed with his name, Pascal, and the words Bienvenue. Benvenido. Willkommen. Welcome. "Bonjour, Madame," he says, waving Lena into his dimly lit restaurant. She accepts his kind gesture. Pascal points to a front table so that the ever-present blues of the sky, the crackled faces of the ancient stone buildings, the vendors' striped tents and handmade crafts, the music, and the passing crowds are set like a stage play in front of her. The streets are covered with cobblestones. Restaurants' tables line both sides of the Cours for as far as she can see. Cigarette smoke, fidgeting kids, quarreling lovers. Cups clinking against thick porcelain saucers. A roving band strums guitars in unison; a troubadour misquotes the lyrics to "American Pie."

"You are perhaps waiting for a friend, Madame?" The young man's accent is melodic. His question is not offensive. He hands Lena an oversized menu written in French and British English, the prices in euros and pounds. "Nope, not waiting for anyone."

Cheryl and Lena, once inside their hotel room, had reverse reactions to the layovers and the twelve-hour flight. Cheryl was enervated. With barely a comment about the room's Provençal décor—the bedspreads' tiny cornflower blue and sunshine yellow flowers, the brass handheld shower head, or the wedge of the Mediterranean visible in a stretch over the ornate balcony rail—Cheryl snatched a black gel mask from her carry-on, put it on top of her eyes, and crawled under the covers without unpacking her suitcase, without taking off her clothes.

"A glass of Beaujolais." Lena is energized. After months of sleeping to forget, she is eager to remember what life has to offer. She shuffles her feet in a careful, congratulatory dance under the table and points to the wine selection. When Pascal sets her glass in front of her, she raises it in a mock toast to him, to the crowd, to the sky and blinks back gathering tears. Last time. Last time. This is the last time she can feel sad in this wonderful place. She downs the entire glass of wine; unable to drink alone, she leaves six euros on the table and rushes back to the hotel.

"You promised you weren't gonna do that." Cheryl stops in the middle of the street and crosses her arms. "I know you're thinking about Randall. I can see it in your face."

Lena scratches her nose and sniffs in that way she's begun to do when she can't think of anything to say. The word *anomalous* pops into her mind. Another Auntie Big Talker word; she'd used it last week when she called to wish Lena well on her trip. While Lena prides herself on her vocabulary skills, she is not sure if what she is feeling is anomalous or just plain normal. The south of France is beautiful, but traveling with anyone other than Randall is something she has never done.

Lena sniffs again. This trip is all about opening up, like a short story she once read where the main character avoided her unhappy present by imagining herself drinking coffee elsewhere. When the character finds a friend, she has a hard time opening up and doesn't realize until the end that in fact she wants to do just that. Lena wishes to be drinking coffee elsewhere. Open up and let me in; not by the hair of my chinny, chin chin.

Adults, teenagers, and even a couple of preteens shout into cell phones. Lena checks her purse to make sure she has remembered to bring her own just as it rings. "Camille?"

"Hey, Mom. Just calling to wish you a good trip. You flying over New York?"

"I'm in Nice." A mass forms quickly in her throat, and Lena speaks slowly to keep her emotions in check. "How's the move going?"

"Dad's pacing outside my door, and Auntie stopped by. She dropped off the stuff you sent . . . you knew just what I needed . . ."

In the months after graduation, Lena repeatedly explained how much she wanted to help Camille move into the dorm. It was a mother's right to usher her child into a new life, just as she had ushered her into life at birth. Their discussions always ended the same way: both of them yelling—the anger of the pending divorce wearing thin on their nerves—leaving nothing resolved.

"Dad is a bit out of it, Mom. He's not doing as well as you are. I don't suppose you want to talk to him, do you?" Camille pauses, and Lena wonders what her daughter wants her to say, wonders if Camille needs to be reminded that her father is no longer her mother's responsibility. "He doesn't know all the little things to get. He even said that the move would be more . . . organized, if you . . . The bedspread you sent was cool . . . and the cookies were good. I . . . I . . . wish you were here. I'm sorry."

"You and your dad will be fine. I love you, baby girl." Because of their problems and Lena's desire to forget, she deliberately chose the day Camille was to move into the dorm as the day of her departure. In the letter sent along with the down comforter, sachets for her drawers, razors, boxes of tampons, earplugs, flashlight, boxes of tissue, paper towels, homemade chocolate chip cookies, and a bone-china dipping pot, Lena wrote that she looked forward to the day they could talk freely again, when they could get past the anger that gnawed at both of them and let their openness lead to a new and better relationship. She wrote that as Camille and her father searched the aisles of the local bedding store, while they lugged and unloaded her belongings into the dorm room, she would be flying over New York, looking through the clouds for the rounded dome and tight square rectangles of Columbia's campus.

Camille and Randall worked slower than she thought. "I'm with you, baby." Lena mutes her sniffs with a tissue so that Camille cannot hear while she tells Lena about her dorm, her roommate, and her class schedule.

"You'll come at Thanksgiving?"

She nods as though Camille can see her confirmation through the phone. "I might even let Bobbie cook."

"Spare us," Camille jokes. "Auntie is better at *selling* cookbooks than she is cooking. Have a safe trip, and bring me back something really French. I love you, Mommy."

"See? Everything's going to be okay." Cheryl hands Lena another tissue while the man next to them pretends not to notice. "Be happy . . . we're in France!"

The knot in Lena's stomach loosens. Truthfully, Lena admits to herself, it unwinds a lot. "Now, if only I could get you to stop thinking about that damn almost was-band of yours." Cheryl's made-up word rhymes with *husband*.

Like Tina, Lena must learn not to dwell in the past.

The bay is lit by thousands of glimmering lights. There is movement everywhere. The ebb and flow of the Mediterranean slaps noisily against the gravelly shore. Nice thrives at night. Tourists meander through the high-end shopping district, restaurants are filled inside and out, and late-evening diners sip dark coffee from small cups, red wine from oversized glasses, and chatter at each other. Filmy smoke drifts everywhere; every man and woman seems to hold a cigarette in his or her hand, elbows on tables, the white stick poised inches from their lips while they appear to ponder the next drag.

"For the life of me I can't understand why everyone smokes," Lena says. "I suppose that's who they are, the French. I mean, look at these women." Lena sweeps her hands in front of her. They are surrounded by tables full of women with hair turned up into flips or smoothed into pageboys, scarves tied carefully around their shoulders, expensive leather handbags, pedicured toes, flat hips and stomachs under skintight dresses, high heels when the rough edges of the cobblestone streets demand something more practical. "French women pay so much attention to everything else. Strange they don't care about their health."

"They're having fun. We're having fun. No preaching, no judging, just fun. Especially seeing as you fit right in." Cheryl cackles.

"Touché!" Lena beams, glad that she sports her not quite so high heels, which make her feel, more than her skin color, that she fits in. She perks her head at the soft background music. Tina sings "What's Love Got to Do with It" on the overhead speakers.

"There's your sign," Cheryl says.

"I love it." Lena picks up her camera and focuses on Cheryl and the gold and green awning above her. *Click.* "It means I'm on the right track."

"So the concert is"—Cheryl counts on her fingers—"eighteen days from now. That means we have time for a little exploring. The light in the south of France is extraordinary. Good for photographs. Lots of artists—Matisse, Chagall, and Picasso—came here to paint. If I visit those museums, I can write off part of our trip. The train goes to Cannes and St. Tropez. And the nightlife in Monte Carlo—"

"Wait." Lena stretches out the palm of her hand like a stop sign in front of Cheryl's face. "You're going too fast for me. Plus, I want to check out Villefranche, where Tina lives. Let's look at our options, then decide."

"Expand your horizons. We need . . . diversion." Cheryl inclines her head in the direction of a dark-haired man on the opposite side of the café's terrace. Diversion for Cheryl, Lena recalls, means more than museums, means more than scouring the streets for historical sites, for the perfect cup of coffee or unusual architectural details. "These Frenchmen look very good, Lena. And who knows what French there is to learn from chatting."

"Men aren't what this trip is about."

"I know that, but let me remind you, like that man's eyes over there, you're not dead. It does *not* hurt to look, Lena Harrison. Should I go over there and introduce myself?" Cheryl scoots her chair back and mocks the panic that stiffens Lena's face. The couple next to them ogles. Their French is cacophony of guttural noises and nasal blends.

"They've probably never seen American blacks before, except on TV. They're probably saying something racist, about ugly Americans or worse—ugly black folks."

"Don't think racism, Cheryl, we get enough of that at home. Maybe they're staring because we're beautiful; maybe they're staring because you're talking so loud."

"You know the French are very racist," Cheryl whispers.

"The world is racist, but I'm not going to let it keep me from having a good time." Lena opens her handbag and pulls out a pen and the little orange notebook filled with things she wants to do, places she wants to see: Matisse and Chagall museums, the early morning markets, a jazz concert in the park atop Cimiez, and a cooking class. On the inside cover she draws a series of horizontal and vertical lines. The lines turn into boxes and she labels them with numbers.

Cheryl reaches over and shuts Lena's handmade calendar. "All we need to know is that Tina's concert takes place in eighteen days. We have our tickets. We'll worry about how to get there when the time comes. Otherwise, no planning."

Lena grins, glad that Cheryl is with her, despite her flamboyance, despite her disorganization and toss-it-to-the-wind outlook.

Cheryl motions to the waiter. "Gauloises, s'il vous plaît."

"Since when do you speak French?" Secondhand smoke catches in Lena's throat.

"Please, everybody knows 'please.' Gauloises are cigarettes."

When the waiter returns, he brings a pack of unidentifiable cigarettes and tells Cheryl that Gauloises are hard to find these days. "C'est la vie," Cheryl says and accepts the compact, blue pack. "It doesn't matter." She opens the box top, pulls out two cigarettes, and hands one to Lena. Putting the cigarette between her lips, Lena strikes a match and leans into its flame.

Chapter 23

Cheryl approaches the last roundabout before Vence: five-foot-wide, circular cement mounds of grass and flowers built at one-mile intervals in the middle of the road to the hilltop city. At each one, multiple thoroughfares converge and crook, snakelike arrows direct traffic left, right, or straight ahead.

Lena points to a tall tower. GARAGE/STATIONNEMENT is stenciled in white letters across its front. The tower's cement angles are almost an insult to the weathered merry-go-round and the frilly, lace curtains in the restaurant windows behind it.

When the elevator lets them off atop a grassy mound, Lena and Cheryl follow a cluster of people to a narrow opening in a fifteen-inch-thick stone wall.

Inside lies a medieval city: winding streets no wider than eight or ten feet, dusty colored bricks, open markets with tables of eggplant, oranges, leafy greens, and more lined in even rows that resemble art more than food for sale; whole, wall-eyed fish and inky squid atop ice-covered bins, pigs' heads, tails, and feet; wine and pungent disks of cheese.

"It's like—" Cheryl whispers.

"We stepped back in time," Lena finishes, "or more like into a fairy tale."

Lena removes her camera from its case, focuses the lens: a whole fish ogling them from atop a bed of greens and ice, the word *traiteur* printed in calligraphy across a striped awning of what looks like a delicatessen, laundry dangling from a window, a small chalkboard with the specials of the day—*plats du jour.*

"Food now, pictures later." Cheryl flips through the pages of a small guidebook and wanders in the direction of a restaurant she read about that serves a great coq au vin.

Lena snaps pictures without compromising Cheryl's search. Each turn reveals more of the city's charm. *Click:* a rusted door. *Click:* a flowering tree beside an old church. *Click:* a watchtower. The stone streets are spotless. Wine shops, clothing stores, bookstores, shops selling postcards and the ever-present images of *cigales* carved into music boxes, the tops of ceramic crocks, and scented soaps; all of southern France loves their melodious cicadas.

At the end of an empty, narrow street that seems to have been ignored by scattered tourists, the sound of sizzling meat and the nutty scent of butter just turning brown beckons them: a tiny restaurant, Chez Philippe.

"This is it!" Cheryl shouts. "This is the restaurant in the guide."

A menu in French and English is taped on the open door. Lena takes pictures while Cheryl scours the two pages. A smiling man with a menu in each hand rushes to the door.

"Bonjour, mesdames. Lunch for two or four?"

Cheryl holds up two fingers. "But, how did you know we speak English?"

"I'd like to tell you it's your shoes or clothes, cherie, because they are *trés chic.*" The man looks into Cheryl's eyes. "But I heard you talking. And women as beautiful as you are hard to ignore."

"Your English is perfect." Cheryl returns his straightforward look.

"I'm from Upstate New York. I'm Philip—Philippe." He exaggerates the French pronunciation—Phil-leep—and cocks his head at a table for two in the corner of the nearly full restaurant. "This is my restaurant."

"California." Cheryl extends her hand. "The land of sunshine and loose women."

Lena slaps Cheryl's arm lightly. "I'm Lena. She's Cheryl."

In between seating new diners and busing dishes, Philip— host, sometime chef and sommelier—returns to their table to chat with the two women as if they are long-lost friends.

"I hardly ever have a chance to talk to anyone from California. We get a lot of people from New York and the East Coast, but not as many from the West Coast." He sips wine from the glass he leaves on their table. Philip is beefy. His clothes are loose and fashionable in a 1920s movie kind of way that makes him attractive though his face is not. His dark brown hair and blue eyes follow Cheryl's while he summarizes his story: he has lived in Vence for almost ten years, and he used to run the restaurant for profit, but since 9/11 there have been fewer American tourists; although business is getting better because he's had some publicity. Now he runs the restaurant for fun and earns his living as an English language teacher at a nearby elementary school.

"He is *so* sexy." Cheryl nudges Lena as Philip guides a couple to a small table near a piano pushed against the back wall. "I love the way he looks right at my mouth when he talks to me."

Lena rolls her eyes in a way that has now become habit and reminds her of Camille and even Kendrick whenever they disapproved of something she did or said.

"Join in the fun." Cheryl pulls out a gold compact and checks her lipstick. Cheryl only wears red lipstick, preferring to draw attention to her heart-shaped lips; her skin is smooth save for a noticeable scar above her right eye—a leftover from chicken pox; her cheeks bear the slightest tinge of her natural blush that flares when she's angry or excited.

Cheryl motions to Philip. Leaning into his side, she points to her lunch selection and smiles. "Are you open for dinner, too?"

Philip shoos away the only waiter in the restaurant. "If you like our food, you must come back for dinner. I sing and play the piano, and there's a wonderful café around the corner that stays open very late."

Lena shrugs and picks at her sweater and pants. "I'm not sure about the roads at night. And . . . we're not really dressed for dinner."

"But you both look fabulous, and my house specialty is on the menu tonight— a pork that will melt in your mouth," Philip says, grinning at Cheryl. "You think about it, and let me know."

Cheryl winks. "Perhaps you can invite a friend in honor of our first time in Vence."

"Mais oui!" Philip holds his chin between his thumb and forefinger and closes his eyes as if those actions will help with his answer. "I think I can arrange something."

A very blond and rather hunched-over man in the corner snaps at Philip. "Garçon," the man calls out, confusing the soft French *C* with the hard American *K*. Philip turns toward the women and makes a face behind his stack of menus. "Duty calls."

"He's being friendly," Cheryl says as Philip walks away. "Besides, if the white boy wants to treat us, what have we got to lose?"

"Nnnnnnn . . ." Lena's tongue rests against the roof of her mouth so that the *N* for "no" buzzes in her nose. She shrugs again and tugs at her hair. Open up. Drink coffee here. "Why not?"

"That's my girl. Remember, we're here to have fun."

"As long as your *fun* doesn't interfere with my plan."

"This *is* the plan."

The Matisse museum in Vence is a short trek from the center of the old city. Lena and Cheryl take the orange trolley across a small bridge to the building where Matisse completed the colorful stained glass windows for the Chapelle du Rosaire and the Dominican sisters of Vence. As the trolley approaches the front of the whitewashed chapel, the last of a queue of men and women load into two large vans topped with bicycle racks and luggage. Once they're all inside, a hand sticks out and pulls the van door shut, then the van pulls away from the curb.

"I swear those people are black." Cheryl waves at the van frantically. "It would be great to make a connection and really have the chance to party."

"Just 'cause they're black doesn't mean they want to party. Or include us. Or, that they're American. This isn't Oakland." Two days in the south of France and, except for Cheryl and the backs of a couple of tall brothers Lena thought she spotted turning a corner in Vence, these are the only people of color she's seen. Or thinks she's seen.

"You never know."

The inside of the tiny chapel is stark white and simple: Matisse's stained glass windows and angled, wooden pews.

"Matisse worked on these windows from around 1948 to 1952. He wanted to convey an easing of the spirit. These windows represent the tree of life." A priest clothed in a white, floor-length cassock holds a finger to his lips as Cheryl describes Matisse's work. Late afternoon light shines through the windows and casts yellow, aquamarine blue, and bottle green rays onto the floor.

"You know so much!"

"Art is, after all, what I do." Cheryl points out a lesser sketch of the windows as they walk through the hall to the small gift counter. "He's my favorite. I love all of his work. There's more in Nice. That museum's larger."

The hallway walls are lined with draft sketches of different portions of the windows: a flower here, a winding vine there, repeated from one frame to the next to show the artist's thought process and practice.

"I wonder if Philip likes art." Cheryl dismisses the thought with a wave of her hand. "Oh, who cares. We'll have a good time tonight."

Lena concentrates on Matisse's sketches. "It says here that

Matisse was searching for one-dimensional movement in this series. What does that mean?"

"You understand exactly what it means, Lena. Don't change the subject, and stop frowning." Cheryl shakes a finger at Lena. "You act like I'm forcing you to pose naked in the town square. You're rusty at the dating game, so just follow my lead."

"If I do that I'll be in bed with a stranger before the night is over."

"And, the problem with that is?" Cheryl pinches Lena's cheek lightly and grins. Postcards line the small glass-topped counter. Lena selects postcards for Lulu, Bobbie, Camille, Kendrick, and Candace, and steps out onto the terrace of the chapel. Camille would love the art and history here; Kendrick would love the winding roads. From the terrace, old Vence is like a postcard: spires and turrets peak above slanted slate roofs clearly outlined against the darkening sky. Lena points her camera at the city and the valley below; she hopes that she has captured the setting sun's rose-tinted cast, hopes that her tingling stomach will calm down or, better yet, that Philip has changed his mind and never wants to see the two of them again.

The restaurant is crowded. Votive candles are everywhere: on the tables, in the windowsills, and on the beam that rests a foot below the low ceiling. Candlelight intensifies the ebony wood. Each table is covered with a soft beige tablecloth and napkins folded into triangle points.

Philip's face brightens when Cheryl and Lena walk through the door. He sits very erect at a small upright piano in the middle of the room where tables were arranged during lunch. The wide lapels of his old-fashioned tuxedo shine in the candlelight. He croons a lazy French song, somewhere between ballad and jazz, in a raspy alto.

"Bonsoir, mesdames," he sings, and all heads in the crowded

restaurant turn with his. "Mesdames et messieurs, je vous presente mes nouvelles amies de Californie." He introduces Lena and Cheryl as if they are celebrities.

"Oh, the one on the left looks just like Diana Ross." An elderly white woman with a distinctive Texas twang points at Cheryl and asks if they are singers, too. "Would you sing 'Stop, in the Name of Love'? I love that song."

Lena and Cheryl roll their eyes at one another. "And *that* is how you can tell *they're* Americans," Lena mutters. "We don't sing—"

"But if you hum a few bars, I'm sure we'll catch on." Cheryl finishes.

Philip sings his own rendition, a muddled blend of French and English, before he joins Cheryl and Lena at their table near the piano. "Tonight you beautiful ladies will have a salad of baby butter lettuce, pork tenderloin sautéed in a reduced red wine sauce *et bien sûr, fromage*—that's cheese to the two of you—for dessert."

"Just what I love—a man who knows his *fromage*!" Cheryl slaps Lena's arm for emphasis. "And soon you will, too."

Two hours later, a dark-haired, puffy-eared man enters the restaurant just as the waiter brings a platter of hard and runny cheeses to the table. The man scans the restaurant briefly and heads for the piano. Philip motions to the man to lean down and whispers in his ear before they both turn their heads to look at Lena and Cheryl.

"I think that's your date." Cheryl tips her head in Philip's direction.

"Don't call it a date, don't call it a date. I'm not ready for a date." Lena glances toward Philip's friend. The man is a parody of an absent-minded professor. His short, very ragged beard is striped with gray, and his glasses slip down his nose so that, in the short time that Lena has to inspect him before he comes to the table, he keeps adjusting them with both hands.

Philip rises from the piano, the professorial-looking man close behind him, and pulls up another chair to Lena and Cheryl's table. He introduces his friend with a flourish as if he were a celebrity, and Lena figures that this, along with his penchant for vintage clothing, is simply Philip's style. "Je vous presente mon ami, Jean-Pierre Dusquesne."

"Enchanté, mesdames." Jean-Pierre lowers his upper body in a feeble bow. His voice is deep and rich like a bassoon. He scoots his chair next to Lena, picks up her knife, and helps himself to a slice of cheese. "Philippe"—he uses the French pronunciation—"tells me that you ladies are here to enjoy the sights of the south of France, and I am available to help if you need me."

Lena hides her amusement behind one of the crisp linen napkins Philip has placed on the table. Jean-Pierre's accent is charming and almost sexy, and, she thinks, if she were to close her eyes this would not be the body or face she would attach to that voice.

Jean-Pierre grazes Lena's hand with his, and she gently moves it away. "And how do you know Philip?"

Without looking at one another, Jean-Pierre and Philip crumple in laughter at the same time. They complete each other's sentences, like only old friends can do, and tell Lena and Cheryl how they first met when Philip came to Vence thinking that he would sweep the French off their feet with his restaurant.

Jean-Pierre leans in to Lena so close she can smell the tobacco on his breath. "He thought we French would permit a foreigner to—*comment dit-on?* . . . how do you say in English?—come in and take over our specialty? *Non?*"

Philip picks up the story. "Jean-Pierre came to my rescue. He was my first chef and my teacher. He helped me improve my French, my cooking, and become a part of the community. *Et voila!*" He slaps Jean-Pierre hard on the back. "I couldn't have done it without him."

"Do you still cook, Jean-Pierre?" Lena scoots her chair to the left and away from Jean-Pierre.

"Ah, cherie, every Frenchman cooks when inspired." Jean-Pierre takes Lena's hand, turns it over and traces the lines of her palm. "I would cook for you anytime, anywhere."

Without a thought to politeness or misinterpretation, Lena yanks her hand away from the Frenchman's and folds her arms across her chest. "I'm sure you would, but we have a plan and we're pretty much going to stick to it." She waits for her friend to come to her aid, but Cheryl turns to Philip and squeezes his arm, which Lena takes as a sign of her plan.

"*Mais non, cherie*, this is France." Jean-Pierre licks his lower lip in a way that looks like it would be better suited to a porno film. "And there is no better way to experience our lovely country than with a French man."

"Okay! Time to go. It's a long way back to Nice." Lena taps her fingers on the table like Bobbie tapped hers against the telephone. "Philip, thank you so much for the lovely dinner. Can you have the waiter bring the bill?"

"No, no, no. Non. You're my guests. But must you leave so early? The night, as they say, is still young."

Cheryl squints at Lena until the tiny knot between her eyebrows is more than a suggestion to her friend; it is an order. "And there's the café Philip mentioned." Her voice is firm, her tone a teacher's scolding a naughty child. She clinks her glass against Philip's and sips until the glass is nearly empty. Their bodies relax into each other's with every additional sip: the more they drink, the closer they sit. The more they touch, the more Jean-Pierre's eyes insist he and Lena should be doing the same.

"And, though there is not much nightlife, perhaps you can stay the night here in our lovely Vence, eh?" Jean-Pierre's eyebrows angle and wrinkle his forehead. "Perhaps I can make a little dessert for you? Dessert," he says, licking his lips again, "is my specialty." He stretches his arm, its direction aimed for Lena's shoulder.

"I take that to mean that you're still a chef?" Lena glowers at Jean-Pierre, uninterested in him or in watching Cheryl play footsy with Philip, the pseudo Frenchman. The last time they went out together, just before Cheryl's first marriage, Cheryl decided to spend the night with a football player they'd met in a hotel lounge after a college game, and Lena had to find her way home because Cheryl drove. Lucky for Cheryl, the player wasn't a maniac. He ended up being her first husband, and then he turned into a maniac.

"Your eyes, they are very exotic." Jean-Pierre leans in closer for a better look at Lena's light brown eyes and brushes Lena's hair away from her ear. "You are like . . . Tina Turner. You American black women are so beautiful." As soon as he presses his hand on Lena's knee she slaps it away and jumps from her chair. "Thank you, Philip, Jean-Pierre, but I'm outta here."

Jean-Pierre motions to Philip. The two men leave the table and step into the kitchen. Through the open door, both Cheryl and Lena watch them; their hands fly through the air, punctuating their rapid French.

"What is the matter with you?" Cheryl pouts. "Look at them. I'm sure they're talking about you. You're rude."

"Good. Maybe he's getting my message. Give me the car keys."

"Jean-Pierre is all talk. You have to learn to ignore men like that. The more you resist, the more they pursue."

"He's a little talk and a lot of pawing, Cheryl. I want to go back to Nice." Lena holds her hand out. Cheryl shakes her bag and the keys to the rental car clink. If they were in the States, Lena would have snatched the keys from Cheryl's bag and let her find her own way back.

"What if I ask Philip to tell Jean-Pierre to get lost? We'll have a nightcap and then head back to Nice. Just do it for me."

Lena stands by the table, grateful that the restaurant is now empty. The night Randall gave her the yellow diamond flashes in her head—a different situation, but the plea is the same. While she waits for Cheryl to come to her senses, the voices of the two men discreetly arguing are still the loudest sound in the room. It is no surprise to either of the women when Jean-Pierre huffs out of the kitchen and heads straight to the front door without saying goodbye.

"Please, please, please, pay my impetuous friend no mind," Philip says, returning to the table. His face is half smile, half know-it-all. "He has another engagement. Let me make it up to you. I invite you, *mes amies,* to my house for a petite nightcap before you head back to Nice."

"I'd love to see a real French home. Well," Cheryl says looking at Philip, "an almost-real French home."

If they were in Oakland, Lena would have fussed at Cheryl and perhaps put distance between the two of them. At home she would still be married. No, at home and in France she is less than one hundred twenty days from being truly divorced. This anger comes from a place she has had enough of: fear.

A fake smile freezes on Cheryl's face while she whispers in Lena's ear so close that only the two of them know what is being said. "What is the matter with you? We are not nineteen, and you cannot be mad at me for doing something you think is wrong. Get it together, Lena. This is the single life. Enjoy."

She shouldn't care what Cheryl does or who she does it with. "I know." Lena stands, arms limp at her sides, eyes blink rapidly to keep back tears, and considers the question she has not thought of before: is this what being single again is going to be like? Backward instead of forward when she needs to move ahead. Here, she guesses, her options are the same: to leave or stay; but she would never forgive herself if something happened to her friend. Fifteen minutes later they arrive at the door of a small building outside the walled city.

"Permit me to give you a tour of my apartment." Philip uses French pronunciation: *ah-par-tuh-MAWN.* "Small by U.S. standards, but good-sized for this part of the world. *Non?*" The place is barely half the size of his restaurant; the kitchen is narrow and neat, with nothing on the single stone counter except a speckled canister, two espresso cups, and a bouquet of yellow daisies. An orderly stack of French, American, and Spanish cookbooks sits atop the small refrigerator. Philip opens the door to his bedroom. "This, as you can see, is the bedroom." He tickles Cheryl, presses his leg into her thigh, his lips to her lips. When he pulls away his lips are tinged with Cheryl's red lipstick.

"Make yourself comfortable, Lena." Cheryl giggles. "I'm going to visit with Philip for a while."

"Fuck on your own time, please. Like you said, we are *not* teenagers."

"The French are so much more civilized about this kind of thing."

Lena cuts her eyes, hoping that her friend will understand that she is serious. "He's not French." Isn't this like being with Randall? Lena muses as she catches a glimpse of a neatly made bed with a white duvet before Philip closes the door behind them. Following somebody else's agenda instead of her own?

Moving through the apartment, Lena peeks into the bathroom. A pitcher on the bathroom counter is heavy with sprigs of dried lavender. Lavender-scented candles edge the basin. Two thin towels hang over a small heating rack beside the sink and, on the shelf beneath it, an unmistakable square box of tampons. In the corner, a shelf in the glass-enclosed shower holds two bottles of shampoo and a shower cap. Tampons, shower cap, the abundance of lavender: Lena figures Philip is cheating on his wife or a woman who spends a lot of time in this *ah-par-tuh-mawn.* Lena storms back into the kitchen. The thick-planked floors deaden the sound of her shoes. Pulling open cabinets and drawers, Lena searches until she finds a wide-blade knife that, if Philip turns out to be a madman, can protect her and Cheryl. Philip does not seem to be crazy, but, Lena knows, men can get crazy when they're denied a roll in the sack.

"Cheryl? I'm going." Would Tina ever allow herself to be in such a stupid predicament? "And I suggest you do the same, since it looks like Phil-leep has a better half who may return at any minute."

Chapter 24

The attendant in navy shorts and a snug boat-necked tee opens the umbrella behind Lena, adjusts it so they are protected from the midday sun, hands them more towels, and sets bottled water and glasses filled with lemon and cucumber slices on the small table beside her.

"Just like home." Cheryl drops her tote onto the lounge chair and motions to the people around the pool. "We're the only blacks around this pool."

The hotel pool, shaped like a long kidney bean, is meant more for dipping than swimming laps. Several bare-chested women stand in the shallow end and drip handfuls of cool water on their shoulders. Sun worshippers recline atop the striped lounge chairs randomly scattered across the marble deck and lawn circling the pool.

"When you're black," Lena reminds her friend in a low voice, "it's just the way it is." Lena adjusts her sunglasses. Through them the pale sapphire sky is clear, and the sunlight is bothersome even with dark lenses. "And, I might add, isn't that bikini a bit risqué?"

"There you go again." Cheryl clasps her hands together like she is about to pray, before plopping onto the striped lounge chair. "Do I have to beg your forgiveness for acting like a grown woman?"

"I told you last night. Pull that kind of act again . . . no. Don't pull that kind of shit again. Period. Dot. End of conversation." Lena gathers her hair and tucks it under her broad-rimmed raffia hat. "Trust me. I'm getting good at leaving people."

With the slightest shake of her head, Cheryl acknowledges Lena's challenge. "Don't get crazy. I guess I could say I had too much to drink, but that's not really the truth. I'm used to doing what I want, when I want, and I didn't give you much thought." Cheryl leans over to Lena and gently pulls her sunglasses away from her face. Without protesting, Lena sighs and looks at Cheryl. "I get it. I'm sorry, so let's not let this ruin our vacation. Now we know the rules." Cheryl lets the straps of her bikini fall down her shoulders and slathers sunscreen on her face, neck, and chest. "Just don't be so damn judgmental . . . and for the record, I look good in this bikini."

"I'm going to be who I am. I thought you understood." Lena adjusts the top of her one-piece bright orange and turquoise floral swimsuit—a maillot, the saleslady called it.

"This is all I'm going to say, and then can we *please* move on?" Cheryl picks up a hotel magazine for tourists and flips through it. "I know the concept of dating all over again is going to be hard for you, Lena, and I'm sorry. But in my mind it simply means you need to loosen up. Randall's ghost isn't lurking in the shadows; you're not obligated to him anymore."

Lena pushes her sunglasses back onto her face and lets Cheryl's words soak in. "If I've learned anything over the last few months . . ." Lena pauses until Cheryl lowers the magazine in front of her face. "If I've learned anything from Tina Turner, it's that I'm the boss of me. But, I'm sorry, too." She relaxes into her chair and into the thought that somewhere, under this Mediterranean sun, Tina is basking as well: two black women from Oakland, Tina, and all the white people in the south of France.

◆ ◆ ◆

"I'll be damned. Looks like we got a party going on." Splashing and flat slaps of stomach against the water rouse Cheryl from her hour-long nap. She nudges Lena's leg: black people alert.

From beyond and to the far side of the pool voices drift in their direction. A man stands at pool's edge. He is long and tall and a shade darker than desert sand. He extends his arms and arcs his back like he knows what he is doing, then dives and swims toward his buddy, in the only square corner of the pool.

Cheryl sits up straight in her chair, strains her neck and stares. His chest heaves after his short swim. "You won't believe who that man looks like." She pushes at Lena again. "That's Harmon Francis!"

The two men, arms stretched over the edge of the pool, chat as much with their hands as their voices. The swimmer appears taller than the average Frenchman, giving Lena another reason, beside his skin color, to be able to see him. Harmon Francis. Definitely. He crossed her mind when she watched the last of a man's familiar walk turning a corner in Vence. Now, the van outside the Matisse museum makes more sense. And here he is again. Harmon Francis. She hasn't seen him in almost twenty-six years, not since the day he'd told her he wanted to get married.

He was the same but different from Randall: street smart. Lena didn't watch Randall's love of designer suits and fancy accessories evolve while he lived on the East Coast, but she enjoyed their benefits when they dated the second time around. Harmon was already grounded in his expensive habits when they met. Unlike Randall, he loved hats—baseball cap, porkpie, beret—and hated jewelry except for the gold watch still hanging from his wrist. Back then he had his hair cut at a salon instead of a barbershop. He collected first editions and world maps; had a great sense of humor, a keen eye for good deals, and a key to an exclusive social club. Within a month of their first date, Lena was in love with Harmon. In the fifth month of their eight-month relationship Harmon told Lena he was tired of being single.

They sat together on the cushy sofa of the restricted club surrounded by football players and real estate tycoons. Under low lights, they sipped Dom Perignon from hundred-dollar champagne flutes and watched the parade of bachelors and flirtatious women on the dance floor. "I'm the kind of man who does better with a woman by his side," he said. Lena figured he was looking for a mother for his two boys. "I've been honest about dating other women." His voice was confident, picking up tempo as he went along; the faster he spoke the faster Lena's heart pumped in anticipation. "I've narrowed my marriage prospects down to two—you and someone else."

Armed with the insight that he was about to pop the question, over the months that followed Lena did what she thought she was supposed to: never let him see her without makeup, introduced him to her parents, had sex with him every day of every other week—her share of him—wowed him with her budding domestic skills. She met his seven-year-old twins. Harmon told her about their difficult mother, revealed his personal finances, took her on a business trip to Las Vegas, introduced her to his law partners.

Harmon was handsome, upwardly mobile, and available. She loved him but never understood that sharing her love with him was her choice, not just his. He broke her heart when he decided to marry her competition, Natalie. It broke her heart even more when she went to his best friend and sobbed on his shoulder, asked why not me, and his best friend said because Harmon thought Natalie was better in bed.

Harmon Francis. Of all the people to run into.

"Let's go over there," Cheryl pulls a makeup bag from her plastic tote and freshens her lipstick. “I can’t wait to see the look on his face when he sees you.”

“Nope! Stay here. Maybe I did learn a thing or two from you last night.” Lena drops her wide-brimmed sun hat onto her chair. Her swimsuit’s colors set off her even brown skin, the suit cuts across the tops of her breasts, like a strapless prom dress, and accentuates the dark mole centered above her cleavage, her favorite. At fifteen, Lena counted the moles on her body, afraid they would multiply into the hundreds like those that dotted her Auntie Inez’s face and hands. “But, I’m doing this my way.”

In the short distance from deck chair to pool, Lena relaxes her hips in a rhythmic sway that is slow and easy. Rolling. From behind her, a long, low whistle signifies someone’s appreciation. She lowers herself on one long leg and dips the other into the warmish water. Eyes focused on the deep blue as if hypnotized by its rippling motion, she pulls her leg out slowly, then squats, dips her cupped left hand into the water, and drips a bit onto her right arm.

As she descends into the shallow end of the pool, pausing after each step, the tiny waves climb her calves, her thighs, her waist. She gazes straight ahead, letting the water envelop her body, then arcs her arms into an inverted V and slips under the surface. Her gentle breaststroke guides her across the pool until she is close to the two men. In one smooth motion, Lena rolls over on to her back, stretches her arms out, and floats like a suspended cross.

The men’s voices are clear, their words jumbled. She knows black folks attract black folks, especially when there are only a few around, especially when there are men and women. She figures they’re deciding who will approach her first. Or perhaps, in all the time she took to get to their end of the pool, Harmon has recognized her.

“Always said you had the best legs in the world.” Her body

bobbles with the tiny swell Harmon's approach creates. He dog-paddles closer. "And here you are in the heart of the French Riviera proving it."

Harmon looks as good as he did in 1978. Full face and body, crinkled forehead, shaved head. When he grins his chipped front tooth peeks between his parted lips.

Still sexy.

"Don't talk to me." Even strokes send her spinning away.

"Stop moving." His gaze travels the length of her body, lingers on her breasts, her thighs, her bright red toenails.

"We're in the middle of the pool; floating is my only choice."

"You know what I mean."

Lena drifts toward Harmon, refuses eye contact. Once upon a time she thought she would scratch his eyes out if she ever saw him again. Time and a good marriage, or what used to be a good marriage, mellowed her anger.

"I guess I should be grateful; I wouldn't have met my husband if it hadn't been for you." People around them laugh at Harmon's raucous response. Lena grins, lets him think that her great life is payback.

"Everything's turned out good for you?"

"Yes." Success is the best revenge. That was what Elizabeth said at their final meeting. Lena never thought it would apply to such an accidental reunion. She spins a half-truth and tells him about her life the way it was when her marriage was good, when she was truly Mrs. K. Randall Spencer and Camille and Kendrick's mother in more than name only.

"Married, children, community work, nice house, fancy car, adoring husband." She pieces together happiness from memories because she wants Harmon to be jealous. "Someone who loved me for who I was . . ."

"I should have married *you*."

Any smart-mouthed comment Lena could make about his decision is unimportant, doesn't matter anymore; but she finds it comforting to realize that the past can become so insignificant and can hardly wait until that happens with Randall. "That's a stupid thing to say to somebody who couldn't care less. What are you doing in this part of the world anyway?" She splashes the water between them, spins and swirls so that the rolling circles eventually smack against him.

"Don't be so mean." He puckers his lips in an unconvincing pout. "Up until this morning I was traveling with a biking group across the south of France. Bruce and I broke off from them. Too much hassle." He pauses, the lines in his forehead crinkle tighter. Lena remembers that face: it is serious, pondering. "I used to ask Jessie about you from time to time. I talked to my buddy about everything. You remember him, don't you?" She acknowledges the man who told her what Harmon would not and lets the sweeping motion of her hands move her around him.

"I talked to Jessie about Natalie, too," Harmon says. "How great she was in bed, how she drove me crazy." Now Lena recalls her biggest disappointment in Harmon: he couldn't keep his business to himself.

"So I heard." Lena slaps the water hard with the palm of her hand so that it splashes onto Harmon's face. "Well, Harmon, it's been good to see you." She starts to swim away. He grabs her leg so that Lena is forced to fold herself into an uncomfortable treading position.

"Don't go." His front tooth shows again.

Harmon announced his marriage plans to Lena the night they took his boys to the circus. The high-energy twins fidgeted all night long while the elephants dumped in front of their prime-dollar seats, while a tiger jumped through a fiery hoop, while the horses pranced with twirling acrobats atop them.

The night was one of those when the Oakland skyline was as

clear and twinkling as San Francisco's. He told her his decision while they were on the freeway, headed back to his place—he was going to marry Natalie. After all, she had a son as well.

The car swerved into the next lane when Lena's hands flew to her face. Harmon grabbed the steering wheel until Lena recovered seconds later. She had volunteered to drive because Harmon had had a long day. Why the hell hadn't he told her before she went to the circus? Before she wiped cotton candy from the boys' sticky fingers, let them share her soda, all the time hoping that Harmon would appreciate her maternal instincts. When they arrived at his house, the kids jumped out of the car. Harmon tried to apologize; she put the car in park and kicked at him until he jumped onto the cement to get away from her spiked heels, then sped off, car door swinging as she drove down the street, leaving him and his whining boys in the middle of his driveway.

"Where are you going with this? It's been—what?—twenty-six, twenty-seven years?" She snaps, aware that there is too much anger in her voice; water under the bridge. At the time his rejection hit below the belt, in more than one way.

"You always did say I talked too much. To make a long story short, I guess I bragged a little too much. Jessie and Natalie had an affair." He shrugs. "Like a soap opera, I caught the two of them in my bed, screwing their brains out . . . she left me for him."

"There's something so ironic here. If I hadn't been here, how would you have gotten all of this off your chest? Why do you think I'd care now anyway?" Her questions tumble lightly like drizzle in May. She truly doesn't care, but truly she is curious. "Are you dying or something?"

"Must be karma," he chuckles. "I'd like to meet your husband. It may sound corny, but he's a very lucky man."

"Randall? Randall's not here." He will never be here with her ever in life, she thinks. "I'm here with a friend. You remember Cheryl?"

"Who could forget Cheryl Jamison?" Harmon motions to his friend, a big man, too, different from Harmon. Flabby yet solid, Harmon's friend, from what Lena judges, appears to be the kind of man who would look skeletal weighing less than 225 pounds. He is well over that weight. He bobbles toward them, lists from side to side like an untethered buoy, unsure in the water. "Bruce Patterson meet an old friend, Lena—the one I let get away. Tell Lena she has to have dinner with us tonight."

"Lena has to have dinner with us tonight." Bruce delivers this line stoically—Lena assumes he is either very witty or lacks imagination—just as Cheryl swims up. When she bobs out of the water like a fish on a hook, Lena sees that Cheryl is right: she does look good in her bikini, regardless of her age.

"*She* has to have dinner with us tonight." Bruce beams at Cheryl.

"I say yes to whatever he wants." Cheryl beams back.

"Sure," Lena chortles, liking the idea of another chance to gloat, to let Harmon see what he missed, even if that life is no longer real. "We'll join you."

"Your husband won't mind?" Harmon asks.

Cheryl cuts a quick look at Lena.

"No, he won't mind. He won't mind at all."

Chapter 25

"Why did you let Harmon think you're still married? He could be your get-over-Randall screw."

"Don't say it. Don't think it. Not interested." Lena lifts her arms away from her body so that nervous perspiration will not create a salty half moon in the armpit of her dark linen dress. Clothes are strewn on the floor, the bed, the chairs, the small table that passes for a desk as if she and Cheryl have hundreds of clothing choices instead of the few they've brought with them. Or the few Lena brought.

"What're you waiting for? You can be guaranteed Randall's not." Cheryl pulls underwear from the elastic pouches around the side of one of her two oversized suitcases.

"That thought turns my stomach." Lena makes a face. "But this isn't about Randall. Let Harmon stew."

"I don't care what you say; Harmon is charming. Harmon is doing well. Harmon is a catch." Cheryl pulls on a low-cut, sheer red dress. "I always liked him. He has a good heart—he invested in the works of a couple of unknown artists I represented when I first started—it got my business going. I'm glad to be here for your first date the second time around."

Energy crackles like electricity in the room and while Lena understands her own, she doesn't quite get Cheryl's. Cheryl dates. There was a time when Cheryl called Lena every weekend with updates on her escapades; that stopped after Kendrick was born. Lena guesses this excitement has to do with Bruce, has to do with the south of France, has to do with an unexpected, free meal at a fancy restaurant and settles with the realization that because she hasn't been around Cheryl this way in a long time, her girlfriend is excited.

"It's not a date—it's old friends getting together." Lena tugs at her dress: black, plunging neckline and back, tight across the waist and hips. It looked good on her in the store. It looks good on her now.

"Hmmm, I like." Cheryl adjusts the neckline of Lena's dress so that it falls lower and exposes more cleavage. "It shows off your chest. And remember: it's okay to flirt, shamelessly."

Wanting to look good for a man this soon is a confusion Lena didn't expect. If she thinks of this evening as practice for when the next real thing comes along, it will make the evening go smoother. No need to worry about small talk: there's always the past to talk to death. Tiny adjustments, another veneer of marriage falls away: Lena twists the bare knuckle of her third finger left hand.

"You do that a lot, rub your ring finger. Stop it."

Lena gives Cheryl a thumbs-up and eases her hand from breasts to waist to hips, wishing she had the guts to expose as much of her chest as Cheryl does. "You look beautiful!"

Cheryl grabs a floral print shawl identical to the fabric of her dress and poses like a runway model. "This is my knock'em-dead alluring. That Bruce may have potential."

Bruce and Cheryl hit it off immediately. They traded quips for the remainder of the afternoon. Even Lena had to admit that Bruce was funny and pretty smart. He knew a lot about wine, food, and foreign politics—a fact he proved with his explanation of the European Union, the conversion to the euro, and its effect on the global economy.

"And one last lecture about last night." In the bathroom, Lena straightens the cosmetics strewn across the counter, fiddles with her hair for the sixth time, smoothes her dress, sucks in her stomach. She is procrastinating. She knows it. Cheryl knows it. Still she takes her time. After all these years, Harmon Francis can wait ten minutes more. "Take your own key. Because if you decide to spend the night, or whatever, with Big Bruce, I'm not getting up to let you in."

Lena would have married Harmon if he'd asked. Two months after their relationship ended, she realized that she'd gotten love, lust, and money completely confused. Yet, there was his honesty, his crooked smile, and sense of mystery that intrigued her. They hadn't paid attention to what they wanted from life—or each other. That's what she loved about Randall—he paid attention.

Out, out damned spot.

Lena wishes that she had her diamond on her finger at the pool to show Harmon that someone thought her performance in bed was quite good, thank you very much. It didn't matter. It doesn't matter. Sometimes old friends come back into your life for a reason, and right now that reason is so she and Cheryl can have some fun.

Bruce, Lena, Cheryl, and Harmon stand in the entryway of Le Chanson. The restaurant is lit by flower-shaped sconces evenly hung along the length of both sides of the room; classical music plays from speakers in the background. White rubrum lilies nestle in a cut-glass vase atop a polished black marble table. Silverware, wineglasses, and large pieces of jewelry around women's necks and wrists sparkle in the light of the candles on each table. Candles, larger and many more than in Philip's restaurant, surround them on ledges, in cubbyholes and windowsills. Lena wishes to be in a restaurant where music blares and bright lights create a glaring, anything but amorous, atmosphere.

"I hope you ladies enjoy this restaurant," Bruce says. "The Michelin guide calls it one of the best in the south of France."

"Oh, you picked this restaurant?" Cheryl nudges Lena as if to say, "See, you're making way too much of this."

"I build all of my vacations around restaurants." Bruce spreads his arms in front of him. "As you can see, I don't miss many meals."

The hostess, whose hips and stomach are equally flat underneath her chic silk sheath, escorts the two couples to a table on the veranda. Cheryl sidles up to Lena and rubs her back. "You're shaking like a virgin. Calm down. Enjoy. That's all this is about."

Lena breathes from her stomach through her chest and nose, blows it out the way she learned in yoga. The remnants of sunset hang in the sky, its warm colors mirrored in the Mediterranean's gently lapping waves. Lena turns to Harmon. Her intention is to lie, to tell Harmon she is sick, bordering on nausea, that it is too cold, that there are shooting pains in her stomach, her chest, her head, anything to persuade him to leave for somewhere less romantic. "All that's missing is a full yellow moon."

"That's for next time," Harmon says, getting her sense of humor like he did when they dated. "It's good to be with you again. And, for the record, you look great."

"Allow me to order for everyone," Bruce says when the waiter hands each of them a menu. "Take a look at the menu, and let me know if there's anything you absolutely veto."

They mull over the bilingual menu: rougets—tiny red mullets—sea bass with grilled shallots, gamberoni, baby octopus and squid, lemons, olive oil, truffles, wild mushrooms. Both men study the pages of the wine list. Bruce orders a white Bordeaux—a 2000 Château 'Y' d'Yquem, Bordeaux Superiore. "There have only been twenty-three vintages of 'Y' since the first one in 1959. It goes well with foie gras, if anyone likes that, and it's a good match for seafood."

Harmon suggests a cabernet from the same region with less

flourish or commentary—a 1988 Léoville-Las-Cases, St-Julien. "This one's a tasty wine just coming into its own." He leans over to Bruce and points to the wine list; they guffaw as if sharing a private joke. "They have one bottle of 1982 Cheval Blanc, St-Emilion—it sells for almost nine hundred dollars back home. I'd love to taste that."

"How do you two know so much about French wines?" Cheryl looks at Bruce, more interested in his response than Harmon's.

"Bruce is the one who decided on the bicycling trip. He wanted to exercise off some of the weight he's gained in two years since his divorce." Harmon points to his buddy's protruding stomach. "Actually, I thought it would be a great opportunity to see the south of France and to drink and buy a lot of wine."

Bruce straightens his tie and leans back in his chair as if he is about to deliver an important message. "Harmon and I are both considering a break from corporate America to start our own business." Which, he explains further, they haven't quite nailed down, but it will have to do with importing obscure French wines to the States and staging pairings with gourmet food. "So I guess you could say that I'm responsible for bringing the two of you back together." Bruce's whole frame wobbles when he chuckles at his good deed.

"And for us." Cheryl bats her eyes at Bruce again. If a big man could bat his eyes, Lena is sure Bruce would. Instead, he grins like a kid and takes her hand.

The waiter, deferential and unimposing, returns to the table and pours enough of the cabernet and white Bordeaux into four glasses for the men to assess. Each takes a glass of red wine by its thin stem and holds it up to the dim light. First, they rest their noses on the edge of the bowl, sniff hard, and nod their approval of the round bouquet. Then they sip loudly and let the wine rush to the back of their throats to let their palates experience the full flavor.

Harmon's and Bruce's faces light up with mutual appreciation, but Bruce is the one whose approval signals the waiter to pour a glass of both red and white for the four of them.

"So, we saw a group of black folks and a van loaded with bikes pulling away from the Matisse museum yesterday. Was that you?" Cheryl asks.

"You mean I missed you?" Harmon sits across from Lena and scrutinizes her face, not for the first time. He has been staring at her since they sat down. Staring with lust and ordinary interest all at the same time, watching her hands as they punctuate her thoughts.

"A toast, to old friends and new. Let's see if I can recall a Yeats poem." Harmon pauses, his lips move in muted preparation. He looks from Cheryl to Bruce and rests his gaze on Lena. The heat of what would be a blush, if she blushed the way Cheryl does, covers her face.

"Forgive me for not quoting the exact words: 'Wine comes in at the mouth and love comes in at the eye; that's all we shall know for truth before we grow old and die. I lift the glass to my mouth, I look at you and sigh.'" He takes his time raising his glass to his mouth, lets it linger on his bottom lip.

"So where's the rest of the group?" Cheryl changes the subject for the sake of Lena's trembling hands.

"We biked near Avignon and the surrounding countryside—Aix-en-Provence, Châteaurenard, Gordes, Châteauneuf du Pape, and Arles a bit farther south. I can't even remember all of the names of the towns, there were so many of them." Bruce massages his thighs. "It was too much."

"City after city full of history. In Arles we walked through a coliseum that was built before Christ was born—avant Jesus. At least that's what I could make out—my French is rusty and wasn't that good to begin with—from the plaques at the entrance." Perhaps, Lena thinks, this is Harmon's version of small talk, and, as he wipes his palms with his napkin, she wonders if he is as nervous as she is.

"Two thousand years ago black folks ruled Africa," Cheryl says. "They probably fought in that coliseum. Bet that wasn't on the plaque."

"Yeah, that's what we said to the guide. He got a little freaked out about African blood mixing with French blood." Bruce adds, "The blood of our ancestors is everywhere."

The waiter appears at Bruce's side and asks in heavily accented, but grammatically correct English, if they have questions about the menu, if they need more time, or if they would like to order now. They don't, Bruce explains, except perhaps to pour a little more wine and a few appetizers to start. Harmon gives the waiter carte blanche to bring a few plates so they can sample the menu's offerings.

"I passed a brother—or what looked like a brother—in the lobby, after we left the pool. I smiled, but he turned his head. Have you noticed black folks don't acknowledge one another over here? I've tried to make eye contact with a few sisters." Lena makes quotation marks in the air; the last time she used her hands that way she was talking to Randall and Dr. Brustere. Stop. "No eye contact. Nothing. It's depressing."

"The only thing I can think of is that they either don't want to be associated with us or that color isn't as important to them as it is to Americans." Harmon speaks to the three of them, but his attention is on Lena.

Bruce goes on with an explanation: "It's simple. They're French, and for them that's what comes first. Heritage. Legacy. Birthright. That's what patrimony is all about." He pauses to let the power of patrimony sink in. "That's what's most important. Someone who looks like us, but is French, treats us the same as they would a white American. They assume we're ignorant because we don't speak their language. They view us not as slaves but as slightly beneath them—wrong word—less than them, because every American black is a descendant of slaves."

"Slavery or not, they're uninformed. They believe stereotypes based on TV and basketball." Cheryl's disposition is demure—meaning only the four of them can hear her—which Lena assumes is her way of being coy. The intense look on Bruce's face says he's serious now, and so Cheryl is serious, too, even as he breaks a chunk of bread from the small freshly baked loaves in front of him and slathers butter all over it.

"They should appreciate our commonality, our connections. If not in language, how about skin color, hair texture?" From the corner of her eye, Lena catches Harmon watching her. "Trust me, they're not as pure as they think. I hear it's the same way in some parts of Africa."

"I never have any problems with the French—black or white—and this is my third time here," Bruce says. "That includes this trip. Everyone's been really cordial, but heads did turn as twenty black folks went bicycling by. Especially in the smaller towns. I bet they've never seen so many of us, French or otherwise."

"Yeah, Bruce does well," Harmon chuckles at his buddy. "His only complaint is the food."

As if on cue, three waiters place dishes on the table with dramatic flare to allow time to admire the food's structured presentation: layered mullets in parsley butter sauce, thinly sliced meat in round swirls roasted tender enough to cut with a fork, delicate, a triangle of fresh anchovies sautéed in olive oil.

"How can someone contemplating a gourmet business complain about French food?" Lena frowns at Bruce. "The food is wonderful. Yesterday, in Vence, Cheryl and I had the best pork loin roast in the world."

"I don't disagree. The wine is great. The food is great." Bruce points to his ample belly with both hands. "It's the portion sizes that bother me."

Dinner is ordinary in the sense that conversation is smooth and entertaining. Bruce grins every time Cheryl asks him a question, answers like he has never told the important facts of his life to anyone but her. She knows more about his marketing vice presidency, his ex-wife, and one kid than Lena has learned about Harmon's recent past. The waiters serve at a moderate pace, giving them time to linger over each dish. All four work through the six-course meal—foie gras like butter; pale, flaky sea bass; salted crabmeat; sautéed sweetbreads with crawfish in a sauce that smells of the sea; a purée of bright green hothouse asparagus topped with dark red sun-dried tomatoes; soft, hard, and pungent cheeses—at a leisurely pace. The evening is less tense than Lena thought it would be. Fresh sea air blows through the restaurant, a pleasant mix of salt and perfume. The breeze is gentle enough to make the candles flicker, refreshing enough to clear cigarette smoke from the air.

Four hours pass, and when the bill comes, Bruce and Harmon insist on dividing the entire tab between the two of them.

"I did some research. Our options are a nearby club with disco music and dancing or the casinos in Monte Carlo," Bruce says, surprising Lena not for the first time this evening and causing her to reconsider him as playful and prepared.

"I pass." Lena pushes back from the table.

Harmon catches her left hand. "Stay. Have a glass of wine with me."

"Yes, stay with Harmon." Cheryl winks in a way that says she wants to do more than dance. "He'll make sure you get back to the hotel."

When the waiter appears at the table, Harmon orders another bottle of wine. "For savoring," he tells Lena. "And reminiscing. I've thought of you more times over the years than I can count on my fingers and toes."

"You should have been thinking about your wife."

"Did you ever think of me?" His face is momentarily innocent, like a young man's.

Harmon's birthday is two days after Randall's. Around that time the occasional thought of him entered into her mind and left just as easily; an empty thought more self-reflection or karmic happenstance than anything else. Although she would never tell Harmon this, doesn't want to give him the satisfaction, wants to keep the illusion going.

Then why is she sitting in this romantic restaurant with this man, this former lover, who thinks she is happily married?

"I worked in public relations for the city of Oakland for a while. I had a husband, kids, a household to run. When, or better yet, *why* would I have time to think about you?"

"Not even a little?"

She admits to the time she took Camille and Kendrick to the circus and an elephant pooped in front of them.

"What does it matter now?"

"I regretted marrying Natalie long before I found her in bed with Jessie. What do you think of that?" Harmon tells her that before their friendship ended, he questioned his buddy about Lena from time to time: Is she married? What's her husband like? Does she have children? What does she look like? Does she still take pictures? "I felt like a fool. I lost the chance to make it up to you." He tells Lena that he saw her once, sitting alone in the lobby of a Chicago hotel. He headed in her direction, but before he reached her, a man—he assumes that it was her husband—joined her and took her hand in his. Harmon considered speaking, meeting Lena's husband, but they appeared to be so much in love, the look on their faces told him they weren't interested in anyone or anything other than each other. He walked away. "I was young, dumb, and horny. Tell me who you are now."

"You've had entirely too much wine, and I need to leave."

"Ah, the elusive Lena. Always so secretive."

Secretive enough, Lena thinks in the silence of Harmon's pause, to never tell him she'd had his baby sucked out of her a month after she pushed him out of the car. Never regretted her decision.

Never told Randall. That wasn't secretiveness. It was their agreement: the past stayed in the past. They were born-again virgins, he said on their honeymoon. No one else mattered.

Harmon reaches for her hands. His are warm, hers cold. She cradles her hands in his for a moment until she tightens and pulls away. "Where's your wedding ring, Lena Harrison? You're not planning to cheat on your old man, are you?"

Isn't she behaving like a married woman? Is there an aroma, a pheromone that says she's no longer married? she wonders. She could change the subject, tell Harmon about Tina, about Camille and Kendrick.

"What the hell, Harmon. I never could lie. I'm divorced, or will be by the end of January."

"Why lie at all?"

"I wanted you to believe my life was perfect. And it was, almost, at least up until this year." She wants to tell Harmon that she hasn't harbored love for him—fondness maybe, but not love. There is a tender spot in her heart for him, but her love was always, is always, Randall. "Too much truth in wine." She raises her glass in a toast and takes another sip of the rich wine that tastes of blackberries and currants.

"I missed you."

"Bullshit."

"Truth."

"How can you claim to miss someone you *happened* to run into on the other side of the world?" She rolls her eyes, finally understanding the intent of her children's favorite response. "If this is your best line, Harmon Francis, you need to go back to the drawing board."

"I should've married you."

"I made my life, you yours." She can't help but chuckle. She wants to tell him that maybe the next time around he'll think with the head on his shoulders instead of the one between his legs, but he doesn't know what she knows. "You're not telling me that after all this time you're still pining for me, are you?"

"I can tell you that if you're game, I am." He divides more wine between the two of them.

"And if you hadn't seen me today, tomorrow, whenever?"

His face takes on that little boy look again. "You're the one that got away."

"Let's talk reality. Or at least if you're trying to seduce me, do it with fewer clichés." When Harmon smiles, Lena turns away to avoid his infectious humor.

"Then start by telling me who you are now."

Chapter 26

Harmon and Lena exchange stories of their lives like two fighters: shadowboxing, ducking, sparring, parrying.

After his divorce, he took a sabbatical from the law and moved, with his sons, to the Caribbean.

Her description of her present life is simple: she is in Nice to see Tina Turner in concert, and she will do whatever it takes to meet her, get an autograph, and take her picture.

He spent three years as a consultant in St. John, studying the potential for start-up technology businesses before he moved to Chicago.

Once she returns to Oakland, there is a new job at the museum and photography classes. She borders him in a frame using the thumbs and forefingers of both hands. Thinks of what angle might best capture the waning candlelight.

The restaurant is empty; the bottle before them half full. The wait staff, in their impeccable French way, stand at a distance yet close enough to anticipate a signal of what to do next. Harmon winks at the waiter, who hands him two clean glasses, corks and wraps the bottle in a white napkin.

◆ ◆ ◆

Outside, the sky is black. The lamps glow yellow along the promenade, lighting the path like mini moons. A cool breeze dusts Lena's shoulders with chill bumps. They walk not hand in hand but close enough to brush against each other and continue their conversation in disjointed phrases.

He loves Shakespeare, reads it, memorizes passages—a relief from the stiffness of legal language.

She takes pictures of buildings, architectural details, vertical lines. Inanimate things: doors, rusty fences, nails. This trip is about finding Tina Turner, about finding herself.

The promenade is edged with planked wood benches with wrought iron arms that swirl and curve and invite. Harmon waits for her to sit before he does.

"I don't want to be seen as spineless. My choices so consumed me, I lost all respect for myself."

"I find that hard to believe," he says, splashing wine into their glasses.

"In retrospect, so do I. But that's behind me now. I'm moving on." She knows this is a lie, or not quite a lie, but a good misrepresentation of the truth when she still thinks of Randall and their life together nearly every day. "Or trying to."

"So, what's your next step? I mean after Tina?"

"Must you ask so many questions?"

"It's how I make my living. And I'm nervous."

"Nervous? You're a big hunk. Why would you be nervous around l'il ole me?"

"It's good to see you. Good to be around you. You always made me a little nervous." Harmon is serious. The lines framing his mouth say take him at his word.

Between the chilly night air, Harmon, and the flittering in her stomach, Lena feels twenty all over again. On a first date with no idea of what to do except stifle a giggle. "I think I should get back to the hotel," she says without moving from the bench.

"You were always a little unpredictable and very demanding. I don't mean that in a negative sense. I mean that you make a man step up his game. Your standards were pretty high. Maybe that's why your husband couldn't handle you."

Now she does laugh. Laughs at the thought of Randall's inability to handle her or anyone. No one has called her unpredictable in a long time. She left it at the altar when she said, "I do," and let unpredictability morph into indecisiveness. "And what about you?"

"I love the law, but I'm tired of it. When you're a litigator, you fight every day. My sons called the knots that come up here," he says, touching the wide space between his eyebrows, "'meanies,' because whenever I was in trial I wore them night and day. I'm looking to make a change. I want to make this next part of my life as good as but as different from the first as I can."

If this were a date, Lena thinks, they would rush to fill the gaps in their conversation. Neither makes the effort. They sip their wine and allow themselves to mull over topics too silly to repeat out loud; the tacit free association of couples comfortable with silence. A family strolls past them oblivious to the late hour the way Americans might be. The parents hold flashlights while the children rush to dig and dump sand into small pails.

"You remember the night I told you that I was going to choose between you and Natalie?" Harmon waits for Lena to signal yes. "Stupid, huh?"

Lena thinks of her own dependence on Randall and shakes her head no. "Most men wouldn't admit it, that's all."

"I've been divorced for thirteen years. I like my independence, but I'd be lying if I didn't admit to something I feel right now, something I thought I'd forgotten. You wear your sadness on your sleeve. Did you know that?" He wants to see her photographs, take her to bed, rid her of that sadness. Make up for his mistake. Create something new. See where it goes.

He is the litigator, she thinks, forger of compelling arguments, and her face smarts in the intensity of his words. She feels it. He feels it. She understands that her first step must be to slow down and not be swept away by supposition. Anything she does, any new relationship she starts, must be on her terms.

"I'm sure I never told you this—I'm only beginning to understand it myself. My theory has evolved over the years; I believe everything that happens is part of a master plan, a divine plan created by a higher being. God, Allah, whomever." He divides the last of the wine between their glasses. "I'm not a religious man, but I consider myself a spiritual one. I've practiced law too long to believe in coincidences."

"You Leos can be philosophical and idealistic about how life should be." Not caring much for astrology until she met with Vernon, Lena looked up the characteristics of the sign to try to understand her Leo husband better. The similarities and differences in the two men are recognizable: they both love the finer things in life, yet uncontrolled impetuosity is a characteristic Randall could never be accused of.

"Don't dismiss me, Lena, I'm serious."

"This is coincidence, Harmon." Lena points at everything around her. "We happen to be in the same place at the same time, and I don't view it as anything else but that."

Harmon explains that if she were to look at coincidence as mere happenstance, random events, or factors colliding, then yes, that would be true. But if she views coincidence as the coming together of a set of predetermined circumstances controlled by a hierarchical being, then no. "This is no coincidence. This is fate."

The beach is far from empty. The crowds are sparse along this path, but groups of roving young people, couples, and a few solitary figures walk the beach and the promenade. The energy, the socializing, the celebration of the warm weather she observed on her first day in Nice continues late into the night. The lights, the wine do not mask or allow Lena to avoid Harmon's intensity, the possibility of his theory as truth.

"What happens when a person doesn't believe in a hierarchical being? What controls fate then?"

"It doesn't matter if you believe or not. Freedom of choice guides us to our inevitable fate. You could have very easily chosen another heroine." Harmon lowers his voice to a level just above the whoosh of the breaking sea. "Then where would you have gone, or would you have gone anywhere? You think fate has nothing to do with us meeting again?"

Someone from your past is waiting for you. Vernon's words, his prediction. Is Harmon that someone?

Tina's performance, that first time around, brought Lena and Randall together; their separation brought her back to Tina, and Tina brought her to the south of France and Harmon. Is that, she wonders, coming full circle, coincidence or fate? "I know that for the longest time, I let someone else make my choices, and when you do that you lose your power. Even though some choices were made from love, there was an element of control, too."

"Yet here you are in charge of you," Harmon says.

"This is my fate because I planned it."

"Or because your plan is part of a larger one."

Harmon provides the opportunity, the dimly lit hallway the ambience. He holds her for a long time. Lena relaxes into his shoulder. Her body aches with his touch, makes her feel her need. It is the touch of his hand on her neck, his hand against her cheek, her arm, his thigh against her thigh. It has been months since a man has touched her—with passion or not. Months since a man has tasted her.

"Invite me in." A meaningful medley of warnings swims around Lena's head: blood tests, condoms, HIV screenings, complications from one-night stands for baby boomers unaccustomed to playing the field after such long timeouts. Harmon holds her; his lips soft against her own seem to fit her mouth. He leans against the doorjamb, holding her hand, and Lena feels like a teenager at the door of her parents' home.

"Why should I?" This is not revenge, she thinks, although it is definitely lust. Her chance to prove him wrong. She wants sex, and she'll have it. Maybe Harmon, maybe not. She is probably overthinking sex—like Bobbie knew she was overthinking Tina.

"We're adults. Adults way over fifty." Harmon slides his forefinger down the length of Lena's cheek. "No need to play games. I want to be with you. I want you to know how sorry I am."

"You've apologized." Lena smirks, thinking back to that long-ago conversation with Jessie. "Why would I want to be with someone who was less than satisfied with my bedroom performance?" Gotcha.

Harmon chuckles. "Like you say, that was a long time ago. I could offer a couple of bullshit reasons to explain my idiocy. Hopefully, I'm smarter than that now." He pulls Lena into his arms and kisses her again. Long. Slow. Hungry. Hard.

Lena slips the magnetic card into the lock; the machinery whirs and the door springs open as Harmon turns to leave. Inside, the lights are on, the room is empty, and Cheryl is nowhere to be found. Why, she wonders, should she deny herself? What difference does it make what Harmon thought twenty-six years ago? She's not the same person she was six months, let alone twenty-six years, ago. Old habits die hard. Break those habits, is what Tina would say. Take the next step to the new Lena.

"We're both too old for games this time around, Harmon." She reaches for his hand and guides him into the room, presses her body, her lips, against his. He tastes like wine: blackberries and currants. She is in control, and his body shows her he likes it.

Slow. Slow. She wants to go slow. To relish what she hasn't felt for almost eight months. Harmon's body, uncannily familiar in this foreign place, molds into hers. He smells like a waning winter fire, like expensive cologne she knows but can't remember the name of.

Not like Randall: pepper and cinnamon. Lena shrinks away from Harmon and moves to the other side of the room. Will she remember how to make love, to screw, to get it on? "I can't."

When he reaches her, leaning against the curtains as if they were the only things holding her up, Harmon presses his fingers to her lips. "You're safe with me." With the rhythm of an easy two-step, they move past the bathroom and the desk and the mess she wishes wasn't there. To the bed. They touch: she his rounded belly, he her rounded hips.

Lena bends beside the lamp and reaches for the switch. Let the darkness hide her imperfections: the scar of her caesarian, the mound of her stomach, her dimpled thighs. Harmon pulls her hand away from the light.

"What do you fear right now?" He makes the moment stop; his way of going slow. Talking. He strokes her neck, glides his tongue across her shoulder, unzips her dress, the metal of the zipper so close to her skin she shivers as Harmon inches it down her back. Her dress slips to the floor with a faint swish.

"My body… I'm not twenty-nine anymore."

Harmon takes off his jacket, unbuttons his shirt, and lets his pants drop to the floor. Stepping out of his pants and shoes, he removes the rest of his clothes and tosses them on the other bed. "And neither am I." He stands, naked, in front of Lena and takes her hand. Like a brush skimming an artist's canvas, he moves her hand to his shoulder. "This is where they cut me when I had surgery on my shoulder." He presses her hand against the thick scar and lowers it to a rough, keloid line of skin near his waist. "And this is from having my appendix removed." His voice is deep and thoughtful. "They thought I might die, I was in so much pain before they took it out."

The memory of sex with Harmon floods back. He likes to mix up the senses of touch and hearing, of taste and sight. The effect of concentrating on mind and body makes the room seem to spin around them. *Randall's hands talked all over her body.* Harmon unhooks her bra, slides her panties down down down, drops to his knees, and nibbles at the scar that crosses her stomach. "Tell me."

"I was in labor sixteen hours before they cut me." Twenty-three years with one man. They grew accustomed to one another; predictable. "Take your time."

Harmon kisses the mole below her collarbone, cups her breasts in his hands, kneads them, blows his warm breath across her nipples, presses his lips to them. Lena's body goes limp, then arches, relishing in this touch, in the here and now.

They go on like this and more. Licking, sucking, swaying in rhythm to the music in her head. He hears the same song; he moves with her. Onto the bed, beneath the sheets, grinding like there is no tomorrow. They are awkward and familiar at the same time.

"Feel it, Lena." He pushes while her body throbs. "Feel how sorry I am."

This is not making love; she does not love him.

Pepper and cinnamon. The thin scar at the base of Randall's throat. Unexpected sadness and joy.

Slow then fast. Fast then slow. "Say you forgive me."

Randall's fingers played her back like a piano. Lena shivers. Old images creep between the sheets and, as hard as she tries, the vision of Randall, of that curve between his shoulder and neck, the knot of his Adam's apple, will not disappear. Will not disappear while her body follows Harmon's moves so strong and sweet.

Until death do us part; loving his body, his mind, forever. Never, never again was she to be with, to feel this good with, another man.

His caresses move from her throat to thigh. Tingling, a moan stirring between her thighs, pulling, moving up her stomach, over her breast, and catching in her throat. It consumes her, that heat, and she holds her breath, releases, breathes into his stroke until she cannot remember where she is. "It doesn't matter. Doesn't matter anymore."

Lena squints at the clock beside her bed and tiptoes into the bathroom. Looking in the mirror, she splashes cold water on her puffy face and prays that Harmon took her tears for joy. She turns the shower on, steps into the oversized tub, and lets the hot water beat against her skin.

"Can I join you?" Harmon asks from the other side of the bathroom.

"Isn't it time you went back to your room?" She grins and summons him with her fingers. In the old days they smoked after sex like in the movies, and she wonders where those dark cigarettes are. Harmon presses against her back. She wants him to leave, wants him to stay. Wants to do it one more time.

His body says he wants her, too, and she wants to say, not so bad after all; but this touch, this rubbing against her, this heat is all she wants. Harmon's hands glide over her body. He turns Lena around to face him. "Seeing ghosts?"

"Now it's my turn to be sorry," she whispers. Slowly, deliberately, she nuzzles with lips, with hand, his swollen organ, the curve of his arm, the scar at his waist, the rise of his chest. Lena nibbles his shoulder, strokes him until he moans and moans. He is a hungry man—her body his buffet: her face, her navel, the crisscross scar on her knee. He sucks at her impatiently while the water beats against his back, enters her sweet wetness, pushes pushes pushes until she believes she cannot breathe; and yet she does.

Chapter 27

"So, did you sleep with him?" Cheryl lets the sugar from the shaker rain into her coffee. "I waited a polite amount of time before I asked. Aren't you proud of me?"

The air is filled with the aromas of everyday life: bread and yeast, croissants, thyme, rosemary, lavender, rose potpourri, orange blossom tea. The café at the old Negresco Hotel is a comfortable meeting spot after their full morning of aimless rambling, watching the tourists and the huge yachts make their way across the sea. Lena grumbles and sips one of the two café crèmes sitting in front of her and dips a flaky croissant into the other.

"Oh, you did! You did!" Cheryl's shrill excitement attracts the stares of the people around her. She lowers her voice. "If you didn't, you would have denied it by now. Hooray! Tell me everything."

Lena flips through *Paris Match,* eyes fastened to the page, even though she doesn't understand one word in the famous French magazine. "Nope. You tell me about Bruce."

"You are sooo chickenshit." Cheryl yanks the magazine away from her girlfriend's hand and grins. "Well, if you won't talk, I will."

Bruce and Cheryl stayed out all night; it hadn't been their intention, but that's the way it ended up. The restaurant hostess told them, on their way out, about a disco for the over-forty, sophisticated crowd. They found their way to the club, danced until one to old Motown music, then left when the deejay changed to techno. Feeling full of energy, they went to Monte Carlo and gambled all night long, with Bruce's money. Cheryl kept her winnings.

"I won a thousand euros at the roulette table. And to top it off, we didn't even sleep together. We found a café and ate a big American-style breakfast. We talked. Can you believe that?" Cheryl slaps Lena's arm. "So. . . did you or didn't you?"

"I wonder if they have cheese?" Lena turns to the side, the side opposite Cheryl's eager face, and scours the chalkboard sign above the bar. "*Fromage*. That's it, right?"

"What are you hiding it for, Lena? You're a grown woman. It's not like you're having an affair. You might as well tell me now. I'll be able to tell when you two are together, anyway."

"You'll just have to wait till then." Lena yawns. "Lighten up."

Bruce and Harmon look like Mutt and Jeff together. Instead of short and tall, they are tall and taller. As the two men approach the café, women on the street turn, their smiles flirtatious and appreciative at the same time. Both men acknowledge the women and keep their eyes on Cheryl and Lena.

"Yep, you did," Cheryl teases. "He stared last night. Today he looks satisfied."

Bruce runs his hand over the top of her head. Cheryl cuddles into him. Lena has never seen any man dare to touch Cheryl's hair, nor has she ever seen her friend's blush appear because of a man's attention. Bruce is different from the kind of man Cheryl dates, perhaps because he is closer to her own age, perhaps because his stomach extends beyond his waistband by more than a little and there is a lot of gray in his thinning hair. Lena thought Cheryl preferred struggling artistic types—she asked for Imara-bartender-artist's number after Marcia's party. The heavy bracelet dangling from Bruce's left wrist, the gold Cartier digging into his right wrist, his alligator sandals—all suggest money. There is tenderness in his eyes when he looks at Cheryl, and his look evokes the same in hers.

"So what's the plan?" Bruce asks.

Fourteen days to the concert; days of moderate heat, cloudless skies, and soft breezes. Four have come and gone since Lena and Cheryl arrived in Nice, and Lena hasn't researched Villefranche or figured out how she can get backstage to meet Tina without seeming like a crazed fan.

"Lena's looking for Tina Turner. I'm just along for the ride," Cheryl titters. "She's her role model."

Lena rolls her eyes, wondering if this channeling of Camille will never stop. Cheryl is a blabbermouth; her quirks are starting to come back to Lena.

"Are you're going to change your hairstyle to match Tina's? Maybe there's a wig shop around here." Bruce howls at this thought. "Or maybe we can find a Thunderdome outfit. The possibilities are endless."

"I don't know you, Bruce. And you don't know me well enough to mock me." Before Tina, before Vence and Philip, before Harmon, Lena knows her first inclination would have been to cut her eyes at Cheryl and stomp off to the barrier that separates the café from the street. Now she hits Bruce's arm with a half-playful, half serious punch.

"Hey, it was funny. No biggie. I'm sorry." Bruce turns from Cheryl to Harmon then Lena with a quizzical look on his face. Lena wonders how it is that such a big man can be so whiny.

"Bruce is only kidding. It takes a while to get used to his sense of humor. You'll get to understand him, once you've been around him longer. But I've got to admit, I'm as curious as he doesn't know how to say he is. Why Tina?"

Traffic horns blare. If she closed her eyes, Lena thinks, they could be anywhere. She prays Harmon's intentions are as sincere as his words. Had he always been this caring? Last night they stayed awake until the drapes lightened with the morning sun. Before she told him he had to go back to his room, he asked more about her than anyone has in a long time. What she wants out of life, what her next steps are. Why she is no longer married. If she is still in love with her soon-to-be ex.

"She conquered fear." Lena takes in the view and releases a long sigh. This is not just anywhere. Everything from the calm sea to the stone-faced mountains is old, historic. The houses, the wrought iron balconies, the massive buildings, sidewalks, the streets. "I don't know why I'm being so defensive. It feels good to say it out loud: Tina conquered fear. She makes me feel like I can do anything, makes me know change is possible, and age isn't a barrier."

If the acknowledgment that spreads over Cheryl's face, even Bruce's chubby face and Harmon's, has not made this trip, this search, worth the pain it cost, then Lena is not clear what will.

"Tina Turner hasn't got a thing on you." Harmon reaches over to hug Lena and, to her surprise, so does Bruce.

"Are you ready to get going?" Maybe, Lena thinks, this is Bruce's apology. "What's the plan?"

"It's not quite eleven." Cheryl bats her eyes at Bruce, who has learned to bat back and seems, to Lena, smitten.

There is a tranquil nature to the aimlessness their vacation has taken that, Lena thinks, she might apply to her life. The lack of purpose evokes a sense of the unknown and freedom and a taste of the unpredictable. In Nice, the Mediterranean anchor is always to the east. Lena cannot get lost here; she has to figure out what her anchor in this new life will be.

"We're off to Eze so Lena can take pictures."

Lena can't recall if they discussed a plan when Harmon phoned earlier that morning, although the high and winding Corniche is a sight she wants to see.

"Do whatever you would do if I wasn't taking your picture. Talk." Lena points the camera lens to Harmon's face and adjusts it to the left and right until his profile is clear through the viewfinder. She waits for him to expose the tips of his teeth, then presses the shutter button twice. "Be serious."

"I'm on vacation." Harmon poses, makes a face like a naughty ten-year-old, and tugs at the sides of his mouth with both hands. He sticks out his tongue. She snaps again. Harmon points to the sturdy metal railing and guides Lena to the potted olive tree in front of it. He entwines Lena's waist with both arms and presses his cheek to hers. They smile while the server figures out how to take their picture and include the dreary sky and smoke-colored clouds at their backs.

When the server places the check and his credit card on the table, Harmon signs the slip, draws a heart, and scribbles the initials HF + LH inside it. "Maybe that's not a manly reaction, but it's me. My sons would whoop up a storm if they could see me. Bruce is having a field day. Blustery lawyer, supposedly adamant and logical. I feel like a kid who found a special something he thought he'd lost, that's been lost for a long time."

"How can you care so quickly?" She asks, praying that he won't ask her to answer the same question.

"I know what I want when I see it, and frivolous youth doesn't count."

"You were thirty-six. I was almost thirty. Since when are the thirties frivolous?"

Litigation, he explains, requires well-timed assessments of facts and circumstances, and strong arguments. "So your unasked question is: if I hadn't run into you would I be paying as much attention to someone else I picked up between my bike trip and my return home?"

Eze is too beautiful, the day too divine to question Harmon's flirtation, but Lena wants answers nevertheless. Once again their deep conversations are surrounded by food and water.

"As a matter of fact, there was a woman on the biking trip. We were checking each other out, on the verge of . . . you know. My point is, you'll notice she isn't with me."

"And she's probably pissed as hell, too."

Harmon shrugs.

"You dog. I better watch myself." Lena shrugs, too, unsure if her sarcastic admonition is for herself or Harmon.

Harmon and Lena wander from the limestone terrace of Château Eza's restaurant high above Nice, closer to Monte Carlo and Menton, and through its arched entryway back to the village. The uneven and narrow streets of Eze are filled, but not crowded, with other tourists wandering about, their single intention to browse. In this medieval town, history has settled in brick walls washed with the acid of time.

Lena focuses her camera. *Snap.* For the most part, the ancient buildings of every street are filled with boutiques and galleries. An iron gate—Porte des Maures—blocks the curious from a craggy path leading down the mountain. *Snap. Snap.* A sign, in French and English, tells all that in the year 900, Moors passed through the gateway to invade the village and occupied Eze for more than seventy years. Lena points out to Harmon that this was probably the last time a multitude of dark-skinned people were ever in Eze or any city around the Mediterranean.

Does it bother Tina that she stands out? Stardom would do that anyway. Perhaps this is a difference between Lena and her celebrity heroine. Oakland and the Bay Area is a melting pot that Lena loves. The lack of diversity, this different kind of diversity, at least in Nice, is what makes Lena know she couldn't live here.

Harmon changes direction and leads them to a small plaza off the main street. The church, Notre Dame de Asuncion, connects to a cemetery where French veterans from the two World Wars lie in rest. From where they stand, even though the sky is overcast, they can see the topography of the land. The dark promontories of the southern coast are stubby like papier-maché hills against the dull gray water. The view is far better than what can be seen from a plane; almost touchable, closer without queasiness.

"It's like having one foot in the plaza and the other in heaven."

Lena plays with the exposure meter on her camera and snaps more pictures with and without Harmon in them.

"I have an idea."

"Just look at the view and act like you're enjoying yourself."

"Let me help you look for Tina's house."

"Even though you're a wonderful diversion, Harmon Francis, meeting Tina is a promise I'll fulfill on my own."

"So, substitute me for Cheryl, or add me to the equation. Take your pick. I'll be your guide."

"I'll think about it."

Inside the church a box of votive candles and wooden matches rest on a creaky table in front of a statue of Our Lady of the Ascension. Wind teases the flames beneath the statue. Lena strikes a match and lights four candles before depositing euros in a metal coin box.

"It looks like a traveler's prayer written underneath the statue." Harmon sticks his face close to the verse and translates. "'Let this light that I offer be my hope before my Lord and the Virgin and guide me to contentment wherever I go.'"

"Now, that," Lena says, teasing and truthful at the same time, "strikes me as divine."

Chapter 28

"Lena!" Cheryl yells from the terrace. Reading on the sunny balcony has become her ritual. Each morning she pores over pictures of European celebrities and decodes the French words that look like English ones. She buys several papers every day from metal-framed kiosks and periodical stores jammed with gossip, crossword, and cooking magazines in layers six inches thick. The covers are brilliant: handsome politicians, gorgeous film stars, lush red tomatoes, bouquets of deep green basil, country châteaus, skinny models clad in outrageous haute couture. "There's a picture in this paper of Tina Turner shopping in Villefranche-sur-Mer."

The only evidence of Lena's presence in the room is the long, crumpled lump in her bed. Apprehension has taken hold of her body; nervous anticipation. The covers hide the top of her head. Can she sink any deeper into the soft mattress? Should she try to find Tina now, before the concert? Does she want Harmon, Cheryl, and Bruce to go with her? What will she say if she's allowed through the gates that surely must protect Tina from outsiders and autograph seekers?

If this were a trip planned for Lena's family, every detail of it would have been written, memorized, and ready to execute. She should have thought through the possibilities: written a letter to Tina and asked for fifteen minutes like she used to grant to community groups seeking an audience with the mayor. Just fifteen minutes, Tina, fifteen minutes to get an autograph, to take a picture and say thanks.

Underneath this six hundred thread-count tent, she checks her cell phone for messages in case Lulu, or one of the kids, has called. Randall's picture appears on the screen—the one she took when she got her new phone over a year ago; he sits on the couch, arms reaching to the camera, thumbs up. He looks like Kendrick or vice versa.

"Lena?"

"It's Randall. He called."

"Ignore him. Leave it to the big shot to spend money on an international call to find out what cleaners you sent his shirts to or the name of the store that carries his precious little-eared pasta. Yuck."

For a minute, one short minute, Lena wonders what Randall needs, how she can help. She presses her finger against the button to retrieve Randall's message: call me.

"Did you hear me? Tina is in town. We can all meet her." Cheryl reaches for the phone. "I'll tell Bruce to get the car."

Lena hits the delete key, thankful once again for Tina—to take her mind off Randall this time—and wonders when finding Tina Turner became a *we,* instead of *me,* quest? Is the *we* she and Cheryl or is it what has now become their almost inseparable foursome? Harmon and Lena have scoured Nice for new sidewalk cafés and local gossip about Tina. They have pondered this question—Lena more than the others—as the captain of the yacht Bruce and Harmon rented sailed along the southern coast. It is their morning routine, familiar if only after five days. They've studied maps and travel books and combined stops at antiques shops that sell old Rolexes, Baume & Merciers, French military chronographs, and Jaeger-LeCoultre watches on the way to visit ancient mansions converted into art museums.

"I'm feeling like this is something that only the two of us, or maybe I, should do."

Cheryl hangs up the phone. "Bruce says to be ready in thirty minutes."

Lena lies back down on the bed. "I'll wait until Harmon and Bruce leave. And what do you think Randall wanted? I wonder if the kids are okay."

"Well, if they're not, he'll call back. Or better yet, call them yourself. Duh. Go with the flow."

"If you'll notice, if you can notice anything other than Bruce and shopping, you'll see I *am* 'flowing.'" She hadn't planned on Harmon, she continues. Hadn't planned to sleep with him, to spend virtually every waking hour with him. Hadn't planned to feel happy—not in this way. They've held hands as they walk the cobblestone streets. Harmon opens doors for her; offers her a first taste of his wine, his main course, his dessert, and she takes it. They talk late into the night, aware that their days together are numbered, and made love more than they should, they've said, for people their age.

"I didn't plan on Bruce—or let's just say I planned to meet a man, and Bruce more than qualifies. That's where the fun comes in." Cheryl flicks her hand.

Randall—what the hell does he want? Last night Harmon asked Lena if she was over her husband. Lena was shocked to hear him refer to Randall, less by his question than how difficult it has been to get rid of thoughts of Randall. She admitted that her soon-to-be ex creeps into her thoughts in restaurants when the menus are full of nothing but the crab, shrimp, and exquisite cheese he loves; on the steep hills of Cimiez that she and Randall would have walked instead of driven. She won't admit what she thinks when they're in bed, though his ghost is fading there.

"I envy you, Cheryl."

"No need to be jealous. Follow my example."

"I'll work on it," Lena says, dialing her phone. "After I touch base with Kendrick and Camille."

"They're fine. Or at least Camille says she is. Kendrick didn't answer his phone." Lena signals to Cheryl before the valet pulls the rental Mercedes in front of the hotel. Harmon eases behind the steering wheel so that Lena can sit beside him and avoid the new sensation of motion sickness she suffers whenever Bruce takes the sharp curves of the winding roads at twice the posted kilometers per hour.

"Tell me what you know about where Tina Turner lives." Harmon drives up a hill toward the middle of the three mountain roads that meander above and away from Nice.

She rifles through a manila folder. The hours spent scouring the Internet have left her with an inch-thick file on the woman, the vicinity of her villa, what she likes and doesn't like. "I don't have a street or an address." Harmon winces, and Lena braces for a complaint like Randall would issue if they were lost or undirected. His eyes stay on the road, and he whistles as they slowly approach a curve.

"Isn't there some kind of map to the homes of the stars?" Cheryl asks.

"This isn't Hollywood, Cheryl."

"Well, what's the plan? If there's no plan, let's head to the casino. I'm feeling lucky." Bruce's loose plans have redeemed him from his rudeness and overeating and helped them see all of Nice. "Thanks to my lucky charm." He wraps his arm around Cheryl's shoulder. Bruce's silk shorts swish with the touch of what Lena sees from the corner of her eye is Cheryl's hand in a place she wishes she didn't see.

"I'm not in the mood to gamble." Lena faces the road ahead and the worn asphalt. The sides of the mountain are sandy white with bits of cactus-like shrubbery protruding from random jags.

Cheryl scoots close to the front seat and Lena's ear. "The mantra is, 'Have fun.' Remember?"

Lena dismisses Cheryl's advice with a wave of her hand. Being with Harmon has been fun; roaming the streets of Nice and all the surrounding hill towns has been fun. This is not fun. It smacks too much of what she came to Nice to forget. Harmon reaches his hand to free Lena's from their tight clasp in her lap. Vernon's words come back to her: delight in what can be. Definitely worth the hundred bucks she spent. Lena takes Harmon's hand and squeezes it. "Okay. Let's do it."

"Then what's the plan?" Bruce asks again. "In my business, success requires planning."

Just like with Randall. She has no plan. Why, she wonders, isn't she learning from all that has happened? "I wasn't prepared for a group."

"What's the matter with all of us looking? That can be the plan." Cheryl rejoins. "I'd like to meet Tina, too."

At the arrow marking Villefranche-sur-Mer, Harmon turns right and down the main road where the city slopes toward the sea. Heat vapors rise from the medieval rooftops blurring together orange, ochre, and blue.

"Since we're here, I guess there's no harm in asking around." Lena releases and relaxes into the leather seat.

"We'll walk around, have a little something to eat. Shop and see what happens." Harmon's words are meant to encourage. "If we do see her, I'll make sure you get to her first. I promise we won't spoil your plans."

This smaller city is as busy as Nice and full of cafés with limestone terraces and smartly dressed women dining on paltry portions of food. Nice, Menton, Cagnes-sur-Mer, Mougins, Villefranche, Eze, Vence all resemble one another: time-stained brick walls connecting the twenty-first century to the Middle Ages;

twisting streets, famous artists—this one Cocteau—a house or hotel marking where each lived and created art. Fortresses that provided protection against invasion that look the same, but don't look the same, and Lena marvels at the beauty man can create when survival is of the utmost importance.

Every city in the south of France has a visitor's bureau. This one is housed on the ground floor of a three-story building. A wood-framed picture window is filled with posters of Villefranche-sur-Mer, the homes along the hillside, and yachts afloat in the port. Inside the bureau, one woman among the staff of five admits to speaking English. "Hello," she calls out from behind her desk.

Harmon steps forward and asks if anyone knows where Tina Turner lives. He carries himself with an air of responsibility and privilege. The woman puts on her glasses, then looks him up and down. Stepping to the counter, she tells him she has heard Madame Turner lives near the top of the Colline du Vinaigrier; that many tourists come to look for the celebrity, but that Madame does not come to town often. It is possible she shops or has lunch in *la vielle ville*—the old town—the woman doesn't know, she is not a fan.

"There are other celebrities that *habitent*—live—in this area as well," the woman says. "Messieurs Bono and Elton John." She lays a map over the counter and bends over it, motioning to Harmon to do the same. She gives vague directions to the hill where Tina's Villa Anna Fleur could be and goes on to say that at each of the very expensive homes in that area there are guards and secured gates. "We French are not secretive, simply very, how would you say, hush-hush, monsieur? There is no way to tell who lives where, but there is a rumor that her villa is higher up the mountain than Monsieur Bono's."

Harmon proffers his full chipped-tooth smile and bows. Lena watches him work his magic on the woman and hopes that he can do the same with Cheryl and Bruce and get them interested in these other famous people's homes, although Sonny Bono is the only Bono she knows, and he died years ago.

"We'll drive around for a while. It won't hurt to do a little reconnaissance preparation." Harmon looks at Lena when he speaks. "Or would you rather get something to eat first?"

"Maybe Tina would like to meet a couple of hip brothers and sisters from the States. That can't happen too often." Cheryl offers her reason why Tina would want to open her doors to them. "There can't be too many black folks that come through here."

"Whatever works," Bruce says. "But whatever we do, we need to make it quick."

Three blocks past the laurier-rose the woman described, up the crest of the hills and past an old stone wall. Harmon cannot follow the signs and drive at the same time. The woman gave Lena a postcard from a website that describes nightlife, shopping, and the celebrities in and around this area. Usually the postcards in Nice show pictures of the sea from a vantage point in the hills. This one is of a building close to the water's edge, marked with a red arrow pointing to a gathering of palm trees and brush on top of the hill. "Tina's villa" is written in block letters.

They drive up and up past many gates with iron forged into initials, flowers, and what look like family crests. The juices in Lena's stomach gurgle from nausea and anticipation. What will she say if they find Tina? She has a vague speech prepared for after the concert, but if they run into Tina here they would appear to be fanatical. Her intention to thank Tina would be lost. So close and so far away.

From this high up Lena observes, like she did in Eze, that the world lies before them, this time from a different angle. Full, thick trees frame the view of Cap Ferrat and the coast toward Monaco.

"Without a street address we could wander aimlessly for hours." Harmon steers carefully from left to right. He opens his window and sticks his head out every time they come to an initialed gate in hope that they will come across the letters TT or a guard who, seeing their fancy car, might feel sorry for them and give them better directions than they have.

"Man, I don't know about you, and you'll forgive me, Lena, but I've about had it up to here with these roads and quaint cities." Bruce yawns.

"I like the snaky roads. It's part of history," Lena says. "Even you said the French take pride in their history."

"I say let's take our pride and get out of the south of France." Bruce looks directly at Harmon's eyes in the rearview mirror as he speaks. Lena catches this coded signal and saddens at the thought of Harmon's departure. All things in their time.

"What's the plan?" Cheryl looks at Bruce, having picked up the signal as well.

"After the bike trip, we'd always planned to go to Paris for four days, then head back to Chicago. Harmon and I were thinking maybe you two would—"

"Yes!" Cheryl's voice is resolute.

"I've got unfinished business here." Lena has seen Paris, twice. Has seen the Eiffel Tower, the Champs-Élysées, wandered through the Père-Lachaise cemetery, and bought handmade umbrellas in the boutique on the Boulevard Saint-Germain. She adores the City of Lights.

"Should we flip a coin? Heads Paris, tails Paris. Either way, I'm going." Harmon swerves the car to the side of the road and searches his pockets for a coin. "It's only a couple of days."

"Only a couple of days," Bruce says. "Nine hours by car, a little over five by train, and, most importantly, a quick trip of about an hour and a half by plane. What say you, ladies?"

Lena is amazed at Bruce's collection of seemingly unrelated facts. If nothing else, she has gained respect for the man. Her Tina Turner folder sits in her lap, research that has led nowhere; no closer to finding Tina than she was when they stepped off the plane. But she cannot deny the calm, the pluckiness that has gathered in her heart and soul since she has been in France. Whether it is Tina or Harmon or whacky Cheryl, she is thankful. "I've been there before. Too many memories."

"No Eiffel Tower, no Notre Dame, no Louvre. We'll go to places neither of us has seen before. C'mon. Tina would want you to take advantage of the moment."

Randall would have demanded; Harmon is asking. Does it make a difference? Because, bottom line, isn't she hitching herself to somebody else's star all over again?

Chapter 29

A limousine whisks the four travelers away from the airport, the cars, jitneys, a cab driver arguing with a gendarme over the parking lot exit fee and whizzes along a freeway that resembles an American turnpike: heavy trucks, modern office buildings, apartments, and factories to the left and right of the road; fields of green, industrial warehouses, Ikea.

"What should we do first? I say: Sacré-Coeur or the Panthéon." Harmon pokes Bruce's shoulder. "No eating."

Bruce's expression implies his difference of opinion. "That's what you think."

"Paris is eye candy," Lena says. "Everywhere is someplace different. Walk and look, that's what I want to do."

Paris is divided into twenty spiraling sections like the chambers of a nautilus shell; each *arrondissement* is different, a city within a city. On their first trip to Paris, Lena and Randall roamed for days in silly search of the red dividing lines so carefully drawn in guidebooks—which were nowhere to be seen. Instead, they ended up with twenty photos of themselves, one for each arrondissement, standing beside the twelve-inch-high blue signs with white lettering that mark the districts.

"I want to taste as many of the four hundred varieties of cheese as I possibly can." Lena reaches for Harmon's hand. "And discover new wines."

As the car gets closer to the center of Paris, the tip of the Eiffel Tower appears in the distance and the city changes. Now the buildings, their slate tiles and zinc roofs and stone in all shades of beige and oyster, become more weathered and wear their centuries proudly. People line the sidewalks from curb to building edges. The Seine splits the city; the spires of churches split the skyline.

"Shopping. Right Bank couture, rue Saint-Honoré, Left Bank hip—that works for me," Cheryl offers. "You get a little bit of everything when you shop—food, views, art."

"The Buddha Bar." Bruce's words are more order than suggestion. "Cheryl will love it. Some of the highest priced drinks in the world—twenty-five bucks for champagne cocktails—food's good, but the people-watching is better."

The limousine driver swings a hard right onto one of the thirty-six bridges connecting the Right Bank to the Left and their hotel. Cheryl twists her neck for a better view of the Louvre's ornate moldings. From this angle the museum's walls—too pale to call mustard, too yellow to call beige—are immense. "If we had more time, I'd spend days in there."

Their boutique hotel sits in the middle of a narrow block named rue des Beaux-Arts. The street, Cheryl tells them, is named for the celebrated art school bordering it where Matisse, Seurat, Caillebotte, and thousands of other famous artists once roamed. Students with backpacks hanging from their shoulders and canvas totes slung like messenger bags across their chests wander in and out of a narrow gate into the school's courtyard. Cars parked bumper-to-bumper like vertical sardines on the curb leave room for traffic to flow in only one direction. There are art galleries—their windows crowded with African masks and iron sculptures and abstract landscapes—small restaurants, retail space on the street floors of buildings meant for multilevel living. Everything is compact, every space occupied; utilitarian.

The limo driver parks the long sedan in front of the hotel. Bruce and Harmon open the wide doors and step out to tip the driver and take care of the luggage. Cheryl yanks Lena's coat as she scoots across the seat to follow them. "I'm staying in Bruce's room."

Lena scrutinizes Cheryl's face as if she hasn't a clue what her friend is talking about and realizes that it's hard to hear what Cheryl is saying. Lena doesn't know, and doesn't care, if it's the French influence or Bruce's, but this new softness is better on her ears. Smiling, she motions to Cheryl to repeat her words, and when she does, Cheryl adds, "You can have our room all to yourself. But, think about staying with Harmon. He's falling in love, and that's not a bad thing."

Lena knows how much truth there is in Cheryl's words. It is in Harmon's eyes when he listens to her plans and his touch when she least expects it; it's in the way he says her name when he holds her, in their silences.

All the buildings on this street, including the hotel, are constructed as if leaning one on the other; each one distinguished and different from the next. Each is composed of three or four even rows of twelve-foot-high rectangular windows and nine-inch ledges beneath them bordered by vine-patterned, wrought iron railings. The facades are washed in faded yellows, grays, and blues, interrupted with carved wooden moldings, closed doors, eighteen to twenty feet high, that lead to courtyards and the apartments above.

The hotel is like this, a beautiful secret behind an ordinary door. The lobby is intimate and welcoming. The walls are covered in rich, maroon velour; striped brown and gold curtains held together with variegated gold-threaded swags create intimate conversation corners; black velvet-covered chairs and the Oriental carpet mimic the same color scheme. A circular foyer and an antique table with claw feet separate the lobby from the bar beyond. The glass vase on top of the table is full of tall curly willow, roses, lilies, and hand-sized exotic purple flowers that Lena doesn't recognize.

"Stay with me?" As they approach the faux-painted front desk, Harmon tugs Lena's elbow. "I booked a room with a terrace."

"*Bonjour, mesdames, messieurs. Bienvenue.* Welcome." A young woman dressed in a tailored beige dress and a Chanel scarf greets Lena, Cheryl, Harmon, and Bruce with an enthusiastic smile. Once the paperwork is complete, she hands the men the keys to all three rooms.

Harmon hands a key to Lena. "Your decision."

What will it hurt, she ponders, to let this sumptuousness, this attention overtake her? She hands her key back to Harmon and takes his hand. Once in front of Harmon's room, the bellman opens the door onto a suite, cozy and luxurious in the way that only the French can create: budding roses, sheer window curtains, crisp linens, books by the bed, and an antique writing desk with curved, spindly legs. A sofa faces the window to the street, and, on the opposite side of the room, a floor-to-ceiling glass door opens to the deck and the rooftops of Paris.

Pigeons nest in the eaves outside the window, their coos velvety and continuous. In the bathroom, the walls are covered with flocked wallpaper, the floors with marble tiles that mix well with the modern faucets, shower, and tub. Lena recognizes, discreetly tucked into a corner of the counter, the labeled soap and perfume vial. They are not the normal gratuitous toiletries; they are gifts of the signature gardenia fragrance of Annick Goutal.

"Lulu loves this stuff," Lena calls out to Harmon and gathers the bottle and bars of soap like Lulu does whenever she stays in a hotel. "These are for her collection."

"There's more where those came from, Lena." Harmon watches Lena stuff the toiletries into a drawer under the sink.

"Go 'way. Shoo!" Lena taunts. "I'm calling Lulu. She'll expect me to bring home more than this once I tell her it's here." Lena dials the 0-1-1+1+ Lulu's number.

"We can buy more if she likes it that much."

"This is much more fun."

Lulu's voice quivers a weak greeting on the other end of the phone.

"It's me, Lulu. Bonjour." Two in the afternoon in Paris is very early in the morning in California and not a problem for Lulu, who can't sleep past dawn. "Cheryl and I decided to visit Paris for a few days. Your favorite perfume is in the bathroom."

"Free?" Lulu's voice changes to an energized pitch at the prospect of more of this expensive perfume that Lena has included in Christmas and Mother's Day presents for the last twenty years. "Then you better make sure you bring a lot of it home and save yourself some money!"

Lena tries to paint a picture with her words, that she will back up with her photographs once she is home, of how different Nice and Paris are from anything Lulu has ever seen. The farthest Lulu and John Henry ever traveled was back to Mississippi to sell John Henry's family's farm and visit the few relatives they had left in the small town they grew up in.

"Cheryl met a new friend. They both like to shop, which means he likes to spend money, and she likes having money spent on her." Lena wonders if this is a temporary arrangement or if Cheryl will continue her relationship with this brusque man after they return home. She is certain that by the time their trip is over, if not any day now, Cheryl will tell her what she wants to know and more.

"She always finds men. Too bad you can't meet someone."

"I'm having a great time, Lulu." Lena won't tell Lulu about Harmon. She's not sure what kind of lecture she'll get: you're still married, or Harmon's a good catch so don't let go.

"That's good, baby girl. Take a lot of pictures. Send a few to Camille and Kendrick so they can let their father know you can still enjoy the good life without him." Lulu snickers at her joke. "You're showing him, Lena. I'm proud of you."

Harmon tiptoes behind Lena as if he, too, is concerned that her mother will find out he is there. As his arms wrap around her waist, Lena is perfectly aware that his concern is not great enough to keep him from distracting her. "Get lost with me."

"I might send a few pictures to Camille, but not for that reason."

"You go on and see Paris, baby girl. Don't waste your money on phone calls. Go out and have a good time." Lena visualizes Lulu stretching when she releases a loud yawn. "I love you."

Out the hotel and to the left of the art school, rue Jacob is the street that leads from the hotel to Boulevard Saint-Germain and the Métro. Shops and cafés occupy the *rez-de-chaussées* of every building. Ground floors house jewelers, antique framers, a furniture boutique, a store full of old watches and penknives.

"I've never seen art supplies look like art." Layers of velvet folded to entice customers: sticks of pastels, chalk in gradations of color from light to dark, erasers, rulers, tablets, single-sided razor blades, and mechanical pencils spread out like a sharp-tipped fan. A costume jewelry store is next to the art store. Pendants, earrings, and necklaces—some in thick ropes of amber, ruby, green, and yellow crystals—gleam in the diffused light captured in the window.

"Let me buy you a souvenir." He leads Lena into the Dior shop a block before the Boulevard Saint-Germain. Two Dior-clad attendants greet them at the door. Clothing, purses, scarves, belts, key chains, and shoes—sometimes one or two to a display case—and more fill the store. "Or we can go across the street." With an outstretched hand, he subtly directs her eye to the tall glass window of the Louis Vuitton boutique.

"Neither. I have everything I need, and what I need can't be bought. Except for that." Lena tugs at Harmon's hand and leads him in the direction of the window of the famous candy maker Ladurée; green and pink square boxes are stacked like a tiered wedding cake and tied with an engraved satin bow. "A box of candy. Maybe two."

The interior of the store is delicate and classy: wood-paneled walls and glass display cases that look like they should contain precious jewels instead of the mounds of confectionary disks and squares inside them. The presentations are perfect. A gloved woman at the front of the line thoughtfully makes her selection, while others in line ponder their choices: to eat the candy then and there or to take a seat in the parlor beyond and enjoy, instead, a cup of thick hot chocolate.

Outside again on the rue Jacob, Lena touches a chocolate to Harmon's lips and waits for him to take a bite. She places her hands, like blinders, beside his eyes, and steers him away from the tempting boutiques. "I want to visit the Marais. It's beautiful. We can start at the Picasso museum and afterward we can walk through the Place des Vosges to the statue that commemorates the Bastille."

She nudges him: past Dior, past Louis Vuitton, past a gray stone church, past the ancient authors' haunt—Les Deux Magots—and the tourists lingering over coffee in the ubiquitous checkered café chairs. The wide Boulevard Saint-Germain runs to the left and right in front of them. Side streets converge diagonally, like spokes on a half-wagon wheel, at the busy intersection; magazine stands, banks, ATMs, more cafés, bookstores, boutique windows full of sexy, trim mannequins.

At the top of the Métro stairs, Lena removes her hands from Harmon's eyes and leads him into the underbelly of Paris. A map four feet wide and as tall as the wall lines all the routes, streets, and stops of the Métro trains. The city is criss-crossed with four lines: yellow, red, blue, and green intersecting at various points, leading north, south, east, and west.

"This is how you tell the direction—by the last stop on the line: Clignancourt, Clichy, Pont Neuf." Lena runs her fingers over the map until she finds the street they seek.

"Nope. If you've been there before, you can't go again." Harmon points to a tiled white corridor and walks in the direction of one of the four turnstiles beyond the map. "Choose." Lena points to the one on the far left.

Saint-Germain is a multilayered station, less complicated than many of the others. They take the stairs to the tracks and wait with the Parisians for the rumble beneath their feet to stop. Within minutes a speeding train comes to a rackety halt in front of them. Lena and Harmon board the middle car; people of all colors rush around them, cram through the automatic doors, shopping bags or briefcases in hand.

Each station's interior, where the trains connect, is covered in white oblong tiles; black tiles form station names in block letters: Odéon, Place Monge, St-Michel. After many stops, starts, and transfers at stations that strongly resemble one another, Lena and Harmon get off the train and follow the crowd up one twisting staircase and down another before they reach the Avenue des Gobelins. The buildings in the fifth arrondissement are reminiscent of those on rue des Beaux-Arts and rue Jacob in feeling, not style. Retail shops, full of nicely arranged but what appears to be less expensive merchandise. Like the rest of France, signs and words resemble English: *pharmacie, hôtel, cinéma, liqueurs, saint, boulevard, restaurant.*

"It's noisy. Buses, cars, the honking horns. If I closed my eyes, we could be in Oakland. I love that this feels like home."

"This is where we're meant to be. Let's pretend like we came here to . . ." Harmon points to the next intersection; the left side of the street is modern, angular. Across the way the change is abrupt. Old Paris, older Paris.

"To find antiques . . . for your apartment . . ."

"Maybe . . . *our* apartment."

In the brief instant that Harmon squeezes her hand, Lena believes the world is full of new possibilities. They take in the wide streets, the balconies, the striped awnings. Their stride is even. They take in the ordinariness of the neighborhood: a store with advertising posters stuck to its windows, a bookstore table full of used books lined in haphazard rows. A rainbow population runs errands, moves in and out of the Métro, takes care of life's day-to-day tasks; Africans identifiable by yards of homeland fabric wound around women's heads and bodies, men in dashikis and long flowing tops; black, brown, and browner faces, eyes round and hooded are difficult for Lena to identify—Paris is a world of new possibilities, too.

"We're on Avenue des Gobelins in the fifth." Harmon nods at a shiny white-lettered sign with a blue background and green border fastened to the side of a building. "That one says rue Mouffetard. Where's your camera? Let's take a picture by the sign."

"No!" Oversized sunglasses slide down Lena's nose when she shakes her disagreement. "The light's better over there." She points to an outdoor market directly in front of a large café: white tents line both sides of the street.

The air is full with the scent of the street: exhaust fumes, the occasional ripe gutter, a scraggly rose bush beside the café, spit-roasted meat, brewing coffee, skinny baguettes. Women scan paper tubs of frilly-capped mushrooms, Italian watermelons bulge at the bottom of loosely woven shopping bags, men with weathered faces lug carts of bright tomatoes, stippled oranges, heads of dark green lettuce, and heaps of paper sacks.

Beside the market a gate-enclosed patch of grass and trees border an undersized cement-block church. Curlicues of wrought iron overlay the weather-beaten wooden door. It squeaks when Harmon heaves, as if they are the first to enter the church in a hundred years. The inside is bigger than the exterior hints. The church is plain; it smells of incense and smoking candlewicks. The immense, whitish marble altar begs to all who enter: pray. Four arched niches on either side of the main aisle frame alcoves enclosing a statue and a votive candle table.

"This is the second church we've visited together." Two times more than Lena has been in church in years. Sermons fail to touch her, focus too much on turning the other cheek. She prefers spontaneous prayer uttered between moments of her life—taking pictures, daydreaming, washing clothes, stopping at a red light, marveling at a gibbous moon.

"If you're not religious, Harmon, why are we here, or does this have something to do with your theory of fate?" Lena distinctly remembers a discussion about religion when his ex-wife put their twins in Catholic school. She thought he was against it, thought he said he didn't want his boys brainwashed or beleaguered with guilt.

"It has everything to do with fate. And architecture. I love these buildings. See this? Harmon's finger follows the line of the long central hall of the church. "The interior of this church is cross shaped. We're standing in the nave, where the congregation sits." He points to the pews around them. "I remember you like words, right? So here's one for you."

Harmon's recollection of this small detail makes her want to do a little dance inside this blessed place, but she refuses to break the spell. She relaxes against him and lets her eyes follow Harmon's finger to the gallery of arches above the side aisles.

"See how the arches vault the nave? That's called a triforium. This church is probably three or four hundred years old." Harmon's face is as serious and sincere as a professor teaching ancient history to college freshmen.

"Nice word. You make a good tour guide." Lena holds her cheeks to keep a straight face. "So, the . . . triforium is the ultimate architectural example of this church's *fate*—to live out man's obsession with immortality." She pokes him gently in the ribs.

"And conceit. The effort to control fate by building structures intended to last forever, even if man can't. Somehow in constructing them man reasons that he can control what fate holds. The completion of the edifice, if nothing else."

The edges of the oak pews are smooth, the seats darkened from years of use. The kneeler is a bare plank screwed onto the back of the pew in front of her, and Lena wonders how anyone could pray on it, especially during a lengthy service. She kneels and blesses herself with the sign of the cross. "These churches are like us. Useful in the old days. Monuments to the past."

"You talking about me, us, or the world getting older?" Harmon teases, kneeling beside her. "Or, us knowing each other before?"

"Both, although these buildings grow better with age. They're eternal. You and me? . . . we're . . . temporary."

"Haven't you enjoyed being with me?"

"If I didn't, I wouldn't be here."

A priest, dressed in a cassock covered by a floor-length white alb and cinched at the waist with a long cord, walks past the pew and nods at them before hanging a narrow confessional stole around his shoulders.

"Pardon," Harmon calls out to the priest and asks, in halting French, if he would give them his blessing. The priest pulls his hands from the full sleeves of his cassock. He makes the sign of the cross over both of them speaking in, what Lena recalls from all of her years in church, Latin. He bows deeply, then disappears into the middle section of a shadowy booth in the far corner where a queue of women and children wait to confess their sins.

"Where do you want fate to take you, Lena?" Harmon asks the question she won't ask herself.

"This trip to Paris sidetracked my fate." Randall distracted her with his agenda; friends distracted her from real conversation with lunches and shopping and spa visits and gossip. Lena slaps her hands against her thighs; she dislikes herself for accepting the detours. "My fate used to be predictable." She supposes that fate occupies itself with longer periods of time. "Like clockwork, I knew what came next, day in and day out. Even those days that weren't predictable still were. An unplanned vacation was always to a warm destination. A spontaneous dinner was always with the same couples, always at the same Mexican restaurant. Fate is simpler these days because there's only me to worry about, and I take my days one by one."

"That's the past." Harmon's eyes crinkle, his back straightens. The professorial demeanor is gone, replaced by the inquisitive litigator. "Where do you want fate to lead you now? Today."

"My life makes me feel weak. Weak like my knees will be if I keep kneeling on these hard boards that pass for genuflectors. Let's get out of here."

Beyond the church garden, farmers sell stalks of celery bound with rubber bands, golden potatoes crowded in a huge wire bin, and strawberries that fill the air from the street to the church's garden and back.

"Think it through. The Lena I knew couldn't have been anything less than a good wife and mother." Harmon wraps his arms around Lena. She inhales the scented soap from his morning shower, amazed at how wonderful he smells.

"I was more determined then." Lena pulls away from his embrace. "The strawberries smell sweet. Let's take some back to the hotel."

Harmon repeats his question as if she is a witness on a courtroom stand. His query spins around and around her brain like the pinball Vernon described rolling toward the one flipper that will move it on to score more points. Push. "Sooner or later you're going to have to answer. You know that don't you, woman?" Harmon takes Lena's hand, kisses it, kisses her as they make their way to the market and past an old man with a pointed, gray beard, a beret tilted to the side.

"L'amour," the old man fusses. "Tout le monde s'embrasse à Paris. Paris est pour les amants."

"He said," Harmon translates, kissing Lena again, this time on her cheek, "something about love, lovers, and kissing in Paris."

Behind the stands, proprietors of hardware stores, pastry shops, and restaurants linger in doorways, beckon them to partake of their goods, too. A farmer winks when she stops in front of his stand. He passes a box of bright red strawberries across his table. "You must have these, and champagne, pour . . . l'amour, eh?"

Lena winks back and tucks the fragile fruit into her tote, not wishing to disabuse the friendly fruit seller of his romantic notion. "Tina Turner's strength helped me—fate holds her in my future. Rebuilding my relationship with Camille and Kendrick—that's my future, too. That's about all I can cope with now. That and my everyday, run-of-the-mill life."

"And what about me?"

The Randall question again.

"We only have so many opportunities. I want our fates to be connected, yours and mine," Harmon finishes.

Lena admires a vendor's attention to detail: a box of thick-stalked, albino asparagus tied with string; apples, oranges, figs, and onions sheathed in smooth orangish skin carefully lined in neat, color-coordinated rows, a presentation for the eyes and nose. Patrons patiently wait in line for the vendors to select the ripest and the best. In Paris the vendors bag and weigh the produce for their appreciative customers.

"That's the weirdest looking asparagus I've ever seen." Lena looks at the vendor, points to the asparagus, then to her camera and smiles.

"Oui, oui," the vendor says, holding the pale vegetable in front of him. Lena snaps his picture. Standing almost on top of the asparagus, she photographs the stalks from above.

The shoulder strap cuts across Lena's chest and Harmon adjusts it. She hasn't taken a picture in days; Harmon has distracted her from Tina and from photographing France. But now the desire stimulates her brain, the synaptic memory commands her fingertips: the uneven cobblestones, the cloudy sky, the artful display some proprietor has taken the time to arrange—flower petals strewn on the street, a perfect row of chocolate truffles.

She shoots picture after picture: purple hydrangeas atop a whitewashed chair, a broken door hinge, a rusted bicycle leaning against a lamppost. Fingers warm against camera's metal, eyelashes flit against the viewfinder. *Whir. Click.* To see what others cannot; light, shading, innuendo. Capturing time. Memories alter with time, but photos never will. Their permanence is to her as fate is to Harmon: preordained.

"This is my fate." Lifting her camera to the sky, she spins in a circle, presses the shutter release so that the camera whirs, clicks, and snaps pictures in all directions. Her dream lodged in the back of her brain, covered itself with Randall's rejection and Harmon's consideration. "A keen eye. A connection to what others want to see. Creating art. Sharing it."

"And me, Lena, let fate bless you with me, too."

Lena stumbles with the realization of Vernon's prediction and kisses Harmon—long, slow, hungry, hard. This old friend has helped her to understand, to put what she wants into words.

Chapter 30

Harmon and Lena run at a steady pace alongside the Seine before the *bookinistes* open their stands filled with antique leather-bound books and twenties-style postcards wrapped in cellophane, before the damp streets overflow with tourists and working Parisians, before the shuttered windows of the ubiquitous apartments open to the dreary sky. It may not be true that Americans are the only people jogging these uneven streets this early in the morning, Lena thinks, but every other voice that greets them carries a distinctive, American twang.

Like they have each of the three days they've been in Paris, Harmon and Lena slow their pace as they approach rue Buci. In the evenings this street's sidewalks are full of music and people dining contentedly under extended awnings. Mornings, the stands are stocked with lemons, plump tomatoes, strawberries, white hydrangeas, red roses, and bread.

"Ça va?" Harmon slaps high five—in the manner of men who have known each other for years—with the African who sells the biggest, flakiest croissants on the street from a cart stacked with tarnished baking trays.

"Tout va bien, mon frère." The African adds an extra croissant to Lena's already full paper sack. "Pour votre amie."

"A perk," Harmon calls this generosity, "of being a brother in Paris with a pretty woman by his side."

The street from the rue Buci back to the hotel has become a classroom. They practice everyday French: *le cordonnier* at the shoemaker's repair shop, *nettoyage à sec* at the smell of the dry-cleaning chemicals, *poissonnerie* at the window where empty aluminum trays will later be filled with fresh fish, *le tabac*. "The fun," Harmon says, "is to figure out what the words mean by looking in the windows."

"Bonjour, monsieur. Madame." The hotel receptionist greets them as they enter the lobby.

"Bonjour!" Lena replies. So much for the myth of French aloofness. Every morning the bellman, the receptionist, the doorman greet them in the same warm way. Is it because their black skin makes them so easily identifiable, Lena wonders, or is it because they look like they're in love?

"Let's see what the kids are up to." Harmon punches the elevator button for Bruce's floor one above theirs.

"What's the plan?" Harmon asks when Bruce opens the door. The question has become both mantra and joke. Beyond Bruce's terry-robed back, a footed silver serving tray sits atop the king-sized bed with two full-bloomed white roses, a silver coffee carafe, the *Herald Tribune*, and a porcelain pitcher artfully loaded on top.

"Montmartre," Cheryl shouts from the bathroom.

"It's hilly up there," Lena shouts back. "You sure?"

After exploring the rue Mouffetard, Lena and Harmon returned to the hotel to meet Cheryl and Bruce. Like first-time tourists, the four rushed through the upstairs gallery of the Musée d'Orsay so Lena could see Gauguin's Tahitian studies; took two Métro trains to the first arrondissement and strolled the Champs-Élysées; walked under the Arc de Triomphe and climbed the interior steps, until Bruce refused to go any farther. From the Métro they wandered past city hall, past bridge after bridge to the golden statue that marks where the Bastille stood before the French Revolution.

Bruce was in charge of food and surprisingly serendipitous in his dinner choice: he peeked into a restaurant that intrigued him and chatted, in broken French and hand signals, with the chef about his food. The cozy brasserie served the best foie gras and paté de campagne any of them had ever eaten, and the chef, after many compliments from Bruce, concocted an original chocolate dessert for them.

Dialing the concierge, Bruce's words are final: "Today, we're taking a taxi."

"*That* is the most beautiful thing I've ever seen." Cheryl sticks her head out the taxi window and squints to get a better look at Sacré-Coeur. The seven domes visible from the front of the stark, white church end in long pointed tubes, like spiked pith helmets. "But, there is no way *this* girl is climbing *those* steps."

The taxi slows at the foot of the funicular and points to a rail car as if he understands. "Six cent escaliers, madame." The motion of the crowd working its way mostly down, not up the flights of steps, is like a winding river of upright bodies flowing away from the highest point in Paris after the Eiffel Tower.

"Six hundred stairs." Assuming the role of tour guide, Harmon steps onto the crowded sidewalk. "We can walk down that street and weave our way past the street where Picasso once lived and back to the top. That way we'll get a two for one tour: neighborhoods and Sacré-Coeur."

Shops surround the base of the stairs, each wooden stall crammed with souvenirs: scarves on hangers flutter in the breeze, postcards spin on wobbly racks, and handsized replicas of the church beckon from the shelves. Harmon picks up a liquid-filled globe with plastic snow that tumbles onto a miniature Sacré-Coeur inside when he turns it upside down. "You'll accept this, won't you?" He passes the souvenir to Lena. The look on his face is devilish, like the old Harmon, who was as funny as he was serious.

"With pleasure."

Harmon and Lena weave past a circular park and stone-colored buildings. Cheryl and Bruce's huffs are audible and labored behind them. The hilly area is the kind of neighborhood Americans understand: a man washes his car in the driveway of a house that could be a mansion or an apartment building, garages attached to houses with gardens, front porches and picture windows, children playing on the sidewalk.

"Give me that guidebook." Bruce takes the green guidebook from Harmon's hand and sits at a rest stop with benches and a dog run behind it. Across the street, a reddish building and its faded sign peek from behind an overgrown bush and a rickety, green-tipped fence. "You walk. I'll find a good place for lunch."

"Rest a minute." Cheryl hooks her elbow into Lena's and leads her across the street. "I want to take a closer look at that building."

Tourists with guidebooks and cameras gather around the brick building and point to the sign: "Au Lapin Agile." Cheryl tells Lena that she suspects that this is the famous cabaret of artists and writers that Picasso memorialized in his 1905 painting. Instead of singing for his supper, Cheryl tells Lena, he painted for it.

Harmon waves from the other side of the street. A dog, no bigger than Cheryl's tote bag, on a long leash held by a frail-looking older woman, sniffs around the men's feet. Harmon is attentive; his smile is constant, and the older woman looks as if she is ready to hand her diminutive pet over to him.

"Well," Cheryl says, "this is a different trip from what we planned."

Lena examines the worn plaque bolted onto the building's side. It repeats the same information that Cheryl has just shared with her. "I love this detour, but I should know where Tina Turner lives by now. I hoped I might run into her."

"Listen," Cheryl says. "When Harmon and Bruce knew they'd had enough of Nice and decided to follow their plan to come to Paris, Harmon explained to his buddy how he feels about you." Cheryl condenses what Bruce told her in between shopping sprees.

In a small wine-tasting bar, twenty-four full bottles in front of them, Bruce and Harmon tried to decide which wines they would send back to Chicago while Harmon confessed that he wanted to be with Lena. That she is a good combination of what he likes in a woman: smart, sexy, and easy to be around. He didn't want to lose that. He had passed the notion of making up for past sins.

"Bruce says Harmon doesn't focus on the past. That when he saw you, something clicked. He knew it was right."

Bruce listened before offering advice. Harmon confessed that Lena's sadness offered an opening and that was what smart litigators look for. "Man, what did you expect? It's like the exclamation point on your damn theory of fate."

"When we first started this trip, Lena, you were sad. Sad face, sad eyes, sad aura. Now you're different. Have you asked yourself why?"

"Because this is Paris! Because I don't have to think about divorce or my kids hating me or my direction—I'm going to see Tina."

"Harmon has a lot more to do with your being happy than you give him credit for."

"I can't deny that he has something to do with it, but my happiness comes from me, from inside." Lena points to Bruce and Harmon. The two men tease the small dog, seemingly content to wait for Lena and Cheryl to decide what comes next.

"Love comes from inside. Go for it. Women like you always end up screwing for love anyway." Arm in arm, Cheryl and Lena move away from the old cabaret. "We haven't had the chance to spend much time together," Cheryl says. "I miss catching up like old times. What do you say to going to the Matisse exhibit at the Luxembourg? Just you and me."

"Deal."

From this location a partial view of Paris spreads out before them in an orderly fashion: flat, no hills between Montmartre and a hilly mass of green on the far side of the city. There are pointed rooftops of varying heights. Notre Dame stands out, as does the Île de la Cité, the island some call the true heart of Paris.

"Richard Wright, Chester Himes, and James Baldwin wrote in Paris. The next time we come"—Harmon looks at Lena who holds his gaze—"we'll take one of the black tours. Every one knows Josephine Baker, but there was a big jazz following here—Sidney Bichet had a nightclub. Black soldiers were here during both World Wars. I wish we had time to see it all."

"I know there must be at least one soul food restaurant here." Cheryl taps Bruce's shoulder lightly with her fist and pokes out her bottom lip like a spoiled child. "Let's have fried chicken in Paris!"

"Fried chicken in Paris. Ha!" Bruce playfully pinches Cheryl's cheek. When it comes to food, he readily voices his opinions. His cheeks and stomach jiggle with his joke. "As long as I can go to my mother's house and eat the best fried chicken in the world, I will not be eating any soul food in Paris."

Two hours later, the plaza in front of Sacré-Coeur is crowded with groups led by tour guides lecturing in Spanish, German, and Japanese. All of Paris—the streets skinny like lines, the gold roof of the opera house, the Eiffel Tower—is within sight. A British guide addresses his group from atop a wooden box.

"Take note of the stone. Sacré-Coeur was built in the late nineteenth century with the stone of Château Landon. The brilliant white is actually the effect of rainwater. When wet, the stone secretes a white substance similar to paint. Thus, it is always a brilliant white." The guide smiles as if this is a fact that everyone in his group, and Lena, and the other English-speaking eavesdroppers around the perimeter of the group, should be proud of.

Lena points her camera at a waddling toddler making his way up the stairs without the help of his parents. "I haven't the vaguest idea how to describe this to Lulu. I'm going to the top and take a picture." Bruce gently taps her shoulder before she climbs to the vestibule of the Byzantine-styled building and points to the funicular. "Cheryl and I are going down." He glances at Harmon. "Sorry, man. It's flat there . . ."

The *libraire's* sixteen-foot walls are covered from floor to ceiling with shelves of books. Lena asks the woman behind a tall desk if she speaks English. "Petit peu," the woman says, holding a space between her thumb and forefinger of no more than an inch.

"I want to buy a gift. A special memory of Paris." Lena points to Harmon browsing the tables on the outer edges of the store. "A surprise."

"Ah, oui, madame." The woman's face fills with glee while she questions Lena on Harmon's likes and dislikes. The woman pauses for a minute, her eyes move from left to right as if recalling her entire inventory. She eases off of her stool and enters the back of the store through a draped curtain. A man comes out and drags a wheeled ladder attached to the shelves until he spots what he is looking for. He climbs to the very top step, his head grazing the ceiling, and pulls a book out with both hands. He holds on to the book loosely while descending the stairs like he seems to have done a thousand times. The shopkeeper holds her arms out to him when he nears the bottom of the ladder, relief visible in her eyes, and places a loving hand on the man's balding head.

Lena flips through the book—the pictures are sharp and show the detail she is looking for. The text is in French, but the pictures need no translation. "Perfect." She thanks the woman three times until the woman steps from behind the tall mahogany pulpit that passes for the sales counter and thanks Lena, in the French way—

cheek to cheek. "I am hopeful your *ami* finds enjoyment with this book."

At three o'clock in the afternoon, this sidewalk café still serves ham-and-tomato sandwiches on crunchy baguettes and hunks of cantal—the hard French cheese Lena loves the most.

"Two more days here and then it's back to the south of France, Tina's concert . . . and home." Lena passes the brown bag from the bookstore to Harmon across the table. "Thank you for sharing Paris with me. This is for you."

Harmon strips away the tape carefully as if his gift is wrapped in expensive paper.

"*Les Églises de Paris.*" He pronounces the words slowly. Lena muses at how much his accent has improved. He traces the outline of the steepled church on the cover with his finger and opens the book to the first page. *Triforium is a word that will stay with me as much as the memory of you and our little church. If that word describes an opening, it is what you have built in my heart. Love, Lena.*

"Don't go back to Nice. Come to Chicago." He reaches his hand to Lena's cheek and holds it there. His touch holds all the tenderness he has shown her over the past days.

"I've already let you take me off track, no matter how much fun it's been." She dips a cookie into her dark wine and bites into it.

"I can rearrange a few appointments. I'll stay longer if you do. Let's see where this—us—is going."

There is nothing she wants more. Nothing she wants less. She cannot help herself because being taken care of by someone who cares makes you feel like chocolate ice cream on a summer day. Lena caresses Harmon's hand. The action, his request, feels comfortable: a promise of security, a predictable future.

"We're moving at the speed of lightning. I'm not done with one man. I have to be sure that it's not this." Lena waves her arms from the curlicued Métro station gate to the ornate buildings rising on the hill beyond the café. "And when the time comes, I'll be looking for a partner, not someone to take care of me."

"I hear you loud and clear."

"This is what vacations are: we laugh, we talk, we fool around. Once we're back home, we'll visit. I'm not going anywhere, and I won't lose sight of my goals. Not this time."

"I love you, Lena. I love your search for change. I don't think you know how indomitable you are." He presses his hand to her mouth. "You can't say anything to me that I haven't said to myself, or Bruce." Harmon looks straight at Lena and searches her eyes for assent. His wide smile, his toothy smile, spreads across his face. "Marry me, Lena. I was going to ask you at dinner tonight. The concierge even found a bottle of that Cheval Blanc, St-Emilion, to celebrate." Frown lines disappear as he pulls a small satin pouch from his pocket and opens it. The ring is a band of diamonds that shimmers in the afternoon light. "I know marriage is a bigger commitment than you're ready for right now. So think of this as a promise ring."

"Too fast, too soon." Can he hear her fear? she wonders.

"I'm not a capricious man, Lena. I know you're still married—even if it's not for much longer. I know what you've got to get out of your system. But, I told you. I assess facts, and I make decisions—business or emotional. I trust my intuition, otherwise I wouldn't be here."

Lena signals with her hand for Harmon to keep his distance. She does not want to cry, does not want to cry. Didn't the optometrist tell her that her eyes were dry? Didn't she laugh and tell him it was because in eight short months she had cried an ocean, a lifetime of tears, that there were no more, that her whole body was dry?

"I love you because it's taken you a long time to realize what you want, and now you're ready to go for it. You admire Tina Turner and, no matter how odd everybody else thinks that is, you hold on to her as role model. I love you because you've let go of thinking of power as the most important thing in your life. I love you because you don't want anything from me. If you go, I'm not sure I'll get the chance to ask again."

Lena swallows hard to wet her throat and checks her fingers for nonexistent hangnails. "I don't love you the way a woman should when her man proposes marriage."

"Yes, you do, Lena. Don't deny it. You wouldn't be here with me right now if you didn't."

Chapter 31

"Take it from your buddy—accept love. It's a gift. Two marriages, and a whole lot of men in between, have taught me that." Cheryl hooks her arm through Lena's like so many French women do. The gesture confirms the importance of alone time with her friend and convinces Lena that encouraging Harmon and Bruce to sample eau-de-vie on their own at a private tasting room near the Place Vendôme was the right thing to do.

The days of this short stay in Paris have toppled like dominoes under a child's heavy hand. Lena has lost count, can barely tell Tuesday from Thursday. All she knows is that they have two days left in Paris and that Cheryl is trying to convince her that love can truly conquer all.

A group of pedestrians moves against the stoplight and across the wide boulevard. Lena loves that Parisians take jaywalking as seriously as they do their coffee. Couples hold hands, smooch, discreetly pat each other's bottoms. "Paris makes you want to be in love, makes you do things you may later regret."

"You. Not me, honey. I haven't done anything I haven't wanted to do. Bruce has been fine company." Cheryl rattles her newly acquired—thanks to Bruce—wide gold bangles. "And besides, Bruce is worried that his boy Harmon is too attached."

"I've finally made some sense of the rues and boulevards. It feels like I belong here." Lena draws an invisible line with her finger on the map to point the way from Boulevard Saint-Germain, where they stand, to the museum at the Luxembourg Gardens. The streets converge at odd angles; at every corner a new rue or avenue sprouts, like tree limbs, in different directions. "Harmon genuinely cares. And that's more important than what he has or what he can give. If it's meant to be, it will."

The museum is separated from the rue de Vaugirard by stairs and a ten-foot wrought iron fence with gold-tipped spikes. Oversized, cloth posters below the sculpted pediment announce the exhibit. Rows and rows of trees jut out behind the building and offer a glimpse of the park beyond. Inside the small gallery, the walls of two rooms are covered with Matisse pieces. The rooms are big enough to accommodate the fifty or so people milling around and small enough to get close to the art and see the brush strokes, the thickness of the paint, a hint of an original pencil sketch.

The exhibit pays homage to Matisse's friendship and correspondence with artist André Rouveyre, who influenced Matisse's creativity in the latter part of his life. Display boxes are filled with the men's original letters. In the middle of the first room, glass cases enclose letters and drawings by both artists. Matisse's envelopes are works of art covered with endearments and sketches of abstract leaves from the tree of life in the chapel at Vence.

"These two artists inspired each other to greater heights." Cheryl loops her finger in the direction of the letters.

"We should . . . correspond. That's what they used to say."

"That's what email is for." Cheryl waves Lena forward. "No one writes letters anymore."

"I still have the letters Randall wrote to me before we were married." The letters were still tied with the ribbon from the first bouquet of flowers (the second time around) he gave her for no other reason than he wanted to.

"Well, that bit of 'correspondence' should go right into the trash."

"Sometimes letters communicate what can be hard to say in person."

"I say what's on my mind," Cheryl declares. They move with the crowd into the next room. "Like, for instance, this: for me this little fling with Bruce is just that, a fling. I don't expect anything more from him than what I've gotten. He's fun and funny and a big spender. Now I've got a friend in Chicago."

In the second room one wall is devoted to "Jazz," twenty vibrant canvases, each one twelve by sixteen inches, working with the same musical theme. Cheryl stops in front of two canvases of the 1947 piece: the stark black silhouette of a man falling through a deep blue field of golden starbursts, an elephant balancing on a ball behind slashes of red.

"You compartmentalize," Lena says. "Work. Relationships. Just like men."

"And I'm proud of it! But I insist on having fun while I'm doing it. I'm determined not to form any connections that have the slightest chance of becoming anything more." Cheryl nudges Lena. "But you, sister girl—you are a one-man woman. You were that way with Harmon when you dated the first time around, and you were that way for all those years with Randall. So, I'm asking you—how does it feel to be in love with two men at the same time?"

"I'm not sure what being in love means anymore. I won't lie; I have feelings for Harmon—maybe love, maybe gratitude. There's a gentleness about him that makes him attractive." Lena moves to the black-and-white charcoal sketches, like first drafts of a novel, that Matisse created for the Vence chapel. "I love the memory of Randall, but I'm disappointed in the present him. I love the present Harmon, but I'm disappointed in the memory."

Cheryl points back to the varying canvases of "Jazz." "The work in this collection is different from what Matisse had done in the past. He always used bold colors and these abstracts still carry his love for color, but they are new interpretations of what he felt. It's artistic evolution. Rouveyre helped him to understand the need to incorporate old ideas into new images and let go of the past." Cheryl paces back and forth between paintings to emphasize her words. "Since I believe that art imitates life, and I'm your friend, I want to remind you that Tina Turner finally made choices based on putting herself first. You're no good to anybody if you can't do that. Tina figured it out, and maybe that's what you're here to learn."

They study the rhythm, the preparation, and implications of Matisse's work in light of what Cheryl has said. Harmon's declaration was not surprising. His attention and affection feel like more than lust. "I wanted this affair to be the first time that love and commitment were *not* my priority."

"And, I might add, isn't that a bit risky for a woman over fifty?" Cheryl teases, mocking Lena's own words.

Lena presses her purse for her book, past the point of writing her thoughts in the margins. There is no longer any reason to compare her predicament. They stop in to the museum's gift shop, its shelves and counters stacked with art books and mementos of the exhibit. Beyond the gift shop window a queue extends down the stairs and around the side of the building. Paris is chilly but bright, its trees are fading from green to gold, and Lena is glad to be alive.

Randall's love meant security, but when it came down to the two of them sitting across from one another, listening to the rain scratch against the window that stormy night, none of it amounted to the kind of love that should have kept them together. Maybe, if she had been more open. But maybe is just a cake that's all eaten up; if wishes were fishes and fishes could fly . . .

While Cheryl decides which art books she cannot live without, Lena waits on the museum steps. She has picked the same card for Camille and Kendrick and jots the same note to them: "The next time I come to Paris, you're coming with me—even if I have to drag you kicking and screaming. You'll love it, and I can't wait to share this city with my two favorite people." Her postcards to Lulu and Bobbie tell them how fabulous Paris is. She will spray

Annick Goutal on Lulu's card when she returns to the hotel. The last postcard, a black silhouette tumbling through blue space and yellow stars, she addresses to herself. On the left side she scrawls her note in capital letters, "ME . . . *THAT'S* WHAT LOVE HAS TO DO WITH . . . EVERYTHING!!"

Chapter 32

Harmon's body is longer than the silk-covered couch. He sleeps, arms folded atop his chest, head on the armrest at one end, feet dangling over the cushioned edge of the other. Lena has come to learn a few of his habits: he catnaps in the late afternoon; he rarely gets into bed before midnight and then without TV, lights, or noise.

Lena tiptoes around the suite, stops to take in the fragrance of the rubrum lilies. Since the concierge discovered they are her favorites, the room has been full of the fresh flowers every other day. Today he has added a spray of a flaxen, star-shaped flower that Lena reminds herself to ask the name of. She smiles at the attention to detail and reminds herself to tell Harmon to be generous when the time comes to tip.

Who can she talk to, she wonders? Who can she tell how strong she feels, not so much loved—in a way she hasn't been in a while—but cared about for who she is, not what she can do, and that makes her feel secure. Her cell phone comes alive to a perky ring tone. Harmon grumbles and turns onto his side before she closes the bathroom door behind her. The phone screen flashes Randall's photo for the second time in five days.

Lena turns the bathtub faucets, pours all of the bath oil into the tub, and drops her clothes onto the floor. In the tub, the slow-running water and bubbles envelop her; the fragrance of the sweet gardenia soap makes her think of Lulu. Her mother would be delighted if she could see her baby girl stepping out on her own. Or almost. One touch of the recall button on her phone makes it easy to call Randall back.

"Why haven't you answered my messages, Lena?" Caller ID eliminates the need for a proper, kinder greeting.

"I'm . . ." Lena takes a second to adjust to the realization that she doesn't have to report in or make excuses.

"How are you?" Manners restored, Randall goes on without her response. "I'm in Brussels."

Close but far away. Her stomach tightens, and she wishes for the thick pink liquid in her suitcase to coat her insides against the acid building there. Getting it might awaken Harmon, and then what would she do? Her heart says to chitchat, to inquire: Did the CEO position come through? Why are you in Brussels? Do you miss me? Do I miss you?

"What do you want, Randall?"

"Camille told me you're in Nice. I have to be in Paris, tonight. Have dinner with me. I can make reservations for your flight, and I'll pay for your ticket and a night at the Crillon."

The elegant five-star hotel is where Lena told him she wanted to stay on their next visit to Paris. From a distance the hotel looked like an extension of the Louvre or an official building meant to house government offices. As they approached the historic Place de la Concorde, where the Jardin des Tuileries ends and the Champs-Élysées begins, they discovered that the building was not what they thought, but rather the famous Hôtel de Crillon. They stood near the fountain of sculpted black bodies with gold turbans and watched the doormen help guests from a line of Bentleys, Maybachs, and other expensive cars neither had seen before. Once inside the landmark hotel, they strolled from the lobby—the floor a marbled black-and-white checkerboard—to the bar. The hotel smelled like money, like extravagance, like someplace Lena wanted to be.

"Let's see. The last time I saw you, Randall, you snarled at me." Lena's voice is a loud whisper she prays Harmon cannot hear. "For months you schemed to keep most of what we had on your side of the balance sheet, now you *happen* to be in Brussels, *and* you conveniently have to be in Paris, *and* you want to have dinner with me?"

Randall chuckles in the playful way she hasn't heard in a long time. "Put that way, my proposition does seem a little farfetched. But what have you got to lose?"

"I already lost it," Lena whispers, "and one dinner in Paris isn't going to make up for that." The soft spot is still there. Eight months since she slept with Randall, eight months since they shared the same bed. Two months, more or less, since they signed their settlement paper. Since she saw the look she never wants to see in his eyes again. Lena kicks the faucet with her foot to stop the water from spilling over the side. The overflow drain gurgles as it sucks up the excess.

Perhaps she is more like that damn Kimchee than she realized. Perhaps that is why she couldn't stand the cat. One day, during what she now thinks of as her foggy time, Lena drove past the grocery store, the yoga studio, the library where she volunteered and parked at the Berkeley Marina to watch the waves crash against the abandoned pier. When she came home from her pretend errands, she found Kimchee strolling across the kitchen counter, tail lifted high, as if the granite were his path to glory. He continued around the counter until he got to the spot where he wanted to jump down. His eyes dared Lena to say a word.

At this moment, Lena feels like she understands that uppity cat. She feels like looking Randall in the eye and daring him to accept her as she is right now, this day, in a hotel room with a man—not him—who claims to love and appreciate her as much or more than he once did. This is her territory. She will not be intimidated by his smile, by the eyebrow that lifts when she walks into a room, by the curve of his lips as they turn from frown to smile. She will not be seduced by his lavish lure. She will strut into that restaurant, if only for the effect.

"I'm in Paris. Tell me where and what time, and I'll meet you."

The bathroom door swings open.

"I'm not going to lie. I heard you talking, heard you say his name. So I listened. That's the problem with being a light sleeper." Harmon closes the toilet seat and sits on top of it. His face is unreadable.

"I'm sorry."

Harmon pauses, his hands folded across his chest. His eyes reflect his thoughts, like the winning attorney he is, of what her last words to Randall mean.

"What does he want?"

"To have dinner."

"And if I asked you not to go?"

"I've been honest, Harmon. I'm still not used to saying no to him."

She lays her phone on the floor and steps out of the tub, extending her arm for one of the plush towels from the counter rack. With her back to Harmon, Lena wraps the towel around her, covering her body from the top of her breasts to her mid thigh so that passion cannot take over where logic should.

"How did he know you were here?" Harmon stands and paces from the tub to the toilet and back. His voice is steady, like a probing drill.

"We have children together, Harmon. Camille and Kendrick know where I am. Camille told him."

He asks his next question, again the strategic litigator who never asks compound questions: "How did he know you were in Paris?"

"He knew I was in France. It's a crazy coincidence that he's in Paris."

"What does he want?"

"He didn't say." And she didn't ask. Old habits die hard.

Harmon walks out of the room.

"It's dinner, Harmon. Nothing more."

"Like we had *dinner* that first night in Nice?"

"That's not fair." Lena shakes her head no and reaches for his arm. He pulls away and heads for the desk where the ring sits in its open pouch.

"I was serious when I bought this. I'm serious now. Think about that when you see him. Your ex is no fool." He grabs the room key, slips into his sandals, and walks to the door. "I'm going downstairs to the bar, and I'm going to stay there until you're gone. I'm going to get drunk. I'm going to hope you remember whose bed you've been sleeping in for the last eleven days. But don't worry, I won't give away your little secret rendezvous." The door slams behind him, but he speaks loud enough for her and everyone else on the floor to hear. "But, I might reconsider my damn theory of fate."

Randall is casually elegant in a tan suede jacket and what looks like a silk shirt underneath. Lena can't tell if he is thinner or heavier than the last time she saw him. She wonders if this were a picture, how she would photograph it. She would call it "Things I Don't Know about the Man I Used to Love" and cover it with question marks: Are his clothes new? Does he play new jazz or old on the CD player in his car? Has he slept with another woman as she has with another man? Did he enjoy it? Did her ghost linger at the foot of the bed as his has? Another corner full of *z*'s: has he thought more about the surgery to correct his snoring? Has he cut back on the three cups of coffee that get his thoughts started in the morning? Who takes his shirts to the cleaners?

"Hey, Randall."

To her surprise he rises to greet her with a bear hug and a grin.

His look is sheepish and tentative. "I ordered for you. Pouilly-Fuissé is a good substitute for those chardonnays you love."

"Actually, I'm into Bordeaux these days." His surprise is obvious. Lena motions to the waiter and asks for his recommendation and ignores Randall scanning her face in a way that makes her want to blush.

The waiter sets a glass in front of Lena with as much flourish as Randall used to present her with gifts. She sniffs the wine, sips, and lets it linger on her tongue the way Harmon does with the first taste from a new bottle.

"Why are you in Paris?"

"I'm here with Cheryl and a couple of . . . friends." Lena watches Randall's effort not to criticize her friend cut lines on his otherwise smooth face. "I enjoy Cheryl's company. I always have."

"It's been a long time since we were in Paris, and if I'm not mistaken it was about this same time of the year."

The second time Lena and Randall came to Paris they held hands and strolled the Seine at midnight so they could see a full Paris moon. He'd held her close, slipped his hands in her pants, and made her want him to do more. They'd made love that night in a way that they never had before or since then; laughed long and hard the next morning, made love again and a baby. When she miscarried, Randall promised to bring her back to Paris, to recreate that night, but they never returned.

Randall is pensive in the way that Lena has forgotten. Two people who, two months ago, could barely stand to be in the same room together, who fought over money and all the possessions they had accumulated and acted as if they had never been in love, didn't have children together whom they adored. The same bitter taste that crept onto her tongue during those sessions is there now. It spoils the desire for food. When the waiter presents the menus, Lena orders a small fish entrée, a salad, no appetizer. Randall's appetite is hearty enough for salad, oysters, and a complicated-sounding entrée.

"Knock, knock," he prompts her like she once did long ago, and she obliges with the proper response.

"Who's there?"

"TIDA's new CEO." Randall slides his hand across the table to hold hers. His touch is different. Understated. Foreign. Now she finds herself comparing Randall to Harmon instead of the other way around.

"I wanted you to be the first to know."

"Not afraid I'll ask for more money, are you? Is this"—her voice falls into the singsong inflection that Randall used to admire, her open arms indicate the beautiful restaurant around her—"another one of your bribes? Did you call Sharon?"

Randall ducks like a boxer, a quick move of his shoulders and head to the left then the right. "Low blow. Two low blows."

"You have a way of getting what you want."

The server sets their entrées on the table and lights the candles. Their talk drifts to Camille and Kendrick. Camille's first semester has started off with a bang; she loves her classes and has already started making friends and concedes to being called Camille again. Kendrick has a clean bill of health from Dr. Miller, though he recommended their son see a campus counselor from time to time. He met a girl from Mississippi. Not his first relationship, but someone he really likes. The irony of Kendrick meeting someone from her parents' home state is enough to make them both chuckle and wonder, if like John Henry and Lulu, Kendrick will marry and live with this girl until death forces them apart.

Lena pursues the details of her children's lives that she should be familiar with. That they have kept from her. She has learned to live with not a word or an email from Kendrick and the one call from Camille—a concession Lena now presumes, with Randall sitting in front of her, to homesickness for the life she, they all, once had. Even though she and Harmon sipped their morning coffee in Internet cafés with the specific intention of checking her email. Even though she has sent long emails to them describing France.

She loves her children: they are worthy of her love, but they do not understand that she is worthy of theirs.

"I won't beat around the bush, Lena, in case you're wondering why I asked you to meet me." He speaks while the server clears away their dishes and presents them with leather-bound dessert menus. Their habit, when they were married, happily married, was to share. One dessert. Two spoons. Lena shakes her head no at the waiter and the luscious pastry described in English on the menu. Randall frowns, waits, and when she repeats her decision he, too, declines.

"I've been mad at you for a long time. Even before we split up. You changed."

"I didn't change, Randall. I grew and you wouldn't keep up with me, that's all. Need I go over our session with Dr. Brustere?"

"I miss family. I miss home. I miss you."

"Why now, Randall? The ink is barely dry on our agreement."

"I let things go too far."

Not exactly an apology. If she still counted days, hours, and more, Lena would wonder how many times she wanted to hear him say he was sorry. She knows this man, knows this is as close as he will come to those words. Did he go too far by letting Kendrick's problems and Camille's insolence come between them? By putting work before his well-intentioned wife? Was seeing her as object, not partner, going too far? The third finger on Lena's left hand pulses, as it hasn't in a while—not that the finger hasn't ached, but she no longer acknowledges it.

"Since when do you flip-flop on a decision? What do you want?"

"It's not complicated, Lena. I want the woman who was with me when I was low man on the totem pole to be with me when I'm at the top. Did you expect some out-of-body experience?"

Their amusement mingles with the conversations around them and, to Lena, it feels precious. She takes Randall's hand. "I'm right here. That woman is, too, but not in the same way. I've slept with someone else who tells me he loves me, and I'm trying hard to get you out of my head."

Randall jerks at Lena's pronouncement and squirms in his chair. Surprise shows in his eyes, his flared nostrils. He raises his open palms no more than an inch from the table. She knows that move: touché, he has done the same. Can they be born-again virgins a second time around?

"Now you sit here and tell me . . . what? You miss me? I have been through hell on a slow, fucking roller coaster." Her words are unhurried and deliberate, and she knows the answer no longer matters because having the strength to say them is enough. "Why wasn't our love good enough two months ago, eight months ago, to make it through the tough time?" She raps her fingers on the table and waits for the answer to the question that has disturbed her dreams on countless nights when she sat in her apartment trying to understand the loneliness, when she made love with Harmon.

Randall leans close to Lena and lets their proximity, their old attraction, take over. She releases into him, smells him. Cinnamon and pepper. It floods. The longing, the heart-to-stomach-to-toes tingle. This is earnest Randall, sexy Randall. She feels the familiar: fine hairs on the nape of his neck, his lips, the urgency of his tongue, his taste. Home.

"Other couples do it, Randall. They lose children, survive disease, infidelity, and they stay together. Their love was strong enough and, at one time, I believed ours was, too."

He releases Lena and hands her a box from his pocket. Cartier is written across the top. Inside a jeweled replica of the Eiffel Tower studded with stones the color of the French flag—blue, white, red—hangs from a platinum link bracelet.

Lena and Randall first visited Paris before they became big spenders, before Kendrick was conceived. They ate ham-and-cheese sandwiches from vendors on the streets, walked to avoid outrageous taxi fares, waited for the free days at museums so they could visit as many as they wanted. Queasy about their mutual dislike of heights, but determined to conquer their fear, they rode the elevator to the top of the world-famous landmark on their last night in Paris. Lena gave a box to Randall that night. Inside perched on a sateen cushion was a miniature replica of the tower, with a diamond chip on its top. It was the kind of gift young lovers shared on a first trip to Paris. He was to keep the inexpensive souvenir, a reminder of how their future would flourish and her promise to buy him a real one from Cartier someday.

He smiles, and his eyes crinkle with the mischievous look that made her love him the first time she saw him. The look that disappeared when he sat opposite her during mediation. "Some of our best loving happens after we argue."

Lena wipes her red lipstick from Randall's lips. "Are you ready for me to start my business? For me to devote as much time to me, to my photography, as I do to you?"

"Walk with me. Come back to the hotel with me. Let's see what happens."

Chapter 33

Paris is a twenty-four-hour city. Troubadours, all night Rollerblade marathons, museum walks. Something goes on in the streets, the parks, the bridges all of the time. This is what Lena thinks as she walks back to her hotel. She feels alive, like the city. The Seine is quiet; the *Bateaux-Mouches*, docked in their slips, await the morning crowd of tourists. She squints at the Eiffel Tower on her wrist and the top of the real one. A rainbow of colors shimmers before her.

At the hotel, the doorman greets Lena without question but holds the door open, expecting, she imagines, Harmon not far behind. Lena smiles at Gaston. He is used to seeing her with Harmon at this late hour but is discreet enough not to inquire. This is Paris. "Madame Harrison, I would have sent a cab for you, if you had called, et voila! You would have not had to walk."

The bolt on the door clicks heavily when Lena turns the old-fashioned key in it. The room lights are on. Harmon sits in bed, in his lap the copy of *Othello* they found at the English bookstore under the arcade on the rue de Rivoli.

"'I do perceive here a divided duty,'" he reads.

The line is exquisitely matched to this moment, and Lena wonders if this is coincidence, fate, or plan. She wonders if Harmon has been up all night long in search of the perfect retort for her long absence.

His eyes trace her body from head to toe. They search her eyes and her clothes for the answer to what she has done.

"Did you sleep with him?" The contentious tone is still strong.

"I was tempted, but I didn't."

"Was that because of me, or didn't he try hard enough?"

"No, Harmon. It was because of me." She climbs onto the bed beside him, resists nestling into his side until he has said all that he has to say.

"Then where have you been?"

"I needed to think, and the bartender at the Crillon was quite accommodating. I guess it was that expensive champagne I kept ordering."

The look on Harmon's face is harsh. His clothes are messy, the room smells of brandy, but Lena sees no trace of intoxication. He seems, she thinks, considering his threats before she left, quite sober. Harmon sniffs at Lena's clothes and hair. Lena lets him, snuggles close to him, disappointed that he doesn't believe her.

"I never thought much about fate before our conversations. Now, you've got me thinking about it all of the time. I sat in that hotel bar and did nothing but think about it. But not for the reasons you believe. I believe that you and Randall are my tests. Brick walls fate has presented to see if I'm truly ready for the life I've been talking about."

"Either I'm a saint or I have an incredibly high tolerance for bullshit—I guess that's why I'm a litigator." The tension in the room, on the bed, breaks when Harmon grins and settles back into his pillow. "What are you trying to say?"

"What I couldn't say to him." Lena fluffs her pillow and sits up straight in the bed, using the time to collect her thoughts, like Randall did earlier this evening. Some habits are hard to break. Now her clothes are rumpled in the way Harmon thought they might be when she walked through the door. "I love you. And, I love Randall. It might've been different if I had waited to leave him when I didn't love him anymore, but I wasn't sure then, and I'm not even sure now that that will ever happen. When I was married, more toward the end than the beginning"—her right hand drifts to her ring finger, and she lets it rest there—"I fell into the habit of doing whatever my husband wanted."

"I'm not him."

"I have a point to make. I loved unconditionally with little or no regard for my own needs." Lena slumps into the bed. Like Lulu did John Henry, she thinks, without the same result. "That was my choice. You understand?"

"That's not who you are now. Not who you used to be way back then, as a matter of fact. You were anything but that."

"Then why the hell didn't you acknowledge *that*, way back when?"

"You made your mistakes. I made mine. The difference between the two of us is that I can forgive mine—even learn from them—and you can't seem to."

She curses him in her head for knowing her truth. If these days have meant nothing more than her gaining her own understanding, she is thankful. Through the window, and between buildings beyond, the hint of the soon-to-rise sun shines through and highlights the last of the double-decker boats on the Seine. She's always wanted to ride one of those and still has not. How many bridges cross that wide river, she wonders.

"There was a point when I wasn't sure I ever would find me. I sat on my bed and counted out the pills . . ."

Harmon scoots to Lena's side of the bed. Her body softens in his arms. When Harmon tightens his grip, she struggles to push him away, and he lets her beat her anger into his shoulders and chest.

"I'm going back to Nice."

Lena is not surprised at his reaction, but the speed at which Harmon jumps out of the bed is unexpected. "Hold on, baby.

Bruce pulled strings to make reservations for dinner tonight. We can go tomorrow. I'll make the changes for us."

"It's done. I'm taking the train." Lena figures it comes naturally to men—pursuing their agendas and expecting women, this woman, to follow. Walking from the bed to the dresser, she collects her clothes. Urgency presses Lena, and she wants to march with the rhythm, boogie to its tune. Do whatever it takes to keep moving forward. The drawers rattle when they roll shut. Clothes spill out of her hands and onto the floor.

"I have to finish what I started." She takes her suitcase out of the closet, empties the drawers of the antique armoire. She stuffs pants, dresses, underwear, and three days' worth of the toiletries Lulu is expecting into the pockets and main compartment.

"And what about us?" If Randall had asked that same question, not tonight, but that rainy night they both seemed on the verge of tears, it might have been him in front of her; now not even his ghost stands off to the side. "Is he going with you?"

"I'm doing this on my own." She chuckles softly. "You've jinxed us both with your theories. It's not over between us, Harmon Francis. But I can't let you entice me back into the same cocoon I just wiggled my way out of."

Harmon steps between Lena and her suitcase. She has forgotten how his thick eyebrows almost meet in the center of his forehead when he frowns. In five steps she is on the opposite side of the room, gazing past the terrace to the rooftops and the Paris skyline she has come to love. Arms folded across her chest, her body language the only signal she feels can convince Harmon; a period to further conversation. Harmon has spent a fortune on this decadent suite. She doesn't want to feel obligated by his generosity or his attention. Paris has distracted her: this affair, the food, the melodious language, the endless waves on the Seine, the quaint streets, and even the Eiffel Tower peaking now in the distance above the tiled roofs. She doesn't want to feel obligated by anyone's love.

"Let me love you, Lena." He whispers his words, softly, seductively, and joins her on the other side of the room. Harmon doles his kisses lightly over her eyes, her forehead, her lips.

"*That*, you can do. But I'm still going. Alone."

She lets him press against her. Lets him carry her to the bed, lets him take off her clothes, wrap himself around her, move with her, pull her with him, suck her lick her love her, until they are one motion of loving, until she can do nothing else but bury her head in his shoulder to muffle her cry.

Chapter 34

The white man sitting across from Lena reminds her of Randall. Not his height or skin color or tone of voice, but his mannerisms. The way his hands slice the air and punctuate his words, how his eyes dart from the window to the train's passengers to her face—seeing, constantly processing. The way he speaks to his teenage son beside him— lecture mixed with love.

Pulling her cell phone from her purse, Lena notices that it is still on. Another text message from Randall tells her that he is delaying his return to the States while she changes hotels. A year ago, eight months ago, she would have been in awe of his confidence, his presumption. *Thanks for the bracelet,* she texts back. It would have been better to tell him in person, she thinks. Thinks again of all of those months he would not take her calls, communicated with her by email and through his lawyer. And now he is as eager, as impatient for her response as he had been when he first proposed. She types awkwardly on the phone's mini-keyboard—thinks if she had them she would send the lyrics from "Silent Wings" so that he would understand: *Good luck, Randall. I always knew you had it in you.*

The train sways from side to side and creates rolling waves of nausea in Lena's stomach. She opted for the long, leisurely ride back to Nice to clear her head and refocus, maybe even the possibility of jumping off along the way for photographs before the train zips off to its next stop. She expected a constant and soothing clickety-clacking motion, a steadiness that would allow her to read. Instead, she catnaps while a different kind of France speeds past her window. Gone are the rows and rows of buildings, museums, and monuments to ancient heroes. Oleander. Laurier-rose is everywhere. It looks like Napa Valley wine country. Brown hills, green fields, grapevines, and rose bushes hide their secrets. Modern skyline turns rustic. Châteaus sprinkled here and there, mysterious steeples, flagstone walls, and empty pastures.

Lena raises her camera to the window and snaps pictures of the passing countryside.

"Are you a photographer?" It is the son who speaks, not the father. This young man's perfect English grounds her to the States, to Oakland, and reminds her of her own son. It makes her feel like Kendrick is near. It makes her know how much she misses him, misses Camille.

"I'm thinking that's what I want to be when I grow up." She pushes at her hair, her gray roots more prominent than they had been when she started her trip. "Sounds funny, coming from a mature woman, doesn't it?" She wants her words to make her seem soft. Young.

"The only thing funny is that you don't think you're grown up."

"What are you? Nineteen?" She doesn't feel any wiser than the youngster in front of her. "At nineteen you think you're grown. At my age you don't want to be grown up anymore."

Eyes still on the passing scenery, the father leans forward in a slight bow of unspoken agreement. The smile the teenager gives to Lena seems to say he understands and that all adults say the same thing. The seats are arranged in groupings of four, two seats facing each other, so Lena can't avoid his eyes.

"Where are you going?"

"I'm on a mission." She likes that he talks to her. Remembers when conversation between her and Kendrick came easily.

"What kind of mission?" He raps the cigarette pack in his breast pocket. This is a no-smoking car. Between the time Cheryl bought the first pack of cigarettes and now she has smoked almost a pack herself. If it didn't kill, she'd keep it up.

"I'm going to the Tina Turner concert." Lena taps Tina's autobiography. "And afterwards I'm going to walk right up to her and ask her to autograph this." Only Cheryl, Bobbie, and almost Lulu have heard her phrase her goal so bluntly. Even with Harmon she'd beat around the bush. Lena fingers the disposable camera. If Lulu could see her now, she'd be thrilled.

"You're doing what, Lena?" Lulu acted as if her daughter said that she was going to the moon to eat cheese.

When Lena explained that she and Cheryl were going to the south of France to see Tina Turner, nothing but the fact that her daughter was traveling without a man shocked Lulu. "I would never do such a thing!"

"This is my life now, remember?" She held back tears so that Lulu wouldn't worry. "I'll be gone for a little over three weeks." She couldn't bring herself to the whole truth, made it more Cheryl's idea than hers. Didn't want Lulu to toss negative vibes her way. Doing her passive-aggressive "No you can't, but you'll sure do great" speech. So she left it at that and figured she would tell Lulu when and if she ever found Tina Turner. Lulu never asked another question about the trip, but she bought Lena eight packets of gum, chewable indigestion tablets, a small package of travel toilet paper, two disposable cameras, a journal, and ten travel-sized packets of detergent.

Nice's station resembles an open-air warehouse filled with trains and people moving in all directions at the same time. Men, women, and children hurry to disembark or board before the trains depart. Overhead signs flash arrivals and departures in military time: 19:00. There are no porters to assist passengers with luggage or directions or translations. Heaving her suitcase onto its wheels, she winds her way through the crowd and down the stairway.

The domed buildings that face the station are older than those facing the sea. Waning daylight does nothing to daunt the crowds milling in and around the station so late in the day. Still no black faces; no yellow or brown faces, either. That was the fun of being in Paris. Of being with Harmon, Bruce, and Cheryl. They made their own community.

Lena waves her hand at a taxi when she reaches the short queue. There was a time when panic, fear of the unknown, would have stiffened her arms and legs, held her tongue in place. Nice is familiar and comfortable. This is the gift, she knows, both Harmon and Cheryl have given her: new perspective on her dream and understanding of the power of doing this alone. That she could leave them and continue on her own makes her understand how far she's come.

The cab driver asks where she is from. He digs America. New York is groovy and he has heard that all the women in California are beautiful. He points to a small U.S. flag pasted on the inside of his sun visor where a mirror should be. His heavily accented conversation is full of slang. "Radical." The driver makes it sound like three separate words. Rah. Dee. Call. "I must be slick with the flag, ya know. Many French people don't like zuh U.S. these days."

He adjusts the rearview mirror so that she can see his smiling eyes and tells her she is a beautiful, sexy American black. "I could make passionate love with you." He says, even as his wedding band gleams in the lights, that he would be more than happy to show her the wonderful clubs in Nice that play the wonderful American jazz.

"Not interested. Just take me straight to the Hotel de la Mer. Now."

"Be careful, madame, these steps are a bit awkward. You must take them one step at a time." The bellman lugs Lena's bag up a short flight of stairs. John Henry used to say that: take one step at a time.

Funny, she thinks, her father would come into her thoughts now as time beats its rhythm against her shoulder. Two days to Tina. Saturday mornings she loved to watch John Henry lather menthol foam over his chin and cheeks. Like a trumpet-less Dizzy Gillespie, her father puffed his cheeks, dragged his metal razor across his smooth skin, and took his time answering Lena's questions. John Henry would smile. "One step at a time, baby girl. One step at a time."

The hotel room is as big as the first one she shared with Cheryl. Lena splurged on accommodations, and while the room is by no means the four- or five-star space she would have if Randall—or Harmon, as he'd proved in Paris—had been around, it is just what she hoped for. Cozy.

Lena reaches for the phone while she calculates the six-hour time difference. Bobbie answers after four rings, her voice alert.

"Bobbie, somewhere outside my hotel the sun hasn't set, the Mediterranean is a color you can't imagine, and there are palm trees swaying over pebbled beaches." A sliding-glass door opens onto a small porch and the rocky side of a vine-covered hill. There isn't a view, but in the morning there will be light and possibly the distant crash of waves. She plops onto the middle of the queen-sized bed, tests the firm mattress with her hand, and settles against the four fluffy pillows at the head of the bed.

"I don't need poetry at this time of the morning. Why the hell haven't I heard from you in two weeks? Don't tell me you got laid."

"Did that and more." Lena holds the phone away from her ear to keep Bobbie's scream from harming her eardrum and describes the last two weeks. She cannot believe them herself.

"Accept it as the gift it is. Fate."

"Harmon said that, too."

"And how about Randall? You still thinking of him? I know you are."

Lena recounts Randall's visit to Paris, the dinner, and his provocative invitation. Bobbie screams into Lena's ear again, when she tells him she kept the expensive bracelet he bought for her. Without bothering to control her glee, her satisfaction, Lena describes what his face must have looked like—or better yet, the shade of red it must have turned when he read her message.

"I'm learning not to let anyone divert me from my course."

"I could have told you that."

"I couldn't have done it without Tina. I couldn't have done it without you. I hope, one day, to do the same for you."

"Must be the guilt for all those years I beat up on you." Bobbie's laugh is loud on the other end of the phone. In the background, a woman's voice, Lulu's voice, asks Bobbie who is on the phone.

"Is that Lulu?"

"Surprise! I'm in California. Been here over a week. Don't ask. Don't lecture. She had a doctor's appointment." Bobbie mumbles into the phone, but Lena is unable to understand what her sister is saying. Bobbie's voice resumes its normal tone. "Pass me that sponge."

"What are you doing? What time is it there?"

"Perfect timing. We're cleaning the bathroom."

"What!" Lena shouts.

"I'm standing in the tub, washing it down. I'm practically naked, and I don't have time to talk because Lulu has a list of things for me to do."

"That's not true, Bobbie," Lulu shouts. "I don't have a list. Besides, your sister doesn't clean as well as you, Lena!"

"I'll call you later," Bobbie says. Lena loves her sister and is glad that for once she is around to take on some of the more tedious tasks in their mother's life.

"You okay?"

"I can think of better things to do."

"Does Lulu need anything? And why *are* you practically naked?" Lena asks. The idea of her sister standing in her underwear in their mother's tub has just hit her. Bobbie hated undressing in front of anyone when she was young.

"Because the tub is *dirty*, Lena. The shower stall is *dirty*, the tile is *dirty*," Bobbie snaps.

"It's not that bad," Lulu shouts again.

"Because," Bobbie continues, "I don't want to get my clothes wet. Because Lulu has a hard time bending over to clean the tub."

"I just wanted to say a quick hi before I grab a bite to eat."

"Hi," Bobbie snaps. "Just call me when you find Tina."

"Definitely. But I have something else I've got to do first."

Chez Gérard, a restaurant the clerk at the front desk recommended, is not far from the hotel. The weather report predicted the rain typical for this early in October. Yet, this evening the air is dry, the wind brisk, and the streets bustle with motorcycles, cars, and people.

Lena heads for the bar and waits for one of the two men behind it to take her order. The bartender is friendly, fluent in English, and, she thinks, barely twenty-one.

"A kir royale, s'il vous plaît. With a lime twist." She asks his name, and he tells her: Armand. The restaurant is crowded. Three couples sit snuggled close at the bar. A woman reading a magazine sits alone two stools over from Lena. The overhead fixtures cast glowing cones of light over every stool.

"I am studying to be a teacher of the English language," he says, passing Lena a bowl of green olives. Armand leans onto the counter and flashes a smile. His biceps are taut, and she can see through his long-sleeved shirt that they are bigger than her neck. Lena laughs. This man is barely older than Kendrick.

"I'm so thankful to hear English," says the woman two stools over. Her accent is distinctly British. "Armand is the only reason I come here." The woman points to Armand and titters delicately into her cupped palm. "He keeps an eye on me, makes sure I don't get hassled. I secretly lust for him."

"Looking is all I can handle right now," Lena says. The two fall into easy conversation, first about the magazine the woman, Margery, reads, then about her life. She is fluent in French and is writing a torrid novel in that language about her ex-husband, his lousy attitude, and his new home in the English countryside. She came to Nice to escape him and the gossip that surrounded their divorce and the homely woman he chose to replace her. Lena muffles a laugh with her hand—as sweet as she is, some might call Margery homely, too.

"And what, may I ask, brings you to this part of France?" Margery grins. "Or to this bar. You're really quite lovely. All alone are you?"

"Alone. By choice." She holds her hand up. The American gesture is foreign to Margery. Lena explains its meaning and shows Margery all the different ways to slap high five: high to low, low to high, and more. "I'm not a good writer," Lena explains. Pictures would be her way of telling her ex-husband's story. Pictures that showed the shock on his face when he understood that she would not be returning the expensive bracelet he bought for her. Pictures of him cursing as he read her last text message.

"Join us," Lena says to a tall, imposing man eyeing the stool between her and Margery. His suit is crumpled, his receding hairline uneven. He orders in French with a German accent. Once Armand places his food in front of him, he slices his plate-sized pizza into bite-sized chunks. "Allow me to buy the both of you another drink."

"Either you haven't eaten all day or that pizza is tastier than it looks," she says.

"Both," he says through his full mouth.

"Do you come here a lot?" Lena flushes at what sounds like flirting. "I'm not trying to pick you up; I'm practicing good conversation . . . I mean, do you eat here often?"

The man looks Lena up and down, hinting that picking him up might not be a bad idea. "The bar is comfortable for a good quick meal. Very few Americans come here."

"But"—another British woman one stool over offers her opinion—"the pizza is good. The tarte citron is better."

The man stuffs more pizza into his mouth, which Lena takes as his endorsement. He pushes away his plate and nurses his beer. "I enjoy this place. I come here at least once or twice a week." He points to his waistline. "I'd come more often, but since all I ever eat is the pizza my waistline would be bigger than it already is if I ate here more often."

Armand stops in front of Lena, leaning against the bar. His lips are thick and moist. "I might do that," she says to his grinning face. "Come here more often, that is."

"I am here from Wednesday to Sunday." He smiles again, exposing even, white teeth.

"Bonsoir," she says to Armand, Margery, and the German man whose name she forgot to ask.

It would be nice to have someone to tell that she stepped out on her own. "Hello, stars. Hello, moon. I did it!" Lena sticks the earplugs of her MP3 player in her ears, zips her jacket, and heads back to her hotel. Tina's "Open Arms" comes in right on cue:

Whatever life throws at you
Your friend is here

Lena smiles at the thought of Cheryl and the image of the old guy, the eavesdropper, from the Magical Café. Although she's sure that this evening is not the context of his comment, he was right: timing is everything.

Chapter 35

This time around, Villefranche-sur-Mer looks as if someone took a giant ice cream scoop out of the hillside and allowed buildings to replace what nature used to cover. Hotels and homes with terraces offer their owners views of the Mediterranean and the yachts docked in the harbor.

The main street is full of boutiques. Lena tries to put herself in Tina's head. Does she need new clothes or sexy underwear or porcelain platters to place on her tables or counters? If she were a famous and easily recognizable person, Lena would send bodyguards or personal shoppers to scan the boutiques before entering to browse. Or perhaps Tina might enjoy the adoration of her fans. Or perhaps she may roam unnoticed, like Lena. She studies faces for a hint of brown to see if Tina is hidden beneath a scarf or visor and follows a petite woman with a full head of hair and shapely legs. The woman, green eyed and tanned face, turns around when Lena calls out "Miss Turner?" and glares.

In the window of a small boutique someone has dressed a mannequin in a sexy and expensive-looking flared skirt and peasant blouse. The style is classic; Tina likes classic. Lena read it on her official website. The fan club president described the interior of Tina's villa and wrote that Tina designed it in a classic style.

"Bonjour," Lena says. In Paris she learned that the French often think Americans' ear-to-ear grins and "have a nice day" salutations are idiotic. She avoids toothy smiles and sticks to French.

The store clerk returns a two-note bonjour and begins, in French, to ask if there's anything in particular Lena is looking for, and since southern French is slower than Parisian, Lena captures a few words and offers a toothy smile anyway. In English, this time, the woman asks again what Lena needs.

"Does Tina Turner ever come in this store?"

"*Mais, non*. How would I know, madame? Sometimes they say she walk around and—how you say? —uh, shops zuh windows?"

"Window-shops." Lena gently corrects and returns the woman's friendly smile.

The blocks are short. Lena does a little window-shopping of her own, asking the same question at four more trendy boutiques.

"Do you know where she lives?" she asks another clerk. "Is there a street number or special marking?"

The clerk shrugs and holds her palms up. No one knows—*on ne sait pas*—all the glitterati have villas here. Madame Turner comes to Villefranche-sur-Mer whenever she pleases, possibly she is here now.

"Perhaps if you try the road that leads up the *colline*, zuh hill, you will find her. You have her address, no?" The woman explains that most of the villas and mansions are gated and plain from the front. "Les Français," she says proudly, "keep the beautiful inside for ourselves."

The hotel's reception area has three Louis XIV writing tables with marble tops angled in a way to greet its guests as soon as they walk through the door. The concierge, Jeanne, has taught

Lena one or two simple French phrases. Jeanne rushes up to Lena and hands her an envelope. The triangular flap is embossed with the hotel's crest; the paper is thick and heavy. Inside, Bobbie's name and cell phone number are carefully written in small block letters on a cream-colored card. 9:30 p.m. is written below the phone number, and Lena is thankful that she doesn't have to decipher military time. Nine thirty in Nice means early afternoon in California. The call came in an hour ago.

Lena asks Jeanne to arrange for a cab to take her to the top of Vinaigrier mountain. Jeanne speaks in deliberate English.

"It is more of a big and steep hill than a mountain, madame."

"Can you find a driver who knows the home of the American celebrity Tina Turner?"

"Of course, I will try to make the accommodations for you, madame." The grimace on Jeanne's face does not match her words. "But, Madame Turner is not simply an American celebrity; she belongs to the world."

Lena continues through the lobby to the elevator while Jeanne explains that she will try her best to find a knowledgeable driver but that the French are very private people, and when the famous Madame Turner is in town, she is French, and therefore her privacy is respected. Lena finds this amusing and completely contradictory to Hollywood, where tours of the homes of the stars are profit makers, and the paparazzi couldn't care less about celebrity seclusion unless it offers a financially worthy photo opportunity.

"I'd like to start early in the morning. I'll need the driver to be available for the whole day." With any luck, she thinks. "Oh, and I'll be going to the concert at Cimiez the day after, so I might as well use the driver for that, too."

From the elevator a phone chimes, and, as she nears her room, Lena realizes that it is her phone ringing two doors down the hall. She runs to the door, unlocks it, and grins at how quickly

Jeanne has responded to her request. "I love this place," she sings aloud.

"Lena, is that you?" Bobbie's is the voice Lena hears when she picks up the phone.

"Who else would it be, Bobbie?" Lena's gold earring taps against the phone in the way that Bobbie and Lulu usually make noise on their end of a call.

"Lena, honey . . . Lulu . . . it's Lulu . . ." Bobbie rushes through the facts: she left the house early to run errands and have brunch with a few of her old friends. Lulu was supposed to go with Aunt Inez to a church barbecue. Aunt Inez rang the doorbell and pounded on all the doors for twenty minutes. When Lulu didn't answer, she called the police. By the time they found Bobbie's number, there was nothing they could do.

Lena slides to the floor in front of the bed, her head falls back against the hard mattress. Breathe. Breathe. The breaths do not come; her chest caves inward like a hundred men are standing on it, the air leaks in small puffs from her lungs to her throat and out her mouth. She tugs the sheet from under the top covering and blows her nose on its edge. "What happened?"

"They found her in bed. She looked like she was sleeping." From six thousand miles away the magic of long distance does nothing to muffle Bobbie's sobs on the other end of the line. "I'm glad I came home. I remembered what you said about her being discombobulated. I called a couple of times after you left and started paying attention. That's why I came out here. When I went with her to the doctor, he said her behavior indicated Alzheimer's. Maybe a heart attack or a stroke? I don't want an autopsy. The cause isn't important, is it?"

"Our mother is dead? I was going to call her today. I came back to the hotel to call her." The phone slips from her neck and tumbles to the floor, leaving the sound of Bobbie's voice far away and tinny.

"Lena, Lena," Bobbie shouts. "Are you okay?"

Images flicker in Lena's head like the 8mm movies John Henry loved to take: mother kissing her dead husband's cheek goodbye; mother tying a Kotex on a sanitary belt at the sign of Lena's first blood; mother laughing at Randall's corny jokes, hugging him as if he were her own; mother running fingers through Camille's hair to twist and braid, and rocking bushy-headed baby Kendrick, tickling his feet, cuddling him close; mother dead on her side of her double bed, alone and stiff.

When Lena picks up the phone, Bobbie talks as if Lena had never dropped it. "Lena, I want you to do something for me. For Lulu."

Lena nods yes as if she were standing in front of Bobbie, better yet hugging her.

"Stay in France. Go to the concert. Meet Tina, talk to her, tell her what she has meant to you for all of these months. Will you do that?"

"I can't. It's selfish. Who will make all the arrangements?"

"Me! I'm not helpless. We'll postpone the funeral. One or two days, a week, isn't going to make a difference . . ."

"How can I have fun when my mother has just died? How can you—"

"Look. Lulu knew how important seeing Tina was to you. She and I had some good conversations over the last few days. I even got her to drink a little of that scotch I brought them twenty years ago."

Lena fingers the disposable camera. An inexpensive gift given with richness of heart that money cannot buy. It is full of Nice and Paris. Lena intended to turn the photos into a scrapbook; Lulu's eyes to the world. Wanted her to see what she had never seen: the Mediterranean's dappled surface, the Eiffel Tower, the boats on the Seine, Notre Dame, her daughter in Paris doing fine. A sprig of lavender is tied around the camera so that Lulu could smell France, too.

"Don't beat yourself up." Bobbie sniffs. "You were a good

daughter, a responsible daughter. Lulu was proud of you. Proud that you could walk away from Randall's money and try to make it on your own. She knew you were doing what you needed to do."

Lena knows all of this. It is the sound of Lulu's voice that she wants to hear saying it.

Chapter 36

"Madame Harrison, I am so sorry that you must leave under such sad circumstances." Jeanne escorts Lena to the awaiting car. "Please accept my condolences on the death of your mother."

"I appreciate your help, Jeanne." Lena hands her an envelope. Inside are the tickets to Tina's concert. "Enjoy."

The driver moves the car in and out of traffic, the static of French over the two-way radio relays to the driver, Lena assumes, instructions for his next pickup. He mumbles then slams the speaker into its cradle.

In the passenger window beside her a spider twirls and scurries from left to right, seeking connecting points on the glass to weave its silken web.

"Oh my God, a spider!"

The cab driver frantically swerves through the traffic to get to the curb. "*Zut alors,* madame. Pardon. The last person in zuh cab carry a tree. Let me kill it for you."

"No, merci." Lena lowers the window. The spider scampers to the top of the glass and crawls over to the other side so that its sticky underside is close to Lena's face. She rolls up the window and lets the French Riviera whiz past: Hotel Negresco, the red double-decker Nice tour bus, the sandy beach where she and Cheryl took their tops off to soak in the sun while Harmon and

Bruce tried to act like the French, not gawking Americans, countless white apartment buildings, cars, and more cars.

Harmon suggested she make her connection to San Francisco in Chicago when she called him. He would join her so that she would not travel to her mother's funeral alone, but she insisted his presence would complicate things. His love is on her mind. Randall is on her mind as well; but, Tina stayed away from Ike. Sometimes the dream is better than the reality. He will be at the funeral, but not beside her. Even in his sadness, she supposes, he will not comfort Lena in the way he might have if they were together. She will watch him console Camille and Kendrick, and Lena is okay with that. Randall will be as upset as she is. He loved Lulu, too.

She unfolds two sheets of Hotel de la Mer's heavy stationery. The pages are full of her list of things to do. Lena and Bobbie have spent hours on conference calls with the funeral home and their aunts making the arrangements. Their aunts have phoned family friends; Lulu's answering machine will fill quickly with sympathetic messages. If this were a cheerful moment, Lena would call it Bobbie's just deserts, since Lena made all of the arrangements for their father. Lena's job is to compose the eulogy on the plane ride home, to compress eighty-one years into a short speech.

Kendrick cried when she told him of his grandmother's death. She waited fifteen minutes while they talked of his classes and his readjustment to the regimen of school before she spoke the words, "Lulu is gone, Kendrick," in order to soften the shock. He called Camille so they could have a three-way conversation. Camille cried, too, at the loss of the only grandmother she'd ever known. Both kids have called her twice in the day it has taken to change her travel arrangements. Funny, she thinks, how kids can become so responsible in a crisis.

His dad, Kendrick said, will make sure their son has something decent to wear—no sagging pants. Lulu used to tease Kendrick about his pants, threatened to pull them down if he didn't pull them up. Camille chased him around her house because Lulu's old legs couldn't move fast enough. Kendrick never pulled his pants up; his grandmother never pulled them down. Camille and Kendrick will miss Lulu as much as Lena will; losing two people you love within a year and a half is hard. Three. Lena adds Randall to her tally: Randall, Lulu, John Henry—losing three people is hard.

The driver parks the car at the curb in front of the airport's glass exterior. Lena doesn't bother to stop the daydreams as she gathers euro coins to pay the driver—tipping him too much to avoid returning home with the heavy loose change—of what it might be like if Randall were waiting when the plane lands in San Francisco. Perhaps he would take her hand, like a friend. At the baggage carousel he would lift her heavy suitcase, carry it like he used to carry Kendrick first, Camille later, in one hand to make their babies laugh, make Lena shake with fear that he would drop the infants, but still have pride that her husband was so strong, her babies and her life so secure.

This would have been possible had she not moved on to her own fate. When she sees Randall at the funeral, when she cries at her mother's grave, he will think all her tears are for her mother, and she will let him; the tears will be for Lulu, but also for her old life. For its death. For what no longer is and will never be again.

Goodbye to Randall. Goodbye to Harmon. Goodbye to the deep blue sea and the smell of baguettes baking in rough ovens. No regrets. She has no regrets.

The airport is straightforward and uncomplicated. Lena wears the only pair of high heels she brought with her and the same sexy dress from that first dinner with Harmon, draped with a pashmina stole in honor of Lulu. On the rare visit to the airport when they were young, Lulu dressed her daughters in pinafores and patent leather mary janes. The sisters believed the airport was a miraculous, mysterious place; its high-glossed floors filled with people coming and going to foreign places they longed to know.

The corridors of Nice's airport are shiny and heavily waxed, too. She has never lost her awe for airports.

Passengers for the trans-Atlantic flight crowd in front of the airline counter; the lines are long but move swiftly. Behind the soon-to-be-boarded travelers, a swarm of people rush frantically toward the exit door. In the midst of all the commotion, Lena catches sight of a brown-skinned woman: hair controllably uncontrolled, red-lipped smile, high heels, great legs.

The woman walks at her own pace, accustomed to the attention, the adoration. The crowd grows thicker as everyone recognizes her. She calls bonjour and hello in a raspy voice like music, like Lena anticipated it would be the first time she heard it up close.

It is a short walk to the glass sliding doors and the curb where a black limousine waits. The crowd falls back and re-forms a line. Several autograph-seeking stragglers remain. *I, Tina* is secure inside Lena's suitcase. She fumbles for a minute to open her luggage. Lena looks up to see Tina Turner walking through the glass door to the limo.

"I love you, Tina," Lena shouts.

Tina twirls around to see the face behind the distinctly American accent. She glances at Lena's sole black face among her adoring fans, and Lena raises both hands and waves.

"Thank you," Lena shouts louder this time.

Tina looks Lena straight in the eye, breaks into a wide smile, and blows Lena a kiss, just before the car door closes, and the limo eases down the road.

Acknowledgments

On this wonderful journey of writing my first novel, I have traveled down and around the paths of discovery, surprise, rejection, and acceptance. With all that is in my heart, I thank God and the Universe for my blessings, for the lesson that family is connected by more than blood, for friendships. My heart and my head have learned so much. I am pleased and privileged to have such wonderful people supporting and encouraging me every step of the way.

My dear friends, The Finish Party, you have taught me that, sometimes, simple words work best, but a simple "thank you" doesn't seem to do justice to your wisdom, help, and love. I am filled with gratitude that each of you smart, witty, talented, and truly wise women is in my life: Farai Chideya, Alyss Dixson, ZZ Packer, Deborah Santana, Renee Swindle, Lalita Tademy, Nichelle Tramble. Wherever you go, wherever you are, I will always value and trust you.

Richard Abate, my agent, and Karen Thomas, my editor. Thank you for believing in me!

The Fourth Saturday crew, Sharline Chiang, Cheo Tyehimba, and Phil Wilhite, you bring me joy.

Felicia Ward, you are an ongoing source of inspiration and wise words.

My friends, my cheerleaders, who believed in me and kept me

on the straight and narrow: Piper Kent-Marshall, Yacine Bell, Arlene Hollis, Brenda Thompson, Pamela Thompson, and Stacy Stone, a big light who shined in my world for a little while.

The Voices of Our Nations Arts Foundation (VONA) workshops, and the fabulous authors in that program, provided a powerful, safe place for this new writer to learn and grow strong.

Reading Group Guide

1. In the beginning of *SFTT,* Lena is scattered and no longer able to manage her life. Were there other ways that Lena could have maintained balance in her life? If she had, do you think her marriage would have fallen apart?

2. What can a younger woman gain from Lena's experience? Does age have anything to do with Lena's situation?

3. Lena chose one aspect of Tina Turner's life as a role model for strength. Were there other aspects of Tina's life that helped her as well?

4. Are role models important? Who are your role models? How have their lives inspired you?

5. What lessons can women learn from Lena's experience?

6. Lena chose to leave the life she and Randall built together. What other ways can women regain "self" without giving up what they worked so hard to gain?

7. Lena and Randall talk to their children separately about their divorce. If the four of them had discussed the situation to-

gether, do you think Kendrick and Camille would have been less bitter toward Lena?

8. Lena tries to explain how she feels about her life to Camille. Can Lena be a role model for Camille? What is it about her mother that Camille should be proud of?

9. Why do you think that Candace comes to Lena's aid at the dinner party? What did Lena learn about friendship from that situation?

10. When Lena picks up Randall from the airport, what could each have done differently to connect with the other? Or was their marriage already over?

11. Lulu offers this advice to Lena: ". . . *make* it enough. Make it enough to last until death do you part. I hope you're not thinking about doing something foolish. There's no way you could live like you do without Randall." Given the generational difference between the two women, what could Lena take from this advice and pass on to Camille?

12. Do you think that Randall was aware that his best friend was flirting with his wife? If so, why didn't he do anything about it?

13. If Lena understood the differences between her and Cheryl, why do you think Lena agreed to go with her to France?

14. How do the differences between Cheryl and Lena help Lena? What does Lena learn from Cheryl?

15. What does Lena learn from her relationship with Harmon? Is he good for her?

16. Lena forgives Harmon for past behavior. Is there an old flame in your past like Harmon? What would it take for you to reconnect with that person?

17. Did Lena do anything that hints to what her future with Harmon could be?

18. What does Bobbie's support mean to Lena? What are the differences between the sisters?

19. Why do you think Bobbie decided to visit Lulu?

20. What, if anything, did Bobbie learn from Lena?

21. If Lena had gone with Randall in Paris, would he have accepted the "new" Lena? How would the two of them have reconciled the changes in Lena?

22. If Lena had accepted Randall's offer in Paris and reunited with him, do you think she would have fallen back into the pattern of their old relationship?

Turn the page for a sneak peek at

Passing Love

a novel

by

Jacqueline E. Luckett

Arm in arm, like sisters, Yvette and Ruby rounded the corner. Buildings, their surfaces chipped and cracked, lined the streets around them: apartments—shutters weathered from neglect, poverty, or both—filled with hundreds, if not thousands, of men, women, and children. A woman behind a table selling small pots of humble flowers that she had cultivated on her balcony. More people walking than riding bicycles. Men with berets, women in straight skirts and sweaters. Repetitions of shallow wrought iron balconies, a geranium pot here and there. A twinkling strand of lights strung between two buildings. Stores where Ruby shopped for food that her mother had never heard of: baguettes, croissants, brioches, bonbons.

Yvette chatted in French and waited while Ruby repeated her words and phrases: How much does it cost? Do you have more? When will my clothes be ready? Can I pay for this a little bit at a time?

"Your French, *cherie*, is getting better every day. Soon you will speak as well as me, and then you will not have a need anymore for your poor *amie*, Yvette."

"*Mais, non,* Yvette. We'll be friends forever."

Yvette lived with a Negro drummer from North Carolina who'd had more success at getting gigs than Arnett. Yvette had convinced the concierge to rent to Arnett and Ruby the apartment two floors below her and walked with Ruby until she learned her way around the neighborhood. Her kindness kept Ruby going, those first days, until Ruby believed she could make it on her own, pointing to what she needed: toilet paper, coffee, milk, sugar, and fruit.

"Regardez!" Ruby pointed to the open seats at a nearby café. Passing men tipped their hats at the two women, different in their looks: Yvette blond and pale, Ruby curly-haired and brown in comparison to her friend. "Arnett will practice 'til it's time to go back to the club. He might take a nap, he probably won't eat, and I know he'll take at least two sips from that bottle of brandy in the back of the closet he thinks I don't know about. We'll pretend we're rich and waiting for handsome men to discover us."

"You are not happy with your handsome Arnett?" Yvette laughed. "Oh, *cherie,* I wish my Freddie loved me so much!"

"*Mais, oui*! But a woman has to know that she's attractive to all men."

"Ah, Ruby, we are in the wrong *arrondissement* for wealthy men. Handsome men, yes. Paris is full of them. Like the ones who wait for the beautiful dancers outside *le Casino Royale* and *les Folies-Bergères.* If they could afford it, these poor men here with their wives and children waiting for them at home, they would stop and buy *un café* for us." Yvette looked at her friend. Ruby could have found the best prices on eggs and bread on the days that that was all their money could buy, and chicken or a little meat on the days that Arnett was paid in more than meals or liquor or drugs that got him high enough to forget that he should have asked for money not the good times a few sticks of reefer could bring. Gaining a friend, a woman friend, surprised Ruby, but once she understood Yvette's kind heart, there was no turning back for either of them. "*Cherie*," Yvette asked. "You have found Paris all that you wanted, *oui*?"

"There's no place else I'd rather be." No fields of dandelions, no lawns green with spring rain, no magnolias or june bugs to catch and bind with string, no lightning bugs to wear on fingers like rings. Not the smell of red dirt or its dust on her shoes. All those years ago, Ruby had known Arnett would come for her. She believed no man could hold a woman the way he did and not want to take care of her. This day, and all of their days together, she felt his love. Ruby's face, a new look she'd perfected, encouraged men without words. "I want to be a woman who lives with no regrets."

"Ruby!" Arnett's voice rang out from the other side of the street. His saxophone hung from his neck. The instrument beat against his chest as he paced from one side of the street to the other. He had been playing for so long that his saxophone blended into neighborhood sounds—the bling of a bicycle bell, the clacking of heels hard against the cobblestones, the patter of rain just beginning to fall. Ruby no longer heard it. "Ruby, where are you?"

Ruby leaned back in her chair and tilted it ever so slightly until she disappeared into the shadow of the walls behind her.

"He will see *me*, *cherie*, and then he will know that you are here."

"One minute more." She scooted farther back, her chair moving soundlessly on the planked wood floor. "Sometimes a girl just needs a minute."

"Ruby!" Arnett rushed to the café, his eyes wide, hair tousled from fingers working through his waves. "I didn't know where you were."

"You were in one of those spells, baby. I'm right here and see? Yvette is with me."

He stood at the edge of the table and eyed their two cups. Two big men sat behind the women. Arnett glared at them. "I didn't know where you were."

"And you found me." Ruby smiled at Arnett in that way that soothed him when he wallowed in uncertainty. She backed away from her chair and waved at Yvette. They would settle the cost of the afternoon coffee later. Ruby guided Arnett back to the rue Ventimille and walked him up the five spiraling flights of stairs, him holding her hand as if he couldn't make it without her help.

"You're gonna be fine, baby. That man today, he liked you. Just play like you do for me. I'll be there. Aren't I always there?" The door to their room was wide open. She made him sit on their narrow bed and lifted the saxophone from around his neck. Carefully, she rested the sax on its case. She took off her dress and set it on his practice chair, then lay beside Arnett and pondered this change that had come over her man.

In her arms, his body was limp and clammy, drained like his practice had taken his spirit. She rocked and sang a little "God Bless the Child" until he drifted off. The street lamplights glowed below the window. Trapped in the half-dark and the length of Arnett's body, Ruby was left with nothing to do except wonder why Arnett had become this way in Paris when never in all of the days they wandered away from Mississippi had he been so concerned about his playing.